LIES

GW00686429

LIES

ANNA DILLON

BROOKSIDE

LIES
First published 1998 by
Brookside
2 Brookside
Dundrum Road
Dublin 14
Ireland

© Anna Dillon

All rights reserved. No part of this book may be reproduced
or utilised in any form or by any means mechanical, including
photography, photocopying, filming, recording, video
recording, or by any information storage and retrieval system,
or shall not, by way of trade or otherwise, be lent, resold or
otherwise circulated in any form of binding or cover other
than that in which it is published without prior condition in
writing from the publisher. The moral rights of the author
have been asserted.

British Library Cataloguing in Publication Data
A catalogue record for this book is available from the
British Library

ISBN 1 873748 05 1

Cover image from Slide File
Cover design by Brenda Dermody
Typeset by Brookside
Printed by Mackays of Chatham plc, Chatham, Kent

All the characters in *LIES* are fictitious.
Briony Dalton does not and never has existed. All the books mentioned in the text are fictitious and any resemblance to books currently in print or now out of print is entirely coincidental.
All of the publishers mentioned in *LIES* are fictitious.

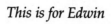

This is for Edwin

At thirty-three thousand feet, in a privately owned Gates Learjet flying from Kennedy International to Shannon, a man made a decision to destroy a woman's life. He had never met the woman and there was no malice in the decision; it was simply a matter of business and expediency.

ભ

Chapter One

The pornographic video was of typically poor quality. The naked, mechanically thrusting bodies were grainy, blurred, the colours shifting slightly on the twenty-nine-inch flat-screen television. The sound track was muted, the voices muffled and distant, occasionally hopelessly out of sync with the picture.

A blunt, slightly ragged nail hit the pause button on the remote control, freezing the bodies on the screen into an untidy tangle that was almost comical.

The woman in the large crimson-framed glasses rested her chin on her hands and leaned forward, staring hard at the image. How long ago was this made, she wondered, and where were the actors and actresses now?

Adjusting the glasses on her straight nose, Briony Dalton began to take notes …

She always found the sex scenes the most difficult to imagine. No matter how ingenious or inventive the rest of the novel, she always blanked on the sex scenes.

The weight of a body atop hers … the sudden pressure of penetration … the movement …

She was the product of a good Catholic environment, brought up in a house where sex was never mentioned and in a society that believed it to be a sin … was it any wonder, then, that her imagination faltered when she had to visualise a couple making love in ever more exotic and erotic ways to satisfy her vast audience?

However, twenty-five novels, the last ten of them international best-sellers, had taught her a few tricks to keep the spice in her books. Her collection of pornographic videos, magazines, and a huge array of erotic literature which she used for reference and inspiration would have shocked and scandalised her few friends … or perhaps not: they had come to expect it. Her own publicity machine had dubbed her the 'Empress of Erotica'. It was a title she hated.

Frozen on the television screen, mouth and legs gaping, a woman whose breast size approximated that of the heroine of her latest novel, was involved in a *ménage-a-trois* with another girl and an extraordinarily endowed young man. Nodding slightly, Briony Dalton noted the positions of the various characters. She could use that in her book. She grinned sourly. If only her fans could see her now, perhaps then they'd realise that the woman *Time* had dubbed 'The Queen of the Red Hot Read' was little more than a sham.

She touched the pause button again and the video moved on, colours shivering slightly before settling down.

Briony Dalton stopped the video again, and made another series of notes, her irregular shorthand crawling across the notebook in her lap. She moved the video on a few frames and stopped when she came to a close-up of one of the women, struck by the expression on the woman's face.

Her eyes were dead, uncaring. Bored.

Briony wondered how anyone could look at pornography before finally coming to the inescapable conclusion that the participants were bored. When she occasionally came across a video where the actors were enjoying themselves, the difference was so immediately obvious, the result so erotic.

She wondered what they had been paid for their talents: a couple of hundred dollars, perhaps, maybe a line or two of coke.

And here she was ripping off their work.

She had been paid a guaranteed advance of two and a half million dollars for the American hardback and paperback rights to her new novel; the deal for the English edition would bring in upwards of a million sterling. Serial rights, foreign language rights and the movie option would bring in another half a million. When the movie was finally made, all the previous figures would begin to look like petty cash.

She looked at the screen again. At least the actors had walked away when their day's work was done, whereas she was trapped in a watertight contract that still had six months to run. On screen, the action moved on, but her attention had wandered, and she caught herself doodling on the spiral-bound notepad. She paused the picture again and tore out the page, tossing it in the general direction of the overflowing wastepaper basket beneath her desk.

The door clicked open behind her and she adjusted her focus on the screen, using it as a mirror, watching a slender female figure move up behind her. The woman leaned forward, resting her hands — long-fingered, slender, with perfect azure nails — on her shoulders. The aroma of Poison caught at the back of Briony's throat, irritating her sinuses. Traces of platinum blond hair tickled her cheek as Gabrielle Royer leaned forward to look with interest at the frozen image.

"I wonder what his nickname is?" she said archly.

Briony stared at the grainy picture and smiled. "I didn't think your interests ran in that direction."

Gabrielle squeezed her shoulders slightly. "I am allowed to look," she said. She spoke in a curious American/French accent. Her lips, painted a deep slashing red, turned into a perfect bow. She nodded towards the screen, "This might be useful for that section in chapter three where …?"

"That's just what I thought." Briony said. She leaned back into the younger woman's body. "I've told you before. You should be a writer."

Gabrielle Royer pressed the pause button on the remote control, allowing the video to play on. She watched disinterestedly as the action came to its inevitable climax. "I haven't got the imagination," she murmured, "that's why I'm a secretary."

Briony indicated the screen. "And you think I have? Jesus," she whispered, half to herself, "I've got to watch porno videos to get ideas for my books."

"But only for the juicy bits," Gabrielle reminded her, "and let's face it, no one writes better juicy bits than you." One of her perfectly manicured hands moved off Briony's shoulders, skin hissing against the silk blouse as it slid down to brush Briony's breast through the thin cloth. "What would the nuns say if they could see you now?"

Briony placed her fingers over Gabrielle's hand, pressing it to her breast. "Frankly my dear, I couldn't give a damn! They never did anything for me."

On screen, two women were performing together in a classic soixante-neuf position while the male lay back on both elbows and watched them.

Gabrielle moved closer to Briony, pressing her breasts against the seated woman's head, both hands draped over her shoulders. She rested her pointed chin on Briony's coal-black hair and smiled. "Now, that's more like it," she said appreciatively looking at the screen.

Briony moved her head slightly, feeling vaguely jealous of Gabrielle's interest. "I'd like a cup of tea."

"I'm your secretary, not your maid!" the younger woman said absently.

"Make me a cup of tea," Briony snapped, her humour changing with its customary suddenness.

Gabrielle gave the woman's breasts a final squeeze before stepping away from the chair. "Yes, Ma'am. Immediately Ma'am. Anything you say, Ma'am. Will that be all Ma'am?" She backed away from the chair, turned and almost — but not quite — slammed the door.

Briony sighed. She hit the stop button and the video whirred and clicked. Gabrielle was impossible; ignorant, rude and arrogant. Briony had come close — really close — to firing her on at least three separate occasions, but she hadn't, realising that the exotic young woman was now an essential and integral part of her life. Gabby was twenty-five years old, twenty years her junior, everything that

Briony was not, and the older woman had been surprised, and initially rather frightened, to discover that she actually felt attracted to the young woman.

Gabby had introduced her to the delights of lesbian lovemaking and that had been a joy, a revelation. Briony didn't consider herself a lesbian. She had been married and had borne two children, and she had never even considered a relationship with any woman before Gabby. Her lovemaking was gentle and passionate; she made no demands, and understood when Briony felt too tired or disinclined to make love. If she had one enduring memory of her first marriage, it was of her husband's sulks when she refused to make love to him.

The video rewound to the start. She ejected the tape and slid it back into its box, automatically checking the title and date: *Sexservice*, 1966.

Nineteen sixty-six was the year she had really started writing. She had been eighteen years old, a few months married, and already pregnant. But that had been a different time, in a different place, in a far different world.

A ghost time.

Old memories, bad memories, wasted times.

Gabrielle came back in time to see the look of anguish on Briony's face. She crossed the room to crouch on the floor beside her chair and took one of her hands, holding it tightly. "Tell me?" she murmured, her French accent in evidence now.

Briony looked into her lover's dark eyes and gently laid her fingers against Gabby's cheek. "Run me a bath, will you? I'm feeling stiff and old today." She shook her head slightly. "Maybe it's looking at all those young bodies forever frozen in 1966. She glanced sidelong at her secretary. "Do you remember 1966?"

"I wasn't even born then. My parents didn't marry until sixty-seven."

"In 1966 I was eighteen, newly married, living in a grotty flat on the outskirts of Dublin, having just discovered that I could write, hacking out any old rubbish for a few bob. Oh, we could have asked my father for the money, I suppose, but we were too proud."

Gabby leaned over and kissed Briony lightly on the lips. "All that's in the past now," she said very softly. "You're not frozen in 1966. You've moved up and on. The good times are rolling."

"Are these the good times?" Briony asked.

"Would you rather be back in that flat? Were you happy then? Are you happy now?"

Briony nodded quickly, refusing to even think about it. "Yes, yes, of course I am. Don't mind me. I'm feeling depressed and maudlin." She nodded towards the blank screen. "Watching this trash upsets me."

"I'll go and run that bath."

છ

Steaming water thundered from the stainless steel taps into the sunken circular bath, and the mirrored wall behind the tub immediately misted up. Emptying half a crystal flask of coloured granules into the water, Briony Dalton watched the bubbles foaming, and smelt the sharp crispness of pine before walking from the bathroom into the adjoining bedroom. She pulled the door closed behind her and the sounds of the filling bath immediately muted.

Unbuttoning her blouse, she crossed to the large plate glass windows and rested her forehead against the cool glass, staring out over Central Park and the reservoir. The park was virtually invisible beneath a thick coiling mist and New York was grey and sombre, the storm that had rolled in two days previously seeming to have settled over the island permanently. Rain twisted and curled down the windows and although she couldn't hear the sounds of the storm outside through the thick glass, she could see the roiling clouds twisting across the metallic sky, and on the small balcony outside the windows, her few potted plants and the small palm she had been cultivating for the past two years had been blasted flat. Soil and mulch were smeared across the balcony where one of the pots had fallen and broken and, as she watched, the rain quickened, drumming into the clay, churning it to mud. Standing on her toes, she looked straight down on to Eighty-Fifth Street and watched the tiny red fireflies crawl through the gloomy street into Park Avenue. Although it was barely two o'clock in the afternoon, the city was lit, the tower blocks pillars of muted light through the low-lying clouds.

Los Angeles, she thought, turning away from the window, pulling off the blouse and dropping it on the edge of the king-sized bed. She would move to Los Angeles. There was nothing keeping her in New York; she didn't even like the city. The weather was usually awful — too hot in the summer, too cold, wet and windy during the winter — and the winters were getting longer. The people were indifferent and she lived behind a security screen that in any other country would be called a prison.

Briony unzipped her skirt and stepped out of it, leaving it on the floor, and strode into the bathroom wearing only her panties. She stopped just inside the door, blinking in the warm steam that billowed around her. The bathroom was decorated in blond wood and silver, with one wall entirely mirrored. She had initially liked its clean, austere lines, but lately she had become increasingly dissatisfied with its coldness. She had been thinking about changing it: browns, oranges, ochre … Mediterranean colours, softer, warmer, more flattering colours.

The carpet beneath her bare feet was damp, from the moisture in the air, she thought and then she realised that the bath had overflowed. Swearing in annoyance, she reached through the mounds of billowing foam that topped the water and snapped the tap off, hissing as the hot metal burned her fingers. The bath overflow gurgled as it drained off the excess water.

Whilst waiting for the water to drain, Briony plucked a towel off the rail and rubbed it down the mirrored wall, wiping it clean. Draping the towel around her neck, holding both ends in her fists, she looked critically at the image before her. She would be forty-five next October and, despite a lifestyle that lent itself to laziness and indulgence, she didn't look too bad. She was not pretty, never had been, never would be now, and her best features were her eyes, which were large and a deep, deep brown. Her hair was jet black — and she ensured it remained that colour — which she wore cut close to her face. She also had the advantage of height: at six foot in her bare feet, she possessed an undoubted presence. Her stomach was flat and her breasts were small. She leaned forward, pressing her long slender fingers to her face, pulling back the skin around her eyes, and the hair away from her forehead. There were wrinkles around her eyes, from staring at a computer screen, from correcting manuscripts and from reading ... always reading: it was one of her earliest and most vivid memories.

Always reading.

Briony ran her fingers through the soapy water; it was hot, but not unbearably so. Slipping off her panties, she stepped down into the bath, the oily water smooth against her skin, the heat rising as she sank deeper into the water. She shuddered as it enfolded her groin and then she suddenly sank into the liquid, cascading water on to the floor, bubbles and foam spinning around the room. Lying back in the water, she surrendered herself to its sensuous caress. She was intensely aware of her own body, the tiny pulse in her groin, the tingling in her breasts, the rivulets of sweat moving down her forehead. She lay like that for about ten minutes while her tight and knotted muscles relaxed and the bar of pain across her shoulders eased and then her eyes closed, flickered open, and closed again.

She wasn't asleep, she was still fully aware of her surroundings, but it was as if she were divorced from them. She had once actually experienced herself looking down on her own body as it lay in the bath tub — it was a classic out-of-body experience — and she had been so tremendously excited by it that she had often deliberately attempted to recreate the experience, but without success.

Images began to flicker across her mind's eye ... discordant pictures ... abstracts ... faces ... and now the sexual images from the video.

She let them come, knowing that if she pursued them, they would twist and turn and then vanish. This was the creative process; she didn't know how it worked, all she knew was that it did work.

She had once explained the process in an interview to a woman's magazine — an Italian magazine — and they had then given the interview to a renowned psychoanalyst. The Sleeping, Dreaming Beauty the article had been titled. The doctor had suggested that the water, as hot as she could bear it, slick with oils, represented the womb, the perfect dream state; the disassociated images were the residue of the conscious mind as it sank into a quiescent state, allowing the powerful unconscious mind to come to the fore, permitting her to dream. At the time, she had thought it was nothing more than trendy bullshit ... now, well, maybe there was a grain of truth in it.

Gently, gently, she began to nudge her thoughts in the direction of the current novel, *A Woman Scorned*.

"Your tea!"

"Jesus!" Briony surged upwards, spilling water everywhere, drenching Gabrielle.

"Your tea," Gabrielle repeated as if nothing had happened, although her platinum-blond hair now hung lank across her face, and her large breasts were clearly visible through her sodden blouse.

Briony took the cup — which was filled with soapy bath water — and laughed. Putting the cup down on the carpet, she reached for Gabrielle's hand, drawing her closer, half-rising from the bath to kiss her lips.

Her secretary responded, her hands reaching for Briony's face, cupping it, turning it slightly.

Briony's wet fingers plucked at Gabrielle's buttons, one of them popping, rattling off the edge of the bath before dropping into the water. And then, with a squeal, Gabrielle toppled into the bath on top of Briony. She emerged, spluttering, dragging her hair back off her face. "This is a three-hundred-dollar blouse."

Briony opened her legs and drew Gabrielle in close to her. "I'll buy you another." She kissed her again. "I'm sorry I snapped at you earlier."

Gabrielle straightened in the bath and undid the remainder of the buttons. She wrung the blouse out before tossing it on to the floor, and then she stood and squirmed out of her black pencil skirt. Beneath she wore nothing but tiny lace panties. She hooked her thumbs into the flimsy material and tugged it off. Kneeling between Briony's outstretched legs, she turned so she was facing away from her and then lay back, pillowing her head on the older woman's breasts.

Briony reached down and ran the palms of her hands down Gabrielle's large breasts. The younger woman shuddered.

"You've made me very happy," Briony said finally. "Kept me sane ... and sober. I'm sorry I snapped at you," she said again.

"Don't worry. I was paying no attention to you anyway."

Briony pinched the woman's flesh playfully.

"Do you want to tell me what's wrong?" Gabrielle asked, watching Briony's reflection in the mirrored wall.

"I wish I knew," Briony said softly, her hands coming to rest on Gabrielle's stomach. She rested her head against the edge of the sunken bath and stared up at the ceiling, where white fluffy clouds had been painted on to a pale blue background. The *trompe-l`oeil* effect was marvellous.

"It's *A Woman Scorned*, isn't it?" Gabrielle asked softly.

Briony grunted but said nothing.

"I've been with you a year now, and you had signed that contract about six months before I joined you. Have you even finished the first draft yet?"

Briony shook her head.

"How long do you have left?"

"What's today?"

"Sunday, first of March."

"The manuscript is due for delivery on the last day of September."

"Six months." Gabrielle twisted her head to look up at Briony. "Can you delay the delivery date?"

"The last three books were all late," she murmured.

"How late?"

"Very. One was six months overdue, one a year and the last one was very nearly a year late."

"But you're a best-selling author," Gabrielle protested. "They'll make an exception for you surely?"

"Once or twice, yes, but not regularly. But that's not the problem," she said.

Gabrielle squirmed around until she was facing Briony. "What is the problem?" she asked.

Briony raised her head and looked into her secretary's coal-black eyes. "I cannot write this book," she whispered. She shook her head savagely. "I can't. I just can't!"

"Well then, don't. Return the advance," Gabrielle suggested doubtfully.

Briony folded her arms across her body. "I don't have it. That's the truth. I don't know where the money's gone — oh, I do, I suppose. A lot of it went on this … all this," she waved a hand in the air, vaguely encompassing the apartment, "and the house in Ireland, and the place in the Greek Islands I've only seen photos of. There were some investments that went wrong. Oh, and the parties, lots of parties, lots of presents, lots of friends," she said bitterly. "My accountant tells me that I owe a little more than five hundred thousands dollars in outstanding debts." She smiled tightly. "If all my creditors were to call in their debts at once I'd be bankrupt."

"Could you sell some of your holdings, your investments?"

"Most of the investments aren't worth shit! The house in Ireland isn't worth that much; I don't know about the

place on Corfu. But if I start selling those what have I got
left? And if anyone ever got to hear of it — one of the
gossip columnists for example — and the news got out,
then it could bring the whole house of cards tumbling
down."

"But I thought your publishers still owed you money?"
Gabrielle said.

"They do. They owe me nearly one and a half million
dollars; half of it due on delivery of the manuscript, the
other half upon publication." She gripped Gabrielle's arms
above the elbow, squeezing painfully. "It's a real Catch-22.
If I had the money everything would be all right. But to get
the money I've got to deliver the book … and I can't. I just
can't write this book. What am I going to do Gabrielle?
What am I going to do? I'm completely blocked."

Gabrielle wrapped her arms around Briony. Kneeling
in the water, she looked down into the older woman's face.
"The first thing you're going to do is to make love to me!"

"Will that help?" Briony wondered.

"It'll help."

Chapter Two

Gabrielle pressed the mute button on the phone and turned to Briony Dalton.

"It's Terri Fierstein; are you in?"

Briony made a face and swung away from the computer screen. She pushed her glasses up onto her hair and reached for the cordless phone. "I'd better speak to her," she sighed. "Terri! What a surprise! Lovely to hear from you!" she lied.

"Briony, how are you?"

"Fine. You?"

"Working hard."

Terri Fierstein's accent was brittle New York, with just enough rasp in it to set Briony's teeth on edge. She extended the aerial on the portable phone, stood up and stretched, pushing the heel of her hand into the small of her back, while simultaneously working her shoulders to free the kinks.

She wandered over to the sliding window and stepped out onto the balcony.

Although she was thirty floors up, she could still smell the bitter chemical stench of traffic. "Pardon?" she said, realising that Terri had spoken to her.

"I was wondering how the book's coming along?"

"Slowly," Briony admitted.

There was a silence on the line, and then Terri Fierstein sighed audibly and deliberately. "Well, you've got six months left to finish it," she said crisply. "Think you can do it? But I'm sure you can," she continued, without waiting for an answer.

Terri Fierstein was Briony Dalton's agent. She had represented her last ten books — all of which had been international best-sellers. She was a tiny, ill-tempered woman, who had married six times, buried three husbands and divorced three: the whole process, she often said, being the ideal if not essential training for any agent. She worked out of an office situated in the loft of a house in Greenwich Village which she had inherited from husband number two — deceased — and managed two dozen of the best-known authors in the world. She also represented scores of other, lesser-known authors, some of whom she occasionally elevated to best-seller status with one of her legendary deals.

Briony Dalton was, in many respects, Terri Fierstein's creation. And Terri made sure she never forgot it. "Is there a problem?" she asked.

"No …" Briony said slowly, leaning on the balcony and looking down into the city. Although the day was crisp and clear, the storm of the previous day having finally blown itself out some time in the early hours of the morning, the streets below looked dirty and grey. "Yes," she confessed, "there is a problem." The silence on the other end of the line made her continue. Terri Fierstein was one of the few people in this world who made her nervous. The woman had made her; she could just as easily unmake her … well no, that wasn't true any more. Four or five years ago it might have been possible, but now Briony Dalton was too well known. However, Terri had the power to damage her reputation within the publishing industry.

"Do you want to tell me about it?" Terri said sharply. Briony shrugged. "I'm having difficulty completing this book," she said, finally coming to terms with the inevitable, admitting what she'd been avoiding for months.

"Blocked?" her agent asked.

"Yes … no … I don't know," Briony hurried on. "Tell me what a writer's block is and I'll tell you if I'm blocked."

Briony could easily imagine the woman on the other end of the phone, the small pinched face with the thin, bloodless lips, the sharp beak of a nose, the deep-set black eyes behind half- glasses.

"The complete inability to write," Terri said immediately. "The inability to see or conceive anything. To stare at a page for days on end with nothing new appearing." She stopped abruptly and then demanded. "Well?"

"Well … .yes, I suppose."

"You suppose," her agent said, keeping her voice carefully neutral.

Briony turned around and walked back into the room. It was still chilly outside. She crossed to sit in front of her computer screen. She was using a colour monitor and had adjusted the colours of the word-processing program so that the text now showed white against a red background, which she found more restful over long periods. Pulling her glasses down off her head, perching them on the end of her nose, she closed the chapter she was working on, and looked at the menu on the screen before her. "Chapters one through eight are written in first draft … that's about twenty thousand words. When I polish and expand it'll come up to around twenty-five. The rest of the novel has been outlined in detail and the last chapter, which will be number forty-nine or fifty is partially written."

There was a long silence on the other end of the phone. Finally Terri Fierstein said, "You have been working for a year and a half and all you have to show for it is twenty thousand words of a first draft. This is a two hundred and fifty thousand word novel! The last few time we spoke, you told me it was nearly finished or that you were three quarters of the way through or that you were nearly done," she accused, her voice rising to end in a shriek. "Now, you're telling me you have a lousy twenty thousand words done. In first draft."

"It was nearly finished," Briony said defensively. "But it wasn't really any good. I scrapped it and started afresh," she lied.

"Bullshit! That's a crock of shit, and you know it. You've screwed around for the past eighteen months being the author celebrity and done sweet fuck all! Well now you listen to me, Briony Dalton, I've invested a lot in you, in time and effort and in cold, hard cash. I stand to make a lot of money out of you ... but you stand to make an awful lot more. I will not allow any dumb bitch to fuck me around. Ditch the dyke secretary and get down to some serious writing. The old Briony Dalton would have turned out this book in six months flat ... and been paid a few hundred pounds for it, and been happy with it. Just remember, this is a two and a half million dollar project ... and you need the money. I don't think I need to remind you that you need that money!"

The phone went dead in Briony's hand.

Gabrielle looked up from the pile of correspondence she was attending to.

"Bad, eh?" Even though she'd been on the other side of the room, she'd heard the woman's voice buzzing down the phone.

"Bad enough. Make me a cup of tea, will you?" she asked tiredly. What was even more galling was that the bitch was right. And why did she have to remind her about the old Briony Dalton? Why did she have to bring that up?

She was right, though: the old Briony Dalton would have been happy to churn it out in six months and been equally happy with a few thousand pounds of an advance.

Briony sat down in the high-backed typist's chair and slipped her headphones on. There was a small portable CD player on the desk beside her keyboard, and she wrote to the sounds of classical music, usually renaissance, medieval or baroque. She thumbed the PLAY switch. It took her a moment or two to recognise the music: Bach, Sonatas and Partitas, with Perlman. The pure, almost ethereal violin music washed over her, and she turned the sound up higher, wiping out the background noises, the hum of the computer, the sounds of Gabby moving around the apartment, attempting to dismiss Terri Fierstein's comments.

The old Briony Dalton would have been happy. She gazed at the screen of her state of the art personal computer and grinned sourly: the old Briony Dalton had written her first novel on a battered Imperial typewriter on the kitchen table of a two-room flat in Dublin's inner city tenements. And the only accompaniment to the clacking of the typewriter had been the wailing of the countless children in the flats, the tinny squeaking of innumerable radios, the voices, the shouts, the cries, the roars, with accents from just about every Irish county.

And, yes, the old Briony Dalton had been happier. The chaos had been something of an inspiration and a spur …

She stopped.

An idea had come to her, complete and whole.

She was smiling broadly as she glanced at the ornate stainless-steel clock over the stone fireplace. She wondered how long she had … about an hour, she guessed.

Terri Fierstein arrived one hour and five minutes later. She was wearing a two-piece grey suit cut in a mannish style and accompanied by the tall, elegant African American, Charles Beaumont Lesalles, who acted as her personal assistant, chauffeur and bodyguard … and, the gossips said, performed other, rather more personal services. The man had never been heard to speak in public and always wore evening dress, complete with bow tie and ruffled shirt.

Briony liked to think she was one of the few people who knew the man didn't speak because of a serious stammer. She didn't think they were lovers: she suspected the man was gay. But she also knew that Terri didn't correct the rumours — indeed, Briony had the tiniest suspicion that she had actually started them herself, because it helped her image.

And Terri Fierstein was very conscious of her image.

"Well it's nice to see you're working," the tiny woman snapped as she strode into the room, leaving Gabrielle standing at the door.

Briony dutifully turned her cheek, but the older woman pointedly ignored it and sank onto the hide settee. Briony said nothing, allowing Terri to continue the conversation. She was well aware of the value of silence. She turned back to the computer and closed the file she was working on, saved the material to disc and then shut down the machine. When the long descending whine had finally ceased, Terri spoke.

"Do you want to tell me about it?" she asked.

"I'm not sure if there's anything to tell," Briony said.

"I asked you earlier if you were blocked," Terri persisted. "Are you?"

"No ... I don't think I am. I think it's just ... the distractions," she said softly, looking at Gabrielle as she came into the room, carrying a heavy-looking silver tray. The tea-service was antique Irish silver.

Terri Fierstein watched Gabrielle bend over to pour the tea. The secretary was wearing a granddad shirt over a pair of soft leather jeans. The jeans were so tight that they looked as if they had been painted on to her legs and it was obvious she was wearing no underwear. Gabrielle glanced up once — deliberately looking into the agent's hard, cynical eyes, and then smiled almost insolently before looking away.

"The last year has been a little crazy," Briony said slowly, as Gabrielle left the room. Terri's companion was sitting on the cane chair on the balcony, a pair of brightly coloured headphones on his head, hand moving to the rhythm of the unseen Walkman. "Even you'll have to admit that."

Terri watched her pour milk into both cups.

"I mean I've appeared on coast-to-coast TV, I've been interviewed in nearly every major magazine, I've guested on countless game shows, I spent a lot of time on the set when they were shooting the mini-series of the last book. I get invited to parties, openings, galas, premières ..."

"What are you?" Terri asked bluntly.

Briony placed her left hand flat against her chest. "I'm a writer."

"Are you a television personality? A media person, a presenter of game shows, fodder for newspaper and magazine journalists? Are you?" she demanded.

Briony shook her head.

"Are you a party person? Do you drink, smoke, snort or shoot up? Do you follow the cinema, the theatre?"

Briony shook her head again; she knew what her agent was leading up to.

"You know I don't."

"Then for Christ's sake, why do you go? Why do you agree to do the shows, why do you accept the invitations to the parties?"

When Briony looked across the table her large brown eyes were bright with unshed tears. "Because I want to. Because I'm lonely," she burst out. "I need the companionship," she added almost fiercely.

The two women finished their tea in silence. When Briony offered more, Terri refused. "Show me what you've done so far," she said.

Briony crossed the room and sat down in the high-backed chair before the computer. She put on her large-framed glasses and turned the machine on, pausing while it blipped softly to itself, red and green lights flashing on the panel set into its body. Text flickered on the screen, too fast to read and then the screen cleared to show the letter C in the top left-hand corner. Briony typed in the coded combination that called up the word processor, loaded the dictionary and thesaurus and opened her files for *A Woman Scorned*. Terri Fierstein came to stand behind her, her left hand on Briony's right shoulder. She leaned forward, staring at the screen; she was wearing a particularly heavy perfume, Opium, Briony thought, wrinkling her nose and resisting the temptation to sneeze.

"Talk me through this," Terri said, nodding at the soft red screen, with its grey-white letters.

"The chapters numbered one to eight are complete. Forty-nine is also nearly complete. The other files are merely synopsis, notes and character files."

"How complete is the synopsis now?" When Terri Fierstein had been auctioning the new Briony Dalton property to the five major American publishers, she had sold it with just a single-page outline in hand ... that and Briony's previous successes. The bidding had started at one million dollars.

Briony's fingers moved across the keyboard, calling up the file labelled SYNOP. The screen cleared and a mass of text appeared. "The synopsis now runs to fifty-two pages," Briony said proudly. "There's a three-page overall synopsis of the entire book, and then single page outlines for every chapter."

"So the major work is done?"

"More or less. All I have to do now is to write it," she added wryly.

"Lots of sex?" Terri asked.

"Lots."

Terri reached over and touched the keys, scrolling the text upwards, silently reading through the overall synopsis of *A Woman Scorned*.

"Excellent," she said finally. "It'll be good."

Briony nodded. *A Woman Scorned* had the potential to be her best book yet ... if it ever got written.

"What about the ending?"

"Two alternatives at the moment. Something happy, but predictable, or dramatic — kill them both off, for example — but I think that might be a cheat."

"Have them murdered, die in each other's arms," Terri suggested, deliberately making Briony think about the book.

"Murdered by the daughter," Briony said, the idea taking shape in her mind.

Her fingers moved on the keys opening a new file, and then she began to type with a speed which Terri always found astonishing. "How about if we reconcile the hero and heroine at the end of the book?" she asked, talking while she typed. "We could have a grand reconciliation … maybe even remarry them … "

"In an exotic location," Terri supplied.

"A Greek island?"

"Tacky, but acceptable. It would film very nicely," she added. "Then have a long, erotic lovemaking scene … fall asleep in one another's arms. And then the daughter reappears and shoots them both!"

"I like it," Terri smiled. "Now, if you can write that, you can write the rest of the book." She squeezed Briony's shoulder reassuringly. "You're not blocked."

That was some consolation, Briony thought. Writer's block was a very real danger for any professional writer. It was the sudden and terrifying inability to put anything down on paper. It was as if whatever well of imagination and ideas had dried up. For some people it was a psychological problem brought on by stress or overwork, and sorted itself out relatively quickly, but with others … she had heard of more than one promising talent disappearing forever.

"You need to work on this book, Briony. And work seriously."

"Yes … yes, I'll try," Briony said, still typing her notes.

"If it is successful, you'll be able to ask your own price for the next one. You'll be able to command Stephen King, John Grisham, Michael Crichton-type advances." She spoke softly, insistently. "But you know what'll happen if you're late. Now there are some agents who believe that you don't put pressure on your author to work. I'm not one of those agents.

"You have to deliver this book; it's as simple as that. Not only for the publishers' sake, but for my sake … and yours. You need the money, Briony. You know that even better than I do."

Briony Dalton turned from the screen. "I know," she said. Terri Fierstein took both Briony's long hands in her own short stumpy fingers. "You've lost direction," she said forcefully. "It happens, and it's partially my fault for not seeing it happen, for not advising you, warning you about it. You were enjoying being a media person, and fame can be addictive, like a drug."

"What can I do?"

Terri smiled sourly. "What's the phrase quack head doctors use? 'Find yourself.' You've got to find yourself, reassert yourself. Go back to your roots, where you started to write. Sometimes that re-establishes the ideals, the reasons why you decided to write. Take a holiday. Take six months off — alone — and come back to me with the book finished."

Briony looked up, a broad smile creasing her face. "I've already thought about that. I was going to suggest going back to Ireland."

"That's an excellent idea," Terri said. "Go back to Ireland. Rediscover why you became a writer."

Chapter Three

Catherine Garrett did as she did with all of Briony Dalton's books. She slowly tore the paperback in half with a great deal of satisfaction. She then tossed both halves in the wastepaper basket beneath her desk.

She sat back, folded her arms across her chest and read through the long review she had prepared on the book. She was amused to find that even though she had written the body of the review weeks before she had actually read *Pavane*, with a few minor corrections, she was quite prepared to allow it to stand. What she found even more amusing was that although she had written the review from the publisher's advance information sheets and the pre-publication sales material, the review was accurate.

Even allowing for her own prejudices, the book was rubbish, absolute, unmitigated rubbish. An implausible story, with a wooden hero, a plastic heroine and a cliché-ridden text that was almost painfully difficult to read. The book was pulp, pure and simple crap. Five years ago it would not have seen its way into print ... and if it had been written by anyone but Briony Dalton, it would never have been published.

And Briony Dalton had been paid an advance of half a million sterling for it.

Catherine Garrett rested her head in her hand and stared out across the rolling Sussex Downs. It was raining over the drab grasslands in the distance, but here, tucked into the lee of a hill, it was still dry. Stray shafts of sunlight broke through the cloud across the distant hills.

"What we have here," she said aloud, "is a little jealousy, I think." Or was it? Catherine shook her head slightly. No, maybe not. Even though she was envious of the huge advances Briony Dalton received, she didn't think she was being unfair in the review.

Catherine Garrett knew Briony Dalton couldn't write. Indeed, in her opinion, Briony Dalton was nothing more than a hack who had been very, very lucky with one particular book — was it *Odalisk*? — and after that a snowball had started rolling which simply couldn't be stopped. The woman could sign her name to a telephone directory and it would sell.

It was unfair; simply too unfair.

The phone rang at the other end of the house, startling her, but she made no move to answer it. Moments later the answering machine cut in, and her own disembodied voice drifted in from the hallway,

" … I'm probably here, but if you know me, you'll know I never answer the phone during the day. However, leave me your name, and a message and I'll try and get back to you after six tonight. Even freelances have to keep regular hours."

"Catherine, why won't you answer the bloody phone? I know you're there "There was a pause, as if the caller were expecting the phone to be picked up. "Anyway. I need this month's paperback reviews by tomorrow. I know I said next week, but the deadlines have been screwed up this month. Give me what you have anyway, and I especially need the Briony Dalton review. We're running it alongside a biographical piece and a photo. I'll try and phone you later. Bye."

She had been half-expecting the call. Briony Dalton was big news. Everything about Briony Dalton was big news. Even the fact that the publishers were putting one hundred thousand pounds into promoting the book had become part of the advertising campaign — a series of full-page ads had appeared not only in all the women's magazines, but most of the male mags as well. *Playboy* had done a four-page interview with what it called the reclusive Briony Dalton, the 'Queen of the Red Hot Read'. Most of the London tube stations carried ads for the book and a series of fifteen and thirty second spots had been appearing on national and local radio.

Bitch!

Catherine turned on her printer, lined up the paper in the machine, and then printed out the two thousand five hundred word review, reading it as the printer head clattered from side to side. When it was finished she tore the paper off at its perforated edge and re-read it.

She carried it across to the fax, lifted the phone and punched out the office number. When the high-pitched warbling changed tone, she pushed the START button and watched the machine swallow up the eleven double-spaced pages one by one.

That would keep them happy for a while.

Catherine returned to her small computer screen and stared at the blocky characters, her face so close to the screen that she could actually make out the dots that made up the letters.

How had the bitch managed to do it? What did she have that Catherine didn't?

"Don't worry about it." Strong hands tightened on her tense shoulders, the fingers squeezing, massaging her taut muscles.

"I'm working," Catherine muttered. "You know I don't like to be disturbed when I'm working."

The hands moved down her back and then under her arms, suddenly lifting her up, turning her around to face the tall young man. He grinned. "You weren't working. You were brooding."

Catherine opened her mouth to protest, but the large hands lifted her higher, bringing her face up to a level with his, kissing her, tongue and mouth working against hers. Catherine resisted a moment, and then responded, relaxing into her lover's arms, her body beginning to respond to his touch. She had lived with Mark Cosgrove for nearly two years and while to the outside world he might be many things — boyfriend, acquaintance, colleague or simply companion — to her, he would always simply be her lover.

Their attraction had been immediate and initially purely physical and it was only later, when they had exhausted that stage of their relationship, that they discovered things about themselves they had in common, things about each other they liked. And of course, Catherine realised, they had also become used to one another.

Mark Cosgrove stood at just over six feet in his bare feet and was broad in proportion. He wore his blond hair shaved so close to his skull that he appeared bald. This made it difficult to guess his age, although few came close to the truth that he was actually only three years Catherine's junior, for he looked much younger. His eyes were bright blue, slightly magnified behind small circular-framed spectacles. She could see herself reflected in the lenses of the glasses, her hair too wild, too much grey in the chestnut curls, her muddy-brown eyes sunk deep into her face, the flesh puffy, with lines around the mouth and eyes. She was dressed in a pair of faded baggy jeans and a chunky cardigan that completely enveloped her.

"Why do you stay with me?" she murmured, her breath warm on his face.

Mark Cosgrove stroked her hair; he had witnessed this scene or a variation of it, on the numerous occasions that Briony Dalton's work came up for discussion. At this stage he could almost write the script. She was looking for reassurance.

"I'm too fat, too old. You could find yourself another woman, a younger woman."

"I don't want another woman," he said. "I like you … no, I love you," he added, the lie coming so easily to him now that he almost believed it. Careful, he cautioned, otherwise you might just end up believing it. The truth was that Catherine Garrett was useful to him, now and in the future, and while she continued to remain useful he would stay with her. "I love you," he repeated.

"Do you really?" she asked.

"Really," he said, hating her in that single moment. Hating her weakness, hating his own. She was not fat, nor was she ugly, although at this particular moment, she was certainly unattractive. She was jealous of Briony Dalton's success, feeling resentful and bitter. And yet, it wasn't as if she was unsuccessful in her own right. Catherine Garrett was one of the foremost literary critics in the country. With her own weekly television book programme, and her numerous reviews for the Sunday papers, the *Times Literary Supplement*, and some of the glossier magazines, it was said that her comments could decide a book's fate.

Mark Cosgrove ran his hands up and down her back, soothing her. He was crooning softly now, murmuring nonsense phrases, but his mind was drifting, and he was already eager to return to work on the manuscript of the novel he was due to deliver at the end of next month. Then the two years of living with this whining woman would be worthwhile; she had already promised him that she would do everything in her power to make the book a success.

"Bitch," Catherine muttered.

"Hmmm?"

"Bitch," Catherine repeated. "She's a talentless bitch; she doesn't deserve it. She's never deserved it. You know we roomed together … did I ever tell you!"

Mark Cosgrove kissed her quickly, his lips pressing hard against hers. If he heard the story of how Briony Dalton and Catherine Garrett had grown up together, lived together, roomed together again, he would scream. His hands moved down her body and gathered up the sloppy jumper, moving beneath it, touching bare flesh. He traced her spine until he encountered her bra strap. He unclipped it and moved his hands around, tracing the slight indentation in her skin …

The phone rang.

They broke apart in surprise, and in that instant the moment was gone. As the answering machine droned out its message, Catherine turned her back on Mark and hooked up her bra again. When she looked around he was gone. Moments later, she heard the faint clacking of the keyboard in the next room.

"Catherine ... Catherine ... For Christ's sake pick up the phone, you dumb bitch. This is important."

The voice shocked her motionless for a moment and then simultaneously she realised it was coming from the phone, audible over the answering machine, and recognised the slight Germanic accent.

"Pick up the phone, Catherine."

Catherine clicked off the answering machine and scooped up the phone in the same movement. "Josef ... Josef Bach?" she said in astonishment.

"Oh, so you know my voice. I should be flattered!" The voice was sharp and clear and for an instant Catherine could see the tall, white-haired, blue-eyed man, whose nickname in the publishing world was the Colonel, because of his resemblance to the American fast-food franchise trademark, and his penchant for wearing white suits.

"There are certain voices you never forget," Catherine grinned. "It's been a while, Herr Bach. To what do I owe the pleasure? It's not often I have a phone call from a multi-billionaire."

"Millionaire, my dear. Multi-millionaire. Accounts of my wealth have been greatly overestimated. We may be able to do one another a favour," he continued pleasantly, and Catherine, realising this meant business, grabbed a pencil and poised it over the notepad beside the phone.

"I owe you more than one favour," Catherine said lightly. He owned several magazines and had helped her get started. Technically, he was one of her employers.

"Yes you do," Bach murmured, the vaguest intonation of his German accent just audible. "You are aware of Briony Dalton's new book?" he asked with his customary directness.

"*Pavane*" Catherine said.

"No, no," Josef Bach said impatiently. "The new book. The big advance book."

"The three million dollar deal or whatever it is," Catherine said, unable to keep the bitterness from her voice.

"I want to talk to you about it."

"Well … yes, of course, the next time you're in London."

"I want to talk to you now. Put your boots on and grab a coat."

"What?"

"I thought we could go for a walk and discuss this."

"Josef … where the hell are you?"

"Look out of your window."

Lifting the phone, Catherine carried it to the window. There was a Rolls Royce Silver Shadow parked on the verge directly outside the front door, a thin plume of white smoke curling from its exhaust. A uniformed chauffeur stepped out of the car and opened the back door, allowing Catherine to see into the interior. Josef Bach leaned forward and waved. He lifted his leg and pointed to his foot, and then, disconcertingly, she heard his voice over the phone.

"Put your boots on, dear, it is a little damp out here."

∞

"Josef Bach, do you want to tell me just what the fuck is going on?"

The big German moved around a puddle on the sodden bridle path, then threw one arm around Catherine's shoulders and drew her close. They had followed the narrow track that led out onto the downs, away from the shelter afforded by the hills. It had been raining on and off throughout the night and the ground was waterlogged, the air damp and fresh with the promise of more rain.

Josef Bach breathed deeply. "Smell that; taste it. If I could bottle it I could make a fortune."

"You have a fortune," Catherine reminded him. "In fact you have several fortunes. I hear you've moved into the retail book trade now."

"I didn't have any choice in the matter. It was the obvious move to make."

Josef Bach had made his fortune in the printing business. He had started as an apprentice in the Hamburg Printing Works just after the war and through hard work and a measure of good luck, he had eventually established himself in his own printing business, from where it was an almost natural move into publishing, first newspapers and magazines, and then books. Recently he had begun buying into the book trade, taking over the smaller bookshop chains and independents, discreetly challenging the larger chains. Catherine had read that the move was generally regarded with disquiet: theoretically it allowed one man to control the life of a book from its manuscript stage through to the sales floor.

"What's on your mind, Josef?" Catherine asked.

"Briony Dalton." He glanced at her. "If my memory serves me, you and she are not such good friends."

"That's putting it mildly," she said, "but you already know that."

"Do you want to tell me why?"

"Not really."

"I could find out if I wanted to," he said mildly.

"I know."

"You grew up with her; you've always hinted that there was some skeleton in her cupboard. Is there? Do you really know her secret?"

Catherine Garrett nodded, and then stopped suddenly. Josef Bach walked on a few paces and then looked back. The smile on his thin-lipped face was anything but pleasant. "So there is a secret. I wasn't sure." He turned away and strode on, his hands clenched behind his back. "You have heard of Hall's?" he called back.

"The publishers?" She ran a few paces to catch up with him. "They're Briony Dalton's publishers. Or about to be."

"Did you know I attempted to buy them out?"

"I had heard something or read something in the trade press."

"They refused my offer."

Catherine wondered where all this was leading.

"I had examined that company very carefully, and I knew they were — they are — in serious financial straits. And yet they have managed to advance Briony Dalton one million pounds sterling for the British volume rights to *A Woman Scorned.*"

"Well, they wouldn't have had to pay out all that money at once … "

The look on Josef Bach's face silenced her. "They don't have the money; they have had to borrow heavily to finance this book. They paid much more than they could afford and that vixen Terri Fierstein tied them into a contract only the devil himself could get out of. They are committed to an extraordinary level of expenditure for the new book. The publicity package alone is worth another hundred thousand. This book has to work for them, otherwise … . "

"You wouldn't be too upset if they went under though, would you?"

"Me? Me? I would devastated … for about two seconds."

"Josef, perhaps I'm being particularly dense this morning, but I fail to see what any of this has to do with me."

"You say you know Briony Dalton's secret?"

"Yes."

"Truly?"

"I know her secret. But it would be difficult to prove. You know there are two faces to her: the brash public face, with all the glitz and the glamour, and then there's the other, rather darker side. Did you know she had two children?"

"Yes," he said, surprising her. He stopped and turned to face her once more. "What would you say if I told you I had discovered the whereabouts of both of them? What would you say if I told you that one is a junkie, mainlining on heroin, whose mother has consistently refused to see him and has refused to give him money for treatment? And what would you say if I told you that the daughter has now made no fewer that thirty hard-core pornographic movies?" Josef Bach laughed at her shocked expression. "Is this the sort of thing the public would like to read?" He raised his hand to forestall her questions.

"I want you to write Briony Dalton's biography. I want you to dig up as much dirt on her as possible. And I want it all, Catherine." He looked away, allowing his words to sink in, and then he continued: "In return, I will pay you an advance of five hundred thousand pounds sterling — that's half a million in real money — on a standard book contract, one third on signature, one third on delivery, one third on publication, with a bonus of fifty thousand pounds if you can deliver the project in under six months." His voice had fallen to little more than a whisper, his accent more pronounced now. "I want to destroy this woman's credibility with the public. I want people to be so disgusted with her that her next book doesn't even move out of the warehouse, never mind sell in the shops."

"What do you get out of it?" Catherine asked.

"This arrangement suits us both," Bach said, ignoring her question. "You get a writing contract and a fabulous advance, and it enables you to shit on your worst enemy."

"Hall's," Catherine whispered, "you get her publishers."

Bach smiled. "When her book flops I'll be able to buy Hall's for a song. Take a few days, think about it," he suggested.

"I don't need to think about it. I'll do it. Go find me that contract!"

Bach reached into his inner pocket.

Chapter Four

"Passengers are requested to please fasten their seat belts…"

Briony Dalton came slowly, sluggishly awake, half-remembered fragments of dreams remaining with her, leaving her disorientated and momentarily confused.

She'd dreamt that she was running away from something formless and horrible, something that threatened to smother her. And just when she thought she'd escaped, the monster had loomed up in front of her and she found she was running back into its embrace.

Ireland.

She was returning to Ireland.

Gabrielle was speaking to her. "When did you leave Ireland?"

She didn't even have to think about the reply. "Fifteen years ago."

"Have you been back often?"

"Briefly." She smiled tightly. "But never for pleasure. I've been back when there was a book to promote and you know what those tours are like, highly organised and so artificial that I don't count them. I really don't have fond memories of the country."

"Why did you leave?"

Gabrielle was chattering because she was nervous, Briony realised with a shock. It was almost amusing to find her usually strong, confident companion trembling with nerves. She reached out and took her hand in hers, squeezing the fingers slightly. "I left shortly after the publication of my first real success," she said, making conversation, distracting her.

"The notorious *Odalisk*," Gabrielle said.

"The notorious *Odalisk*." Briony smiled fondly, remembering that strange, crazy time. To her it had been just another book — perhaps a little more commercial than her previous writing, but to some people it was a scandalous attack on the very fabric of Irish society. "I left shortly before it was banned."

"Why was it banned?"

"You've read *Odalisk* haven't you?"

"I thought it was wonderful."

"Well, my dear, you must bear in mind that fifteen years ago Ireland was a staunchly Catholic country and *Odalisk* was a highly explicit, if somewhat satirical look at the sexuality of the Catholic clergy. It offended far too many people. People claimed that they recognised political and clerical figures of the day in some of the major characters in the novel … and perhaps they had," she added with a wicked grin, "perhaps I hadn't disguised them well enough. I remember one reviewer claiming that the whole tenor of the book had been too factual to be fiction." Her smile faded and, involuntarily, her grip tightened on Gabrielle's fingers. "It also made me something of a *persona non grata* with certain factions in the country."

She remembered the threats, the obscene phone calls, the hate mail that had made her life a misery. But she also recalled the sudden flurry of television and radio appearances that had helped push her into the public eye and keep her there. The book had been a best-seller.

And what was it Oscar Wilde had said about being talked about and not being talked about … ?

She had been denounced from the pulpit, and booksellers were urged not to stock the novel: those who chose to carry the title had been picketed and boycotted by various religious factions. The furore had eventually resulted in the book's official banning by the Irish Censorship Board … and the resultant publicity had helped hype the book into its multimillion-copy best-selling status all over the world.

Less than twelve months later, when the sequel to *Odalisk*, *Harem* had appeared in print, most of the major book wholesalers in Ireland had refused to handle the title, and although the book was widely reviewed, and well received, it never featured on the Irish best-seller lists, although it topped the *New York Times* best-seller list for ten weeks, and appeared in the top twenty best-selling novels in Britain for twenty-four weeks. It was placed number fifteen in the top one hundred books of 1978 and even now, fourteen years later, both books remained in print. Paradoxically, *Harem* which was if anything even more explicit than its predecessor, was never banned in Ireland.

The Irish newspapers had dubbed her 'The Pornographer' and, while it wasn't true — her books were erotic rather than pornographic — it was a reputation which had remained with her to this day.

On her few previous visits to the country she had been hounded by the press, virtually besieged in her hotel; on her last trip, her television interview with one of the country's most popular entertainers had been abruptly terminated when a section of the audience had begun chanting 'Pornographer' and 'Blasphemer'. The publicity had done wonders for the book's sales.

"I've never been to Ireland," Gabrielle said excitedly, looking out over the bright green fields intersected with a flat, grey ribbon of road as the plane banked for its final approach to Dublin Airport.

"You'll like it," Briony said quietly. She hoped there wasn't going to be a scene at the airport. No one knew she was coming, not even her English publishers; no arrangements had been made. This was not work, there would be no interviews, no signings, no promotional appearances; this was simply Briony Dalton returning to Ireland for a holiday, a break, a chance to recharge her batteries in the country that had inspired her to write.

Her mouth twisted in a wry smile. She had about two chances of achieving that, she thought: slim and none. Why, she hadn't even managed to leave New York without an argument.

Terri Fierstein had been absolutely furious when she had learned that Briony was taking Gabrielle along with her. Her agent had even gone so far as to meet her at Kennedy Airport in a last-minute attempt to bring her to her senses.

But Briony had been adamant.

She needed Gabrielle, she claimed; she was essential for her work, necessary for her peace of mind.

But in truth, Briony was frightened to return to Ireland on her own.

As the Aer Lingus Boeing 737 dropped in the dusky evening sky, Briony leaned back into the seat and wondered what awaited her in the land of her birth. There were some who claimed that she had betrayed the country and everything it had given her, pillaged it for material for her books … and what was wrong with that, a small voice asked, a writer writes from personal experience. There was nothing wrong with that, she knew … nothing except in the way she had used that material. She had made the Irish, with their quaint, sometimes curious and often downright puzzling customs and manners, a laughing stock, she had mocked the institutions of the Church and State.

But did anyone care?

No, not now maybe; the fictional events in her books had been surpassed by the Church's own sexual scandals, but in the mid-seventies people did, and she was still living with the results of the passions she had aroused then. Writers had come after her who had written worse — much worse — about Ireland and the Irish, but no one had ever aroused that same sense of outrage as she had.

Briony knew that her publisher's publicity departments had mined the banning of *Odalisk* and the subsequent protest about the book's 'pornographic' content for all it was worth. Newspaper column inches, no matter how good or bad, but preferably the more dramatic the better, sold books. She had never protested at how they used her name — indeed, initially, she hadn't realised what they were doing. And even if she did, she wasn't sure if she would have cared. All she knew was that they were selling her books, and the more books that sold, the more money she made.

She hadn't yet learned the valuable lesson that everything has a price, and some fees are paid without money.

The plane touched down with the barest shudder and Gabrielle's fingers locked painfully around her hand before finally relaxing. "We've landed."

Briony smiled tightly: she wondered if many people would recognise her.

And prayed no one would.

She had last been in Dublin a little more than a year previously to sign copies of her latest book, *Pavane*, which had just been published in hardback. She had appeared on television and radio chat shows and had been extensively interviewed, but the single book signing that had been arranged had been a disaster. A picket outside the shop, accompanied by a monotonous chant of `Pornographer' and `Blasphemer' had ensured that few people had even entered the bookshop, and of those only two had bought copies of the book. As one stage there had been a brief flurry of young men and women in the bookshop who appeared with a copy of the book for her to sign, but they had all only asked for a signature and not a dedication, and she immediately knew that these were the bookshop's own employees, disguised as customers in an attempt to save her embarrassment.

The newspapers had had a field day. All the old stories had been raked up then: the stories about her marriage and its subsequent break-up, in which she treated her husband so badly, her numerous affairs, her much publicised lifestyle ...

" … Thank you for flying Aer Lingus."

"We've arrived," Gabrielle said unsnapping her seat belt. "Aren't you glad to be home?"

Briony looked at her and shook her head slightly. "I don't know," she said. "It hasn't been my home for a long time."

Gabrielle squeezed her fingers tightly, confidence fully restored now they were on the ground. "Nervous?"

"A little."

"Don't be. We'll have a lovely holiday, and you'll be able to work on your book. You could even find time to visit your family," she suggested.

"There's none I'd want to visit, and even if I did, I'm sure none of them would want me to visit."

"What about your father?"

"Especially my father," Briony said grimly.

∞

It was unusual to step through the sliding doors into the arrivals lounge of Dublin Airport and not be blinded by camera lights and the flash of lightbulbs. The lounge was surprisingly quiet, almost deserted, which relieved her greatly. Briony had taken a few elementary precautions coming back to Ireland. Instead of flying directly from New York to Dublin, she had first flown to London and then back to Dublin. She was travelling light, having sent her baggage on ahead a few days previously by courier and, whilst she was not exactly in disguise, she had gone to some pains to dress in a rather less flamboyant fashion than usual. Her thick, coal-black hair was hidden beneath a 1920's-style cap and she was without her trademark large-framed spectacles, wearing the contact lenses she detested, but occasionally found useful and often necessary.

She stopped in the arrivals hall to wait for Gabrielle, who was somewhere behind her. She was abruptly aware of a presence standing right beside her. Conscious of the pounding of her heart, she turned quickly, and found herself looking up at a tall, bulky man, who was smiling pleasantly at her. She put his age at close to fifty, although he could have been older. His black hair was cropped close to his skull, his wide and innocent eyes were slate grey, looking like a child's eyes in a mature man's face. He was casually dressed in jeans and a chunky roll-neck jumper beneath an anorak that had seen better days.

"Miss Bernadette Dalton?" he asked softly, his American accent putting him firmly in the Southern States.

Bernadette was the name she had been born with. When she had begun writing she had changed it to Briony, deciding that Briony was rather more exotic. No one ever called her Bernadette any more. In fact, she was unsure just how many people actually knew her real name. However, she had a good idea what was happening. The only person other than Gabrielle who knew she was coming here was Terri.

"It's Briony," she corrected him, walking past him and moving towards the Hertz car-hire desk. She spotted Gabrielle hurrying after her.

"Let's stick with Bernadette," the big man suggested quietly. "It's a lot less conspicuous."

"Let me guess," Briony said, the bitterness evident in her voice, "Terri organised you."

"Miss Fierstein did ask me to look after you." He smiled, his teeth white and strong. He turned to look at the younger woman as she hurried up. "And you must be Miss Royer. I have a car waiting for you both."

Briony rounded on him. "Look, Mr?"

"O'Neill." He smiled again and extended his hand. "Charles O'Neill. Most people call me Charley."

Briony ignored his hand. "Look Mr O'Neill," she said pointedly. "I have come here for a holiday; I would prefer if you left me alone. I'm sorry if I sound rude, but I didn't ask Terri to interfere."

The smiled faded from his face, and the big amiable man suddenly became menacing. "I am a private detective, ma'am. I have been hired by Miss Terri Fierstein to look after you during your stay here. That is what I have been paid to do … and that is what I am going to do." He shrugged and smiled again. "It is not open to discussion."

Gabrielle rested her hand on Briony's arm. "Let's get to the hotel and you can phone Terri from there. We don't want to make a scene here and attract attention."

"The young lady's right," Charley O'Neill agreed. He lifted Briony's overnight case from her hands and began moving towards the door. "Car's parked out front."

The two women followed the big American detective. Briony was furious with Terri. She knew the woman had done it with the best of intentions, but she bitterly resented the interference, bitterly resented the fact that Terri thought she could meddle in her private life as well as her business affairs. She was her agent for Christ's sake, not her mother.

And it wasn't the first time it had happened either.

Perhaps it was time she considered getting rid of Terri; maybe it was time for a new agent. She was a big name now and there would be no problem about finding someone to represent her. Some of these new agents were hot, managing to get huge advances for their clients … even when some of these clients had never written a word before. She also needed someone who would be able to get her more film contracts. Four of her books had been made into movies, two for the big screen, two for television mini-series; the mini-series had been disastrous, but the movies had been all right. There should be more movies … but Terri was a little old-fashioned about that. Yes, she decided, it was about time she got herself a new agent. This nonsense with the private eye was the final straw.

Charley O'Neill was talking to Gabrielle as Briony caught up with them. "I think you'll find that the pace is different, slower, gentler than back home, especially in the country. Will you be doing a little touring?"

Gabrielle nodded. "Oh yes, definitely."

They walked out of the terminal building, blinking in the watery sunshine.

"Why you?" Briony asked him rudely, as they waited by the small pedestrian crossing that led into the car park.

"I beg your pardon, ma'am?"

"Why you? Why did Terri pick you?"

"I think Miss Fierstein thought you would be happier with an American, ma'am."

"Do you have an agency here?" Gabrielle asked.

He nodded.

"And what exactly did Miss Fierstein want you to do for me?" Briony persisted.

"I'm supposed to look after you, chauffeur you around, keep you out of trouble. You've got something of a reputation, ma'am."

"And how detailed will your reports be to Miss Fierstein?" Briony demanded. "Exactly how much does she want to know?"

"I think she's merely protecting her investment," Charley O'Neill said, crossing the narrow road. After a moment's hesitation, Briony and Gabrielle followed him.

The car park was enormous, but O'Neill seemed to know where he was going. Without hesitation, he turned off to the left.

"I suppose I should ask to see some sort of qualifications," Briony snapped.

He dipped his hand into his breast pocket and showed her a laminated card. "I was a master sergeant, Marines, Vietnam service, Purple Heart, then Army Investigations Unit followed by a twelve-year stint in the FBI. When I got out of that I had my own agency in New York for a while before I came over here."

"Why did you leave all that to come over here?" Gabrielle asked, obviously fascinated by the man.

"For health reasons," he said with a grin, fishing in his anorak pockets for his car keys. He thumbed the alarm and the lights of a steel-grey Saab in the long line of cars ahead of them flashed once. "I decided I wanted to keep my health."

They drove in virtual silence into the city along a narrow stretch of motorway, past the occasional factory, until they reached the suburbs proper where the road was lined with houses.

"City's expanding," O'Neill remarked. "Must be quite a change since you were last here," he added, glancing in the mirror.

Briony ignored him.

"Lady, you don't have to like me, you don't even have to like what I'm doing, but the least you could do is to be civil to me. That costs nothing."

"I resent the intrusion into my privacy and freedom," Briony said primly.

"Sure you do. And what happens if a crazy person decides to intrude into your privacy, eh?"

"And is that likely to happen?" she asked, unable to keep the anxious note from her voice.

He shrugged. "Look, lady, the last time you were here, you managed to upset a lot of people. I've read your file. Every time you come over here, you upset a lot of people. Now, I know that's probably some sort of publicity stunt, and I'm sure it sells lots of books, but when you go around bad-mouthing people, talking dirty, swearing on national TV and radio, you're going to get notorious. Some of these people have long memories."

"You swore on national television?" Gabrielle asked in astonishment.

"Prime-time Saturday night television," Charley said. "Even I can remember it."

"What did you say?"

Briony shook her head. "I honestly don't remember."

Charley O'Neill grinned. *"I couldn't give a fuck what people think about my books"* was the sentence that did it. You then went on to speculate why, if so many people disliked your books so much, how they were all number one best-sellers. You added that you thought it highly likely that people were … ahem … arousing themselves by reading the erotic passages."

"You didn't!" Gabrielle breathed.

Briony shrugged. "I don't remember, but I suppose I must have."

Gabrielle threw back her head and laughed. "You must have been drunk or high or something."

"Probably."

They had passed out of the suburbs and were now into the rather run-down outskirts of the city proper. As they drove into Dorset Street, Briony suddenly leaned forward and pointed to the left. "Up here, into Belvedere Road."

O'Neill dutifully turned to the left and as they neared the top of the hill, which was lined on both sides by tall four or five-storey buildings which had seen better days, Briony pointed to a house almost on the corner. "I had an aunt who lived there …" She tapped the American detective on the shoulder and pointed to the right. "Follow the road round, then turn left, down past Sean MacDermott Street and then up into Gardiner Street," she instructed him.

They drove through an area that had obviously been razed to the ground and was in the process of being redeveloped. "Everything's changed," Briony muttered. They were almost opposite the ruin of what looked like a school when she tapped him on the shoulder again. "Slow down, slow down." He obediently slowed the car to a crawl.

"There … " Briony leaned across Gabrielle and pointed to a blue-painted door. "There, that's where I was born, fifth of October nineteen forty-seven. I didn't think it would still be here." The sense of awe and wonder in her voice surprised even herself.

"Have you ever been back?" Gabrielle asked, looking at the door again, and then up and down the street.

"No. The last I heard an aunt — my father's sister — lived in it, or in one of the rooms, rather. My father has his own little house."

"It doesn't seem a very wealthy district."

Briony put her arm around Gabrielle and squeezed. "My dear, when I was growing up in Dublin in the fifties, we were poverty stricken … or rather we were until my father got the pub. Every stitch of clothing I had was a hand-me-down, and I got my first pair of new shoes when I was making my Communion. I was six years old. This whole area, and the area we've just driven through, Mountjoy, Gardiner Street, Sean MacDermott Street were all tenements." She laughed at her secretary's horrified expression.

"You've seen lots of changes then," Charley O'Neill remarked.

"Lots," she said absently.

"What do you miss most from the old days?" he asked.

They had stopped at the traffic lights at the corner of Talbot Street. Briony rolled down the window and then turned her head slightly, listening. The incessant noise of city traffic percolated into the car. "The sound of children's voices," she said softly.

Chapter Five

"Bitch!"

Briony Dalton sat on the edge of the bed wrapped in a dressing gown, the phone held in a white-knuckled grip. Gabrielle stood behind her, naked except for a towel that had been tucked loosely between her breasts. She was towelling Briony's hair dry.

"Is there something wrong, Briony, dear." At the other end of the line, Terri Fierstein's voice was crystal clear, the triumphant edge coming through distinctly.

"This private detective you've hired … " Briony raged.

"What about him?"

"What gives you the right … ?"

"I am merely protecting my investment … and your future," Terri said primly. "I don't want anything to happen to you — and you do remember what went on in that terrible country the last time you were over there?"

"That was all publicity," Briony snapped.

"Not all of it." There was a pause as something distant and hollow clicked along the transatlantic line. "Mr O'Neill knows his job. He's there to make sure nothing happens to you."

"Well, I won't permit it."

"My dear, you don't have any choice."

"Nothing is going to happen to me."

"You are in Ireland for one reason, and that is to work. No other. You don't want any distractions, any disturbances … and that includes that secretary of yours. Now, since this phone call is costing you money, I'll be brief," Terri said icily. "These are the facts of life. If you fail to deliver this book, the publishers will sue you for the million dollars which you have already received; they will also sue for damages, loss of earnings, negation of investment, breach of contract and goodness knows what else. The damage to your reputation will be irreparable, and it will tie you up in litigation for years. And then, when they are finished, I'll sue," she added vindictively.

"You'd sue?" Briony asked, shocked.

"Breach of contract, loss of goodwill, loss of earnings, and of course, the time and effort I've put in on this project. The costs would run to millions. You don't have much left as it is; when I would be done, you'd be back in the slum you started from. And you don't want that, do you? Now, you're over there to write — so write!"

In the long silence that followed, static clicked and hissed on the line. At last, Briony said, "Fine, thank you." She hung up. "Bitch," she said again, but with a little less vehemence.

"What did she say?" Gabrielle asked, tilting Briony's heavy head of hair backwards, continuing to towel it dry. "It needs a colour," she added, noting the faint white line appearing along the roots.

"Bitch," Briony murmured. But what really galled her was she knew everything Terri had said was true … and that was one of the reasons she couldn't generate the proper amount of outrage. She closed her eyes and attempted to relax, deliberately working her shoulders to loosen the taut muscles along her shoulders, breathing deeply to ease the feeling of tightness in the centre of her chest.

And so what if the bitch sued her? It was an empty threat; whatever was left of her once considerable fortune would be swallowed up by the lawyers. Briony wasn't sure what she was worth now — there was money due from the sale of foreign language rights to her books, the television rights, magazine and serial rights; there was the house in the west of Ireland, the apartment in New York, the villa on Corfu; they were all worth money. Then there was the jewellery, the antiques she had collected, some savings in accounts which not even her accountant knew about. If she was to realise everything, she might be able to put her hands on a couple of hundred thousand ... but according to her accountant and Terri, she was virtually bankrupt, her debts outnumbering her assets.

Where had the money gone? She had once been listed by *Time* magazine as the highest grossing author of all time.

It was gone now, and the only way she could achieve the level of earnings that would keep her in the style to which she had become very accustomed was to write. She had to finish *A Woman Scorned*.

She had ... what?

She had twenty thousand words written, which left around two hundred and thirty thousand words to go, and she had six months to write it in. She visualised a blackboard in her head with the figures chalked on to it, and she slowly did the long division: six months equalled roughly one hundred and eighty days, and two hundred and thirty thousand divided by one hundred and eighty came to ... one thousand two hundred and seventy- seven. Now one A4 page of double-spaced manuscript came to roughly two hundred and fifty words, which meant that she needed to produce around five pages every day.

Now that wasn't so bad, was it?

Five pages; one in the morning, two in the afternoon, two in the evening. And that was just the minimum. If she really put her mind to it she should be able to produce twice that amount which meant that she'd complete the book in half the time, which was only three months.

No problem.

"Well ... did it work?" Gabrielle's voice jerked Briony back to the present.

"Pardon?"

Gabrielle leaned over her head and kissed the tip of her nose. "When you hung up on your favourite person you were as tense as a board, and over the last few minutes you've relaxed. I could actually feel it happen here and here." She touched Briony's bare neck and spine. "It was as if you were reciting some sort of mantra, or doing a yoga exercise."

Briony smiled at the upside-down Gabrielle. "I suppose I was. I was working out how many pages a day I'd have to write to bring this book in on time."

"How many?"

"Five, but that's in double spacing."

Gabrielle moved around the bed to stand before Briony. "That's not too bad. You can do that, can't you?"

"I can do it." Briony reached out, wrapping her arms around Gabrielle's waist, pulling her close, pressing the side of her face against her stomach. "But I'll need help. I'm going to need you; I won't be able to do it without you."

"You know you have my full support. I'd like to think you didn't have to ask."

"If I don't get this finished on time Terri says the publishers will sue, and then she'll sue. I'll have nothing." She laughed shakily. "I'm writing for my very survival now."

"You can do it," Gabrielle said. "You've done it before, haven't you?"

Briony nodded slowly. "Once … a long time ago. A mile … two miles from here, and a lifetime ago."

"Why did you write then?" Gabrielle asked, watching Briony carefully, attempting to gently ease her out of the despondent mood that had wrapped around her like a damp cloth.

Briony's eyes were unseeing, looking inwards, looking at another time, another place. "I wrote to feed my children, to pay the bills … to escape," she said softly, her Dublin accent — flat, vaguely nasal — suddenly surfacing. "It was a way out. The only way."

"Were they good times?"

Briony's eyes flickered, blinked, blinked again, and she sat forward, nodding. "They were good times." Without pausing, she suddenly stood up and added, "I'll write now."

Briony followed Gabrielle into the large sitting room. Crossing to the window she looked out over the rather uninspiring view of the corner of Grafton Street, sandwiched between Harry Street and Anne Street. Terri had booked them rooms on the top floor of the exclusive Westbury Hotel in the heart of Dublin. Although magnificently appointed, it was set just off Grafton Street, Dublin's main shopping thoroughfare, and the views from any of its windows were anything but scenic. The stone and glass facade of the St. Stephen's Green Shopping Centre dominated one side, while the other three were a collection of rooftops looking down over the numerous back-streets that led off and fed on to Grafton Street.

"What do you want?" Gabrielle asked, opening one suitcase and lifting out a smaller zippered case. From another suitcase, she lifted another nylon case, larger and obviously heavier.

"The usual."

Briony had brought two laptop computers with her to Ireland. One — 'the usual' — was for her exclusive use. It was an eleven-pound, twenty-megabyte Hitachi laptop. It was big, and slow and completely out-of-date by present standards, but it had been the first laptop Briony had purchased, and she felt curiously attached to it. The second machine was the latest Compaq, a high-speed marvel that Gabrielle adored, but which Briony found just a little too small, the keyboard a little too cramped for her fingers. When the two women travelled, Briony would work on the bigger machine and pass her work across to Gabrielle so she could check the spelling, grammar and internal consistency, and do whatever rewriting was necessary. Briony would then work on this corrected material.

Gabrielle placed the large black box on a small occasional table close to the window, pressed the studs on either side and flipped up the top, revealing a large, square green-tinted screen. She attached the machine to its power adapter and plugged it in to save its batteries. The machine chattered to itself deep in its workings, the green screen lit up and the computer came alive with an ascending hum.

Gabrielle then took Briony's portable CD player from another suitcase and plugged it in, leaving it on the table beside the computer. She checked the disc in the machine — Anne-Sophie Mutter playing Brahms' *Concerto in D Major*, with the Berliner Philharmoniker, under Von Karajan — and decided to leave it alone. Briony worked to music, usually classical, preferably loud. She considered the CD to be the greatest invention since auto-reverse had been put on cassette tape recorders.

"All set."

Humming distractedly to herself, still wearing the dressing gown, Briony sat down before the machine and took out the detachable keyboard. Sitting back in an easy chair, with the keyboard on her lap, she picked up the CD's headphones and adjusted them over her head. Moments later, Gabrielle heard the faintly scratchy sounds of the elegant violin concerto. She watched fascinated as Briony's fingers moved — slowly at first and then with increasing speed — calling up the word-processing program, shifting into the directory where *A Woman Scorned* existed. She opened the last chapter she had been working on, and her fingers began to dance across the keyboard, the keys chattering quietly, the letters green on green, the backlit LCD screen virtually unreadable unless one was staring directly at it. Gabrielle looked at Briony's face, but it was blank, expressionless and, although she was staring at the screen, the young woman knew from experience that Briony wasn't actually seeing it.

Gabrielle nodded slightly, pleased. She had seen these sudden changes of mood come over Briony before. Depressed one minute, followed by either elation or bouts of intense concentration. When she worked then, it was as if the book just opened up like a flower and swallowed her deep into it. But it was a delicate, nervous bloom, it had to be carefully nurtured. The slightest disturbance and the moment would be gone. Oh, Briony would continue working at it, typing away, but the spark would be gone, and she was simply hacking it out then, putting words down on paper.

Moving away quietly, Gabrielle retreated to the bathroom. She allowed the towel to fall to the floor and stepped into the shower, wondering how long this burst of energy would last. They had become rarer of late and they never seemed to last as long as they once had.

The young woman turned the water on as hot as she could bear. The thin needle spray stung her skin, but she revelled in the water's almost painful touch. Tilting her head back, she allowed the water to run through her platinum blond-hair, plastering it to her head, giving it a vaguely yellowish tinge. She breathed deeply, absorbing the damp air, allowing the tension to seep from her knotted shoulder muscles. She knew if Briony got in a little work today, she would be in good humour later, and then they might get a chance to go out to dinner or maybe take in a show, or even merely take a stroll around the city.

Gabrielle reached for the shower gel and began to work it into her upper arms. She had been with Briony Dalton for just over a year now, and she had realised long ago that Briony Dalton did not conform to her image of what a best-selling author should be.

For a start, she seemed to find the actual process of writing extremely difficult. It was a fitful, often erratic process, although, by all accounts this was a somewhat recent development; her earlier works had been written — churned out, was the phrase most often used — at a frenetic pace. It was only with the previous book and now this current work that she had found it difficult and often impossible to write. Gabrielle had also come to the conclusion that Briony Dalton had not been entirely responsible for *Pavane*, her current best-seller. The manuscript had been returned three times from the publishers for extensive revision and rewriting, and she knew that, in places, the finished book bore no resemblance to the manuscript version that still existed on

Briony's files. Extensive editorial work had obviously been carried out on the novel, and perhaps it was significant that her new book, *A Woman Scorned* was not being published by *Pavane*'s publishers.

She snapped off the shower and then stood for a few moments, steam rising from her lightly tanned flesh. Brushing water from her body, she stepped out on to the luxurious shower mat and pulled the monogrammed bath towels from the heated rail. Wrapping one around her head, and another around her body, tucking it down between her full breasts, she cracked open the bathroom door and peered out into the room. She was delighted to find that Briony was still sitting before the small computer, her fingers shifting quickly across the clicking keys.

Gabrielle watched the older woman for a few moments and then stepped back from the door. Brushing the edge of a facecloth across the mirror, she leaned forward and stared at her reflection, checking for lines around her eyes or wrinkles at the corners of her mouth. For a single instant, she saw Briony's face, the wrinkles beginning to edge in now, despite regular beauty treatments and the best of cosmetics.

Gabrielle stared into the mirror, looking into her wide black eyes, attempting to sort out her feelings towards Briony. The writer was twenty years her senior, a mature once-married woman with two children, one of whom was older than she was, for Christ's sake! She'd started out feeling sorry for the lonely woman, and ended up liking her, genuinely liking her.

And loving her?

Shaking her head, Gabrielle turned away, and pulled the towel from her hair. Dropping her head forward, she began patting the thick, silky strands dry. She wasn't sure she knew what love was.

Gabrielle Royer had come to Briony Dalton as a secretary through the same agency that Briony's publishers used to recruit their own staff. When Gabrielle had been put forward for the post, she thought she was going to work for the publishers and even later, when she ended up working directly for Briony Dalton, she thought that it would be a one-off job and she would return to the publishing house when the book was finished. But gradually her duties with Briony had expanded as her role developed, the position of secretary changing to that of a personal assistant. Eventually it became convenient for Gabrielle to move into the New York apartment, where Briony was quite willing to allow her to organise the countless tiny details that she was disinclined to take care of. Gabrielle became Briony's constant companion, and there were whispers on the literary and party circuit of a liaison between them long before it actually became fact. Gabrielle Royer became something of a minor celebrity in her own right, her ambiguous sexuality adding to her newsworthiness.

Although she used the name Royer and spoke with a French accent, her real name was Gabrielle Rogers, and she originally hailed from Austin, Texas. Her mother had been French and Gabrielle had grown up in a bilingual household, although she herself had never been to France. And when *The National Enquirer* had unearthed and published this titbit of gossip, rather than harming her, it only added to her notoriety.

Despite what she might whisper to her in the throes of passion, Gabrielle wondered if she really loved Briony Dalton?

She looked up, raking her fingers through her damp hair, pulling it back off her face, and stared into the mirror.

No, she didn't.

But she felt a genuine affection for her. She had seen Briony when her defences were down, when all the money, the fame and the success meant nothing; she had seen her in the dark hours of the night, when she had cried in her arms, crying for her lost husband, her lost children, crying for what might have been.

The success had destroyed her — was destroying her. She was writing fiction she despised for money she had already spent.

And, Gabrielle knew, if Briony Dalton didn't finish this book it would destroy her totally.

Chapter Six

The interior of the pub had been completely remodelled and, in Charley O'Neill's considered opinion, the atmosphere had been completely destroyed in the process. Now, smart young men in shapeless — unstructured was the word they used — Italian suits and haircuts that cost more than some men earned in a day, sat on buttoned leather seats behind genuine hand-carved wooden tables. They drank designer water or alcohol-free lager.

In his shapeless anorak, and his clumpy, steel-toecapped boots, drinking Guinness, or Bourbon if he was celebrating, he looked totally out of place, like a labourer who had wandered in off a building site. Once, one of the smart young people, in an attempt to impress his girlfriend, had suggested precisely that. Charley had smiled innocently as he had pressed his two hundred and thirty pounds on to the young man's paper-thin, silk-soft Italian loafers, and then walked away without a word. The young man had lost three toenails and still walked with a limp.

Charley was reading the previous day's edition of *The Irish Times*. The Thursday edition came with the property supplement and it amused him to read through the properties on offer and choose one. Not that he would ever move from Dublin, but there was always his retirement ...

He glanced at the old Rolex on his wrist. He would give him another five minutes, then he was out of here ... and this time he was sending the son of a bitch a bill for his wasted time.

"Sorry I'm late; traffic on the quays was shitty as usual." Marcus Holland slid into the booth opposite Charley. He pushed another pint of Guinness across the table towards the big American and poured some Ballygowan Spring Water into his own glass.

"I was just about to leave," Charley grumbled.

Marcus nodded sympathetically. "Traffic," he mumbled. They both knew that — despite whatever Charley might say — he wouldn't have left. He was a seller and Marcus was the buyer with the money.

Marcus Holland was a freelance reporter specialising in scandal and gossip. He had co-authored two very successful titillating biographies, one on the lesser known Royals, the second on the children of pop stars. Five years previously he had come to Ireland on an assignment to cover the story of the runaway daughter of a British cabinet minister who was living with a religious sect on an island off the west coast. Marcus had broken the story that the sect practised black magic, including animal sacrifice, and for a while the press had had a field day with various snappy headlines. But during his brief stay in Ireland Marcus had actually fallen in love with the country. After the noisy excesses of New York and London he found Dublin slow and lazy, almost quaint, and the Irish countryside completely charming. His journalistic pedigree and qualifications opened many doors, and after a brief affair with radio he ended up appearing on and eventually hosting a popular arts programme on RTE television with surprisingly high viewing figures. And he exploited the power his ratings gave him to the best of his ability.

"Have you had a good day, Charles?" Marcus asked easily, only the faintest trace of his American accent still audible.

"Not bad, not bad." Charley O'Neill reached for the second drink and drained half of it in one long swallow.

"Meet someone interesting?" Marcus asked shrewdly. He ran his fingers through his slicked-back blond hair, pushing strands off his forehead. His eyes were stone grey and completely humourless.

"Somebody very interesting."

Marcus passed across a folded magazine. Within was an envelope with five twenty-pounds notes: standard finder's fee for an exclusive lead.

"This is worth more," Charley said, not looking at him, not touching the magazine.

"Depends on who it is, doesn't it?"

"This is good ... there's got to be another hundred in it."

Marcus nodded slightly. "If it's good, there's another hundred in it. But you'd better be telling that the Pope is coming back to Dublin."

"Better than that." Charley O'Neill said. He reached for the magazine, tucking it into his inside pocket without opening it; they both knew Holland wouldn't even think about cheating him. "Briony Dalton has come to Ireland to finish her latest book. She's here with her girlfriend staying at the Westbury," he finished with a triumphant smile.

Marcus Holland's eyes glazed as he considered the possibilities — the countless possibilities. "What about security?" he murmured. He glanced sidelong at Charley. "Not you?" he asked in astonishment.

"Me!"

When he looked at Charley again, his face had relaxed into a broad grin. "There's another two hundred in it!"

Chapter Seven

Catherine Garrett sat in a contoured leather chair that was too concave to be called comfortable, facing Josef Bach across the smooth slab of veined black marble that he used as a desk. The desk was completely bare with the exception of two copies of the small stapled contract which he had placed directly before his stubby fingers.

"You were happy with the contract?" Bach asked, his bright blue eyes wide and concerned. "Did you get some legal advice on it?"

"Do I need to take legal advice on it?" Catherine asked. "You told me yourself it is a standard contract. And besides," she added, "I trust you."

The big German smiled slightly. "Your trust is gratifying … if unnecessary. And as for this being a standard contract, well, in view of the amount of money involved it is not quite as standard as a — shall we say —a ten thousand pound contract."

"How does it differ?"

"Minor changes."

Catherine moved forward in the bucket seat, but still couldn't see across the desk. She finally rose to her feet and came around the desk to stand beside Josef, turning the contract with the tips of her fingers, looking over it quickly. She was wearing a white silk blouse with a French collar over a pair of skin-tight black leather trousers. Black buttoned ankle boots completed her simple dress. Her choice of the simple — almost stark — look had been deliberate, knowing Josef's taste.

The big man moved back in his chair, watching the woman carefully. He recognised in her something which he knew existed to a greater or lesser degree in every human being — greed. Few, however, admitted to themselves or to others that they were greedy ... few except the successful ones.

Josef Bach was greedy — he knew that, had known it from an early age, and he had used that greed to make him a very wealthy man.

Catherine Garrett was greedy, and her greed was tempered with the desire for revenge. Bach found the combination almost irresistible; it made Catherine malleable, purchasable, and manoeuvrable. When she signed the contract she was his in all but name.

"This contract looks fine to me," Catherine said slowly, aware that Josef was looking at her, giving him time. She leaned forward, allowing her small breasts to press against the silk of her blouse, the nipples prominent.

"Your perfume," the German asked, "what is it?"

"*L'Air du Temps*," Catherine said. She looked at Josef, smiling, then moved away from him to stand before the enormous glass windows that took up one wall of Bach's London office. Directly north, close enough to pick out details, was the Post Office Tower, looking like a badly designed special effect, while below her London spread out in its haphazard sprawl. She turned slightly, showing him her best side.

Josef swivelled in his chair to watch her. With the light behind her, her blouse had turned translucent, clearly outlining her breasts.

"I want us to be very clear on what we are doing here," Josef Bach said. He touched a button on the arm of his chair and a series of hidden cameras and microphones began to record everything in high-fidelity stereo on VHS video.

"I am commissioning you to write a book on Briony Dalton, the number one best-selling author in the world. I want this book to be factual. I want all the facts in the book authenticated, noted and referenced in case of a possible libel. Leave nothing to chance. I want to know how a girl from the slums of Dublin ends up writing blockbusters for extraordinary amounts of money that sell more copies than the Bible. I don't want a smear job ... No," he shook his big head dramatically, "I do want a smear job, I just don't want it to be obvious. I told you I know the whereabouts of her two children. Use them. Use their testimony. Record it on tape, video too if you can."

Catherine nodded. She knew about a lot of Briony's skeletons. Maybe it was time to open those cupboards that contained them.

"In return, I am paying you an advance of half a million sterling, payable one third now, one third on delivery of the manuscript and one third on publication. There is also the bonus if you bring the book in early."

"But even if I bring the book in within six months, by the time we have it proofed and set, the cover designed and the hundred other tasks that need to be completed before the book appears in the shops Briony's new book will already be in print."

Josef held up one stubby finger. "One week — one week exactly — to the day after you deliver the manuscript, it will hit the shops."

"That's impossible!"

"With money, my dear, nothing is impossible." He reached out with both hands. "Now come here and sign."

Catherine returned to the table and took the heavy Mont Blanc fountain pen from Josef's hand. Deliberately leaning across him, she dated the first page, initialled the bottom of every page and signed a short neat signature on the last page. He handed her the duplicate which she also dated, initialled and signed. Straightening, she handed the pen back to Bach and then stood with her hands in her pockets as he slashed his name across the bottom of the last page of both copies. Pushing one aside, he lifted her copy of the contract in both hands, and blew gently to dry the ink, his eyes on Catherine's face. Finally, he folded the twelve-page contract and handed it across to her.

"Will you do a good job on this book, do you think?"

"I will."

"You hate her, don't you?"

"More than you will ever know," Catherine whispered, her eyes flat and distant.

"Hate is a dangerous emotion. It can cloud your judgement."

Catherine shook her head. "Sometimes it allows you to see things clearly. There are two grand emotions, hate and greed." She lifted the contract in her left hand. "What about my advance due on signature? When will I get that?"

Josef back threw back his head and laughed. "I like you." He pressed a button recessed into the side of the desk and the door at the far end of the room opened almost immediately and a slender Japanese woman appeared. She advanced a few steps into the room and then waited.

"Kaho, my personal chequebook, please."

The woman bowed slightly and left the room without making a sound, her eyes fixed to the floor.

Bemused, Catherine watched her. "You have her well-trained, don't you?" The contempt in her voice was not quite disguised.

"That is how Japanese women are," Josef said mildly. "She is a superb secretary. Miss Kaho Tomita reads, writes and takes shorthand in six languages. She has a degree in computer sciences, and a masters in business studies. She is currently studying political history."

"And in her spare time?" Catherine asked sarcastically.

"In her spare time she is married with a husband and two children living just outside London. She has an apartment in Kensington and a boyfriend in the city whom she sees every second day for lunch and dinner twice a week." He saw her look of surprise and the corners of his mouth turned up in a humourless grin. "I like to know about the people I employ."

"I wonder what you know about me?" Catherine murmured.

"More than you think."

The door opened and the woman reappeared. She crossed the huge expanse of floor silently and laid the long chequebook on Bach's marble desk without a word.

"Thank you, Kaho."

The woman bowed and left the room. She hadn't looked at Catherine once.

"She seems almost frightened of you," Catherine said.

"Most of my staff are, my dear."

"Are you sleeping with her?" Catherine asked, her directness taking Bach by surprise.

"No," he said simply, and Catherine believed him. "Not now, anyway." He opened his chequebook, folded back the cover, and then produced the Mont Blanc fountain pen again. Unscrewing the cap, he looked directly at Catherine and said, "I always find large sums of money a great aphrodisiac, don't you?"

"I wouldn't know," she said. "I've never had a great deal of money." She stepped closer to the desk, and watched Josef's harsh, angular script bite into the page. It didn't need a handwriting analyst to work out the man's personality from the writing. It was so like himself, quick, violent and forceful, and yet some of the letters, the loops of the *g*s and *y*s were almost decorative, indicating a sensuous nature.

"Pay to the order of Catherine Garrett," he said slowly, watching her approach out of the corner of his eye, "the sum of one hundred and sixty-six thousand, six hundred and sixty-six pounds ... and sixty-six pence," he added with a smile. His signature this time was not quite so jagged as the signature on the contract. He pulled the long cream-coloured cheque from the chequebook and passed it up to Catherine who was now standing by his shoulder. "One hundred and sixty-six thousand pounds," he murmured.

She took the cheque in both hands and stared at it, for one brief and terrifying second thinking this might be some huge practical joke. But the cheque was genuine, the signature real.

One hundred and sixty-six thousand, six hundred and sixty-six pounds.

She looked at Josef Bach and suddenly found that she didn't know what to say. Her mouth was dry, her heart was pounding and she felt almost breathless. Bach stared up at her, a smile twisting his lips, his hands folded across his stomach. Finally, she simply said, "Thank you," and leaned down to kiss his cheek. But he turned his head and her lips met his, and they parted and she felt his tongue against her teeth. For a moment she resisted and then her mouth opened and she kissed him with a passion that surprised herself. Her arms went around his bull neck, her fingers closing into the thick mane of hair at the back of his head. His hands rested on her hips, where the leather of the trousers met the silk of her blouse, then slowly moved upwards, the calluses on the palms of his hands rasping against the silk. He touched the sides of her breasts and stopped. Catherine pulled her head back and looked into the German's cold blue eyes and then she closed her eyes and kissed him again. With one hand locked onto the hair at the back of his head, her right hand moved down his shirt buttons, twisting them open, sliding the palm of her hand across his thickly furred chest, rubbing the ball of her thumb against his nipple. Her hand went lower, across his stomach and then fumbled with his belt, sliding the loop free.

Josef Bach waited while her hands roved over his body. Her tongue was still probing, flicking against his lips as his hands moved against her blouse, gently working the buttons free. He pulled the ends of the blouse up out of the waist of her leather trousers, and allowed them to hang free. He moved his rough hands up beneath the blouse to cup her small breasts, flattening them against her chest. Her nipples hardened against his hands. He moved to the waistband of her trousers, gently unhooked them, and then slid down the zip. The trousers were moulded so closely to her body that he had to pull them down. His breath caught at the back of his throat. He had been correct: she hadn't been wearing any underwear.

Catherine Garrett and Josef Bach made love on the cold marble of his desk. It was brief and uncomfortable, though the excitement of the moment did much to counter that. It was only afterwards, when Josef had finished and pulled away, leaving her lying on the table while he went into his private bathroom to wash himself, that she realised she was still holding tightly to the contract and the cheque. She dressed quickly and had left the room before Bach reappeared. And as she made her way down in the private elevator to the ground floor she realised that what she had done might make her a whore — but at least she was a very well-paid whore!

Chapter Eight

"Did he fuck you?"

"Jesus!" Catherine Garrett swung around to face Mark Cosgrove, suddenly glad that the room was in semi-darkness and that he couldn't see the colour that had flooded to her cheeks.

Mark had been unusually quiet since she had returned from London earlier that afternoon. However, knowing that he could be moody depending on how his own work was progressing, Catherine had left him alone. They had eaten in silence and when Catherine had attempted to tell him about the details of the contract she had just signed with Bach, he had clearly shown that he was completely uninterested. The idea that he might be jealous had only occurred to her as she was washing the dishes, standing before the window, looking out at the night creeping in across the Downs, the gritty twilight growing to a deeper, softer night.

After the initial snap of anger, she had tried to place herself in his position and the realisation that, while he had no right to feel angry, she could at least understand his jealousy.

With her assistance and advice, he had managed to obtain a five thousand pound advance for his third novel. Again, with her assistance, the publishers had agreed to pay fifty per cent up front but, since he had been working on the book for the best part of a year, it meant that his total earnings for the last tax year came to two thousand five hundred pounds. When he delivered the manuscript he would receive one thousand two hundred and fifty pounds, but the final portion of the advance, another one thousand two hundred and fifty pounds, would not be paid until publication of the book. And publication was about fourteen months after delivery.

Whereas here she was, with no published books to her name — although she did have numerous articles, reviews and scripts to her credit — earning half a million pounds for her first book. Was it any wonder that he was upset and jealous? If the situations were reversed, she'd feel bloody angry herself.

Somewhat relieved that she had discovered the reasons for his sulks, Catherine made her way from the kitchen into her study. Give him a little time, let him do some work on his own book: that would calm him down. She'd take him in some tea later, and she'd talk about what they were going to do with the money, make it plain they would be spending it together. Maybe when they were both finished writing their books, they would go on a holiday together … a world cruise.

She turned on her computer and allowed the grey light from the screen to illuminate the room. Sitting on top of the keyboard next to the screen was the contract and atop that was the cheque. She couldn't resist the temptation to look at it for a final time. She didn't hear Mark come into the room, but his abrupt crude question stopped her cold.

"I don't know what you're talking about," she replied finally, swivelling around in the chair to face him.

"You do," he hissed, and his circular glasses took the light from the computer screen and turned them into grey mirrors. "You let him fuck you, didn't you?" he said savagely, making the sentence an obscenity. "Or maybe you even initiated it. I saw how you were dressed this afternoon."

Catherine took a deep breath. Swallowing hard, she said, "Let's not have an argument."

"Who said anything about an argument? I simply asked you a question!"

"You made an accusation!" Catherine said, more harshly than she intended.

"Which you didn't answer."

"It wasn't worthy of an answer."

"So you did fuck him," Cosgrove said triumphantly. "I knew it. When you came in here this afternoon, I could smell him on you. I could see it in your face, in your eyes. For Christ's sake, I've lived with you for nearly two years now; I know what you look like after sex."

Catherine lowered her head and took a deep breath. She knew if she said anything now it would be something she would regret, something that couldn't be easily retracted.

"Mark…" she began.

He snatched the cheque from her fingers and waved it in her face. "Why did you do it, eh? Did he make you … no, no, no. Someone like him thinks that money buys everything … and in your case he was right. He's paid you to destroy another woman. Bach has bought you, Catherine Garrett, bought you body and soul in order to destroy someone who stands in the way of some grand scheme of his. You're his now." He crumpled the cheque and dropped it at her feet. "He's made you his whore! I only hope for your sake that it's worth it," he said. His voice cracked and he turned suddenly and rushed from the room.

Catherine sat in the semi-darkness for a long time afterwards. She had no answer to his accusations, because they were too close to her own thoughts.

Finally, she picked the crumpled cheque from the floor and smoothed it flat. She would lodge it first thing in the morning.

Chapter Nine

She was going to call the book, *Lies*.

Catherine Garrett sat before the glowing computer screen and slowly typed the first words of Briony Dalton's biography:

> *Briony Dalton was born Bernadette Margaret Dalton on the 5th October 1947 in Dublin. Her roots were very firmly fixed in the Dublin working class of the period ...*

ଓ

Briony Dalton and Gabrielle Royer walked arm in arm down Dublin's fashionable Grafton Street, enjoying the unseasonably warm day. Although they had done nothing so dramatic as disguising themselves, they both felt confident that they wouldn't be recognised. No one in the city had been alerted to their presence, no one would expect to see them walking around Dublin, and Briony especially knew that it was very difficult to recognise someone out of place, out of context. None of the staff in the Westbury Hotel knew her true identity; Briony had checked in and was travelling under her married name of Moriarty. When she had finally split with her husband, she had kept nothing of his — except the use of his name, and the passport which she regularly renewed.

The two women stopped outside elegant Brown Thomas, in its new home where Switzers used to be, and stood admiring the latest beach fashions from the Continent — one-piece, skin-tight, almost transparent fabrics cut high at the crotch, and low in the bust, designed to reveal and suggest more than any bikini ever could.

Gabrielle moved the Porsche sunglasses down on her straight nose. "Why don't we go to the villa on Corfu?" she suggested. "The weather would be just right, and the tourists wouldn't have started to arrive yet."

Briony nodded, a smile twisting her lips. "The only problem with that is that we'd spend all day in the pool or on the beach and I'd get nothing done."

"Oh, you would. I'd see to that."

Briony considered the thought. "It's a nice idea."

"And what's even nicer is that you wouldn't have to tell Terri where you'd gone."

Briony's smile broadened. "I think I'm beginning to like this idea more and more … " She caught the fleeting glimpse of a face reflected in the glass and she suddenly stopped and whirled around.

"Good day, ladies." Charley O'Neill stepped up to the two women and touched his index finger to his forehead in salute.

"You have been following us," Briony accused him, her voice icy.

The detective smiled, but said nothing.

"Go away, or we will call the police," Gabrielle hissed.

"You could do that," the big man said. "But you won't. It would cause an unnecessary embarrassment, draw attention to you, and you, ma'am, can afford neither embarrassment nor attention at the moment." He looked up and down the crowded street and shrugged. "I'm just doing my job. I'm just keeping you safe from harm, that's all. You needn't even know I'm here."

Briony gripped Gabrielle's arm and turned back to the window. Reflected in the glass she saw Charley O'Neill turn and walk away. As soon as he had his back to them, she dragged Gabrielle into the shop. "Come on," she murmured, "let's see if we can lose him." She hurried past the perfume and jewellery counters, pushed through a gaggle of teenagers and out a door that led to Wicklow

Street. Briony turned to the right, crossed Grafton Street, raced through a narrow arcade … and Gabrielle suddenly found herself in a bookshop. "How did we do that?" she asked in astonishment, looking over her shoulder.

Briony marched her in a straight line through the bookshop, down a flight of steps, across a large foyer and out into another street. Unlike Grafton Street, which had been packed with Saturday morning shoppers, this was quieter.

Briony took Gabrielle to the edge of the pavement and the young woman found she was facing a second bookshop. A life-size cardboard cut-out of Briony Dalton holding the *Pavane* paperback dump bin dominated the window, and the book jacket's dominant colours of green and gold had been cleverly duplicated by the window-dresser with bunches of daffodils and ferns. "Where are we now?" Gabrielle asked as they crossed the road.

"This is Dawson Street," Briony said shortly, "there are four bookshops on this street alone, with a fifth just around the corner. I'm hoping the detective will think that the last place we'll go will be anywhere near a bookshop where there is the remotest chance of someone recognising me." She stopped to look at the window display. "I still don't like that cut-out," she muttered in an aside. The cut-out depicted Briony Dalton wearing a black leather Boss jacket and skirt, leaning forward, displaying a cleavage that she did not possess, but which had, rather obviously, she thought, been airbrushed onto the photograph. Briony still thought that the illustration cheapened the book, but her publishers felt it was a suitable image of 'The Queen of the Red Hot Read'.

"Have we lost our friend?"

Briony smiled thinly. "I hope so. With luck he'll think we're still shopping in Brown Thomas."

"What'll we do?"

"What he least expects us to do." She took Gabrielle's arm and turned down the street. "That's Trinity College," she said as they walked towards a high stone wall. At the corner they turned to the right, into a street that was in deep shadow. Out of the sun, they both shivered, suddenly glad of the warmth of the heavy leather coats they were wearing.

At the side of the road, with her back against a parking meter, a small dirty-faced child crouched, swathed in a blanket. There was a torn cardboard carton by her feet, a few coins lying tossed in it. She looked up as the two elegantly dressed woman approached, and for a single moment, they both felt the raw intensity of the envy, and the desire that flashed in her eyes. Even though she couldn't have been more than six or seven, she radiated an almost tangible sense of anger and hurt, as if she had already realised that circumstances had dictated she could never possess what these two women had. Gabrielle's hand went to her pocket, but Briony squeezed her arm. "Don't," she said. "Give the children food, but never money."

They walked on in silence, the presence of the child beggar having disturbed them both. They stopped briefly outside a third bookshop. Here too, there was a full window display of *Pavane,* although without the cut-out, and there was a ten-by-eight glossy photograph of Briony signing books. "I remember a signing in here for one of my books." Briony said.

"Was it successful?"

"They sold close on two hundred copies in an hour and a half. There were people queuing down the street; the police had to be called to control the crowd." She smiled. "The demonstrators arrived as I was leaving. They contented themselves by haranguing those queuing, but they gave as good as they got."

The two women continued down the full length of Nassau Street, until it became Clare Street, where they passed yet another bookshop, this one with book-filled trays stretching out into the street. Briony turned to the right. "I hope they still do lunch," she said enigmatically.

"Who?" Gabrielle asked, but the older woman simply smiled and said nothing.

Briony led Gabrielle into the grounds of the National Gallery of Ireland. Once within the impressive foyer, Briony took a great delight in leading an increasingly bemused Gabrielle through a series of small oval rooms until they reached what looked like a dead end. When they turned to the right they found themselves in a large restaurant. Although it had just gone twelve, the room was busy and filling rapidly. As they joined the short queue, Briony turned to Gabrielle, "When I was a child, and later as a young adult, this gallery was my favourite place. I used to wander through the rooms for hours, sometimes not even looking at the paintings, merely enjoying the silence, and the smells. It always smelt so clean."

Gabrielle laughed softly. "I've noticed that you've a thing about smells. You're so aware of them. I've also noticed that every one of your books has a strong 'nosy' content. Wherever you grew up must have smelt rotten." She turned towards the young woman behind the counter, and didn't see the curious expression that froze Briony Dalton's lips into a twisted parody of a grin.

☙

The smells of sweat, sawdust and vomit remained with her for years afterwards.

She had grown so accustomed to them as a child that they failed to register with her, although she was always sensitive to the sweeter, sharper odours of the scents of perfumes. There were other odours, too, from her childhood — the toilets in the yard which always overflowed, the beer slops that were spilled into the gutters every morning, the manure from the horses that delivered the barrels and kegs of beer and the stench of the wharfside, the bitter sickliness of the sea, the smell of the scum of diesel oil that drifted on the surface of the water

Briony Dalton's father was a publican, a tiny wizened man with a fearsome temper who ran a wharf bar deep in the heart of Dublin's dockland. She had known her mother only briefly and she retained an image of a tall, rather severe woman, dressed in black with her hair swept back off her face, but it wasn't until many years later that she realised that this mental picture was actually of one of her father's sisters. She had grown up believing that her mother had died while she had been young, but again, much later, she had discovered that her mother had simply walked out after yet another beating at the hands of her father. Only this time she had retaliated and driven a six-inch bread knife through the fleshy part of his thigh with enough force to actually pin his leg to the wooden chair he was sitting on. While Mick Dalton had howled in anguish and struggled to free himself, her mother had calmly walked around the room, gathering her few belongings into a single suitcase. She had walked out of the room and never returned. Briony Dalton was one year old at the time. The woman never made any further contact. Later, Briony was to say that while she forgave her mother many things she had never been able to forgive her that.

Briony had grown up in the two-room flat her father held rent free above the pub. The rooms were small and always dirty, and the smells from the pub directly below — especially the sweat, the vomit and the sawdust — permeated everything. One room was the bedroom, a tiny box of a room with a single window that looked down over the small enclosed yard at the back of the pub that was always piled high with kegs and casks. Beyond the yard, the cobbled quayside was criss-crossed with tram tracks right down to the water's edge. There were two beds crowded into the room, a double bed up against the window for Mick Dalton and the women he occasionally picked up, and a narrow cot for Briony behind the door. There was a small table beside the larger bed and a chest of drawers at the foot of her own bed. There was a wardrobe, but it was out in the 'sitting' room. On the wall above her father's bed was a plain wooden crucifix, and above her own bed was a picture of the Sacred Heart that terrified her and gave her nightmares for years: Christ opening his red robe to expose a bleeding heart wrapped around with thorns. The sitting room was dominated by an ancient sofa in a faded floral pattern and a hideous dining-room table with six chairs that was far too big for the small room, but which Mick Dalton had received as a wedding present from his parents and dare not throw away. A clock ticked solemnly on the mantelpiece above the fire, while two china dogs stood guard on either side. A set of china ducks in flight were forever frozen above the fireplace. On a small table beneath the window there was a large Philips radiogram; it was one of her father's most prized possessions.

Occasionally Briony Dalton would sit in the overstuffed armchair with the radio turned to 2RN, which would later become RTE, the national radio station. The young girl would have a notebook on her lap, and she would delight in making notes on the topics she heard discussed on the radio, or create word pictures of the radio speakers.

And it was her father's proudest boast that his daughter would be a writer some day ...

ଔ

"Madam ... madam?"

Briony blinked, abruptly returning to the present.

"Can I get you something to eat, madam?"

"Oh, I'm sorry. A chicken salad please," she said.

"Are you OK?" Gabrielle asked.

"I'm fine. Just remembering, that's all."

"Remembering what?"

"Remembering the past. Thinking that perhaps I might just see my father while I'm in Ireland."

"Is that wise?"

"Probably not," Briony said quietly, "but you know that'll not stop me doing it anyway."

ଔ

And it was her father's proudest boast that his daughter would be a writer some day...

Catherine Garrett hit the key that saved what she had written in the machine's memory and sat back in her chair. She wasn't entirely satisfied with it, but that could be fixed later. What was important now was to get all the details down on to the page - or into the machine - and then it could be worked upon.

Mark Cosgrove strode into the room without knocking and dropped a large padded jiffy bag on to her desk. "The postman's just been." He tilted the bag to show the label and postmark. "Looks like a present from your boyfriend," he said nastily.

Catherine Garrett waited until Mark had left the room before tearing open the bag. There was a thick spiral-bound report inside, and a black, untitled three-hour VHS video cassette.

Chapter Ten

Catherine Garrett read through the spiral-bound report with a growing sense of disbelief. It was an eighty-page single-spaced typed brief documenting the activities and whereabouts of Matthew and Rianne Moriarty, Briony's two children, over the past number of years. The last entry was dated seven days previously, the 30th April.

There was a series of shocking ten-by-eight black-and-white photographs of both children, although neither of them was a child any longer: Matthew was twenty-six and Rianne, twenty-two. Neither of them had been aware that they were being photographed, and Catherine suddenly wondered how long Josef Bach had been planning this campaign against Briony.

Catherine placed the photographs on the desk before her, looking at each one a final time before turning it face down. She shook her head slowly. She remembered bouncing both children on her knee: she was Matt's godmother. She gazed at the skeletal, haunted-eyed figure of the young man in the photograph and shivered: how had it come to this? Why had it come to this?

She stared out through the rain-spotted window, looking into the past. If the past could be changed, was there any one particular moment when the future could have been altered?

There was …

There was a moment back in 1966 when, if she had had the courage to do what was right, then all of this — Briony Dalton's great wealth and success, the destruction and degradation of her children — would never have occurred, and of course her own job, the very fact she even lived here in England rather than in Dublin, and the half million pound contract — none of that would have happened either.

She had once hated Briony Dalton, but hate, like most great passions, couldn't be sustained indefinitely. Over the years, the hate had dulled, become muted, changed into a simple loathing and disgust. A new book by the writer could still enrage her, but Briony was no longer the ruling passion — the obsession — that she had once been. Until now.

Catherine Garrett lifted the photographs again, tilting them to the light. She didn't want to know how much Josef Bach had paid for the photographs and wasn't really interested where he had obtained them. But she wondered if he knew what he was doing when he sent them to her ...

Yes, she fancied he did.

She picked up the photograph of Rianne and looked into the girl's eyes. Beneath a false, tight smile and too much make-up, her resemblance to her mother was marked. She had Briony Dalton's eyes, the strong determined set to her face. The girl in the photograph was twenty-two now; at that age, Catherine Garrett had known Briony Dalton for nearly twelve years ... and they were inseparable.

Chapter Eleven

Josef Bach read through the single-page report a final time before touching the button on the side of his desk. "Send the gentleman in now, Kaho," he said softly into the air. The sensitive directional microphone in the desk relayed the message to his secretary in her office down the hall.

The small Japanese woman stood up, pulling at the hem of her severe Lauren suit. She smiled at the room's only other occupant, and said in perfect, virtually unaccented English, "Josef Bach will see you now, Mr Holland."

Marcus Holland followed the Japanese woman down the plush, silent corridors. Although he could feel the cool air on his skin, and taste the ozone in the air, he was sweating slightly, and his own nervousness made him angry. He had covered some of the world's hottest trouble spots and was noted for his ability to remain cool under fire, but certain situations, certain people, had the power to upset him. His brother, who was a four hundred dollar an hour analyst in New York, had diagnosed the problem.

"You may be a hotshot reporter, but in your heart you're still a good Catholic boy from the South Bronx, whose father worked in a Jewish deli and whose mother took in laundry. You — we — owe them, and you can't forget that. You feel guilty because they worked their butts off to give us a lifestyle they would never even have dreamed about. You're also carrying some guilt because they both died before you could do anything to repay them. I'd say you see every authority figure as a manifestation of parental stereotypes." His brother had then sent him a bill for professional services. Marcus hadn't been able to work out whether or not it was a joke, though he hadn't paid the bill.

Nor had he been able to decide if the call from Josef Bach's secretary to his Dublin home late Friday evening had been a joke. Initially he had decided that it was, but on Saturday morning he had begun to have second thoughts and had actually rung to confirm his appointment with Herr Bach. The woman on the other end of the line — the Japanese secretary he realised now — had sounded almost surprised that he should even question the invitation. Even so he hadn't really believed it until the letter of confirmation had arrived by courier later that day. It included a first-class return ticket for the Monday morning seven a.m. Aer Lingus flight out of Dublin into Heathrow. The letter had stressed absolute confidentiality and secrecy and that, more than anything else, had prompted him to take up the invitation.

He had been met at the airport and driven in a limousine chauffeured by a singularly uncommunicative driver to Bach's central London offices. Holland had been vaguely aware of an elaborate security ritual as he entered the building, but it was carried out so discreetly that he chose to ignore it. He had been met in the foyer of the impressive silver and gold office block by the Japanese secretary who had given him her name, but had said it so quickly that he hadn't quite caught it, and he hadn't dared ask again. She had presented him with a laminated security pass that was impressive in the detail it contained about him, and included a very recent colour photograph that he did not remember posing for. The word VISITOR was clearly stamped in solid red across the card.

"Please wear this badge at all times within the building," the woman had said softly. "It will save you unnecessary embarrassment."

As he had been brought up through the building, he realised that the place was a fortress. There were security cameras everywhere and while the majority of these were visible — and intended to be so — he had been in enough embassies and military installations to recognise those which were rather more discreet. Everyone wore a security badge, each of them colour coded which, he assumed, determined access to various floors and departments.

He had been kept waiting exactly five minutes in the secretary's large modern office and, although he hadn't seen the woman touch anything that might alert Bach to his presence in the room, nor — to the best of his knowledge — had she passed on any message to him, he had heard the simple message from Bach come through the speaker phone on the desk.

If it had been designed to put him off balance, it had succeeded.

He followed the Japanese woman down a pale, featureless corridor. She opened a pair of tall metal-sheathed doors which were embossed with the Bach logo, and stepped to one side. When Marcus Holland walked into the room she stepped out pulling both doors closed behind him. Although they looked like fortress gates, and he expected them to clang together, they closed without a sound.

Marcus Holland walked the length of the room in silence towards the tall black leather chair behind the desk facing away from him. He had almost reached the black marble slab of a desk when the chair swung around and Josef Bach surged to his feet, his shock of white hair and his gleaming white suit almost a physical blow. Marcus stopped and Bach thrust out his right hand.

"Josef Bach," he said simply.

The reporter had to lean forward across the desk to take the man's hand. "Marcus Holland," he said, annoyed at the tremble in his voice.

Bach gestured towards a chair. "Please, sit down. A drink? Kaho," he said, without waiting for an answer, "coffee; Colombian, and Mr Holland likes his black with two sugars."

Marcus nodded, impressed. "You've done your homework," he said, attempting a smile.

"I know all about you, Mr Holland." The German resumed his seat and folded his hands together. He rested his forearms on the table and leaned forward, impaling the American with his bright blue eyes. "I will get straight to business, Mr Holland. You know me, you know my reputation."

"I know of you. And that's why I cannot imagine what you want with me."

Bach leaned into the high-backed chair and regarded Holland steadily. The American felt tiny beads of sweat pop out on his forehead; he tried to hold the man's gaze, but failed, and he concentrated instead on the office. It was stark and cold, without any humanising or personalised item in it. It was very much a reflection of the man.

The door opened and Kaho appeared with a tray of coffee. She walked the length of the room in silence and placed the tray almost exactly between the two men. Without a glance at either of them, she left. The tray was solid silver, but the two mugs were thick — obviously hand-crafted, hand-painted earthenware. There was milk and rock sugar in matching bowls. Bach leaned forward, pushing the tray in Holland's direction. When Marcus reached for the sugar, Bach shook his head. "Kaho, my secretary, will have added two sugars," he said. Marcus tasted his coffee and found it had indeed been sugared.

"I find if you tell the Japanese to do something," Bach said, pulling the tray back in his direction, "they will invariably do it. They make excellent employees. Loyal and obedient."

Holland sipped his coffee. "I'm quite sure you didn't bring me all the way from Dublin just to talk about your staff."

"You're quite right, I didn't." He slid a rectangular slip of cream paper across the table. "And, for your time, here is a cheque for five thousand pounds sterling. I trust that will recompense you for the inconvenience I've put you to. I trust it will suffice?" His lips curled in a smile, but his eyes remained cold and hard.

Completely off balance, Marcus muttered, "Yes … yes, of course."

"And now to business." Josef Bach finished his coffee in one long swallow and pushed the mug away. Leaning across the table, he said, "You are in a position to do me a service, Mr Marcus Holland. In return, I am in a position to advance your career quite spectacularly."

"I really don't see ... " Marcus began.

"I know for example," Josef Bach continued, ignoring the interruption, "that you have a desire to become something in the publishing world. I know you have toyed with the idea of setting up a publishing house in Dublin catering to small, limited editions. Let me ask you ... do you see yourself as a publisher Mr Holland?" He stopped, considering his own question and then nodded. "Yes, I think perhaps you do." He ran one hand through his thick shock of hair. "There is — or rather, there will be — a position for an editorial director within one of my publishing houses in the very near future. I would certainly be pleased to consider — most favourably — your application. There is also the possibility of a vacancy as a features editor in one of the newspapers in which I have a controlling interest ... "

"Editorial director," Holland said thickly. "I think I'd like to apply ... "

"Ah yes, I thought that might suit you."

"Why?" Marcus asked.

"Why? Because, as I said, you are in a position to do me a service. I know my reputation is that of a tyrant, but I reward my staff very well."

"I would be delighted to be of any ser..."

"I know you are currently attempting to gain an interview with Briony Dalton who is in Dublin. Charles O'Neill, a private detective who occasionally feeds you information, advised you that she was in town, and I would imagine you will use his services in an attempt to get past the hotel security to her room."

Marcus Holland opened his mouth to speak, but Josef raised both hands, palms facing outwards. "Bear with me. You see, I too have an interest in Briony Dalton. I have just commissioned — for one of the highest advances ever paid for a non-fiction work to a previously unpublished author — the biography of Briony Dalton. It will tell the full story of how she came to her present position of prominence, it will tell the story of her children — did you know she had two children?" he said, as Holland shook his head. "It will tell how she came to write her first book, her marriage and subsequent divorce. There will be a chapter on her parents; her father ran a sleazy pub in Dublin. He beat his wife until one day, when she couldn't take any more, she stabbed him and ran away. She ended up selling herself in Camden Town here in London, and was eventually fished out of the Thames. The day her husband was told her body had been found, he proposed to his barmaid." He smiled thinly at Holland's expression. "Wonderful material for a book, you will agree. This new biography will show Briony Dalton as she really is. I am offering you an exclusive interview with the author; I am offering you the opportunity of reading the manuscript and excerpting those sections which we agree upon. I am offering you the literary scoop of this century."

Holland swallowed hard, nodding dumbly.

"Naturally all I have said to you is off the record for the moment. This campaign must be carefully organised and orchestrated. Dalton mustn't know that this book is in preparation, and she certainly mustn't know my interest. When your Dublin detective reports to you, you will report to me. When you give Kaho your name she will put you through to me. And you will report to me, regularly, daily, twice, thrice daily if necessary. I want to know everything this woman does, everyone she sees. You never know, it might have some bearing on the book.

"Now," he continued briskly. "Briony Dalton has returned to Ireland to work on her latest book, *A Woman Scorned*. However, although she has only six months left before she delivers the manuscript, she has barely started the work. Goodness knows why she's gone back to Dublin; perhaps she hopes to rediscover that original spark of talent. Anyway, leaving that aside, she has returned to

Dublin to work." Josef Bach smiled, a mere twitching of his lips. "I want you to make sure that she doesn't have the opportunity to work. Interview her, hound her, leak details to the press of her whereabouts and activities ... do whatever you have to. I do not want her to finish *A Woman Scorned*. I will go through the details of this campaign before you leave."

"But why?" Marcus whispered, awed by the arrogance of the man.

"Personal reasons. Personal reasons which don't really concern you. In return for all of this, you will have the exclusive, as I have said, and then later, the editorial director's job will be yours. I will also instruct my bank to debit five thousand sterling per week directly to your account to cover whatever expenses you might incur."

In the long silence that followed, Holland's question was almost lost. "Why me?"

Bach's smile was chilling. "For several reasons Mr Holland. You already have an interest in Briony Dalton; therefore I am not asking you to do something against your will, or something you have no interest in. You know my motto, 'the right people for the right job.' "

"And I'm the right person for this job?"

"Indeed you are. You are ambitious and greedy. Now, while the two traits are not always mutually exclusive, I find it extremely useful to discover them in the one person; it makes that person malleable. What else? You are bisexual, although you have been living a celibate life for the past thirteen months. You have had three blood tests in that period. All of your tests have been negative to date; however, one of your male lovers in New York died from the hepatitis infection, so perhaps you have a reason to be concerned. You have used heroin, though not recently, though you still habitually use amyl nitrate. Speed, I believe it's called. You also appeared in a gay magazine when you were seventeen; I've seen the photographs: they would do nothing for your reputation." He shrugged. "So you see: you are exactly the type of person I like to employ. Your loyalty is guaranteed."

Marcus took a deep breath. "Are you threatening me, Mr Bach?"

"I never threaten," Bach said simply. "I don't have to," he added.

Marcus Holland believed him.

Chapter Twelve

The two women strolled arm in arm through the National Art Gallery of Ireland, walking from room to room without speaking. They had known one another long enough now to remain comfortable and companionable in silence.

"You know your way around here," Gabrielle said eventually.

"I spent my winters here as a child — spent a lot of my summers here too with … with a friend." She smiled fondly, remembering, "Sometimes we would come here on our way back from school — we both went to the Loreto Convent on St Stephen's Green just around the corner — and we'd stop here on the way home, pretending to be copying a painting. We always took our time looking at the nudes, especially the male nudes." She laughed aloud, the sound echoing off the floors and walls, and heads turned to stare at her. "Ah, we had such fun together."

"Would I know this person?" Gabrielle asked, standing back to admire a small Manet.

Briony glanced sidelong at her. "You might," she said, walking past her, "it was Catherine Garrett."

℠

Catherine Garrett was a year and a week older than Briony Dalton and yet, almost from the moment they were introduced, they discovered an affinity with one another that brought both girls even closer than sisters.

Catherine Garrett's mother was a widow when she began working as a barmaid in Mick Dalton's pub. Briony was ten years old at the time, a peaceful, often curious but contented child. According to Catherine's mother, one of the main reasons the two girls got on so well together was because they were both Librans, well-balanced, artistic types, and that they were both interested in writing. Like Mick Dalton, Brigid Garrett knew that her daughter was going to be a writer.

For a while it seemed almost inevitable that Briony's father and Catherine's mother should marry, and almost from the very beginning the regulars in the pub and the neighbours speculated on a romance. But there was never a romance: there was companionship certainly and, if the circumstances had been different, perhaps there could have been a wedding. But Mick Dalton was a devout Catholic and he could never even contemplate marriage, not while he was unsure of the present whereabouts of the wife who had run away.

However, the day the local police sergeant came to him with the news that the body of a woman who had been identified as Sheila Dalton had been dragged out of the River Thames, Mick Dalton had put on his best suit and walked across the cobbled square to the tenement where Brigid Garrett shared a single room with her daughter.

Brigid Garrett had opened the door and stepped aside without a word. Mick Dalton sat in the chair beside the window, looking down over the square, with the dirty line of the wharves visible beyond the houses. His pub was opposite and, like the rest of the street, it was shabby and run-down. Brigid, a stout, unattractive woman well into her forties, but comfortable with her appearance, made a pot of tea without saying anything. She instinctively knew why he had called.

"I'm a free man," Mick said as Brigid poured the tea.

She nodded.

"They've found … that is … the police were with me. They found a body in the Thames … in London," he added. "It was Sheila. She was still using my name. She had been living rough, whoring for the price of a bed at night. And drinking." He spoke so softly that Brigid had to lean forward to hear him. "The police said she might have fallen in the river while she was drunk." He shook his head and looked away towards the pub that had been too poor for his dead wife's ambitions. "She could have come back to me at any time, you know that. She knew it too, but I suppose she was too proud. May God have mercy on her soul." His eyes flickered up at Brigid's impassive face. "I beat her, but God alone knows she drove me to it, constantly whining, bickering, moaning and groaning. I know it's no excuse, but sometimes the only way to shut her up was to hit her a skelp."

Brigid Garrett nodded again.

"Anyway, now that I know she's gone for good, it means I'm free."

"You've been free a long time, Mick Dalton, only you didn't want to admit it to yourself."

He drank his tea, suddenly unsure of himself. His marriage to Sheila had never been entirely happy. She had been too fond of the bottle — an especially unfortunate affliction for a publican's wife — and far too fond of other men's company. Although she had been born not four doors from where he grew up in Corporation Street in the heart of Dublin, she had always had airs and graces above her station. When he'd been younger, he had seen her as the perfect wife: pretty, intelligent and interesting, the perfect mate. She was also interested in him. Later, much later, he realised that she had obviously seen him as a soft touch, a publican with the money to allow her to indulge herself. It must have come as quite a shock to her to discover that all of his money had been sunk into the pub. She had borne him one child — Bernadette — and Mick always claimed that the child was the greatest gift he had ever received and had given him some of the happiest moments of his life. He always said he found it easier to forgive Sheila for all she had done to him, for all the pain she had caused him, when he thought of Bernadette.

He realised that Sheila had always wanted to be someone else, to be something more. She wanted something, some indefinable thing which he couldn't give her. She had dreams; he had none. Well, he hoped she was happy now.

Mick glanced up over the rim of his teacup at Brigid Garrett and he knew she would never try nor pretend to be anyone else. He knew she would be domineering, but not demanding, and he knew he wouldn't love her — not the way he had loved Sheila — but at least he liked her and he knew he would be content in her company. Surely that was enough?

"I suppose I'm asking if you want to be wed," he said eventually.

"I know you are."

"I can't offer you much." He shrugged. "Well, you can see for yourself what I have."

"You've enough for most women, Mick Dalton." She sipped her tea. "Why me?" she asked.

He shrugged again. "You're a good sort, Brigid Garrett. I wish I'd met you ten years ago: I think things would have been different. Things would have been better."

"This will be better," she said by way of accepting his proposal.

There was a small church ceremony a month later. Both Bernadette and Catherine were flower girls in matching pink dresses with pink bows in their hair. They both thought it was the happiest day of their lives: the day they became step-sisters.

ভ

"Company." Gabrielle Royer stopped, her fingers closing around Briony's arm, pulling her back.

When the two women left the National Gallery they had turned to the right walking past the Natural History Museum and government offices, before turning right into Merrion Row, heading back towards their hotel. Gabrielle had stopped almost at the top of Grafton Street, less than fifty yards from the Westbury.

Briony followed the direction of Gabrielle's eyes and found she was looking at the imposing figure of Charley O'Neill. He was deep in conversation with two other men, one of whom was laden with cameras.

"Now it could be coincidence…" Gabrielle muttered, looking at the cameraman.

"And then again it might not," Briony added.

"Has our watch dog sold us out to the paparazzi?"

Briony hissed softly. Her strong white teeth nipped at her bottom lip as she looked around, hands deep in her pockets. Suddenly she walked away from Gabrielle, heading toward the imposing gates to St. Stephen's Green. There was a group of punks standing outside the gates, chatting quietly together, a silent ghetto blaster on the ground between.

Briony stepped into the group and all conversation immediately stopped.

"Who do I speak to here?" she demanded, playing up her Irish accent.

One of the girls stepped forward. "What do you want to speak about?" she asked in a surprising Cockney accent. Her hair had been dyed a deep purple, which matched the vaguely purplish hue to her make-up. Her clothing seemed to be mostly army surplus, except for the obligatory Doc Martens which looked sparkling new.

"I have a problem," Briony said easily, concentrating on the girl. "There is a man following me, an American reporter who wants to photograph me for his raggy newspaper. Now I've come home to Ireland for a little holiday, to escape people like him. I've had a bit of publicity in the States because my boss was caught doing something he shouldn't … you've probably read about it in the papers. Anyway, now I get people like this scuzzy reporter following me around everywhere I go. It's as if I'm some sort of freak for him to photograph."

The girl nodded. "I can relate to that." Other heads nodded around her.

Briony took a fifty-pound note from her purse. "I'd like to try and get into my hotel without being photographed. I'd be very grateful if you could ... distract him."

The fifty-pound note disappeared almost magically. "That buys you a lot of distraction. Now where is that creep?"

Briony turned. "The big guy with the tight haircut in the blue anorak. He's standing beside two guys, one of whom is carrying a lot of cameras."

"I see him. You wait here, we'll take care of him," she said confidently,

Briony stepped back into the shadow of the gate and watched the dozen punks move through the lunchtime crowd. They lacked the aggressiveness of the New York punks — although punk as a style in New York had been taken up by the best designers, and the clothes had been priced out of the market.

The cockney girl walked up to Charley O'Neill and stood on her toes to whisper something in his ear. She saw the startled look on his face ... and then suddenly the girl grabbed hold of the man with both hands and began screaming. Briony saw her leg hook around behind the big man, and then she pushed hard, tumbling them both to the ground. She had used the American as a cushion as she fell, but now she rolled off him, hauling the heavier man atop her. Her screaming reached an extraordinary shrillness, and now the other punks were circling around the pair, shouting and screaming. The photographer turned to walk away, but he suddenly crashed to the ground, camera equipment scattering all around him. One mohawked young man walked smartly away from him, a camera — a Nikon, Briony thought — clutched under his coat.

Two well-dressed young men appeared out of the crowd that had materialised around the couple on the ground and attempted to drag Charley off the girl. One grabbed his hair, another his arm.

Briony later realised that Charley must have reacted
instinctively. Reaching up he wrapped one hand around
the fingers locked into his thinning hair and squeezed. His
left arm grabbed the same arm at the elbow and tugged it
sharply downwards. The young man hit the ground
shoulder first, smashing his face on to the street. The
American rammed his elbow into the second man's solar
plexus and then punched him hard in the groin, the force
of the blow sending him reeling into the crowd.

By then the police had arrived.

慘

"You did what?"

"I paid them," Briony said with a smile, stepping into
the lift and pressing the button for the top floor. She
waited while the lift moved upwards, discharging its
passengers at various floors. "Mind you. I didn't expect it
to be quite so spectacularly successful," she added when
they were alone again.

"You're incredible," Gabrielle said. They walked in
silence down the thickly carpeted corridor and then she
asked, "What do we do now?"

"We move. It's time we looked for another hotel."

"Agreed."

"Do we need to look for someplace in the city?"
Gabrielle asked.

"Probably not, but we'll stay in Dublin anyway." She
slipped her coded keycard into the lock and the door
clicked open. "Now you get everything packed. I want to
be out of here before that detective makes bail."

The call button was flashing on the phone and Briony
and Gabrielle looked at one another. "Terri," Gabrielle
said. "She's the only one who know's where we are."

Briony pressed the call button for the switchboard.
"This is Mrs Moriarty, room 708 … was there a call for
me?"

"Yes, ma'am. A Ms Terri Fierstein phoned from New York at twelve thirty, Irish time. She asked that you return her call the moment you came in."

Briony glanced at Gabrielle who had pulled the suitcases out of the wardrobes and was busy packing. The younger woman caught the look and stopped, eyebrows raised in a silent question. "Did Ms Fierstein leave any message?"

"No, ma'am. But she said she would be in the office all day, and asked that you phone her the moment you came in. She left her number."

"Will you make that call for me, please?"

"Yes, ma'am. Immediately."

"Call collect," Briony added and hung up. "Terri phoned from New York; sounded urgent. It must have been urgent if she phoned here at twelve thirty ... that's seven thirty in the morning in New York. It must be important to get her out of bed so early."

"I'll continue packing," Gabrielle murmured.

"Yes ... yes," Briony said distractedly. "We'll need to get away from here soon." Two minutes later the phone rang. Briony snatched it on the first ring. "Hello?"

"I have Ms Fierstein on the line from New York now, Mrs Moriarty."

"Thank you. Terri?"

"Briony ... Briony. Thank God." There was a faint transatlantic echo on the line, but otherwise it was perfectly clear.

"Is everything all right?"

"No. Definitely not all right," Terri said, sounding slightly breathless. "How near are you to completion on *A Woman Scorned*."

"Terri, for goodness sake, we've already had this conversation. I've only been here a couple of days; I haven't done much more since we spoke in New York. Look, I've six months left to complete the contract. I'll bring it in on time." She felt a sudden snap of anger; was this the emergency?

"You've got to bring it in sooner than that."

"Impossible."

"Make it possible."

"Why?" Briony asked, curious now. "What's happened?"

"I had supper yesterday with … well with someone you wouldn't know. But he told me — in strictest confidence — that Josef Bach has just commissioned or is about to commission your biography."

"What's wrong with that? Shouldn't I be flattered?"

"Depends what sort of biography this is going to be, doesn't it? Depends who is going to write it."

"Come on, Terri, spit it out. What have you got? What about this biography?"

"It's going to be a smear job … written by your good friend Catherine Garrett."

Briony sank down on to the edge of the bed and closed her eyes. Catherine was the one person who could hurt her, really hurt her. "But surely if there's a biography, that will only help the sales of the book?"

"If the biography goes to print first, and it is scurrilous enough, and manages to turn public opinion against you, then it might damage the sales of *A Woman Scorned* quite dramatically. From what I was told, this is going to be a real muckraker."

"How much can it harm me?" Briony asked very softly.

"You received a two and a half million dollars advance for the American hardback and paperback rights. If your book fails to sell, the net loss to the publishers could be catastrophic. They could even go under. You'd become a pariah. No publisher would ever touch you again. You don't need me to tell you, my dear, that you've developed a lifestyle that would be difficult to support working behind the counter in some store."

"I hear you."

"I know you hear me, but do you understand what I'm saying?"

"I think so."

"Well, let me spell it out for you. Deliver *A Woman Scorned* in record time, and it will see publication ten days after the delivery of the final manuscript."

"That's impossible," Briony Dalton said flatly.

"It's a matter of survival — and not just yours any more. Now we are talking about the future of the British and American companies who bought your book. We're also talking about the damage to my reputation. Fuck this up and you will never write again."

"What can we do?"

"Deliver the book. Nothing else will do. This biography will hurt."

Something clicked into place, and Briony suddenly said, "How about countering with an official biography, an authorised biography?"

There was a long silence on the other end of the line.

Briony hurried on, warming to the idea. "Once you have the publication date of Garrett's book, we could publish ours exactly two weeks beforehand. If it was written properly, we would be able to refute her every argument … before she had even made them."

"I like it," Terri said very quietly, and then, more excitedly, "I like it a lot. I think it's a stunning idea. But who would we get to write it?"

"Why, Gabrielle of course. Who else?"

"Brilliant! A superb idea. I'll float it right now with a couple of publishers and get back to you later today."

"No," Briony said, "I'll phone you. We're about to go shopping. We won't be in for the rest of the day. I'll speak to you later." She hung up without another word and turned to Gabrielle, who was looking at her intently.

"What was that all about?"

"You're going to write the authorised biography of Briony Dalton . . . or at least my version of the authorised biography."

"Why?"

"Because my step-sister, Catherine Garrett, is writing the unauthorised, and hence unvarnished version. And that's a story I don't want told. I need to destroy her book and her credibility before she gets her book into print ... before it destroys me!"

Chapter Thirteen

Catherine had put off looking at the video cassette which had accompanied Josef Bach's report for several reasons. From reading the text she had a very good idea of what it contained, and while, in principle, she had no problem with pornographic videos and indeed had watched them with Mark Cosgrove on a couple of occasions while they drank wine and later made love, she didn't feel she could watch it critically, coldly ... and especially not when she would be looking at someone she knew.

She also felt that there was something inherently wrong in watching a pornographic movie so early in the day. She remembered standing outside a sex shop off Piccadilly Circus at noon one day and watching a middle-aged business man actually waiting for the shop to open. When he reappeared about five minutes later he had a brown paper bag under his arm. For days afterwards she wondered what he had bought, what had been so important.

She hefted the black video box in her hand. Why was she so reluctant to view it? Was it her good Catholic upbringing? The nuns had instructed her that sex was bad and dirty, something only conducted at night, under sheets, with the eyes closed, and only then for procreation, never for pleasure. She liked to think she was liberated, but underneath ... deep down, the good Catholic upbringing of her childhood still held her in it's thrall. Deciding that she might find it easier to watch the video at night, she slid it back in to its cardboard case and tossed it onto her desk.

Catherine turned to the computer screen and lifted the keyboard on to her lap, her fingers resting lightly on the keys. She wondered what the nuns who had educated both

Briony and herself thought of them now. She pressed the
two-key combination that opened up a little notepad on
the screen, and wrote a short sentence to herself.

Interview one of the nuns.

With a bit of luck — and a little coaxing — they would
give her a usable quote … and the more outraged and
outrageous the better. And that shouldn't be too difficult:
Briony Dalton attracted outraged comments. Catherine
stared at the screen, idly picking at the rent in the knee of
her jeans. There were a number of people she needed to
talk to: the children, of course, although, bearing in mind
what she now knew of their lifestyle, that might be
difficult. It would be important to speak to Briony's father,
her own step-father, but again, that was going to be
difficult. Catherine hadn't spoken to Mick Dalton in over
ten years, and she knew Briony had bitterly disappointed
him. And then there was Niall Moriarty, Briony's ex-
husband. There would be no problem getting him to talk,
and while she thought of it, she suddenly wondered why
he had never given the story to one of the Sunday rags,
since it was exactly the type of thing they delighted in. She
made another note on the screen: Bach might know the
answer to that, and if he didn't know, he'd certainly be
able to find out.

There were other people whom she would love to
interview, people like Terri Fierstein, who had made
Briony Dalton the multi-millionaire household name she
was; there was her personal secretary, Gabrielle Royer; she
could use the story about the girl really being from Texas,
she decided, adding another note to the screen.

And then, of course, there was Briony Dalton herself.

Interviewing her was out of the question, but Josef Bach
had supplied her with a complete listing of all the
interviews which Briony had given over her entire writing
career. A couple of days spent in the library would be of
immense worth … she could use the quotes as headings for
the chapters, and if she used a quote that was diametrically
opposite to the material in the chapter, that would show
Briony up for what she was. There was one which

Catherine particularly remembered, "Our children are the culmination of our past, the harbingers of our future." It was attributed to Briony by the First Lady of America when she was launching a youth-orientated drugs awareness campaign. Well now, that would make a perfect quote for the chapter which dealt with the present whereabouts and activities of Briony's two children. The thought sparked another idea, and Catherine noted down, "See police record for Matt." She had a friend who had access to the records section who might be able to get her a copy of Matthew Moriarty's arrest sheet. Indeed, she was rather surprised that Josef hadn't included a copy of the file in the otherwise almost encyclopaedic report he had prepared on the two children.

Catherine folded her arms and leaned back into the chair. Some of the most damning evidence against Briony was to be found in the present predicament of her two children.

When her marriage had broken up, Briony — obviously — had received the custody of the children. But what sort of life must they have had? Briony had immediately left Dublin to settle near London, close to the heart of the publishing world. The children were given into the care of a series of nannies and tutors and rarely saw their mother. Her routine then was to start 'work' at eight in the morning and finish at nine at night. They were living in a five-bedroomed house in Hemel Hemptsead at that time, with Briony having two of the largest bedrooms to herself. During the thirteen hours she worked, she rarely moved from the room. There was a bathroom en suite, and she was able to make tea for herself at any time. And if the work was going well, she would often continue through the night. She also demanded complete silence while she worked, no voices or noises to distract her.

Truthfully, she wasn't really interested in the children; she found them a nuisance. She had contested custody as a matter of form, and it came as quite a shock to her when she discovered that the children had been granted into her custody. Briony Dalton found most things about the real world intrusive and annoying. Only the worlds she created, the worlds of imagination in which she was god, held any real interest for her.

She had neglected her children in as much as she had had no real interest in them. She had been content to allow other people to rear them and in return they had gone their own way at the earliest opportunity. Was it any wonder they had ended up as they had?

And Catherine felt she was not entirely blameless either. She had had the opportunity to stop Briony and yet she had done nothing.

The children were her step-niece and step-nephew, if such a thing existed. And, even though she hadn't seen them for many years she still felt guilty and more than a little responsible for what had happened to them. But her split with Briony effectively prevented her from seeing them.

Too late now. Too many might-have-beens and should-have-beens.

The phone rang down the hall, and the answering machine clicked in. Even before her own message had run out, she knew it was the office. She glanced guiltily at the two shelves of books she currently had for review. Since Josef Bach's extraordinary offer, she had done no reading.

"*. . . I need those reviews by close of business tomorrow. And I'll need you to read through the guest list for Saturday night's show . . .*"

"Jesus!" She replaced the keyboard and stood up, flicking through the books. Most of the paperbacks were rubbish. There was some new fantasy and science fiction which she reviewed under a pen name for one of the science fiction magazines. Most she could dismiss quite easily, reading the opening and the ending, simply scanning the text. The rest of the review she could take from the publisher's blurb. There were a couple of new pieces of fiction: a new Salman Rushdie, a Paul Theroux and an enormous family saga by some unknown author who was currently being mega-hyped. She knew, even without reading it, that it would be awful.

The temptation was simply to forget about them: with the half a million advance she need never work again. And yet ... and yet ...

Catherine Garrett had spent years building up her name and establishing her reputation as a serious literary critic. She had fought long and hard to achieve her own radio programme and later the sometimes controversial *This Week I Read. . .* on BBC2 where celebrities were invited to discuss the book they had read the previous week. Because topicality was essential, the programme went out live, which besides lending itself to the numerous dangers of live television, was often used and misused by its contributors. The show had helped make her famous ... and she wasn't prepared to throw it all away.

She might never write another book, although she wanted to write, desperately wanted to see her name in print — always had — but she doubted if she could. Every time she put pen to paper — or finger to keyboard — that first terrible, terrifying disappointment would pop up, dredging its emotional cocktail of hate, anger and envy.

She stopped suddenly.

No. Not yet. She wasn't prepared to explore that particular memory just yet. That would come later and she would probe her pain as she wrote about it, as she put it down on the page, maybe even exorcise the memory. But right now she was determined to keep her day job alive. The *TLS* had once said that hers was possibly the most powerful and influential voice in book publishing in Britain today. She had thought there had been an element of sarcasm in the article, but it was true that she could make or break a book with her reviews and coverage.

Catherine spent the next couple of hours phoning various friends of hers, people she was certain had read this month's crop of best-sellers. Most were booksellers. Booksellers, like reviewers, were in the sometimes enviable position of reading a current best-seller weeks before it appeared for sale, either in proof or presentation form. If a publisher decided to push out the boat on a particular title, copies would be distributed to every major bookshop or chain, so that by the time the publisher's representative arrived to sell in the forthcoming titles there would already be an awareness of the book.

A quick call to three of the specialist science fiction and fantasy bookshops disposed of the fantasy titles: none of them was up to much. She jotted quick notes on each; they could be dismissed in a brief paragraph.

Finding someone who had read the Theroux and Rushdie took a little longer, but eventually she struck lucky. The trick of course, was not to let her contacts know she was pumping them for information.

By seven o'clock, Catherine had finished the rough drafts of the various reviews, bulking up the Salman Rushdie with snippets from reviews of some of his earlier works. She would rework the reviews early in the morning and fax them down the line by lunchtime. She saved the work to disc and replaced the keyboard on the table before the screen. There was a dull throbbing at the base of her skull, and her eyes felt gritty and hard. She spread her arms out on either side and stretched, fingers outspread … and she jumped when two hands came to rest on her shoulders.

"Jesus, Mark, but you scared me."

"I'm sorry." He kneaded her shoulders, loosening the taut muscles. "I'm sorry," he said again.

"Why?" she asked.

"For … for what I said. The things I said. I didn't mean … that is I had no right."

Catherine reached over and exited from the programme she was using. She used the disc parking programme and they both listened to the soft whirling clicking as the cylinders on the hard disc were parked one by one. When the machine flashed the message, HARD DISK UNIT PARK PLEASE TURN THE POWER OFF, Catherine pressed the power button on the screen and then on the computer. The power died with a long descending hum. In the silence that followed she said, "But you were right."

"I know," he said very softly.

Catherine began blinking hard, the back of her throat beginning to burn.

"But we're not tied to one another ... I mean it would be different if we were married ... but we didn't want to be married, we wanted the freedom. Didn't we?"

She nodded.

"The freedom to have other friends, other relationships. So it's not as if you did anything wrong ... or anything like that ... " he finished helplessly.

Large tears rolled down Catherine's cheeks, splashing warmly on to her hands which were folded in her lap. In the darkness behind her, Mark Cosgrove bit the inside of his cheeks to prevent himself from smiling. He had written out this speech at least half a dozen times before getting the tone just right. He must be seen to be apologising, but she must be made to feel guilty — that was the difficult part.

"It just happened," she sobbed.

"I know," he said, understanding, forgiving.

"I don't even know why it happened."

Because he gave you a cheque for more money than you'd ever seen in your entire life, Cosgrove thought, but kept his thoughts to himself.

"I've made some tea," he said finally.

"That would be lovely." She stood up and stepped away from him, looking out over the Downs. "Let me ... wash my face and change." She glanced back over her shoulder. "Do you want to go to the village for something to eat?"

"Not really. We can pop something in the microwave."

"Fine. How is the book?" she asked awkwardly, turning to face him.

He shrugged, smiled his little-boy smile. "Coming along."

"Good." She paused, as if she was about to say something else, but then suddenly turned and left the room. Cosgrove remained leaning on the back of her chair watching the dusk gathering outside the window. Jesus, but she was such a pathetic creature. She disgusted him. He'd walk away from her tomorrow if he could ... but the problem was he needed this woman, she was going to make his career. He had been so angry with her when she had come back from Bach with that cheque. And it really was the cheque that was at the centre of the argument. He hadn't known she had made love to Bach although, knowing the man's extraordinary reputation, he should have guessed. His accusation had been a shot in the dark. The truth was that he was jealous of the huge amount of money she was receiving for a book which she would very probably have written for nothing.

He'd seen this happen before, with other authors, other personalities: the big advance had nothing to do with talent, but everything to do with connections. However now he was making his own connections. His new book was going to be different: it was going to make his fortune. Catherine would review it on her programme and in her column. She should be able to wangle him on to the programme either as an author for interview, or a guest reviewer, and after that well...

He was going to look for a hundred thousand pound advance for his next book.

And to achieve that he was willing to sacrifice a little — like some of his self-respect. He was also willing to lie a little and, distasteful as it was, he was also willing to sleep with her. He was using her, he freely admitted that. But only in as much as she was using him, for sex, for comfort, companionship and the constant reassurance she craved.

He picked up the video which was lying beside the computer and shook it out of its box. It was untitled. He tapped the box with the back of his fingers, remembering the package that had arrived from Bach; there had been something hard and oblong in the jiffy bag. He had seen Catherine reading the report, but she hadn't offered to show it to him and he hadn't asked. Obviously the video had something to do with the Briony Dalton book.

Mark Cosgrove took the video into the sitting room and knelt on the floor to plug both the TV and video in. When the television picture appeared he shoved in the video. The machine swallowed the black box and clicked on. The grey haze on the TV screen was replaced by a multicoloured sunburst logo. The colours shivered as he played with the tracking and the sound trembled slightly, but otherwise the quality was fine. He had seen enough pornographic videos to immediately recognise the type. The film's dialogue was in English, but it was subtitled in Dutch. It was set in a hospital or clinic and within minutes the two nurses had climbed into bed with two patients and the action had begun to a slightly off-key piece of classical music which Cosgrove couldn't identify.

He heard Catherine come back into the room and knew by the sudden odour of perfume that she would be wearing her negligée, probably the transparent black one. He glanced up, and found he was correct.

He jerked a thumb at the screen. "Not bad," he remarked.

Catherine looked past him, her eyes dull and expressionless.

"The blonde's pretty," he remarked, "but the black-haired bird is the business, and she can certainly…"

"Don't!"

"Why?" Her tone had been shrill, almost hysterical. "What's wrong? It's only a…"

Catherine knelt on the floor and took the remote control from Mark's fingers. Pressing the pause button on the video she froze the picture of the pretty raven-haired girl who was at that moment kneeling between two well-endowed young men.

"That is Rianne Moriarty, Briony's Dalton's daughter." Her voice was a flat monotone. "She is twenty-two years old. I was once like a mother to her."

Chapter Fourteen

It had taken Charley O'Neill nearly five hours before he had finally convinced the police that he had not assaulted the girl. He knew — and they knew too — that they had nothing to hold him on. They were simply enjoying themselves at his expense, and getting some of their own back.

He stood outside Pearse Street Police Station, breathing deeply, and then coughed on the acrid exhaust fumes. He grinned at his own stupidity: taking a deep breath when you stepped outside a prison was, he was sure, an instinctive reaction. He had watched POWs and hardened criminals do exactly the same thing. He'd never thought he'd be doing it himself.

He had spent the last five hours trying to work out what had happened, trying to make sense of the sequence of events. It had all the hallmarks of a scam, and yet he couldn't figure it. Why should this punk girl, whom he'd never seen before in his life, suddenly have picked on him? Sure, one of the photographers had had his camera stolen, but it seemed an awful lot of work just to steal one lousy camera.

Unless, of course, stealing the camera had been a blind, or someone being opportunistic.

Unless, of course, the attack had been deliberate, pre-meditated.

The big American dashed across Pearse Street, and made his way through the grounds of Trinity College, which faced the police station. He strode through the college grounds, exiting out into Dawson Street where Briony and Gabrielle had walked a few hours previously.

At the top of Dawson Street, he turned to the right and slowed down. Slowly, casually, he went past the United Services Club until he could see the impressive gate to St Stephen's Green.

And she was there. It was difficult to miss that haircut.

There were a dozen outrageously dressed punks in the group outside the entrance to the park, passing around a brown plastic bottle of cheap cider amongst themselves. Charley O'Neill tucked his hands into his pockets and hurried past on the opposite side of the street, deliberately looking down Grafton Street away from the group. He ducked into the enormous St Stephen's Green shopping centre and pounded up the escalator. He bought a pot of coffee and a pastry in a restaurant that overlooked the park, and then he settled back to wait. He had no worries that the group would suddenly split up; there would be an elaborate parting ritual before they each went their own way.

And then he would have her.

It was nearly an hour and a half, and four cups of coffee, later when the departure dance began. Feet were shuffled, shoulders shrugged and some of the group moved away a dozen steps before returning to finish their conversation. At the first indications that the party was breaking up, Charley hurried down the stairs, abruptly realising that he desperately needed to pee. He stopped in the entrance to the shopping centre in time to see the female punk saunter down Grafton Street, her arm around the shoulder of a dishevelled young man with greasy spiked hair. Charley followed her down the length of the narrow, crowded shopping thoroughfare. He had no real plan in mind, other than to catch up with her in some quiet place and ask her one simple question. Close to the bottom of Grafton Street, the pair turned to the left into Wicklow Street. They briefly examined a display of handmade jewellery on a stall before continuing. Charley O'Neill paused at Weir's the jewellers, allowing them time to move on. As they moved further and further down Wicklow Street, pedestrians became fewer and he had to hang back.

Luckily the punks' brightly coloured haircuts were relatively easy to follow at a distance. As they neared the end of the street, he increased his pace. They turned to the right into Georges Street, and Charley at last had an idea where they were going. As he rounded the corner he saw them turning into Marx Brothers' restaurant. He crossed the street and stood in the doorway of some anonymous government office watching them buy coffee and then make their way downstairs. He had them now: there was only one entrance to Marx Brothers. Taking his time, he crossed the street and entered the café, buying himself a mug of strong black coffee. He went down the stairs cautiously, holding the cup before him. He spotted the couple sitting in the corner of the low-ceilinged room, the girl with her back to him.

The boy looked up as he approached, frowning, wondering why the big man was crowding them. There were plenty of empty seats downstairs and no need for him to come so close.

Charley hooked his foot around a chair and pulled it over, dropping into it and immediately draping his right hand over the girl's shoulder, his broad hard fingers tightening around the back of her neck. "Scream, and I'll snap your neck like a chicken's."

Her eyes — dull, muddy green, the whites yellow-tinged — widened, but she said nothing.

"You remember me, don't you?" he hissed. "You did a number on me earlier today."

"Hey, mister." The young punk leaned over and grabbed the front of Charley's anorak.

Without taking his eyes off the girl, the American lifted the scalding cup of coffee and held it before the young man's face. "Take your hands off me before I throw this over you." As the punk subsided into the chair, Charley squeezed the back of the girl's neck for emphasis. "Now, I have two questions: why did you do it? Who put you up to it?"

"Fuck you!"

The American's blunt fingers found the nerve at the side of her neck and began to squeeze. "Don't make me hurt you," he whispered. "Why did you attack me today?"

"A woman," the girl said tightly, tears glistening in her eyes.

"Which woman?"

"I don't know. Honest, I don't." She felt the fingers tighten. "Well dressed, American, I think. She gave me fifty quid to distract you ... said you were following her."

With his arm still around her shoulders, Charley O'Neill drank his coffee in silence, then stood and bent down to the girl, making her draw back in fright. "Don't ever let me see you again," he snarled.

So, he'd been right, but he'd had to make sure. Now he owed that bitch a return favour. She was about to learn that you didn't fuck around with Charley O'Neill.

The call button on his phone was alight when he returned to the car, but he ignored it and drove back to his office in Fitzwilliam Square in complete silence, idly working his way through a dozen plans that presented themselves. Why couldn't she have just let things be? He was watching her for her own protection: what was wrong with that? Why did she have to get smart and involve him with the police? And she was going to make him look like a fool when Marcus Holland got to hear of it. He ran his hand through his grizzled hair; maybe she thought this was some kind of novel, a nice neat piece of fiction where the heroine manages to give the villain the slip. She was about to find out that life did not copy art.

Marcus Holland was at home by the time Charley O'Neill got around to phoning him. The detective was gruff, tired after the long battle through the snarled evening traffic.

"You were looking for me?"

"How is our case progressing?"

"So-so," he said, noncommittally. He sat at his desk in his darkened office drinking a sour cup of instant coffee, determined to spend another hour here before venturing out into the traffic again.

"We're going to step up observation on the woman."

Charley shook his head, but said nothing; this guy thought he was the fucking CIA.

"I'm going to do a documentary on her, the whole works, interviews, the lot," Holland lied. "However, I'd like to discuss it with you before we proceed any further. I'm going to need some material on the subject."

Detecting something in the other man's voice, Charley straightened. "So, discuss it," he prompted, half-guessing the answer.

"In person."

"I'm in my office."

"Can you come around here tonight?"

"Not tonight," Charley said capriciously, although he had nothing on tonight or, indeed, any other night.

There was a pause on the other end of the phone, and then Holland asked, "How long will you be in the office?"

"Another half an hour or so."

"It will take me that long to get across to you. Will you wait?"

"I'll wait," Charley said, keeping the surprise from his voice. Whatever Holland was planning it was obviously more important than a series of interviews. He realised the phone in his hand had gone dead and gently replaced it on its cradle.

It took Marcus Holland less than thirty minutes to make it from his Dun Laoghaire address to O'Neill's office. He used the time to work out exactly how much to tell O'Neill, how much he needed to know. He also had to decide how far he trusted the American detective. His decision was tempered with the knowledge that if O'Neill was willing to sell out his present employer then what was to stop him selling out Holland if the price was right?

Finding a parking space directly outside the building which housed O'Neill's offices, he used the television

presenter's trick of sitting for a few moments, rehearsing
his speech, practising his expressions. With a final breath
to calm himself, he climbed out of the car and walked up
the steps to the glass-panelled door. The foyer door clicked
open the moment he rang without waiting for him to
announce himself. He made his way through the deserted
building, his rubber-soled Nike runners making no sound
on the parquet hallway. Somewhere in the distance he
could hear a woman singing loudly off-key: cleaning lady,
he guessed.

The detective's office was in semi-darkness, O'Neill a
vague shape against the windows which looked out over
the south side of Fitzwilliam Square.

"You could do with a light in here."

"I prefer the dark," Charley murmured. One of the
reasons he could afford rooms at the prestigious
Fitzwilliam address was because from about one o'clock
onwards the two connecting rooms descended into
perpetual gloom and the offices were discounted
accordingly. "I charge extra for after-hours work," he
added.

"This could make you quite a bit of money," Holland
remarked, discerning the vague shape of a chair in the
gloom and settling into it.

"Must be dirty."

Marcus shrugged. "Certainly none too clean."

"What do you want?"

"I want Briony Dalton."

O'Neill shifted in the chair. "I thought that's what we
were doing."

"Sort of. We're stepping up the operation. Can you get
me access to her suite in the Westbury?"

"What for?"

"I'd like to talk to her ... with a television crew," he
added.

"What? Look, let's just cut the shit. I'm tired; I've had a lousy day. You tell me exactly what you want to do and then I'll tell you exactly whether or not I can do it."

"I'm going to persecute Briony Dalton," Holland said simply.

"Why?" O'Neill asked.

"Publicity." Holland leaned forward, squinting into the darkness. "I'm going to rake up everything I can on this woman, make a big splash with it, stir the shit, and then I'm going to ride the wave of publicity that'll undoubtedly follow. If I do it right, it'll make me — and you — wealthy. It'll also open lots of doors."

"How are you going to do this?"

"This woman stirred up a lot of resentment with her various books … "

"That was a long time ago, as I remember."

"Not that long. She was particularly outspoken about the church and various public leaders. And some of these people, as you know, have very long memories. Now, we know she crept back into the country under a false name, so obviously she thinks she has something to hide. What I want to do is try to get her on national television and interview her live. In the meantime, I want to leak photographs, articles, titbits — all scurrilous of course — to the press and in general inflame public opinion about her." He sat back into the chair. "But I'll need your help. I want you to get me the dirt on the woman. Can you do that?"

Charley O'Neill threw back his head and laughed. "I worked for the FBI. When you were still in diapers I was getting the dirt on people, militants, communists, peace marchers, actors, political candidates, and when we couldn't get the dirt, well sometimes we got a little creative. You want her high-profile and dirty, leave it to me. And you know something else? I'll even do it cheaply, because I reckon it's going to be a labour of love."

Chapter Fifteen

"I think you should go back to New York immediately," Briony said to Gabrielle.

"Why?" The younger woman looked up, astonished. She was sorting through a pile of clothing that had been spread out on the bed. A half-filled suitcase lay on the floor by her feet. "Terri said she'd get back to us when she'd drummed up some interest in the book."

"Go back," Briony said firmly. "If you're there it might put a little more pressure on her to hurry it along, but remember, sign nothing without referring to me first."

"Of course."

"Go to the apartment. There are some old notebooks, scrapbooks, box files and other bits and pieces on the top shelf in the study. Go through them, use whatever you need for your biography: they'll give you excellent background material. I think there's some old photographs as well … take those also."

"Hang on a sec, dear." Gabrielle came around the bed to stand before Briony. She took both her hands in hers and stared into her eyes. "We're forgetting one thing. I've never written before. I can't write."

"Bullshit!" Briony snapped, breaking the contact and turning away. "You can write. I've seen the work you've done on my own writing."

"I don't"

"You do!" Briony went to the window, and looked down over Harry Street into Grafton and South Anne Street. "You might think you're just tidying up the text, correcting the spellings, but you're doing more than that. I keep a copy of my first draft and when you give me back the corrected version I've often compared one against the other. You're an excellent editor."

"An editor is not a writer."

"Listen to me. Once you've done the background work, and prepared the notes and chapter breakdowns, I will dictate my life story to you, and you can then write it in any way you wish. You see, all you'll be doing is editing my work again."

Gabrielle nodded doubtfully.

"While you're gone, I'll buy myself a little tape recorder and begin taping my memoirs so you can start work on the book the moment you come back."

"But…"

"No buts. Now phone the airport and make a reservation." She turned around, smiling broadly. "You know if this book works for you, it might launch your own career as a writer." The smile turned wistful. "Don't tell me you don't want to write, I know the signs." She crossed the room and wrapped her arms around Gabrielle. "You can do it, I know you can." She brushed her lips to Gabrielle's forehead. "Believe me, if I can do it, then anyone can."

"You rob it of it's glamour," Gabrielle said.

"There is none. Tell me where's the glamour of sitting staring at a blank page or at a screen for hours on end? The only secret to writing is to get yourself a comfortable chair, because, by Christ, you'll be spending a lot of time in it."

"You sound as if you regret it," Gabrielle said quietly.

"Sometimes."

"It's given you everything you have now."

"I sometimes think it has taken away more than it gave. The problem with being a writer is that I'm blessed — or cursed — with a writer's imagination, so it's easy for me to imagine what it would be like to be just another nobody."

"You're only a nobody if you believe you're a nobody. Everybody is somebody," Gabrielle tried to smile, but she recognised the very real hurt behind the older woman's eyes.

Briony lowered her head on to Gabrielle's shoulder. "Wouldn't it be nice, though, to have a house in the suburbs, a nice husband in an undemanding job and two grown-up children?"

"You'd go mad."

Briony shook her head. "If you knew no better you wouldn't know what you were missing. If the biggest worry in your day was wondering what to make for dinner that night, then how could you even begin to contemplate what it must be like to lead any other sort of life?"

Gabrielle kissed her quickly on the lips. "You'd read books," she laughed.

Briony nodded and stepped away, turning to look out over the street again, watching the people bustling by. "And then you'd imagine a world where money is the cure for everything, the women are beautiful, the men are handsome and everyone is happy." She glanced back over her shoulder at Gabrielle. "And who writes these books?"

"People like you," Gabrielle suggested, though she knew it was not the truth.

"No. Not people like me. People like that housewife, dreaming of another life. You know that only a tiny percentage of authors make it to the really big time, the rest of them go on churning out books for their publishers, hoping against hope that one day this one will be the best-seller. And when that happens, what does it do? It changes their dull lives, and suddenly they think they're living the big time."

She crossed the floor and slumped down on to the bed, lying back on the crisp sheets, her feet still on the floor. With her hands locked behind her head, she stared wide-eyed at the ceiling. "And then what happens? Suddenly they have to deliver the next book … and the next … and you're only allowed one failure, do you know that? Just one." The bitterness in her voice was almost palpable now.

"Now they're no longer writing for pleasure, they're writing to survive."

Gabrielle crossed to the portable computer and lifted up a box of discs. Opening the hard plastic box, she pulled out the ten grey discs and then carefully lifted out the white glassine envelope that was hidden in the bottom of the box. Sitting at the dressing table, she opened her purse and took out her gold American Express card. Using the edge of the card, she eased about a quarter of the white powder from the envelope on to a hand mirror. Resealing the envelope she popped it back into the disc box and dropped the discs back in on top of it. Returning to the mirror, she divided up the pile of white powder into four regular lines. She dipped into her purse again and pulled out an Irish twenty-pound note. Rolling the note into a tight tube, she carried the mirror across to the bed and knelt on the floor behind Briony's head, so that she was looking — upside down — into the older woman's face. "I've got something that will cheer you up."

Briony turned over on her stomach and cupped her face in her hands. Her eyes went from Gabrielle's face to the small mirror in her hands. Without saying a word, she lifted the rolled note, placed one end alongside the first line, inserted the other end in her left nostril and inhaled sharply. Switching the tube to her right nostril, she repeated the procedure.

The dust hit the back of her throat, and blossomed into her head in a solid ball of buzzing white noise and sparkling light. She closed her eyes and breathed deeply, savouring the rush, feeling the tingle along her flesh.

Gabrielle inhaled the two remaining lines of cocaine, and then licked the tip of her index finger to gather up the remaining particles of white powder. She rubbed the dust in under her gums. Sinking to the floor, she lay stretched out, her head against the side of the bed, while the cocaine worked through her system.

Briony too could feel the drug work its magic on her taut muscles, feeling them relax, feeling the bitterness that had threatened to smother her vanish beneath the white cloud. There was a warm glow in the pit of her stomach and the knot that had tightened in her chest loosened and she began to breath more evenly. Her eyes closed, opened and then closed again and a smile appeared on her lips.

Moist air brushed her face and then equally moist lips brushed against her eyelids. A tongue, wet and soft, touched along her lids, against her cheekbones, against her lips. With her eyes still firmly closed — she would never open them! — she parted her lips, felt the tongue brush against her teeth, rasp against her own tongue. She opened her mouth wider as the tongue probed, then moved down across her lips again, down the long column of her throat. Fingers plucked at the buttons of her silk steel-grey Dior blouse. With her eyes still squeezed shut — spirals and glittering sparkles of colour dancing behind the reddened lids — she rolled over on to her back. She felt the sudden touch of cold air on her ultra-sensitive flesh, and then what felt like knives touched her skin. She jumped and her heart began thrumming beneath her breast. Her arms were being forced apart exposing her small breasts. Again the touch of moist air against her skin, and she could feel her nipples puckering, hardening in response. A tongue, liquid and warm, and then lips, feather-soft, traced their way across her breasts before finally coming to rest on her taut nipples.

Intensified by the drug, each caress, every touch, was magnified a thousand-fold and as her lover worked on her, Briony could feel her orgasm building deep within her; she imagined it as a tiny spark, growing into a smouldering fire, then flaring, before rising to consume her totally, unconsciousness washing over her, rising up in a warm, welcoming tide, swallowing her...

⟡

Gabrielle sat in the easy chair and looked at the naked body of Briony Dalton. The older woman was sleeping easily now and when she awoke, she would feel tired, but relaxed. Hopefully the negative spiral into which she had been drifting would have been forgotten. Gabrielle had seen it happen before. Sometimes it could take days for her to snap out of its depressive grip and, of course, while it worked its evil spell on her, she couldn't write.

Gabrielle shuddered as her taut muscles contracted. The residue of the cocaine was still in her system. She would have liked Briony to have made love to her, but she had been quite happy to allow her to lie there while she worked on her, arousing her again and again, using her own responses to wash away the threatened depression.

She looked at Briony Dalton again. What made a woman of forty-five, once married with two children, take up a lesbian affair with a woman half her age?

She remembered the first time she had touched Briony Dalton in an intimate way: they had been in the sauna together, one of the new herbal saunas where the steam was scented with various exotic odours and spices, the moist air almost a caress in itself. Briony was sitting with her back against the panelled wall while Gabrielle was lying stretched out, her head in Briony's lap.

At some stage Briony had dozed off and the towel she had wrapped around her torso had slipped off, exposing her small, taut breasts. Gazing at them Gabrielle had become unusually aroused. She was not exclusively gay, though it was true she preferred women as lovers.

Turning on her stomach, it had seemed the most natural thing in the world to begin stroking Briony's breasts. By the time Briony awoke, her breathing and pulse had quickened and while her initial reaction had been one of shock and disgust, she had been only too aware of her body's arousal and had eventually yielded to the younger woman's attentions. Initially, she simply lay there, not moving, not touching, but before that first orgasm had taken her, she had clutched at Gabrielle's shoulders, digging her fingers into the soft flesh. She had dragged the younger woman up, delighting in the touch of her breasts against her flesh, holding her tightly as she had kissed her with surprising passion. They had made love long into the afternoon, their lovemaking gentle and undemanding. Shared.

They had come a long way since then.

Gabby pulled off her clothes and crossed to the bed to slide in under the covers alongside Briony, wrapping her arms around her. The older woman snuggled closer and murmured in her sleep. Gabrielle thought she heard her murmur Catherine Garrett's name.

Chapter Sixteen

Briony Dalton awoke feeling alert and refreshed. No headache, no hangover, no nausea. She lay in the centre of the double bed and stretched in the sheets, spreading her arms wide. Paper rustled beneath her right hand. She turned her head and found a folded sheet of cream hotel notepaper on the pillow beside her.

Sitting up, she called out, "Gabrielle ... Gabrielle?"

There was no reply and she knew, even before she opened the note, that Gabrielle had gone.

Took the seven o'clock flight. You looked so peaceful I didn't want to wake you. Will phone later. Do some writing. Love, Gabrielle.

Briony laughed as she swung her long legs out of bed and padded naked into the bathroom. She turned on the shower and while waiting for the water to warm up, she ordered a continental breakfast from room service, asking for it to be delivered in twenty minutes.

She showered quickly with the water on full, turning her face into the needle spray, revelling in the sting of the water. Today was going to be a good day: she could feel it. Already she was beginning to think about *A Woman Scorned*. If she started now, she might be able to work through until lunch without a pause ... though maybe it would be a mistake to go out for lunch, that might break the spell. No, she would stay in, work on through the day, have a light lunch sent up to the room. Then dinner — probably in the hotel, or in that marvellous looking Indian restaurant behind it — and then she might be able to put in another couple of hours before bed.

She stepped out of the shower and began patting her thick coal-black hair dry, noticing the numerous threads of silver running through it. Gabrielle was right. It did need a colour.

If she could do say ... two thousand words in the morning, another two in the afternoon and maybe even just a thousand in the evening, well then that was five thousand words, which was twenty pages. Her daily target was only five.

Room service arrived exactly twenty minutes later, orange juice, croissant and coffee on a hallmarked silver tray, but she barely noticed its arrival and forgot to tip the waiter. She was buzzing with excitement about the book. She needed to write.

It happened. In the beginning, after her first novel was published, it happened frequently, sometimes the excitement of getting the ideas and words down on paper overriding everything else. Lately, however, it had become more and more infrequent, the buzz giving way to something approaching monotony.

The early stages — especially preparing the synopsis — was always the most exciting part: one of the few things she could do was to write a single or two-page précis of an idea that would make it read like a best-seller. Once she sold the novel on the précis, she would set about preparing a more detailed synopsis of the book with individual chapter breakdowns, before finally moving on to actually writing the book itself.

She usually enjoyed writing the first draft. It was exciting seeing what came out on paper and often the story drifted away completely from the prepared synopsis or the characters developed traits and peculiarities of their own. She found the second draft incredibly boring, although this was the stage where the book actually took shape, when the dross was cut away, certain scenes padded, others trimmed, characters re-shaped in the earlier chapters along the lines they developed closer to the middle and end of the book to give them consistency. The final draft was pure hell, the slow, sentence-by-sentence reading of each chapter again and again to finally fix it — checking through the novel for inconsistencies, mis-spellings and grammatical mistakes. It was tedious, and it helped rob whatever pleasure she had had out of writing the book.

But there were still days — like today — when the buzz returned and the excitement was there, and the desire to read on, to continue writing to see how the novel presented itself became almost overwhelming.

Briony sat down before the portable computer and popped the lid. She turned it on and while it chattered to itself she drank her orange juice quickly and then poured herself a cup of strong black coffee: she hated coffee, and especially hated it black, but she wanted the surge of energy.

When the screen cleared, she opened her word-processing program and changed to the directory which held *A Woman Scorned*.

A Woman Scorned was to be her most ambitious novel to date. When she had prepared the original synopsis — how long ago now? Two and a half, three years? — she had decided it would be about a large Italian family returning home for their mother's funeral and wake. The book would then tell the mother's story as well as each child's tale in alternate chapters. There were twelve principal characters and numerous historical ones who appeared in the mother's story, she being the woman scorned of the title. Briony had initially loved the idea and she especially liked the thought of writing about a strong female character who had exacted her revenge for the wrongs done to her and then brought her children up to believe in the same eye-for-an-eye morality that she herself possessed.

Portions of it were semi-autobiographical. One of the daughters was a successful novelist who had left the Italian village of her birth and made her way to America where she had established herself first as a children's writer, then as a serious novelist.

It was originally going to be the mother's book, but Briony gradually felt the emphasis shifting and discovered she felt easiest writing about the youngest daughter, Rachel. Some of it was so close to home she felt almost uncomfortable — even guilty — about putting it down on paper. It was almost as if she were betraying something. Although she hadn't started out to write about her in this way, she found that Rachel's life paralleled her own. Like herself, the character in the novel had borne two children — although at least hers had grown up happy and contented — and she too had had an absolute bastard for a husband ...

In the book Rachel would murder her husband.

Briony smiled. How many times had she thought about killing Niall, her ex-husband?

Her fingers began to move across the keys: she decided Rachel would kill him with a kitchen knife ...

Chapter Seventeen

There was a smell of damp and mildew on the stairs, the paint on the walls was flaking and large patches were scabrous with lichen. The stairs had once been carpeted, but large threadbare patches had been worn through, and the remaining rags were filthy.

"This place is a tip," Marcus Holland said loudly.

Charley O'Neill put his finger to his lips, shaking his head warningly.

There were at least a dozen doors on each floor. Most of those they passed were boarded up, although some were obviously still in use, and on the second floor, a telephone shrilled monotonously in the distance, the sound echoing in an empty room. There were only two glass-panelled doors on the top floor. Barely legible in flaking gold paint, Marcus Holland made out 'The Benson Literary Agency', while the door next to it bore the legend, *The Irish Literary Magazine*. The pane of frosted glass was cracked right down the middle, ancient sellotape hanging off in curling yellow strips.

Charley O'Neill didn't bother knocking. Twisting the slick handle he simply walked right in. The empty reception room looked like a doctor's surgery, with a dozen mis-matched wooden chairs and a pile of mouldering magazines — *The Irish Literary Magazine* — scattered across a scarred table. Faded magazine covers lined the walls in wooden frames.

Charley O'Neill went into the adjoining room.

A gaunt-faced man was slumped behind an old desk, leaning across a pile of typewritten pages. There was a bottle of Jameson's Irish Whiskey beside his left hand and an empty tumbler was clutched in his right. Although he was mostly upright, he was asleep, snoring fitfully. The sour reek of whiskey fumes tainted the close atmosphere of the musty room.

"He's all yours," Charley murmured, walking around behind the man and staring out through the grimy window onto the quays. Beyond the window the sluggish River Liffey wound its way past the imposing facade of the Four Courts which was almost directly opposite. Marcus Holland stood in the doorway, looking warily at the drunken man. "Jesus," he commented. He glanced at his watch: it was a little after eleven o'clock in the morning.

Charley turned around and kicked at the rickety wooden chair with his steel toe-capped boot. The sleeping man came awake with a start, the open whiskey bottle tumbling to the floor. It didn't break, but the sour smell of whiskey intensified as it leaked on to the greasy rug.

"What the fu..?" He looked around in alarm. "What do you want? How did you get in here?" He attempted to rise to his feet, but Charley pushed him down.

Marcus Holland came into the room and closed the door behind him. He dragged a straight-backed chair over in front of the desk, swivelling it around with its tall back to the desk. He sat astride it, his arms draped across the back of the chair, chin resting on his arm. It was obviously a position he had practised. "You are Niall Moriarty?" he asked as if he didn't quite believe it.

"Why? Who wants to know?" He squinted at Holland, watery grey eyes blinking rapidly, frowning, almost as if he recognised him.

"Just answer the question," Charley growled from behind him.

"Are you Niall Moriarty … Briony Dalton's ex-husband?" Holland asked.

At the mention of Briony's name, something like defiance appeared in the man's eyes. "You're newspaper, fucking newspaper. Right. Now let's get a few things straight. I don't give interviews, and I don't discuss Briony

Dalton." He attempted to rise from his chair again, but Charley pushed him down, more forcefully this time.

"We're not journalists," Holland said. "My name is Marcus Holland ..." Moriarty's eyes opened wide in recognition. "The other gentleman's name need not concern you."

"Yes, yes, yes! I thought I knew you," Moriarty said quickly. "I watch your show every week. We're in the same business, you and I — discovering new literary talent."

Holland bit back a retort: there was no point in antagonising this man, not just now, not when he needed him. "That's exactly why I'm here. I'm preparing material for a new show," he lied easily. "I was wondering if you would care to appear — either as an author or a publisher ... or, as you've said yourself, a discoverer of new talent."

Moriarty's mouth opened and closed soundlessly as his heart began to pound forcefully. He had been waiting for an opportunity like this all his life. He had known his talent would be recognised some day.

Niall Moriarty was forty-seven, but looked older. His face was haggard, deeply lined, his nose a network of broken veins and burst capillaries. His eyes were a pale translucent grey, constantly moist, his teeth yellowed and stained. He had been editor and publisher of the ILM since 1975. The magazine, which had originally been monthly and which had initially enjoyed an excellent reputation, had become quarterly, then bi-annually, and finally only occasionally. In the last ten years, no author of any real note had submitted material to it. It had always been Moriarty's dream to discover a great writer, an Irish talent to rival Yeats, Joyce or Beckett. Recently, however, the rate of submissions had fallen to such a degree — and what he was receiving was often such patent rubbish — that he had taken to filling the magazine with his own writings under a variety of pseudonyms. There was also a very good chance that the magazine's Arts Council grant — which, along with a minuscule advertising revenue, enabled it to survive — would not be forthcoming this year. He was due for a bit of good luck.

"What can I do for you, gentlemen?"

"I think the first thing we'll do is get out of here," Charley O'Neill growled. "The smell's screwing up my sinus."

"Yes … yes … I've spoken to the landlord about it. But he's holding off doing anything in case a compulsory purchase order is slapped on the place and it is levelled. This whole section of the quays is due for redevelopment," he added hurriedly. "His excuse was that he didn't want to throw money away on it." He scrambled to his feet, gathering up the manuscript which was scattered around the desk.

"Something interesting?" Holland enquired.

"Well … actually, it's mine. I've been working on this book for the past few years. I'm just correcting what I hope will be the final draft before sending it off to a publisher."

Holland nodded, smiling. He had heard the same story innumerable times. The next thing Moriarty would do would be to offer to let him read it.

"Perhaps you would care to read it?"

"I'd be delighted to," he murmured.

"Perhaps you might be able to make a few suggestions … maybe you'd know someone in a publishers … " Moriarty rambled on, moving around the room, finding a jiffy bag for the bulky manuscript, looking for his coat.

"I don't know anyone in any publishers," Holland said quickly, his stock answer. "Well, that's not true, I do know a lot of people in the publishing business but unfortunately the only way to get a manuscript published is to submit it. The days when someone would publish your book as a favour are long since gone. It's all big business and accountants now."

"But you'll read it?" Moriarty asked, almost fearfully.

"I'll read it."

They made their way down the rickety stairs, with Niall Moriarty in the lead, chattering excitedly. He saw this as being his big chance: possibly the opportunity to appear on television, and if he was successful, then there might be a weekly spot, possibly as a guest reviewer. If that happened, then there would bound to be a resurgence of interest in the magazine.

Moriarty led them across the river to a shabby pub almost facing his dilapidated offices. It was dark inside and virtually deserted and they found a corner table that was comfortably in shadow. O'Neill ordered for the three of them, a whiskey for Moriarty, black coffee for Holland and mineral water for himself. When he returned to the table, Holland was speaking earnestly, Moriarty hanging on his every word.

"I see this series as being a tribute to the forgotten men of Irish letters … people who have been left behind or passed over for various reasons. We've already interviewed several and some of their stories are fascinating. For example, we have a young man whose entire family — father, mother, brother and sister — had been published, and while he was a fine writer, the publisher didn't want another member of the same family on his list. Ironically, no other publisher would touch him because the name was so firmly established with the first publisher. We talked to another author who had submitted a book to a publisher and had it accepted for a very respectable advance. But then the publisher was sold, and sold again, and the book was lost in the shuffle … unfortunately he hadn't kept a copy. Then there was the case of another young man — again, a brilliant writer — whose brother was a best-selling author who rather stole his limelight … "

Niall Moriarty grunted.

"I would imagine that's what happened to you, eh?" Holland said gently. "Briony Dalton did that to you, didn't she?"

"Something like that," Niall said very softly. He swirled the amber whiskey in the glass, breathing in the heady fumes. "I was the writer in the family. I had even been published." He shook his head. "But somehow it never came together. She started writing … I even gave her some ideas, and she stole others. That last book of hers, *Pavane*, that's based on an idea of mine. I can clearly remember writing it down and discussing it with her." He drank his drink in one long swallow and Charley went to get him another.

"It must gall you to see her achieving the success which should rightfully belong to you," Holland suggested, not looking at him.

"Yea … yea."

"You started writing before her, didn't you?"

"I did." He took the new glass Charley put down on the table and downed half of it, grimacing as the whiskey seared his throat. "I was writing before I met her. I had had some work published … sold my first novel soon after we were married."

"I believe I've read it," Holland lied. "Where did you meet Briony?" he asked, before Niall could be side-tracked.

"In her father's pub." Moriarty grinned suddenly, and looked around, taking in the drab surroundings. "A pub very much like this one … "

ଔ

The pub in the heart of the docklands had assumed something of a reputation as a literary and theatrical haunt. Mick Dalton, with Brigid's encouragement, had realised that their pub had little to offer that was different from the hundreds of other similar pubs in Dublin. So, as a publicity gimmick, they had begun to discount drink prices to authors and actors. The drinks had been watered down in any case so it wasn't so much of a loss, but the word spread, and the tiny pub quickly drew the traditionally impoverished literary and theatrical crowd. To be able to buy alcohol at the reduced prices authors had to present a copy of their latest work to the pub's `library';

actors would present a playbill, preferably signed by themselves and as many of the cast as possible. The books were placed on shelves behind the bar, protected from the smoky atmosphere by glass cases, and the playbills were framed and hung around the lounge and bar.

Many years later, when Dalton's public house's rare first editions in original dust jackets had gone under the hammer, they had established record prices, some of which were still unbroken. Only after very stiff bidding had the collection gone to the National Library of Ireland.

Like most of the young Dublin writers of the sixties, Niall Moriarty had been attracted to the literary pub. He had had a couple of poems and an essay published in *The Bell*, the foremost Irish literary magazine of the day so he qualified for the cheap drink prices. He had pretensions to being a writer and he felt that mixing with this crowd — his fellow artists — would somehow bring him closer to achieving his ambition.

Soon, however, he discovered another reason for visiting Dalton's pub: an eighteen-year-old beauty named Bernadette. He had seen her serving behind the bar and their attraction was immediate and mutual. He used every opportunity to engage her in conversation, making small talk, boasting, before he finally worked up the courage to ask her out for a date. She had told him she would have to ask her father's permission — and he had been horrified when she had turned round and spoken to Mick Dalton: Niall Moriarty hadn't realised until then that her father owned the pub.

He quickly discovered that they had a lot in common. She too enjoyed the literary crowd, appreciated their sometimes cruel and obscure humour, and the extravagances of the actors and actresses. They had read the same authors, seen the same movies, listened to similar music. She wrote, she confided in him one day, but only for herself. He convinced her to allow him to read some of her work: it turned out to be a maudlin collection of poems, and a turgid six-page love story written on copy paper. But he praised it, acclaiming its clarity and crispness and in return he presented her with examples of his work, which she spent hours reading and discussing with him.

Against the wishes of his parents — who had imagined something better for their son than the daughter of a publican — they were married in September of that year, 1965. Bernadette Dalton was eighteen, Niall two years older.

He found them a flat in the square directly across from the pub; maybe it was a little too close to her home for comfort, but it was cheap and convenient. Bernadette continued to work in the pub while Niall remained at his job in the Post Office. Those early months were idyllic, and he remembered them as amongst the happiest times in his life. He was writing constantly now, sometimes at his desk in the Post Office, snatching every opportunity to put words on paper, then in the evening, often working long into the night. And he was now living with someone who was proud that he was a writer; his parents had always dismissed his writing as being unimportant and trivial.

In December, three months after their marriage, Bernadette became pregnant. He remembered the day clearly: it was a red-letter day on several accounts.

The morning's post had brought a letter from Victor Gollancz publishers in London. It was terse, badly typed, on flimsy paper, but the simple three lines were to change Niall's life irrevocably. Gollancz had accepted his novel and were prepared to offer him the princely advance of £50 against royalties. It was an extraordinary feeling. He didn't know whether to cry or shout, but he was finally on his way. He was going to be a writer. An author.

When his superior had reprimanded him for his flippant attitude to one of the senior staff, Niall had simply handed in his notice on the spot, quitting his reasonably well-paid, pensionable job.

Later that night Bernadette told him she was going to have a baby.

He took it all in his stride; the omens were good. The novel was going to be a best-seller. He could feel it. and it would just be the first of a long string of best-sellers.

The novel was never published.

It was his own fault. He knew that now, but he'd been young and arrogant then. His ego had not allowed him to even consider that his novel might need some work; he'd refused to rewrite any portions of the novel and ignored the editorial suggestions. After months of haggling the contract was cancelled and he found himself back at the beginning — out of a job with no prospects and no money. He had sold some short stories during that period, but had concentrated all his efforts in writing his great work, an enormous history of Ireland as seen through the eyes of a single family. He hadn't been overly worried when the publishing contract was cancelled, since he was confident that he would be able to place the novel with another publisher. But he had established a reputation in the small and clannish world of British publishing and no other publisher was prepared to work with him.

With no other money coming into the house, Bernadette had been forced to continue working. She was nearly eight months pregnant when she found she could continue no longer. Mickser Dalton continued to pay his daughter until Niall discovered it and refused to accept the charity. He was the man of the house — he would support his wife.

Niall realised later that it must have been around then when she began to write. It was always done in secret, when he was out of the house. Using the expensive Royal typewriter that he had bought for himself, she churned out a succession of short stories, articles for newspapers and magazines, she even wrote letters to magazines which paid for the best letter. She used a score of pseudonyms, except for her short stories where she still used her maiden name.

And she was published, time and time and time again.

She would never be a great writer — she lacked his skill, his style — but she was a published writer ...

ଔ

"She stole a lot of my early ideas. I kept them in a big ledger beside my bed. I used to dream, you know." Niall nodded his head vigorously. "I used to dream in colour … whole stories, complete plots. And she stole them."

"Greedy talentless bitch," Holland murmured softly, egging him on.

"Yeah, you said it." Moriarty was talking to himself now, holding a conversation he had gone over countless times in the past. "And as soon as she could she left me. She claimed I was stifling her talent … would you believe that? She went to live with that creepy step-sister of hers. Not that they have any time for one another now. They used to be so lovey-dovey I'd often wonder about them …
"

Marcus Holland glanced across at Charley O'Neill, who was barely visible in the shadows, and raised his eyebrows in a silent question. The big American shook his head.

"And who was her step-sister? Maybe we could talk to her," Holland said.

"Who?" Moriarty asked dumbly.

"Bernadette Dalton's step-sister."

"Why Catherine Garrett, of course." Moriarty looked up in drunken surprise, "I thought everyone knew that."

"Of course … of course … for a moment there I thought you were talking about someone else," Holland said quickly, thinking furiously. How had he missed that piece of information? "I think she has treated you shabbily," he pressed on. "But anyway, would you be interested in appearing on the television programme discussing your own writings, and your publishing ventures?"

Niall Moriarty nodded eagerly. "Yes, yes, of course."

"We could meet at a later date and discuss details. Maybe you'd like to talk about how Bernadette, or rather Briony Dalton, stole your success." His smile turned icy. "You never know, there might even be a book in it."

"A best-seller," Niall slurred.

Chapter Eighteen

Catherine Garrett checked the address a final time as the cab slowed to the edge of the kerb. The cabby — a huge Puerto Rican in drab army fatigues — swivelled in his seat to stare in at her through the stained glass screen. "You sure this is the address, lady?" He spoke Bronx-English with a strong Spanish accent.

Catherine waved the slip of paper in his face. "That's what I have written down here."

The big man rubbed the back of his neck with an enormous hand. "Hey, lady, you should know that this ain't a particularly nice neighbourhood. Look around you; this ain't no tourist attraction.

"I lived in New York for nearly eight years," Catherine said with a disarming smile.

The cabbie was unconvinced. "Lady, we're two minutes from Times Square, but you might as well be two hundred miles from civilisation."

Catherine sat forward. "Thanks for the advice. I know this isn't a good neighbourhood. But I do know what I'm doing, I do know where I'm going."

"You're a reporter, aren't you? Either that or a cop, though they usually use their own cars … and they usually travel in pairs, or more in this neighbourhood," he added with a grin.

"I'm a reporter."

The Puerto Rican indicated a dilapidated, graffiti-scrawled house at the end of the block. "A reporter went in there to do a story on a crack house … " He stopped, letting the sentence hang.

"And?" Catherine pressed, not sure that she wanted to know.

"Gang-raped." He paused and added quietly, "And he was a man!"

Catherine looked at the house again. "How safe would it be for you to wait?"

"Not very." The cabbie leaned forward and produced a gleaming silver revolver. "But I reckon I can hold my own for a while anyway."

"I appreciate what you're doing. I'm going into number thirty-two. It's that house there." She pointed.

The cabbie nodded. "The porno-picture factory."

"You know it," Catherine almost accused.

The man smiled broadly, displaying four solid gold teeth. "T'aint no real secret. You should'a told me, I wouldn't a been that worried. But I still reckon I'll wait. I'll circle the block. How long do you reckon you're going to be?"

"Could be five minutes, could be an hour. I'm going to interview one particular girl who works there. If she's not in, I'll be out immediately."

"I'll wait five minutes. Then I'll circle back every ten minutes or so. Don't wait on the street for me. Stay inside the building until you see the cab. You got that?"

"Got it." She opened the door and stepped out. Standing at the driver's door, she leaned in. "And thanks."

"For what? I expect a very good tip for all this free advice."

"Count on it."

Catherine quickly surveyed the filthy street. Two young men lounged on the stoop of number thirty-two, identical in their cut-off jeans and bodybuilder tops. One was an albino, his hair swept back into a mohawk; his companion was black, his hair hanging in scores of tiny braids. They came to their feet when they saw Catherine heading in their direction. When she was still about six feet away, she said loudly, "Mr Cutter is expecting me." When she was closer, she added, "He told me to say, `That's entertainment' to the doormen. Are you the doormen?"

"That's us, lady." Both young men laughed and moved aside, the albino opening the fire-scarred door into a darkened hallway. "Straight through to the door at the end," he said, his accent sounding vaguely Germanic.

Once she stepped into the hallway, the door closed behind her leaving her in almost total darkness. She reached into her slim pocketbook and produced a mini-mag light, a slender aluminium-bodied torch with an intensely powerful beam. She twisted the head, turning on the torch and adjusting the light at the same time. The hallway was filthy, though on closer inspection, she discovered that what she had first taken for dirt was actually paint and layers of graffiti sprayed and painted onto the walls. There were bare floorboards beneath her feet, the skirting board was flaking and peeling away from the wall in places, and she fully expected to hear the scuttle of rats. However, she was about halfway down the hall when she realised that there were none of the usual foul smells she would normally have associated with a hallway like this.

There was a second door at the end of the corridor. She knocked once, flinching as her knuckles rapped on metal instead of the wood she had expected. An intercom squawked static on the wall beside her. "Catherine Garrett for Bernie Cutter," she announced to the shadows. Electronic bolts snapped and the door clicked open, sudden light lancing out into the hallway, blinding her. Blinking furiously, Catherine stepped into a foyer that would not have been out of place in an office in any major city in he world.

Although there were no windows, the combination of the cream and gold colour scheme, numerous potted plants and subdued lighting softened the rather stark outline. A pretty Chinese girl sat behind a slender smoked glass table, a series of tiny television security monitors on a shelf to her left, a small computer terminal on the table before her, an intricate electronic switchboard on her right. There was no paperwork visible.

Completely disorientated by the switch from dingy corridor to ultra-modern office, Catherine stopped in astonishment. The Chinese girl came to her feet, smiling.

"Don't worry, it affects everyone like that the first time." Her accent was very British, though just a little too perfect for her to be from England. Hong Kong, Catherine speculated.

"You are Miss Garrett." It was a statement, not a question. "We've been expecting you." She turned and led Catherine down a short door-lined corridor to an unmarked door at the opposite end. Without knocking, she opened the door and went inside.

"Miss Garrett," she announced and stepped aside, allowing Catherine into the room.

The small stout man behind the desk stood up and hurried around the desk, hand outstretched, all in one fluid movement.

"Bernie Cutter," he announced, in an almost comical cockney accent, "delighted to meet you." He pulled out a chair for Catherine and then scurried back around behind his glass-topped desk. "Coffee?" he asked, and then looked at the secretary who was still standing by the door. "Two coffees, love." When the door closed, he turned back to Catherine. "So, how was your trip?"

Catherine Garrett shook her head and attempted a laugh. "Now, hang on a moment. Slow down a bit, just let me get my bearings. I came here looking for porno movie studios … I was expecting … Well, whatever I was expecting it certainly wasn't this … So, you'll pardon me if I'm a little confused." She looked around the small boxy office, which had been made to look larger than it actually was with clever lighting and mirrors. There was an enormous flat-screen television in one corner with a video neatly tucked away beneath it. One wall was completely covered with video cassettes.

Bernie Cutter sank deeper into his high-backed, studded leather chair and smiled expansively. "Most people are surprised. Take your time. Take all the time you need. All this still surprises me sometimes too." He gazed appreciatively at her. "You ever done any movie work?"

Catherine laughed. "Don't even think about it. I haven't heard that chat-up line since I was a girl."

"Yeah, but most of the guys who'd give it to you couldn't put you in movies — the difference is I can."

"Am I not a little too ... too mature for the type of woman you're looking for?"

"'Ain't no such thing as being unsuitable for the type of movies I make. There's a growing market for mature women." The small stout man folded his be-ringed hands across his stomach and smiled, displaying too-perfect, too-white teeth. Catherine decided that just about everything about him was too perfect, from the too-perfect toupee to the perfectly cut three-piece suit in the most appalling check she had ever seen, to the Rolex she thought might be an imitation, to the enormous diamond pinkie ring that she knew certainly was,

"You know why I'm here, don't you, Mr Cutter?"

He nodded vigorously. "I do. Mr ... well, shall we say a mutual acquaintance contacted me personally. He told me to extend you every courtesy."

Once again Catherine found herself wondering at Josef Bach's sources and contacts. When he had sent her the file on Briony's children and the pornographic video of Rianne Dalton, he had added a simple typed note which contained the address of the movie company. He had scrawled across the bottom of the note that he had spoken to the producer of the movie and suggested that it would be the most likely place to start looking for Rianne.

The Chinese girl reappeared with coffee and Cutter fussed about for a few moments, serving them both.

Catherine sipped the hot black coffee, wincing as it burned her tongue. "I must admit that even with the little I've seen I'm very impressed."

"Thank you. Thank you very much. Well, we are one of the largest producers of high quality adult movies in the States now … well, on the East Coast anyway. We're selling into the European market, and the Oriental and Arab markets are opening up to us."

"You're talking about a multi-million-dollar operation?"

"We're talking about a multi-*billion*-dollar operation. When I started making porno movies back in the fifties in Soho — they were called stag movies then, shot on eight millimetre, though usually without sound — it was for dollars and dimes. In those days anyone could make a stag movie, all you needed was a couple of hundred dollars, a camera, lights, actors — never any shortage of actors then — film and an editing board. Make it quick, sell it cheap. They were good days then," he added, smiling fondly. "Of course adult movies have always attracted the attention of undesirable elements, especially when … " He leaned forward and whispered conspiratorially, "especially when the mob began pouring money into it. They gave it a bad name. They brought in hookers to play the female parts, started laundering money through the movies, paying off the actors and the crew with dope. Ruined the trade." He shook his head sorrowfully.

"But that's changed now?" Catherine raised her cup to hide her smile.

"It's got professional again. We went through a good patch in the seventies. Porno became respectable. Deep Throat made it respectable, and then the line between erotica and pornography became blurred. You began seeing more and more explicit sex in mainstream movies. People got used to seeing couples getting it on: it's made my business a lot easier."

"So you set up here to produce movies?"

"No, lady. Set-up costs here run to … well they run to a lot of money. I only work here, like the rest of the actors. We shoot about a hundred shorts a year, as well as maybe ten or twelve main features."

"All hard-core pornographic movies?"

"Yes," Cutter said proudly. "We do straight and gay material, some soft bondage, but no rough stuff, no animals, no children, nothing like that."

"But those sort of pictures are being made?"

"They are, but not by us. That stuff's filth. I've got a family, Miss Garrett, I attend church on Sunday. And — surprise, surprise — I've got some morals. I don't use people who've appeared in that type of filth; I don't even use the crews."

Catherine finished her coffee. She felt she had entered some sort of twilight zone. Everything had been out of sync since the cab driver had started giving her advice. She opened her pocket-book and took out the photograph Bach had supplied of Rianne Moriarty. "I need to speak to this girl." She slid the small photograph across the table.

Cutter touched it with soft fat fingers. "I knew the girl. Ryan, she was called..."

"Hang on. What do you mean, you knew her?"

"She used to work here. Until very recently, too. Look, if I'd known this was who you were looking for I could have saved you the trip, but Mr B didn't give me no name, just said I was to help in any way."

Catherine raised both hands to stem the flow. "I understand; it's not your fault; you weren't to know. It would be helpful if you told me what you do know about her."

Cutter stood up suddenly and waddled around the desk. "I can do better than that. Come with me and I'll introduce you to some of the girls she worked with. They'll be able to tell you a lot more than I could."

Catherine remained seated. She folded her hands in her lap. "Mr Cutter, you wouldn't be holding something back from me, now would you?"

The small, fat man shook his head unhappily, his toupee shifting slightly. "Of course not."

"Because you know I report directly to Mr B, and he would be very upset if he thought you weren't telling me everything."

"I know, I know. But listen to the girls first and if there's anything else you want to know after speaking to them, then come back to me."

Catherine rose and followed Cutter down a corridor. The corridor was lined with silver-framed porno movie posters. Catherine was intrigued to discover that many were in French, German and Dutch.

"All our movies are silents. They're made without sound," Cutter said. "Then they're dubbed into whatever language the customer wants. We do a lot of business with Germany, and we intend using it as a springboard into Eastern Europe. And we've recently started selling to the Arab countries." He pointed to a poster in twisting Arabic print. "We cater to all tastes, and we make movies for particular markets. The Arabs, for example, like their women blond, busty and aggressive." He tapped a poster printed in Japanese characters. "The Japanese on the other hand, like their's blond, busty and submissive."

He indicated to the doors as they moved deeper into the building. "Each of these rooms is a studio; some have fixed sets which we can adapt to whatever film we're shooting. We rarely work outdoors, and even then it's usually a straight continuity shot. Here we are."

He stopped outside a door identical to all the others and cracked it open a fraction. Peering inside he waited a moment and then pushed open the door and stepped in. Catherine followed him. Two young women and a young man in jeans and a T-shirt were standing before a trio of microphones, staring intently at a large screen where an intricate *ménage-a-trois* was taking place. The actors were dubbing on the sound effects, panting, groaning and moaning at the appropriate times.

"Take a break, folks; five minutes, everyone. Girls, girls." Cutter attempted a warm friendly smile, which failed to advance beyond his lips. "Come here, girls." He draped his arms around the girls' shoulders and manoeuvred them until they were standing before Catherine. "Girls, I want you to meet a friend of Ryan's. She wants to talk to you for a few moments and I want you to talk to her. You can talk to her," he added, squeezing both their shoulders for emphasis. To Catherine he said, "I'll be back in my office if you need me. One of the girls will bring you when you've done."

Catherine waited until Cutter had left the room before turning to the two young women. They were both in their late teens or early twenties, wore little or no make-up and were both dressed relatively conservatively. Neither looked like the sort of girl who would appear in a porno movie.

Since no introductions had been made, and Catherine thought it best to leave it that way. "I'm Rianne — Ryan's — aunt," she began and then added hastily, "I'm not trying to take her back home or anything like that. I'm just trying to find out if she's all right."

"She's all right," the blond-haired girl on the left said.

"Would you know where she is?"

Both girls shook their heads.

"Would you know anyone who would know?"

Again the same shaking of heads, though this time a slow, insolent smile crept across the blonde's thin lips.

Catherine abruptly changed tactic. She stepped up to the young woman and snarled, "Think again, bitch — or by Christ I'll make sure you never work again, unless it's selling yourself on the street corner. Now you answer my question, or I'll go back to Cutter."

"She's gone," the girl on the right said suddenly.

Catherine rounded on her. "Gone where?"

"We don't know. Everything was fine last week. She'd just finished a movie, said she was feeling tired — we all were, it had been a hectic few days. The following day she didn't turn up for work. We were doing some dubbing earning some extra bucks, doing this sort of thing." She nodded towards the screen. "And we knew she needed the money. When she didn't call in we went around to see her, 'cause she's a friend. She was in her apartment all right, but she was packing."

"Packing a bag?"

"No, not just a bag. Everything."

"And how was she? Was everything all right?"

"She looked OK but you could tell she was wired. If she'd been a user I'd have said she was strung out, but she doesn't do drugs."

"What happened?"

"She told us to take what we wanted from the apartment, said she didn't think she'd be back for a while."

"And?"

"And that's it. She's gone."

"But surely she said something?"

"Nothing."

"She must have," Catherine snapped. "People don't up and walk away from everything without good reason.

"There was a card on her dresser," the blonde said sullenly.

"Yes, yes ... what sort of card? Jesus, it's like pulling teeth. Do I have to drag everything from you bit by bit? What has the card got to do with anything?"

"I don't even know if it's relevant. It was from Holland. From someone signed "M". It just said, The worst possible news." She shrugged. "That's it."

But it was enough. Catherine Garrett suddenly knew where Rianne had gone ... and she had a very good idea why.

Chapter Nineteen

The phone was ringing.

The sound was distant and muted through her headphones and Briony Dalton attempted to ignore it and concentrate on the small computer screen in front of her. However, the insistent shrilling was naggingly intrusive. Finally, annoyed that her train of thought had been broken, she pulled off the headphones and snatched up the phone.

"Yes?" she snapped. Whatever it was, it had better be an emergency.

"Miss Dalton, I wonder if you could spare a few minutes of your time … " The voice was male with an American accent.

"What? What for?" she demanded, a thread of panic in her voice as she realised that the caller knew her name.

"For an interview. My name is Marcus Holland, and I present a weekly books programme on … "

"No!"

"No?"

"No." She was about to hang up when she heard the voice on the other end of the line say, "Your husband has agreed to an interview, Miss Dalton."

"I don't have a husband," she said, and immediately regretted it. The trick with reporters was to give them nothing.

"I do understand that, Miss Dalton, but Mr Moriarty has claimed in our interview that you stole some of your ideas from him. Furthermore, he claims he has the evidence to back up his assertions. We felt it would be only fair for you to have an opportunity to refute these allegations? Have you any comment you'd like to make?"

Briony closed her eyes, pushed her glasses up on to her forehead and pinched the bridge of her nose. "No comment. Compare my work — most of which was prepared after he and I were divorced — with the number of books which he has had published in the same period and draw your own conclusions." She paused and added into the silence. "And you may tell Mr Moriarty that if he persists in these baseless allegations I will sue. Good day, Mr ... "

"Holland."

"Mr Holland." She broke the connection and then left the phone off the hook. She was almost amused to find that her hands were trembling slightly. The sheer gall of the man ... both men. She didn't know who this Holland person was, obviously another reporter out to make a quick name for himself by doing an exposé about Briony Dalton. Well, he wouldn't be the first and better reporters than him had gone over that ground. Finding her ex was a neat trick, though. She wondered if the reporter had been telling the truth, or had he been just fishing? But she thought it was too serious an allegation to make unless he could back it up. If Niall carried on with the accusations, though, she'd be forced to refute them — which wasn't a problem, since the weight of evidence was on her side — but she simply couldn't afford the time nor the distraction ... not now.

She returned to the portable computer and replaced her headphones. Bach's *French Suites*, usually amongst her favourite pieces of music, now sounded harsh, the harpsichord jangling, discordant. Her mood had been destroyed. She stabbed the STOP button and the music ceased instantly.

Cupping her face in her hands, she squeezed her eyes shut. She had known that sooner or later the press would catch up with her — it was to be expected. But she hadn't been expecting Niall to surface.

She opened her eyes and looked at the small screen. Funny; she had been thinking about him in a roundabout sort of way. She had been writing the section in *A Woman*

Scorned where Rachel, her heroine, meets her future husband and whereas Rachel had come, almost accidentally, to be based upon herself, there were certain elements of Max, the husband in the novel, that were deliberately based on Niall's character — so much so, in fact, that she had been seriously considering changing them, making him less like her ex-husband.

Briony sat back and folded her arms across her chest. She closed her eyes again and concentrated, attempting to draw up her last mental image of Niall. Her earlier images were clear; she remembered the first time she had ever seen him, but curiously she couldn't remember the last. She recalled the occasion though: it would have been when he had attempted to claim custody of the children in the High Court in Dublin.

What would he be like now?

It was said that one only remembered the good times out of any relationship; well, she had discovered that was so much shit. She remembered both the good and the bad, and unfortunately there had been too much bad. And she could justify the bad times, she could give the reasons for his behaviour towards her and the children. There were many reasons: his disappointments, his failures, the drink. She could make excuses for him, but she didn't excuse him. Nothing could. She could never forgive him.

And yet, everything had started out almost idyllically.

∞

Bernadette Dalton noticed him from the beginning. He seemed almost too young for the crowd he was mixing with — authors, journalists, poets. He looked like a student, and yet she didn't think he was a student. The students tended to stay to one side of the pub, showing off, talking too loudly — although it was difficult to out-shout a drunken poet — or else they sat in silent, sometimes morose groups hunched over a single drink all evening, pretending they were part of the literary scene.

He always lingered over his drink, making it last, as if he hadn't got much money, but she noticed that he always stood his round. She also noticed with wry amusement that when he came up to the bar he always made sure she served him. He had a quick smile and his eyes were kind.

"I don't think I've see you in here before." he said one evening, watching her shyly.

"Only every day for the past week — that's how long you've been coming in," she said tartly.

"Oh, so you've been watching me. I'm flattered."

"Don't be. I notice all the newcomers," she said with a cheeky grin.

He paid for his pint at the cheap rate. "I'm an author," he explained.

"Are you now?" she said, as if she didn't quite believe him.

"I've had some stuff published."

Bernadette decided to stop teasing him. "Go on then, show me." If she'd been a gambler she would have put money on the fact that he would have a copy of his latest — or possibly all of his — published work with him. Most of the writers, especially the new writers, did. The young man reached into his pocket and produced a small square magazine, which Bernadette immediately recognised by its distinctive cover.

"*The Bell*," he said proudly. "And you know you've got to be good to appear in *The Bell*."

Bernadette Dalton nodded. In the bar at the moment, there were at least four authors who had appeared in *The Bell* literary magazine.

He folded it back about halfway and turned it for her to see. "There you are, *The Dark Crusade*, by Niall Moriarty." He tapped himself in the centre of the chest. "And I'm Niall Moriarty." He stopped and then, rather self-consciously, stuck out his hand.

Equally self-consciously, Bernadette Dalton shook it: she was not used to customers introducing themselves.

She saw him nearly every day after that. He always had a few words or a joke and he always made a point of telling her what he was writing. She knew he was trying to pluck up the courage to ask her out, and about four weeks after they had made their first introductions, she put him out of his misery by saying, "Are you never going to ask me out?"

Completely dumbfounded, he had finally said, "Yes. Would you like to go out with me?"

"Yes."

He gazed at her, mouth open.

She made a face, tilting her head to one side, considering. "I suppose I'd better ask my father first, though."

She had seen the expression on his face as she had turned and spoken to Mick Dalton.

Niall looked at Mick Dalton, suddenly seeing the resemblance. "He's your father?" he asked in a horrified whisper.

Bernadette grinned broadly. "Don't tell me you didn't know?"

"I didn't." He finished his drink and stood up. "When are you free?"

"I'm free Saturday. Meet me here around one."

"Do you not have to work on Saturdays?"

"Don't worry, I can get Saturday off. I'll meet you outside."

Niall Moriarty had met her at one o'clock precisely and they had taken the train to Bray, the small seaside town south of Dublin city. The long promenade was thronged with couples and families, and the amusement arcades and fairs that lined the seafront were loud and busy. Niall and Bernadette strolled down the promenade eating ice-cream and candyfloss and toffee apples, giggling like children. Towards evening they made the climb up to Bray head, the low mountain overlooking the town which was topped with a tall cross. They were easy in one another's company; his initial shyness of her gradually disappeared to be replaced by a boastfulness she found almost amusing. He was going to be a writer some day, a great writer. He was already working on a novel and, even if he said so himself, it was good. So good, in fact, that it was going to make his name. But until then, he was going to keep his job in the Post Office. The pay wasn't good, but it was steady and secure and it would do until he made it as a writer, and besides, many writers had to do menial jobs until they finally achieved their ambition and, by the way, what was she doing next Saturday?

Caught in the flow of his dream, Bernadette had hesitated a moment too long. Niall had taken her hesitancy for reluctance, and had added quickly, "Of course, I realise a young woman like you must have lot of boyfriends and you've probably got a date, and..."

"There's no one else, and, no, I'm not doing anything next Saturday, and, yes, I'll go out with you."

"Fine." Niall had looked at her with obvious admiration. She was the first girl he had ever met who was so self-confident. She knew what she wanted; she knew her own mind and she wasn't afraid to speak it. And she was the first girl he had ever met who seemed genuinely interested in his ambition to be a great writer ... and who wasn't bored by him.

They had an early tea in a café on the seafront. The food was disgusting, but Bernadette didn't mind. She enjoyed the company of this nervous, boastful, too-serious, funny young man, who seemed always on the verge of apologising for something. Although he didn't wear glasses, Bernadette felt he should. It would give him something to do with his hands. She knew if he wore glasses they would be the type which were always slipping down his nose.

On the train back from Bray, crammed in tightly in the overcrowded carriage, with tired, sunburnt screaming children, their mothers and fathers surly and exhausted after a day that had started out as a good idea and ended up something else, Bernadette had asked him, "Why do you write?"

"Because … " he said immediately, and then stopped, and Bernadette realised he couldn't answer the question.

"For the money?" she suggested.

"Never!" he replied, shocked by the very suggestion.

Bernadette said nothing while the train thundered through a short tunnel. "But are you paid for writing?" she persisted.

"Yes. Not a lot, mind," he added with a laugh.

"But it is possible to make a lot of money writing?"

"There are some writers who make a lot of money," he conceded, "but you have to ask yourself are these people really writing? Most of this best-selling stuff is just hacked out. It might sell, but is it art?"

"Does it put food on the table?" she asked with a wry smile.

"Well, there is that," he admitted. "But I want to create great literature. Readable literature, of course," he amended. "I mean I want it to be accessible."

"Of course," she agreed, "but it still has to sell."

"You make it sound so commercial," he had accused her lightly.

"Isn't it? Is it not a job?"

He had looked at her in horror. "No, it's never a job. It's an art."

That was the only difference to emerge in an otherwise perfect match. They read the same writers, listened to the same music, liked the same cinema, adored the same artists. They were married five months later.

Although Bernadette was eighteen and Niall twenty, there was never any doubt who wore the trousers in the relationship. Almost from that first date, Bernadette knew she was Niall's superior in all things. She was practical and down-to-earth, whereas he was quite the opposite. She began to gently shape the direction his writing took, attempting to make it more commercial. She read every literary magazine, both local and imported, and made suggestions about storylines and plot ideas that might be suitable for them.

Niall was initially delighted and flattered by his wife's interest in his writing. Perhaps he found her leanings slightly more commercial than his own, and she seemed obsessed with the fact that writing should pay. She maintained it was a job, not unlike any other, and the labourer was worthy of his hire. It was a constant source of disagreement between them, but their first real argument about it didn't take place until they had been married for nearly three months.

Niall had been selling reasonably regularly to the local literary magazines, and although the pay was a pittance — and non-existent in some cases — he continued to submit material to them. The money meant little or nothing to him; he simply enjoyed seeing his name in print. When the magazine appeared he bought dozens of copies — which usually cost him far more than the meagre fee he would eventually earn from the piece — and distributed them amongst his friends and relatives, showing them what a great writer he was going to be.

Bernadette was working in her father's pub, saving every penny she earned, trying to live on Niall's Post Office wage, to stretch it as far as it would go, suspecting — even though she was only a few weeks gone — that she was actually pregnant.

Niall had come home late from the pub. He had taken to drinking with his literary buddies, often standing them round after round to show what a wealthy author he was. Bernadette was waiting for him, sitting at the kitchen table of the small flat they had found almost directly across from the pub. She was reading through a pile of Niall's short story manuscripts, correcting them for grammatical and spelling mistakes, editing out the inconsistencies. He could write, she couldn't deny him that, and he could be a very successful writer if only he directed his talent towards more saleable, commercial subjects instead of intensely introspective prose pieces that he lacked both the vocabulary and the experience to write.

"You're still up," he said, stepping into the room which served as both kitchen, dining room and sitting room. The only other room was their bedroom.

Bernadette had divided the manuscripts into two piles. She pushed both forward without a word.

Niall sat down opposite her. "What are you doing?" he said

"Have you any money on you?" she asked disconcertingly.

"What ... well I ... " He reached into his pockets, but his hands emerged empty.

"You went out of here this morning with four pounds," she said.

"I don't know how much I had ... " he began sullenly.

"You had four pounds," she stated. "And now you've nothing. I know where you've been. I can smell it from here. I know you've been buying rounds for your drinking buddies, playing the successful author, but unfortunately you cannot afford to do that just yet." She touched the right hand bundle of manuscripts. "This stuff here is saleable."

He turned it round and leafed through a few pages. "It's rubbish. Half-baked ideas. They're not even polished."

"They're saleable," she said. "This pile here is pretentious and unsaleable."

Niall reached out and turned the second pile around, reading down through the typewritten pages. "Hey ... this is some of my best stuff."

"Unsaleable," Bernadette said shortly. "And you need to be writing saleable material — especially at the rate you're drinking it." She leaned across the table and stared into his grey eyes. "Niall, we need the money."

"We have the money," he insisted. "We've got two, no, three salaries coming in. Mine, yours and what I earn from my writing."

"Yours is small, mine more so and what you earn from your writing is negligible."

"Well, Gollancz are reading my novel. We'll have a lot of money when they buy it," Niall said.

"The novel is good, but it needs a lot of work."

"It does not. I've worked very carefully on each chapter."

"It needs work," she persisted.

"Now listen here! What do you know? Just what do you know about writing? You don't write, you don't know how to write. All I've seen is some shit verse and an even shittier story written in a child's copybook. So how can you judge my writing? All you talk about is the money. Writing is more than cash."

Bernadette Moriarty smiled coldly. "Why do you write?"

"You asked me that before," he muttered.

"And you couldn't answer me. Well, I've got the answer for you. You write to see your name in print. Simple vanity."

He started to shake his head and then stopped.

She pressed on. "A writer writes because he has to, I know that, but he also has to be paid for it."

"You're mercenary." Niall staggered to his feet. He placed both fists on the table and leaned forward. "I'll tell you one thing though, Bernadette Moriarty: you'll never be a writer!"

Chapter Twenty

Josef Bach accepted the thin sheaf of envelopes from his secretary's hands and spread them out one by one across the black marble desk. The Japanese woman stood behind and to the left of his chair, unmoving, unspeaking, awaiting instructions.

"All the fish are darting about, it seems." His blunt fingers pushed the first envelope out of the pile and he opened it slowly. There were a dozen ten-by-eight glossy black-and-white photographs inside, along with a single typewritten sheet. "Ah, here we have Mr Holland and that must be Mr O'Neill, the American detective." He flipped the photo over to confirm his guess. There were long-distance grainy shots of the two men entering a dilapidated building, and then sharper, crisper photos of them leaving the same building with a third man between them. "Ah, a new player." He turned the photo over, reading the name, frowning until it suddenly made sense. "Of course, Niall Moriarty, our famous author's ex-husband." He looked at the photo of the dilapidated building again. "And fallen on hard times too, it seems. Excellent. I'm sure Mr Holland is treating him properly."

Josef Bach opened the second envelope. "Now let us see. Miss Garrett. In New York too; so she followed up that lead ... excellent. But with no results, I see," he added, reading the typewritten sheet. "And now she has gone to Holland to continue her investigations. Excellent."

The fourth envelope contained two shots of Gabrielle Royer boarding a plane at Dublin Airport. The report added that she had flown directly from Dublin to JFK International. There was no other information.

"Find out where she's gone and why," Bach snapped. He didn't like people doing things he didn't know about. This was a huge game of live chess, with Briony Dalton as the prize. If he was to win the game she had to fall. And he was going to make sure she fell.

There were no photographs in the last envelope, although this time the neatly printed sheet ran to three pages. It was a detailed report on Briony's movements over the past few days — not that she had done much: kept to her rooms, received no one, saw no one and — after the call from Marcus Holland the previous day — accepted no other calls. News of her presence in Dublin had got about, and although the media were paying court there had been none of the religious backlash that Holland had promised there would be. Bach was wondering whether she was old hat; had time and an increasingly permissive morality wiped away whatever claims to fame she might have had?

Well, if so he would have to do something about it.

"Find out when the book pages appear in the Irish newspapers," he announced to his secretary without looking around, "and then bring me all of Briony Dalton's books."

Briony Dalton deserved a little free publicity.

Chapter Twenty-One

He threw her upon the rumpled sheets, catching the front of her bodice, ripping it away, exposing her small, tender breasts. And then he was upon her, straddling her on either side, holding her flailing arms down, pressing his manhood between her breasts. She opened her mouth to scream, but the savage look in his eyes silenced her.

She shut her eyes in shame and pain as he entered her roughly and without warning. Her wide blue eyes snapped open again as he fell forward, across her. She twisted her head as he grunted atop her, and she suddenly found she was looking at his clerical robes tossed across the back of the chair. She wept for shame then ...

Briony Dalton, *Odalisk*, 1977

In the silence of the chapel the strains of the Christmas Oratorio rang out sharp and clear, each voice raised in exultation to heaven. Most of the nuns had their eyes closed, praising God in prayer as well as song, others had their heads draped forward across the edge of the seat.

Sophie allowed her forehead to rest on the pew in front. There was no one behind her and the nearest sister was four seats ahead, which was just as well. Marie's fingers were buried deep inside her, touching where only her own fingers had explored before. She shuddered, trembling on the verge of orgasm, her mouth opening and closing in a parody of the hymn as she shuddered.

And part of the pleasure was knowing that she would have to repay the older nun, licking, sucking, kissing and caressing her fuller body to its own passionate orgasm. But that was for later, now ...

Squeezing her eyes shut, her fingers wrapped tightly amongst her beads, she allowed the pleasure to take her. And she would always remember that particular moment, that orgasm, that shuddering forcibly silent orgasm in the chapel on Christmas morning. It was the most passionate, the most forceful, she had ever experienced.

Briony Dalton, *Harem* (sequel to *Odalisk*), 1978

"People are well aware of my views about the clergy: they are repressive, vindictive, and downright dangerous. Far too many of the priests display homosexual tendencies and the nuns are obviously lesbian. Do we want these people teaching our children ...?"

Briony Dalton, interview, *The Irish Times*, 1981

"There is graphic sex in my books and no, I do not think it offends people. People who are easily offended should not read my books. Unfortunately, you will find that these people will only be offended after the last page."

Briony Dalton, live radio interview,
The Book Programme, 1983

"Of course I make money out of sex. People would not buy my books if there was no sex in them. I sell sex like any tart on the street corner, only I don't have to open my legs for it ..."

Briony Dalton, live television interview,
The Late Late Show, 1985

"I am one of the wealthiest women in the world. And, yes, most of that wealth I have achieved through my writing and, yes, my writing is about sex. So sex has made me wealthy. It has also enabled me to live exactly the way I want to live, to eat what I want to eat, to sleep with whom I want to sleep, be they male or female. Great wealth places one above the law."

Briony Dalton, interview, *The Bookseller*, 1988

"I don't give a fuck what people think about me. I don't give a fuck about them."

Briony Dalton, interview, *The New York Times*, 1990

Chapter Twenty-Two

"I cannot agree. I think it would be a disastrous move."

Gabrielle Royer sat back in the chair and stretched out her long legs. She glared at Terri Fierstein. "But Briony is in trouble. She needs me."

"She has a problem," the small woman snapped looking at Gabrielle over the rim of her half-glasses. "But it is a problem of her own making. Indeed," — her thin lips twisted in a humourless smile — "you might say it is her own sins coming home to roost."

Gabrielle frowned, shaking her head slightly. Sitting forward, she rested her elbows on the edge of Terri Fierstein's battered desk. "Explain that to me," she suggested.

"Briony Dalton is — always has been — a commercial writer in every sense of the word. Her books have always been carefully targeted to certain markets. And of course, we had the advantage that Briony was always her own greatest publicist. She was controversial. She was outrageous. What was it Oscar Wilde said about being talked about...?"

"Better to be talked about than not talked about," Gabrielle supplied.

"Exactly. And Briony loved to be talked about. Newspaper inches sell books, she said, and she's right. So when we decided that *Odalisk* was going to be a best-seller — this was back in 1976 when she had finished the book, about a year before publication — it was decided that one way of doing it was to make the author as controversial as possible. Briony then set about coolly and deliberately attempting to raise as many hackles as possible. She was living in Ireland then, and it was easy to make a big splash in a small pond. She insulted church and state leaders in public and in print. She was rude and sometimes downright boorish on television and during radio interviews."

The small woman suddenly began laughing and continued until tears came into her eyes. When the laughter threatened to become uncontrollable, she swivelled around and stared out through the huge picture window behind her desk over the New York rooftops while she dried her eyes with a surprisingly feminine lace handkerchief. Without turning around, she added, "If you get the chance, do try and see the infamous Ed Sullivan interview she gave over here and the Michael Parkinson interview which she gave in Britain the following week. They're almost identical: both men asked her all the obvious questions, and she gave them the obvious answers. They both asked her what was the magic ingredient to writing a best-seller. 'Fucking every five pages,' she replied. You'll probably never see two men so completely horrified as they realised that millions of people all across America — and Britain — had just heard this pretty and vivacious young woman use the terrible F-word." She swung around to face Gabrielle.

"And Briony did that deliberately as an advertising stunt?" Gabrielle asked, her eyes wide in astonishment.

"Precisely that. Crude, but very very effective." Terri Fierstein shrugged eloquently. "It made Briony's reputation. The book was talked about, spoken about, speculated upon for months before it appeared. And when it finally came out it became an instant best-seller." She leaned forward, wagging her finger in Gabrielle's face. "Because Briony made it a best-seller by selling herself. She never stopped selling herself, going too far too often." She sat back, seeming suddenly exhausted. "I warned her she was going too far too fast. Now people only know her by an artificial reputation. And people have long memories. That's what's happened now," she murmured.

"Has anything else happened? When did she speak to you?"

"Late last night."

"She must have phoned you after she'd spoken to me. I know when she was speaking to me she was very upset."

Terri nodded unsympathetically. "It was really only a matter of time before the word got out that she was in Dublin. It was a calculated risk how much of the animosity and ill-feeling she had generated would remain."

"Obviously quite a lot."

"Yes and no. Interestingly, this started four or five days ago when she was contacted by a journalist named Marcus Holland."

"I don't know him," Gabrielle said.

"Neither do I. But I contacted Charley O'Neill and asked him to see what he could find out about him. Apparently, he's very well known in Ireland. He's an American journalist working in television, with his own chat and book programme. He's written a book or two, and seems to be genuine. Anyway, on Thursday, he contacted Briony and asked for an interview, which she refused. The following day she was contacted by half a dozen journalists working for the daily newspapers and the national radio, all looking for interviews. Of course she said no, but they continued to badger her and she's now reached the stage of refusing all calls."

Gabrielle examined her long azure nails. "She should have agreed to at least one interview."

"She should. It might have cooled things down. However, later that day — Friday — some time in the evening, one of the fundamental Christian groups who would, of course, be violently opposed to Briony's views, demonstrated outside the hotel. The following morning there was another group outside the hotel. This crowd were handing out hand-printed bills with quotes from Briony's interviews and excerpts from her writings." She slid the single sheet of fax paper across the desk. "Some of the quotes were reproduced in the evening newspapers, and it was front page in most of the Irish Sunday papers."

Gabrielle read the blocky, smudged text carefully. "This first quote from *Odalisk* is taken completely out of context. The man making love to the girl is not in actual fact a priest."

"I know."

"And I don't recognise the second quote from *Harem* — although I've read the book."

"That is actually quite interesting. That paragraph, the lesbian love scene between the two nuns in the church, appeared in the manuscript but I felt — as did the editors — that it was completely unnecessary"

"Briony being controversial again."

"Exactly. So we cut it out."

"Then someone in the publishers must have passed it on."

"Very possibly, but there's nothing we can do about that now."

"What about the rest of the quotes?"

"They're genuine, although some have been slightly edited and rearranged to make them read even more aggressive and belligerent than they were intended or sounded in the original."

Gabrielle read down the page again. "They make her sound like a horrible person."

"They do," Terri said noncommittally.

"I really think I should go back to her."

"If you return it will only add fuel to the fire. More newspaper inches. Lesbian lover returns..." she said, showing her teeth in a humourless smile.

Gabrielle ignored the gibe. "So what is the situation at the moment?"

"We've got groups protesting outside the hotel. The hotel management are — as you can imagine — less than pleased. It's great media and the place is swarming with journalists and news crews. The net result is that Briony is getting no writing done."

"Bring her back here," Gabrielle said decisively.

"That's what I suggested last night, but she'll have none of it. I think she feels it would be like running away, admitting defeat after all these years. That's not what she said, of course," Terri added. "What she actually said was that when she did write it was going really well, she had rediscovered her joy in writing. And we both know that that is so much bullshit!" Terri turned to looked out over the shabby New York rooftops again.

Gabrielle glanced around the woman's office. It reminded her in some strange indefinable way of her father's study, even though it looked nothing like it. It was a long, incredibly neat room, one wall completely covered with bookshelves holding the works of the numerous authors Terri represented. Briony occupied a shelf and half, Gabrielle noted, and there seemed to be one copy of every edition of the books published, including foreign language and book club editions. The opposite wall was covered with photographs of Terri Fierstein meeting famous authors and dignitaries. Gabrielle didn't recognise a lot of the faces, but there were some surprises: a trio of photographs of her shaking hands with Richard Nixon, Jimmy Carter and Ronald Reagan. An extraordinary photograph of Terri presenting a book to the last Pope, alongside an equally extraordinary photograph of Terri being presented to Queen Elizabeth. Gabrielle had to look hard before she discovered the picture of Briony Dalton: it was of Briony at least ten years ago, looking slimmer and prettier. It was almost lost beneath a large autographed photograph of Jacqueline Susann, and alongside it was a large black-and-white shot of Norman Mailer with his signature scrawled across the bottom corner.

Terri swivelled her chair around. "Our hands are tied because we cannot phone her — she's refusing to accept any calls — but when she calls you, try and convince her to return here."

"I'll do my best. You don't think she's in any danger, do you?"

Terri shrugged and spread her hands. "I don't know. I don't think so. But the world is full of crazy people. And, remember, she's insulted these people's religion."

"But hang on a minute. Ireland is a predominantly Catholic country; it's not as if they're fundamentalist or extremist or anything."

"There are extremists in every walk of life," Terri stated flatly. "I don't think she's in any danger, but let's not expose her to the risks. Remember, there is a lot of money riding on her at the moment. She has to deliver that book."

"I know. And she knows. When I left her she was working hard."

"She should have worked hard months ago. But never mind, never mind." Terri pulled open a drawer and reached inside, dragging out a manila folder. "I've done some work on the proposal you submitted for the Briony Dalton biography. There is interest, naturally, and we've got some good offers on the table, but with this added publicity surrounding Briony I was wondering if we should wait for a few days to see what develops."

"Every cloud having a silver lining, eh?" Gabrielle asked cynically.

"Let's face it, dear, if Briony wasn't in her present predicament she wouldn't be news and no one would even consider a biography of her. She's news at the moment, so your book can be placed; if she becomes bigger news in the next few days, then the price for your book goes up. It's rather like dealing in shares: we have to judge the moment to sell."

"How much do you think you'll get?"

Terri smiled her professional business smile. "Briony taught you well, eh? Everything has a price." She sat back into her chair and took off her glasses. "I don't know yet. I'm trying to tie up a hardback-paperback deal, but at the back of my mind I'm wondering if we should try to tie in a movie option as well. I might get you to prepare a treatment for an agency I work with on the West Coast. If we have a movie deal then the book's success is guaranteed." Terri lifted the synopsis and re-read it quickly. "The only problem is that this is an authorised biography, which sometimes — no, usually — tends to be a whitewash, and because of your rather intimate association with Briony, it would be seen to be even more so. So I was thinking: rather than do an authorised biography, why not sell this as a kiss-and-tell biography, full of sex and scandal?"

Gabrielle started to shake her head, but Terri ignored her and pressed on. "The problem with that is that Briony has led, with minor deviations, a rather uneventful life. It's only in the last few years that her life-style has become dramatically high profile. Even back in the seventies when she was attempting to establish herself as a media personality her public and private personae were very different. The public Briony Dalton might say and do outrageous things, but the private Briony Dalton never went to the all-night rave-ups; she sat in at night and wrote." Terri allowed the synopsis to fall to the desk. "Another point you might look at closely is the problem of the children. Have you decided how you're going to handle them in the book?"

"To be honest, no. I was going to ask your advice about that."

Terri looked mollified that Gabrielle should have considered seeking her advice. Her dislike of the younger woman had, if anything, intensified over the past few days of their association, but she was professional enough to realise that she needed Gabrielle for the moment.

"My advice to you is to tell the story exactly as it happened, without embellishment, without additions, and without mawkishness." She shrugged. "There's no easy way around it; Briony treated her children appallingly and no amount of whitewash is going to make her look anything but a complete bitch."

"Have you any idea where they are now?"

"None. Matt, the elder, was a rather morose young man. He was never in any trouble in school. He just didn't seem interested in his studies and ran away a couple of times. The last time he didn't come back. Rianne, however, was wild, completely wild. She would be a year or two younger than you," she added without changing her expression, her barb almost, but not quite, slipping past Gabrielle. "She was expelled from two convent schools because of her outrageous behaviour. Eventually she too ran away. Matt's running away had obviously put the idea into her head. I know she idolised her older brother. I have no idea where either of them is now. I don't even know if they're still alive."

"Does Briony?"

"There has been no contact between them in years. The only person who might know is their father, Niall Moriarty. I know Rianne kept in contact with him on and off for years after the break-up of the marriage. But there's no way he's going to speak to you."

"If he knows who I am, he won't," Gabrielle said calculatingly.

"Don't even think about it," Terri warned. "Niall Moriarty doesn't give interviews; never speaks about his ex-wife. He's very bitter about it."

"Why? Did he want the children?"

Terri nodded. "He did, and I reckon he would have been a better parent to them than Briony — and I don't think I'm being disloyal in saying so. I think Briony sued for custody to spite him. Because of her income and because she was the natural mother and all that, she got custody. He once promised to tell the real story, but he may have forgotten about that. He was always very fond of the bottle," she explained.

"Anyone else you would advise me to speak to?"

"The obvious person would be the journalist and broadcaster, Catherine Garrett, Briony's step-sister … you did know they were step-sisters?"

"I discovered only very recently. I was astonished. Though I suppose it makes some sort of sense when you consider how vituperative Garrett is about Briony's writing. Jealousy."

"No," Terri said, "there's more to it than that. It's more than just jealousy, I'm sure of it. But don't ask me what, because I don't know."

"Would she speak to me? I mean it's hardly likely if she's writing the rival book."

"Don't forget, my dear, Catherine Garrett will want to interview you for her book. Trade. Lie to her. Tell her you're writing a magazine article about famous literary siblings or something like that. Flatter her."

"Have you any idea how far she is into her own book? How much work has she done to date?"

"I don't know. But I wouldn't imagine there'd be much. The early material wouldn't present much of a problem; after all her mother married Briony's father. But any biography of Briony Dalton must include the children's stories, and Catherine Garrett wouldn't have a clue where to even start looking for the children!"

Chapter
Twenty-Three

Catherine Garrett had originally decided to fly directly to Amsterdam, but at the last moment changed her mind and stopped over in London. Before beginning the search for Rianne Dalton she needed to make certain arrangements, and it was easier to set up contacts at this end. She had had some dealings in the past with NTV, the Dutch television service, and it was time to renew those contacts. Maybe someone there would be able to arrange an interpreter, preferably a reporter who knew the sleazier side of Amsterdam or at the very least had good police contacts.

She used the hour-long tube ride into the centre of the city to jot down some notes for *Lies*, the biography of Briony Dalton. She smiled at the irony: she would have to be very careful that she told no lies about Briony. The facts would have to speak for themselves, and the facts were damning enough.

She got out at Piccadilly Circus and picked up a taxi on Regent Street. It was a five-minute ride to her office.

There was a new man on the door who didn't recognise her and consequently refused her admittance because it was after five-thirty and she made a point of never carrying her laminated security pass. She spent a frustrating fifteen minutes until a second security guard from another part of the building was called down to vouch for her. The new man apologised profusely, but Catherine waved it aside, "You were doing your job. I can't fault you for that." She smiled humourlessly. "I suppose it's very vain of me to expect everyone to recognise my face — especially in the office where I work," she added as she walked away, toying with the idea of having the man fired and deciding that she simply couldn't be bothered going to the trouble.

The offices were almost deserted. The large, open-plan floor spaces were in semi-darkness except for the occasional pools of light where someone was still working, faces washed in stark computer light, writing up last-minute reviews or finalising copy for the next issue of the magazine. Her office was locked and for a moment she thought her electronic card key was out of date — they were changed every month — but the door clicked open when she swiped it through for the second time. She stepped in and palmed on the lights. As usual, she found herself confronted by a pile of mail.

Catherine Garrett rarely used her office. All of the important material was sent directly to her home, and she usually went straight from home to the studio to present her book programme. All her reviews, articles and editorial comments were prepared at home and sent by fax or modem to the office computers. She detested the journey up to London; hated the time she wasted travelling to and fro, loathed the disturbance to her routine.

She went over to the window and peered out through the half-closed blinds at the streets now washed with evening twilight. She realised — once again — that she could finally give it up. She need never work again. The deal she'd done with Bach ensured that.

She didn't need to work. But she did have to work. It was a subtle, but important distinction.

She cast a cursory glance over the mail, Jenny, her secretary, had already sorted into various trays. The smallest pile, those letters needing her particular attention, would be sent on to the cottage. There was another pile which Jenny would handle and send on for signature, and finally there was the huge junk element. Brochures, advance information sheets from publishers, advertisements, time-wasting letters, some fan mail. Propped up in one corner of the room was a pile of proof copies, some of which had been boxed to be sent on to the cottage, and alongside them was the most recent crop of pre-publication review copies.

Perched on the edge of her desk, she turned her appointment book towards her, flipping it open to the back where she kept business cards and addresses. She had done a programme on Dutch writers and writing about a year ago ... what was the name of that woman producer she had worked with?

A red blinking light distracted her and she looked up in surprise. It was the message light on the answering machine. The machine was usually cleared every day, important messages being relayed on to her and during office hours her line was redirected into Jenny's office next door. The message must have come in just after closing time. Without thinking she pressed the answer button.

"Good evening Miss Garrett. My name is Gabrielle Royer, Briony Dalton's secretary. I'm currently doing an article on Briony Dalton's background for *Writer's Digest*, the American writers' magazine, and I was wondering if you would care to talk to me. In return, I understand that you are doing a book about Briony; naturally I would be willing to speak to you. An exchange of information. I am staying at Briony Dalton's New York apartment and may be reached at that number if you are interested."

The machine blipped and stopped. Catherine listened to the tape rewind, and then replayed the message. She wondered why her heart was pounding. If Gabrielle Royer knew about the biography, then so did Briony ... and probably the entire publishing world. Josef had said it would remain secret, but the publishing trade was so small, so self-centred, that it was hardly likely that something like this would remain secret for long.

Catherine tapped her perfect teeth with a pencil. What was far more interesting was that Gabrielle Royer was willing to talk to her. Had there been a dispute with Briony, a lovers' tiff? Possible — probably! — knowing Briony's uncertain temper. But if they'd had an argument, then she'd hardly be staying in Briony's New York apartment. And what was it she had said about writing an article for *Writer's Digest*? That was highly unlikely. *Writer's Digest* would not be interested in a piece on Briony Dalton written by her lover; that was Playboy or Cosmopolitan material, and besides, they paid better.

Catherine Garrett moved around and sat down behind her desk for the first time in weeks. The call from Royer was intriguing, but how truthful had she been? What was the hidden agenda? There was one simple way to find out: fifteen minutes later, having spoken to one of the editors of the *Writer's Digest* in Cincinnati, Ohio, she had confirmation that Gabrielle Royer had not been commissioned to write anything for them.

Catherine sat still for a few moments longer, before finally coming to a decision. It took her several minutes to find Josef Bach's number in her Filofax because for some paranoid and by now forgotten reason she hadn't put his name alongside his number. Still unsure if she was making the right decision, she slowly tapped out the number on her phone. She glanced at the clock high on the wall to the left of her desk. It was after seven, and he had probably gone home.

The phone was answered on the second ring by the Japanese secretary, Kaho. In her soft, virtually unaccented voice she merely repeated the number and then said nothing, waiting.

"This is Catherine Garrett."

"One moment, please," the woman said immediately, not allowing her to continue.

Josef Bach was on the phone seconds later, his voice gruff and hearty, sounding for all the world like a favourite uncle. Catherine remembered what she and he had done the last time they had met and was abruptly glad they were speaking at the opposite ends of the telephone line. The very memory of it sent a shiver down deep into her groin, and she felt herself blushing.

"Catherine, my dear, how are you? Is everything all right?"

"I don't know," she answered. "Is this line secure?"

"From my end, certainly. From yours I wouldn't be so sure. Why? Is there a problem?" A note of caution had crept into his voice.

"I'm phoning you from my office. When I got here this evening there was a message on my answering machine. I'd like you to listen to it." She brought the handset of the phone closer to the machine and touched the answer button. Gabrielle's message unfolded into the silence.

When it had finished, she said simply, "Well?"

"Interesting message. You will, of course, speak to the lady."

"Of course," she snapped, "but how did she find out about the book in the first place?"

"I suppose it was too big to keep a secret," Bach said. "It's not a problem, though, since now that it's out in the open it allows us to begin the pre-publicity campaign."

"I've checked out her story about doing an article for *Writer's Digest* and it is completely untrue."

"How interesting. But why does she want to speak to you?" he mused. "Perhaps she simply wants to find out how much you know." There was a long pause on the other end of the line and then Bach said, "She's in New York at the moment?"

"Yes, in Briony Dalton's apartment."

"Have you got the number?"

"It's in my book somewhere."

"Phone her. Find out when she's coming to London; arrange a meeting."

"I'll do that."

"Weren't you going to Holland?" Bach enquired pleasantly.

"I'm on my way there. I just wanted to set up some contacts at this end rather than arrive cold."

"And your work on the book?"

"Proceeding. I've done a lot of work on the early chapters," she lied. To date she hadn't advanced much beyond the first chapter.

"You will keep in touch," he said and then hung up as she was saying, "Of course … "

Catherine looked at the dead phone in her hand for a moment before returning it gently to its cradle. What an ignorant man.

Catherine sat at her desk for five minutes working out her strategy before she picked up the phone and tapped out the New York number. It buzzed for what seemed like an eternity before it was finally answered.

"Hello?"

Catherine recognised the faintly French accent. "Gabrielle Royer? This is Catherine Garrett."

There was a long — and she presumed shocked — silence on the other end of the line. Static hissed and howled across the transatlantic connection.

"Are you there?"

"Yes, yes. I do beg your pardon. I phoned you about an hour ago, I must admit I didn't expect you to return my call … so soon," she added quickly.

"It was a fortunate set of circumstances. I came into the office to pick up some mail and I caught your message."

"Would you be willing to speak to me?" Distance and a bad line robbed the voice of nearly all its nuances, but Catherine thought she detected the eagerness in it.

She doodled on her notepad with a red marker, deliberately wasting time, allowing the other woman to sweat a little before finally answering, "Yes, I think I would. An exchange of information, as you suggested."

"I will be in London on Wednesday afternoon. That's the day after tomorrow. Would it be possible to meet then?"

"Have you details of your flight yet?"

"No."

"Well, if you contact my secretary, Jenny, with the flight details, I'll leave instructions that you are to be collected from the airport and brought to my office ... no," she said suddenly, "why not come down to my place in Sussex? We can talk over dinner without interruption."

"That's very kind of you," Gabrielle said, sounding startled.

"I'll see you the day after tomorrow then. I'll look forward to it," she added and broke the connection. She always believed in being the first to terminate a conversation. And then she smiled: she realised she had just done to Gabrielle Royer what Josef Bach had done to her.

She would delay her trip to Holland for a week, she decided, and picked up the phone to call a taxi. She debated phoning Mark and telling him she was on the way, but decided not to: she'd surprise him.

⅓

Catherine stood in the driveway and watched the taxi drive away, its headlights disappearing down the avenue of trees that led up to the cottage tucked into the lee of the hills. She supposed she should have invited the driver in for a cup of tea after the long journey, but to be perfectly honest she simply felt too tired.

There was a light on in Mark's room: he was obviously still up, working on that blessed book of his. What a closed, incestuous world the publishing and book business was. You met with book people, lunched with book people, talked books to them, you read books, reviewed books and now here she was writing a book and living with a man who desperately wanted to be an author. Sometimes, in her darkest moments, she couldn't help but wonder if Mark truly loved her or if he was perhaps using her, hoping that in some way she would be able to promote and hype his book. She shook her head as she turned her key in the lock. She was getting cynical in her old age; she was so used to using other people that she assumed that everyone else was the same.

Although he must have seen the light of the car's headlights — his study was at the front of the house — Mark hadn't come out to meet her. Catherine stopped in the hallway. She could hear the hissing of the television. Dropping her bags and pushing the door closed, she turned to the right and walked down the short corridor to his room. She was about to knock, but on impulse, simply turned the handle and walked in. The room stank of stale beer and sweat. It was its usual mess, clothes, books and papers scattered everywhere. Mark Cosgrove lay in his armchair, head thrown back, snoring loudly, his glasses perched on the end of his nose threatening to fall off at any moment. There was the remains of a six-pack of beer strewn about the room, crumpled cans tossed on to the floor, the last intact one hanging loosely from his nerveless fingers, a puddle of beer on the carpet beneath it. His computer was still running, an animated chess program playing endlessly against itself. The small portable television was on in the corner, grey fuzz hissing from it. She frowned; it wasn't late enough for all the channels to have gone off the air. Catherine was about to turn it off when she realised it was connected up to the video and tuned to the video channel. Glancing sidelong at Mark, she pressed the play button. The screen flickered and the images appeared ...

The surge of anger that whipped through her was completely irrational, she knew. She had no basis for it, no right to it, and the very extent of the rage surprised and rather frightened her.

On the screen Rianne Moriarty's naked body writhed in simulated ecstasy.

Chapter
Twenty-Four

Briony Dalton was going to give an interview. And, by God, she was going to make it an appearance neither the media nor the public would ever forget.

The campaign against her had intensified. She was now convinced that it was a deliberate campaign, orchestrated and organised by someone, though Terri said that this was simply paranoia. She was a virtual prisoner in her hotel room, and the management were beginning to express serious reservations about the huge media circus now in full swing. She felt it was only a matter of time before they would ask her to leave.

For the last few days the newspapers — especially the English tabloids who had picked up on the story — had carried articles about her, dredging up all the old stories. In one of the English papers, she had read a long piece — with salient examples — about the 'disgraceful pornographic content' of much of her books. It had been published alongside a picture of a topless page three girl.

But there is no such thing as bad publicity. Not only *Pavane*, but also *Odalisk* and *Harem*, and the two books known as the *Seasons Quartet: Spring & Summer, Autumn & Winter*, were currently riding high in the fiction best-seller lists, with *Pavane* actually at number one.

Her initial fear and anger had given way before the realisation that all this publicity was exactly what she wanted, what she needed to sell books; every book sold made her money, and already speculation had begun in the press about her forthcoming book. She recognised a feeling which she realised she hadn't experienced in a long time. She had looked into the mirror — and instead of the rather complacent middle-aged woman looking back at her, she had seen someone harder, colder, determined. The type of woman she had been right at the start of her career, or at least when *Odalisk* was published. That had been her first true best-seller and she had worked so hard to make it a success. That Briony Dalton had been a fighter.

What had happened to her in the meantime? She had grown old and fat. Not physically fat, she had too much pride in her appearance for that, but she had grown lazy, the fire had gone. The need, the desire, the overwhelming passion to succeed at all costs had been swept away with success and the money and lifestyle that came with it.

Well, now her back was against the wall. Everything she had worked so hard to achieve was in the balance.

She claimed that she had come to Ireland for peace and quiet, to rekindle the spark that had driven her to be a writer. Well, she had certainly done that. She had rekindled the spark, but it wasn't the spark of her creativity — whatever that was — it was the spark of her defiance, her need.

She stood naked before the full-length mirror in the bathroom with her hands on her hips and deliberately straightened her shoulders. Staring into her eyes, she forced herself to relax, easing the lines off her forehead, the tightness around her lips. With both hands she pulled her hair back off her forehead, looking critically at the quarter inch of white hair that showed close to her scalp. She did need a colour!

She wondered what she would have done if she'd been faced with this situation ten years ago. She would have fought, as only Briony Dalton would have fought, in the press and on television, judging her results in column inches and air time, gauging her success in book sales.

She padded into the bedroom and opened the newspaper to the books page. The best-seller listings were alongside a brief article about 'The Queen of the Red Hot

Read.' *Pavane* was number one, *Odalisk*, number two and *Harem*, number four. And that had been achieved without trying. What would she be able to do if she really tried?

So she'd grant an interview. She'd phone Terri and have her make arrangements for interviews with both the BBC and RTE, the Irish television station.

Briony Dalton suddenly laughed aloud. She was feeling good, she could feel her old form returning. She hadn't been able to write for two days, but right now she was bubbling with energy. Pulling on her dressing gown, she popped the lid on her portable computer and turned it on. As it powered up, she realised what had been missing from her life over the past few months: stimulation, excitement. Oh, there had been plenty of false party thrills, the buzz of TV interviews, but there'd been nothing that had set the adrenaline pumping. Thinking back on it, maybe that had been the initial attraction of taking Gabrielle as a lover; those first few weeks had been so exciting. If anyone thought this aggravation was going to stop her writing, they were quite mistaken. In fact, she was beginning to think that she actually needed the stimulation, the aggravation, to write. Certainly when she had started writing she had had enough aggravation ...

ᴄ⳹

Her own orgasm had taken her five minutes previously, stealing almost secretively upon her, a fire blossoming deep in her groin, spreading upwards in a warm rush that left her breasts feeling heavy and tender, the nipples hard, almost painfully sensitive.

But Niall Moriarty hadn't noticed.

He was still moving urgently atop her, eyes shut in concentration, fingers biting into the soft flesh of her shoulders, intent upon his own satisfaction.

Bernadette had already lost interest, her attention having shifted, Niall's body now an irritation. But she knew from experience that when his own orgasm had passed he would roll over and in that semi-conscious state between sleep and wakefulness he would be amenable to suggestions, hints, new ideas.

It was about time she told him that she had been selling short stories and articles for the past few weeks with an almost frightening ease. In the last week alone she had sold one short story and four articles. She hadn't been paid for them yet, but there was nearly fifty pounds due. Niall had sold three short stories in the past three months.

She was also going to tell him that she was pregnant.

That was the real reason for her sudden interest in writing: they were going to need all the money they could earn. She had to work, but she didn't want to continue in the pub with the noise and the smells, the constant lifting and carrying, on her feet all day. But finding another job had proved to be virtually impossible. Her standard of education was as good as the nuns could make it, but she had no special qualifications and of course she was married. A lot of employers did not like to take on married women — especially young married women. The employer fully expected that they would become pregnant after a few months and leave. The only thing she could turn her hand to make some money was writing. Bernadette differed from Niall in that she chose her markets very carefully before submitting a piece, and she never wrote unless she already had an expression of interest from a magazine editor, either for an article or a short story. She employed a variety of pseudonyms and although she knew that she really should let the editor know her full and proper name she still kept the pen-names, cashing the cheques when they arrived in the pub. She had done some rough figures, based on her earnings coupled with Niall's regular wage and whatever money both their writings brought in, and they should have quite a few bob saved before the baby arrived.

And she was going to tell him tonight.

Niall's climax shuddered through him, his fingers tightening spasmodically on her shoulders, his breath catching in his throat, holding there for long seconds before he finally breathed again in a great gasping breath.

The first time this had happened it had terrified her: she thought he had died.

When he rolled off her he snuggled down, his head resting against her breasts, his arm around her waist. "I've got some news," he muttered hesitantly, almost shyly.

Bernadette was immediately on the alert. "What sort of news?" she said, feigning sleepiness.

"You know I've sent *The Dark Crusade* to Victor Gollancz in London?"

"Yes." *The Dark Crusade* had been Niall Moriarty's first sale as a short story to *The Bell* magazine. In her opinion he had never written anything better, and she had tried to convince him that it would make a novel almost from the beginning.

"Well, I got a letter from Gollancz today," he said slowly and clearly. "They said they wanted to make an offer for it. They've offered ..." he paused dramatically, "a one hundred pound advance. What do you think of that, eh?"

"But that's marvellous, absolutely marvellous!" She wrapped her arms around him, hugging him tightly.

"I'm going to be an author ... "

"You are an author," she reminded him gently.

"No, a proper author, I mean." Without changing his tone, he added, "And I handed in my notice today." He waited a heartbeat for her reaction and when none was immediately forthcoming, he hurried on. "I mean, now that I'm a proper author, I'm going to need time to write. And writing a few lines every evening after a full day's work is no fun. There's no way I can develop my creativity."

"You're full of shit!"

The cold vehemence in Bernadette's voice shocked him speechless. "You fucking eejit." She sat up, pushing him away, slapping at his hands when he reached for her. "You've given up a full-time pensionable job because you've got a book contract for ten weeks' wages spread out over two years. You'll get fifty pounds when you sign that contract. That's five weeks' wages. What do we do when that money runs out, eh?"

"Now hang on a minute," Niall began, vaguely frightened by this sudden change in mood and temper. Two minutes ago he had been making love to this woman, now she was practically spitting at him. "You're forgetting we have your money … "

Bernadette shook her head savagely, her lips drawn back from her teeth in an almost feral snarl. "Not for very much longer, Niall Moriarty. I'm pregnant. You're going to be a father!" She flopped back on to the pillows and turned away from him, biting the inside of her cheek to prevent the tears from coming. They were tears of rage and frustration. She should have known he'd do something like this. It was his greatest wish to be a real writer, a full-time author. This was something he could brag about to his pub cronies — most of whom were so-called authors, but only two of whom were full time writers: one of them wrote detective thrillers under a variety of names, the other was reputed to write pornography for an American publisher, again under a variety of names. And yet both men — who had published more than the combined totals of all the others present, and were able to live very comfortably off their earnings — were rather looked down upon by the others. What they were doing wasn't real writing. It wasn't art.

Like hell it wasn't. Any writing which paid was real writing.

Later, much later, Niall touched her shoulder with his fingertips. "Is it true?" he asked.

"I'm pregnant, if that's what you mean."

"When?"

"Middle of next year."

"How long have you known?"

"A while. It was confirmed yesterday."

"Why didn't you tell me?" he asked, sounding almost angry.

"I wanted it to be a surprise for you."

"Well it's that all right."

"Can you take back your resignation?" she asked into the shadows.

"No," he said shortly.

"Why not?"

"I just can't, that's all."

"You said something, didn't you?" she accused. "You said something or did something you can't go back on."

"Well, maybe I did say a few things, tell a few home truths. But I'm not someone who's afraid to speak his mind."

"You a bigger fucking eejit than I thought," Bernadette snapped. "Do you have any solution to our problem?" she asked.

"Problem?" he asked.

"The problem of you with no job and us with no money."

"But I do have a job," he said. "I am an author; that's a noble profession."

"My arse!" she swore.

"There'll be other books," he said almost fearfully. "And there'll be magazine articles; they'll bring in some extra money. And I can maybe find a part-time job, and ... and ... you can work for a few more months surely. Things won't be as bad as you think." He sounded as if he were trying to convince himself. "And we'll save. No unnecessary spending, I promise. I won't go to the pub. I'll write. Every day I'll write." He crept closer to his wife and wrapped his arms around her, resting his chin on her shoulder. "Everything will work out, I promise."

Bernadette didn't believe him.

Chapter Twenty-Five

Gabrielle Royer used the long transatlantic flight to sort through her notes. With the small Compaq computer perched on the table before her, she began assembling all the scraps of history, items of information, titbits of news and gossip she had gleaned from Briony Dalton's extensive files into something approaching order. Most of the material she had transcribed directly on to the computer in Briony's apartment, only taking away an envelope full of photographs which she felt might be suitable as illustrations in the book.

She worked steadily almost from the moment she boarded the flight. A young man with an accent that was so British it sounded put on had persistently attempted to engage her in conversation, until she had rounded on him, and said, quite simply and distinctly, "Please leave me alone, or I shall scream."

He looked completely nonplussed and attempted a smile, not sure if it was a joke or not. But looking into the blond woman's hard black eyes he had decided that it probably wasn't worth putting it to the test.

By the time the flight eventually left the ground over an hour later, having sat on the tarmac for some unaccountable reason, Gabrielle had blocked out the structure of the book, creating the chapters and their headings. Some were going to be easier to write than others, and she had the idea that she might actually start with the last chapter, or second last chapter which would begin when she had joined Briony. She wondered whether to write openly about her intimate association with Briony and decided to wait until she had first talked to Catherine Garrett to see how she was going to handle the relationship. Her love affair was part of Briony Dalton's life — Gabrielle liked to think it was an important part — but it needed to be portrayed properly and sensitively, not with a snigger as something dirty and obscene.

Gabrielle opened her briefcase and pulled out the single sheet of information Terri Fierstein had supplied on Catherine Garrett. What was there was little enough: born on 25 September 1946, she was Briony Dalton's step-sister, her mother, Brigid Garrett, having married Mick Dalton, Briony's father. The two girls seemed to have been the best of friends in their youth, closer than full sisters, but something had happened which had sundered the relationship completely. The break-up seemed to have occurred shortly after Catherine had returned from America: this would have been around the time that Briony's first book, *Summer's Song* had been published to rave reviews. Gabrielle had read *Summer's Song* and found it to be a very beautiful, rather lyrical book ... and completely unlike any other Briony Dalton title she had read.

What had happened between the two women? Gabrielle wondered. And would Catherine Garrett tell her? She doubted it; if there was a dark secret, Garrett would want it in her book, but she was determined to make the effort to find out.

Gabrielle turned off the small computer and closed down the screen. She shook out the photographs on to the top of the slender computer, sorting them into some sort of order.

The oldest she had been able to find was a dog-eared, creased snapshot of a man and a woman standing smiling fiercely at the camera. The style of the clothing was late thirties or early forties and while the man was short and soft-featured, the woman was remarkably like Briony, with the same hair, the same eyes, the same determined set to her mouth and Gabrielle guessed she was looking at a photograph of Briony's parents.

There was a second photograph of two young women aged about fifteen or sixteen, one blond, one dark: Briony was recognisable and she guessed the second girl was Catherine. This time the smiles were genuine and the girls had not only wrapped their arms around one another's shoulder, they were also holding hands. They were dressed identically in grotesque floral print dresses.

The third photograph was a street photographer's snap. A young couple — the woman was Briony certainly, and was the man Niall Moriarty? — caught on a bright summer's day, crossing a bridge. She recognised the location; it was O'Connell Bridge in Dublin.

Gabrielle tilted the photo to the light. Briony hadn't changed that much, except that a certain softness around her features had been pared away, polishing the harder, sharper lines of her face, giving it character.

The final photograph was the only one in colour, and was of two young children, a boy and a girl, sitting on carpeted stairs, the girl higher than the boy, both staring solemnly into the camera, neither smiling. The girl looked to be about six, the boy maybe ten or eleven. They both resembled Briony to a remarkable degree, especially the girl. Matthew and Rianne. Gabrielle returned the photographs to the envelope. The chapter on the present whereabouts of the two children was going to be the most difficult: Briony wouldn't be able to help since she didn't know where either of them was, and Terri had also denied all knowledge of their present whereabouts. Did Catherine know where they were? And would it be worth asking?

Gabrielle sat back and closed her eyes; she wondered where the two children were now, she wondered what they thought of their mother. Her eyes snapped open. She wondered what their mother thought of them! That was a question that begged an answer.

The plane arrived nearly two and a half hours late into Heathrow. It was another forty minutes before she finally cleared customs and collected her baggage, and she fully expected whatever transport Catherine Garrett had provided to be long gone. But as she came out into the arrival hall there was a tall, rather bored looking young man holding a cardboard sign, which read ROYER in shaky capitals. She walked up to him and smiled and he looked at her in surprise. "Miss Royer?" he asked in a nasal Cockney accent.

"Yes, that's me. Gabrielle Royer."

"Yes, of course, Miss." He reached down and lifted her single suitcase while she held on to the briefcase containing her notes and computer. He grinned. "I was expecting someone … " He paused and shrugged.

"Older?" she supplied.

"Different," he said, and then he grinned again. "Older."

"I'm sorry for keeping you waiting so long," she said as they walked through the terminal.

"Not to worry, love. I always make a point of phoning before I set out. I knew you were going to be late."

"Have you been waiting long?"

"An hour or so."

It had been raining and as they stepped outside the smell of damp air, tainted with diesel fumes, bit at the back of her throat, but she breathed deeply, relishing the dampness after the antiseptic dryness of the flight. The car was a long gleaming Mercedes limousine, and Gabrielle hid a smile: she was getting the star treatment. The driver opened her door and pointed out the facilities as she settled herself into the comfortable leather seats.

"Television — though lousy reception — stereo, radio and phone. Bar, icebox. Help yourself to whatever you want."

Gabrielle waiting until the driver had moved around and climbed in behind the steering wheel. "Have we far to go?"

"An hour or so, depending on the traffic."

"Does Miss Garrett know I am going to be late?"

"I phoned earlier." He lifted a handset off the dashboard. "I'm about to phone her now, let her know you're on the way. Any message?"

"No ... none. Thanks." Gabrielle wondered how she was going to approach Catherine Garrett. When she had initially contacted her it had seemed such a simple idea: phone her up and ask. But she had fully expected that to be the end of it. When the woman had actually returned the call, no one had been more surprised than Gabrielle. And now that she was about to meet her ... well, what could she say? She could hardly ask her to dish up the dirt on her step-sister, could she? Whatever dirt the woman had she was going to keep for her own book, and even if, for example, she did know the whereabouts of the children, she was hardly likely to share that information, was she? Gabrielle turned on the small overhead reading light and opened her briefcase. She had prepared a list of questions she was going to put to Catherine Garrett. She reached for her pen and added another question at the top of the page: why had she agreed to talk to Gabrielle in the first place?

At some time on the long car journey, she fell into a light doze. She was still aware that she was in the car, conscious of the street lights slipping past, knew when they became fewer and fewer and guessed they were moving deep into the country. She experienced a curiously vivid waking dream. Both Briony Dalton and Catherine Garrett were in the car with her, sitting facing her. They had their arms around one another's necks and were holding hands. It was the pose from the photograph, but the two fifteen-year-old girls were gone and had been replaced by two mature women. But as Gabrielle watched the two smiling faces became masks of hatred and the arms around one another's necks tightened, squeezing, choking, strangling. Their hands, clasped firmly together, tightened, the fingernails digging deep, tearing flesh, drawing blood.

Silence.

Gabrielle came awake as the driver said, "We're here, Miss." He held open the door and Gabrielle stepped out into a cold, fresh night. The air was sharp, scented with moist growth, faintly tinged with the plume of grey smoke from the car's exhaust. The silence was almost unnerving.

She shivered, and pulled her coat around her shoulders.

"Cold, miss?"

"Not really." She smiled. "I'm a city girl. Too quiet for my liking."

The driver glanced up into the cloudless sky, stars sparkling hard and cold. "I know what you mean, miss," he said feelingly.

Gabrielle turned as the door to the long sprawling bungalow behind her opened, shafting a bar of light out into the night. A shape moved in the doorway, throwing a shadow across the gravelled driveway.

Gabrielle walked up to the doorway, squinting in the harsh light, followed by the driver carrying her case.

Catherine Garrett came out to meet them. "Thank you, Will," she said, looking over Gabrielle's shoulder at the driver. "You will pick up Miss Royer in the morning."

"Of course, Miss."

"Any particular time?"

Catherine glanced at Gabrielle who shook her head. "Around noon. That will give us a chance to talk in the morning if we don't cover everything tonight." She came closer and extended her hand. "Catherine Garrett."

Gabrielle took the proffered hand, surprised by the strength in the grip. "Gabrielle Royer. It really is most kind of you to receive me into your home this way," she said, emphasising her French accent slightly.

"My pleasure. Please come in." She stepped aside and allowed Gabrielle to precede her into the hallway. "This way." Catherine touched her left elbow, guiding her down the hallway towards an open door. The dining room had been prepared for dinner, the table set for three, although one of the settings had been used.

Catherine saw Gabrielle's gaze flicker across the table. "A friend, Mark, had hoped to join us for dinner, but unfortunately when we knew your flight was delayed he had to eat and go. He had a late appointment," she added, turning away. Relations between herself and Mark had been strained since she had discovered that he had watched the pornographic video of Rianne Moriarty. In some way she couldn't truly identify, she felt it was a betrayal. The ongoing simmering argument had blown up again earlier this evening when he had discovered that Gabrielle would be staying overnight. He resented the intrusion, he claimed. He wouldn't be able to work, wouldn't be able to concentrate knowing a stranger was in the house. He had eaten about an hour previously, and then left — presumably for the pub in the village. Catherine was secretly dreading his return when he'd probably be very drunk.

Gabrielle turned, seeing Catherine Garrett for the first time in the light. She was surprised at how old the woman looked; although she was only a year older than Briony, her hair was shaggy and grey-streaked, and she wore no make-up which added at least five years to her age. Her eyes were red-rimmed and Gabrielle wondered if the woman had been crying. She was dressed rather surprisingly in black silk Chinese pyjamas, with flat slippers which meant she was inches smaller than Gabrielle.

"I thought we'd talk over dinner," Catherine said. "If you'd like to freshen up, I'll have everything ready by the time you're back. Bathroom's down the corridor to your right. Your room is next door."

The bathroom was decorated in soft pine and cork tiles. Hanging baskets draped greenery from the four corners of the room, and one wall was taken up by a full-length smoked-glass mirror. Gabrielle — who usually only wore the lightest of make- up — spent a few minutes removing it entirely. She added a touch of colour to her lips, dabbed some Opium behind her ears, touched it to her wrists.

Pine had also been used in the guest bedroom to lighten and brighten what Gabrielle guessed would otherwise be a dull room. Off-white, bronze and gold had been used on the wardrobes that lined one wall, the same colours carrying on into the dressing table. Her bag was on the floor beside the double bed. She changed quickly, choosing a black suede mini-skirt and a white silk blouse, no bra. Low-heeled boots added the few extra inches to her height, which, along with the simple elegance of the outfit, she felt gave her a psychological advantage over Catherine Garrett. She ran her fingers through her platinum-blond hair, pulling it back off her heart-shaped face, deftly securing it in place with a pair of ivory combs.

Gabrielle Royer smiled into the mirror, forcing her black eyes to sparkle. She was going to be charming, and she was going to be so, so interested in everything Catherine Garrett had to say. She turned to her bag and pulled out the bottle of Seagram's Canadian whiskey — Terri had told her that Catherine drank whiskey — and if her charm wouldn't work, then maybe the drink might.

She needed the information this woman had, and by Christ she was determined to get it.

Ten feet away, down the hallway, Catherine Garrett's thoughts were identical.

Chapter Twenty-Six

"I suppose you're wondering why I agreed to meet you," Catherine said, surprising Gabrielle. Throughout the light meal the conversation had been vague, and they had chatted about authors and publishers they both knew, books they had read, movies and videos they had seen — and both had been surprised to find that their tastes were remarkably similar.

It was only as the coffee was being served — a harsh bitter Colombian coffee that Gabrielle instinctively knew was going to keep her awake all night — that Catherine had finally broached the subject of Briony Dalton.

"I must admit I didn't think you'd even reply to me," Gabrielle said. "Why did you?"

Catherine sipped her coffee from a tiny cup, and stared at Gabrielle over the rim. "I was curious."

"Curious?"

"I had read some of the stories about you and your ... relationship with Briony."

"Don't believe everything you read in the press," Gabrielle smiled, her eyes fixed on Catherine's face.

"Oh, I don't; believe me, I don't!" Catherine looked at Gabrielle Royer, wondering what her stepsister saw in her. Why, she was nothing more than a jumped-up secretary, but there was something about her — a self-confidence, almost an arrogance — that she found unsettling. "Tell me how you learned I was writing a book about Briony," she said.

"Terri Fierstein — Briony's agent — contacted Briony and told her. I don't know all the details, but I understand that Terri had lunch with the editorial director of one of the big paperback houses who had been approached and offered the American paperback rights to the book." Gabrielle shrugged. "She was naturally concerned, so she contacted Briony."

"Why? Surely a biography of Briony Dalton would only help sales of her books," Catherine said, peering at Gabrielle over the rim of the coffee cup.

Unsure where the line of questioning was leading, Gabrielle answered truthfully: "There are certain … aspects, shall we say, about Briony Dalton's life — the episode with her husband and her relationship with her children especially — that are less than savoury. Both Terri and Briony felt an unauthorised biography would harm her reputation, and possibly the sales of her books."

"I understand Briony is in some sort of financial difficulty at the moment," Catherine said casually.

"I wouldn't know," Gabrielle said easily.

"So you were asked to write the authorised biography?" Catherine continued, not looking at the younger woman. "I too have my sources," she added.

Gabrielle allowed herself a smile. It would be a mistake to underestimate this woman. "Yes," she agreed. "I was asked to write the authorised biography. But I felt if I told you that over the phone there was no way you would agree to see me."

Catherine poured herself another cup of coffee, offering the pot to Gabrielle who put her hand over her cup and shook her head. "I'll be up all night."

"Of course you would be in the perfect position to write the authorised biography," Catherine said. "Briony would give you access to all her letters, papers, manuscripts and photographs."

"Yes, everything like that. And there is an awful lot of it."

"She always was a hoarder."

"But I can find nothing about her husband or her children, or you for that matter. In fact I didn't even know until recently that you were step-sisters. But I'll obviously need to include something about her husband and the children. Terri Fierstein suggested I contact you; she said she knew you had kept in touch with them after the break-up of the marriage and later when they both left home."

Catherine nodded. "I kept in touch with them for a while, but they haven't contacted me in the last few years."

"Then you don't know where they are?" Gabrielle asked, sounding disappointed.

"I didn't say that. I do have vague hints of their whereabouts which I'm currently looking into."

"I don't suppose you'd be willing to share some of that information with me, would you?"

"What would you be willing to trade me for it?" Catherine asked.

Gabrielle rested her elbows on the table, cupping her chin in her hands, her long-nailed fingers framing her face. "What do you want to know?"

Catherine put down her coffee cup, leaned back in the chair and folded her arms across her chest. "I tell you what I'll do. You tell me about you and Briony; what you do for her, how she works, that sort of thing, and in return I'll tell you what Matt and Rianne Moriarty currently do. I won't tell you where I think they are, though when I've told you what I know you may be able to work it out for yourself. In fact, I'll even be able to show you what Rianne Moriarty does. Sound fair?"

Intrigued, Gabrielle Royer nodded. "Sounds fair."

"Let's move. I hate talking over the remains of food."

A fire had been lit in the sitting room next door. It had died down to a few glowing embers, but the room was pleasantly warm. Catherine switched on the concealed wall-lights and turned the dimmer down until the room was in shadow, and then pressed the play button on a neat CD unit.

"Brahms," Gabrielle said decisively, "the Concerto for violin and orchestra in D major."

"I'm impressed."

"I'm surprised."

"Why?"

"It's one of Briony's favourite pieces."

Catherine poured them both two large shots of the Canadian malt whiskey, dropped ice into her own and again into the second glass when Gabrielle nodded. She settled herself into one of the high-backed chairs close to the fire. "Briony Dalton and I once shared many things," she said quietly. "She had a great love for classical music, especially violin music. I take it she still has?"

Gabrielle sat down facing her, spreading her long legs towards the fire, the warm light burnishing her smooth skin a deep copper. She rested the Waterford crystal whiskey glass on her flat stomach. "She has a huge collection of CDs — they're all classical or instrumental pieces, and most of those would be violin music. That's how I recognised the Brahms piece. Briony has taught me to appreciate the beauty of classical music."

"When I write I do so to music, usually with headphones on."

"Briony does that too," Gabrielle said.

Catherine nodded absently. She sipped her drink, watching Gabrielle over the rim of her glass. "Tell me about your relationship with Briony," she said.

"I am her secretary," Gabrielle said simply.

"You seem far too close to her to be nothing more than a secretary."

"I am a friend too. She hasn't got many friends," she continued. "And if you're asking if we're lovers, well then the answer is yes. Occasionally," she added softly.

"Has she no male lover?" Catherine asked staring into the fire.

"There have been men in the past, yes, but there's no one I'd call close. Writing is essentially a lonely, lonesome job."

"I know," Catherine said, more forcefully than she intended.

"Briony once told me that not many relationships can stand the strain. I wasn't sure whether I believed her then, but I've seen Briony so wrapped up in a piece of work that she becomes totally uncommunicative, not speaking, not eating, barely sleeping. I don't know how a normal relationship — if there is such a thing — would survive."

"I know what you mean," Catherine muttered. She caught the undisguised look of disbelief on Gabrielle's face and continued: "I live with a young writer. We've been together now for nearly two years. He's not a great writer, but he's a good writer ..."

"I'm not sure of the difference."

"Well, he won't win any prizes for his writing, but he'll turn out workmanlike stories time after time. And he's committed. I've seen him do what you describe: become so totally immersed in his work that everything else ceases to matter. I know the symptoms."

"Was Briony like that when you knew her?"

Catherine shook her head. "She didn't start writing until after she married in 1965. When she came to live with me after the first break-up early in 1966 she had written a few short stories, but she mainly did articles in those days. She tapped them out on the kitchen table on an expensive Royal typewriter Niall, her husband, had bought for himself," she added, smiling fondly at the memory.

"When did she start writing fiction?"

Catherine's expression closed. "*Summer's Song* was published in 1966."

"What was she like when she was writing it?"

"I don't know. I never saw her writing it."

"Oh. I suppose she must have written it in 1965 then. Why did she leave her husband?" Gabrielle asked.

Catherine shrugged. She drank quickly. "They married too quickly. They barely knew one another. They could only talk about writing together: he desperately wanted to be a writer, and she worked as a barmaid in her father's pub, which, as you may know, had a reputation of being a literary haunt. He was charming and articulate, handsome too. The day he sold his first novel — to Gollancz, I think — he quit a good job in the Post Office. I think that's when the rot started."

"I didn't know Niall Moriarty had ever published anything."

"Short stories only; he was always in the process of writing the great Irish novel. He was running some literary rag in Dublin the last time I heard of him. It's really a shame, too — I've read some of his earlier work, and he had genuine talent."

Gabrielle seized the moment to ask one of the questions she'd hoped to get an answer to. "What happened between you and Briony?" she asked quietly.

"Didn't she tell you?"

Gabrielle shook her head.

"There was an argument."

"It must have been a very serious argument."

"It was, I suppose."

"Do you want to tell me about it?"

"I can't. Ask Briony."

"I have. She won't say." She smiled tightly. "I suppose you're keeping that for your book?"

"No, I don't think I'll be including it," Catherine said surprising her.

"What did she do, commit murder?"

Catherine swirled the remainder of the whiskey around in her glass, and then drained it. "Tell me, do you like Briony?"

The question startled Gabrielle. "Yes, yes I do."

"Do you love her?"

She hesitated, and then realised that the hesitation had already answered the question. "I don't know," she said.

"Do you sleep together often?"

Slightly off balance by the abrupt change in questions, and feeling that she was losing control of the situation, Gabrielle answered, "Not often, no; we're not lovers in that sense of the word. But you were going to tell me what happened to Matt and Rianne."

"Yes, I was, wasn't I? Would you like another drink?"

"Yes, why not?" She rested her head back against the chair, her eyes closed. She was close to something, she could feel it. What was the secret between the two women, what had caused the break-up? What had turned two close friends into the bitterest of enemies? Catherine had been drinking steadily through the evening: maybe another couple of drinks would give Gabrielle the answers she wanted.

"You're not what I thought," Catherine said. Gabrielle hadn't heard her come back into the room. As the older woman handed across the tumbler of amber whiskey, her hand trembled, splashing whiskey on to Gabrielle's fingers.

"What did you think I was?" she murmured, delicately licking the alcohol from the backs of her fingers.

"Oh, I don't know. I've heard all the stories about you. I thought you were either a gold digger or a bull dyke. I suppose I'd imagined you as harder, colder … more masculine."

"I started out as Briony's secretary; I ended up as her friend and lover. It happened naturally. What's wrong with that?"

"Not a thing. Not a single thing. Sometimes you need friends."

"That's a lonely cry if ever I heard one," Gabrielle said sympathetically.

"Matt and Rianne Moriarty," Catherine said abruptly, ignoring the invitation to unburden herself. "Matthew Moriarty was born about a year after Briony's marriage. He's my godson," she added, almost defiantly. "Briony — she was still called Bernadette then, of course — left Niall shortly after she became pregnant, and although she was living with me when the child was born Niall came to the christening. The boy was named Matthew after his great-grandfather. Briony and Niall reunited about six months after the child was born. The girl, Rianne, was born in 1970. After the marriage broke up for the final time, Bernadette supported herself solely on her writing. She wrote under about a dozen pen names — even I'm not sure of all of them, and I'm quite sure she won't admit to half of them anyway. She did a lot of Gothic horror and Gothic romances … it was more or less the same story, but she managed to keep changing the elements. I do know that at one stage she wrote four a year. She did some humorous soft-core pornography, true-life confessions sort of thing, featuring a busty blond named Candy or Sandy. She wrote a long-running western series for one of the American publishers; there were actually four or five writers writing under the name of Colt Remington, or something like that. The series ran to twenty-two or three books before it finally finished. I know Briony accounted for five or six. When she was finished those she did an occult series featuring some evil Satanist called Diablos; there were five books in that series. They were incredibly gory and vaguely erotic, and they sold extremely well. I know Briony got the idea having read Dennis Wheatley … "

Gabrielle listened, fascinated. This was a side of Briony's nature which she had never even dreamed about, had never imagined even existed. Briony kept her own books on a shelf in her bedroom, but there was certainly nothing like this there.

"Sure, she was turning out crap, but it was paying the bills. There was a price, of course. The children paid that price. They rarely saw their mother, who worked extraordinary hours to meet her deadlines — and at that stage, doing the work she was doing, meeting a deadline was essential. She was a hack, and if she couldn't bring the book in on time then the publisher would find another hack who could. I'm surprised it didn't kill her, or give her a nervous breakdown. She often worked on into the night, writing while the house was still and silent and the children were asleep. And then, in 1977, she published *Odalisk*, her breakthrough book. And the rest, as they say, is history. She was a superb publicist, and when the book was published it was an instant best-seller in Ireland. That success spilled over into the British market making it an enormous best-seller there too. Once the ball started rolling, it just didn't stop."

"Tell me about Matt and Rianne," Gabrielle said, trying to keep Catherine on the subject.

Catherine cupped her whiskey in both hands and stared into the fire. "A series of nannies and housekeepers looked after the children. If the weather was fine the children would be allowed out into the garden; unfortunately Briony often sat in the garden and worked, so they weren't allowed to disturb her. If the weather was inclement, and they were forced to remain indoors, she would stay in her study and again the children weren't allowed to make any noise." She stopped and sipped some of the whiskey to ease her throat which was beginning to grow ragged.

"What did they do all day?"

"Watched television. And then, later, when they were old enough, they were sent off to boarding school. But neither was a particularly good pupil, and I know that Rianne was expelled at least once."

Catherine looked up and smiled at Gabrielle's bemused expression. "Remember, these children had no real parents to look after them. Although they were living in the same house as their mother, they rarely saw her and when they did she was often distant and aloof. I know she often took stimulants to stay awake while she wrote at night, which meant that she was usually in foul form the following day. They saw their father infrequently, and he was drinking very heavily at this time. He was the classic failed writer: always talking about the book he was going to write, but never actually doing it."

"What happened to the children?"

Catherine's face fixed itself into a mask. "Matt dropped out of school, ran away from home when he was fifteen and again when he was seventeen. On both occasions, the police picked him up and he was brought back. He ran away in 1984 when he was eighteen and he hasn't been back since."

"What did he do, where did he go? What did Briony do?" Gabrielle asked, genuinely interested now, forgetting for the moment her ulterior motives.

Catherine stared once more into the fire, the light etching the lines deeper into her face, ageing her. "He was living rough in London for a while; he had a squat up in Camden Town. He contacted me a few times, and I sent him some money. I know he went on the Continent for a while. I got a card from Greece on one occasion, another from Rotterdam, and there was even one from Malmo. But he never gave a forwarding address, and he never asked for anything."

"Do you know where he is now?" Gabrielle asked gently, and then she shook her head. "No, don't answer. What about Rianne?"

"Rianne was a little smarter than her brother. In the summer of 1987, when she was seventeen, and home for the holidays, she simply vanished. No one knows exactly when; her mother wasn't around when it happened. One of Briony's mega-selling books was launched that year; money was beginning to come in as the various subsidiary rights were sold, and she was away doing publicity stunts, signings, radio and television interviews. The woman who came in to cook and clean the house was the first to notice that the girl hadn't been home for three days. She raised the alarm. Initially, the fear was that she had been kidnapped — Briony was causing quite a stir at the time and there was a lot of speculation in the press about her earnings — but when there was no ransom demand that theory was abandoned. Then Briony got a bank statement. She discovered that over the three month summer period, just short of twenty thousand pounds had been taken from her accounts, drawn on cheques. When she demanded copies of the cheques she discovered that they were all made out in her daughter's favour and signed by Briony Dalton." Catherine grinned. "Rianne had forged her mother's name on the cheques — and done it cleverly enough to fool the bank. The girl had never taken an exact amount. It was always in odd figures and pence, some of it taken in cash, some of it transferred directly into Rianne's account. Obviously the girl had been planning her escape for quite a few months."

"Do you know what happened to her?"

"She went to London in search of her brother, but by that time he had gone to the Continent. I know she went to Amsterdam and then on to Germany, and the last I heard of her she was in America. She spoke to me twice, a reverse-charge call on both occasions. She didn't ask for money, she just wanted me to know that she was well."

"What is she doing now?" Gabrielle asked.

Catherine stood suddenly. "Let me show you." She turned on the television set and switched on the video. Lifting an unlabelled video from the shelf above the TV, she slid it into the machine. Catherine fast-forwarded through the titles, horizontal lines racing across the screen. Figures appeared, comic and ludicrous in high speed, like a silent movie.

A man and a woman talking in a hospital ward, the woman lying on the bed, a doctor entering, the woman stripping naked to be examined by the doctor …

"It's a porno movie," Gabrielle whispered, looking at Catherine in astonishment as both the doctor and the second male proceeded to undress.

The young woman kneeling between the two men, fondling them both, the camera moving to her face, a close-up of her eyes closing, her mouth opening …

Catherine froze the image of the woman's face.

Gabrielle stared, comprehension dawning. "You mean …?"

"Rianne Moriarty now makes pornographic movies. Ryan Divine is her working name." Her voice was trembling.

"Have you watched this movie through?" Gabrielle asked, her eyes on the screen.

"A couple of times. It's hard-core pornography, but at least it's straightforward pornography. There's nothing kinky in it." She wrapped her arms around her body and shivered. There were tears sparkling in her eyes. "I held that girl as a child," she whispered, genuine pain in her voice.

Gabrielle crossed the room to stand before Catherine's chair and took her hands, squeezing them tightly. "It's her life," she said. "She's made her decisions. There's nothing you could have done."

"Oh, but there is ... there was ... "

"There was nothing you could have done," Gabrielle insisted.

"There was, there was ... " Her voice was thick, eyes huge behind unshed tears.

Gabrielle reached for her glass and passed it to Catherine. "Drink this." She stood up and moved towards the drinks cabinet. "I'll get some more."

Catherine lifted the glass and drained it in one long swallow and then gasped for breath, coughing as the liquid seared her throat. "I'll hate myself in the morning. This stuff doesn't make you feel better; it just stops you feeling."

"Tell me about Briony," Gabrielle said, returning with an almost full bottle of malt whiskey.

Chapter
Twenty-Seven

A door opening.

Footsteps.

Gabrielle, always a light sleeper, had blinked awake. There was someone moving in the hallway outside. There was a fleeting moment of disorientation and panic, then she put the pieces together and realised it must be Mark Cosgrove, Catherine's boyfriend. She glanced sidelong at the clock on the bedside locker — 4:05 blinked in red — and she wondered where he'd been 'till this hour. Floorboards had creaked as he had made his way down the corridor and then she heard a door opening. A second or so later, the door had closed.

She smiled grimly; he had been checking to see if Catherine was in her bed.

Moments later another door opened and closed as he went into another room. A toilet flushed, the sound distant and muffled, and then there was silence. Feeling vaguely disappointed, Gabrielle drifted back to sleep.

It was close to six when she had awakened to sounds of movement at the other end of the house. She had heard padding, scuffing footsteps in the corridor outside and again the door down the corridor had been opened. This time there was a longer interval before it was closed.

Now he was wondering where Catherine was. He was probably checking the bed to see if it had been slept in.

Knowing what was going to happen next, Gabrielle gently pushed the duvet off the bed, exposing both their naked bodies. The two women were lying facing one another, Catherine's face pressed to Gabrielle's breast, her lips inches from the nipple. Gabrielle's long legs were between Catherine's thighs. Chewing on the inside of her cheek to prevent herself from laughing aloud, she closed her eyes and waited.

Seconds later, as she knew it would, the door to her room cracked open.

And then silence.

Well he was certainly taking his time, and getting an eyeful. Murmuring unintelligibly, Gabrielle rolled over on her back and spread her legs, allowing him a good look at the body which neither he, nor any other man, would ever possess. She peered at him through slitted eyelids, and the look on his face was priceless.

She abruptly opened her eyes and regarded him coolly.

"Just … just … just … what the fuck do you think you're doing?" he suddenly shouted, staggering into the room, his face ashen.

"We were sleeping," Gabrielle murmured. "What are you: a voyeur, a pervert? Do you get off by just looking?"

Catherine came awake slowly, groggily. She was still exhausted after a night of fierce lovemaking, where her orgasms had been so intense they had left her feeling bruised in every muscle. She looked from Gabrielle to Mark Cosgrove and the flash of alarm and shame in her eyes lasted less than a second. She slowly and deliberately stretched out in Gabrielle's arms enjoying the experience of the younger man's rage, delighting in his jealousy.

He suddenly strode into the room and roughly grabbed Catherine's arm, attempting to pull her off Gabrielle, his fingers biting into her flesh. Gabrielle rolled over on the bed and punched him squarely in the groin. He crashed to his knees, his face inches from the mattress, eyes bulging. Her long-nailed powerful fingers found the hinges of his jaw and she squeezed.

"Fuck off," she said very softly. "You touch this woman again, and I'll feed you your balls. Understand me?" she squeezed his jaw for emphasis and he uttered a strangled squawk. Wrapping her hand around his face, she sent him sprawling across the room.

Cosgrove backed away from the bed, his eyes smouldering. He looked from Catherine to Gabrielle as if unable to decide who was to blame. "You're a whore!" he spat, glaring at Catherine. "First you fuck Bach to get your precious book contract and now you fuck her secretary to get the dirt on her."

"And the only reason you fuck me is to ensure that your book will be well reviewed," Catherine blazed. "You're as much a whore as I am. Well let me tell you something, Mister Cosgrove. I won't be reviewing your book, and I'll damn well make sure that no one else does either! You can kiss your writing career good-bye."

Cosgrove slammed the door with enough force to knock one of the pictures from the wall. Seconds later the hall door opened and closed with equal force.

Catherine dropped back onto the pillow, shivering. "Jesus," she whispered, "what have I done?"

"What's right," Gabrielle soothed. She ran her hand down Catherine's stomach onto her thighs. Almost involuntarily the older woman opened her legs slightly to allow her easy access.

Gabrielle Royer brought Catherine Garrett to orgasm quickly and efficiently, but her thoughts weren't on what she was doing. She had been intrigued by the mention of Josef Bach's name. Just where did he fit into this picture? She had a feeling it was an important connection: but this was a giant jigsaw and she didn't possess all the pieces. But she was close. She felt she was damn close to something.

Terri Fierstein. Terri would know.

Chapter
Twenty-Eight

"I am quite capable of looking after myself," Briony Dalton said defiantly. "Is that clear, Terri?" she demanded.

There was a long silence on the other end of the line and then finally Terri Fierstein sighed audibly. "Whatever you say, but it is most irregular." She attempted a laugh. "People will think I'm not looking after my author."

"I promise you now," Briony said firmly, "if you send anyone to me, I will consider it to be a breach of contract and sue you. Is that understood?"

"Understood."

Briony caught the hesitation in her voice, and pressed on. "But ..? "

"But I'm afraid I've already told Charley O'Neill to meet you in the hotel. It's for your own good, Briony. You told me yourself that there are people protesting outside the hotel. Charley will be able to take care of you in case the situation gets out of control."

"Fine … fine," Briony snapped. "All right then. Just to satisfy you I'll have Charley. Happy?"

"Not happy, but happier!"

"I'll phone you later and let you know how it goes." She broke the connection and dropped the phone back on to its cradle. Secretly she was rather glad that Charley O'Neill was going to accompany her to the television studio. There had been a small group of protesters — it had gradually dwindled — outside the hotel for the past few days. She thought that most of the rather fresh-faced men and women would have been too young to remember her when she was completely outrageous. However, with the approach of her much-publicised interview and her expected appearance, the numbers had swelled and there were now about eighty people demonstrating with placards.

Briony had spent the morning being interviewed by the BBC. Although she had initially planned to fly to London, she had decided she couldn't be bothered with all the hassle and, with a little stage management by Terri, the BBC had arranged for members of their Dublin staff to interview her. The interview would be edited and worked on, and Briony Dalton would later be seen speaking 'live by satellite' on one of the weekend chat shows. The advantages of the taped interview, of course, was that mistakes could be snipped away — live television was not so kind. Tonight she would be appearing live on one of the highest rated chat shows in Ireland. She would be talking about her life and work, and would then take questions from the audience.

She hadn't asked about the make-up of the audience, but she could almost guarantee that it would contain representatives of the major religions, and would be heavily biased in favour of the moral majority. There would almost certainly be a small group of what might be called her supporters — although they were very probably the type of people she neither wanted nor needed as supporters.

There would be an argument, but that made good television.

Briony glanced at the clock; she had about an hour before the hairdresser arrived for the second time that day. She went into the bathroom and turned on the shower, setting it to a fine needle spray and about as hot as she could bear. She undressed slowly, wondering what she was going to wear. After all, she did have her *femme fatale* image to maintain.

She stepped into the shower, gasping as the hot water stung her body, and then raised her face to the spray, allowing it to wash away the remnants of the morning's television make-up. The interview had gone reasonably well; the young male reporter had gone through the questions with her beforehand and she had had her answers worked out by the time they were making the final take. She spoke briefly about why she chose religious protagonists in her novels and then treated them so badly, she discussed the sexuality of the books, and the difference between erotica and pornography. She had given hundreds of similar interviews — 'nothing interviews', she called them. She had made no outrageous statements this time ... except, perhaps, when she said that everyone enjoyed pornography, only very few people actually admitted to enjoying it. The question had led naturally on to the exploitation of women by pornography, and Briony's answer — which she regretted now, because it sounded almost too glib — was that the women appearing in the magazines or videos were paid, some of them extremely well for relatively easy work. So where was the exploitation? She knew instinctively that that was the remark which would be taken out of context and highlighted in the press, because, of course, it wasn't true: only a tiny percentage of women could command the huge fees, while the vast majority of their sisters earned a pittance for their degradation and so many ended up diseased or junkies. It was a remark that would have been typical of the younger Briony Dalton: speak first and then think. She turned off the shower and stood for a few moments in the stall, allowing the water to drip from her body. She hadn't made a mistake like that for ages. She reached out for a towel and wrapped it around her hair before stepping out onto the mat. She wrapped a second large bath towel around her body, tucking the end down between her breasts. Perhaps the BBC wouldn't use that bit ... but no, that would be too much to hope for; of course they would use it. It was controversial, it made for good television. She smiled slightly. She must be getting old: actually worrying about what people would think of her remarks. When she was younger it was something which never bothered her in the slightest.

ભ

"You look stunning!" Charley O'Neill was genuinely astonished by the woman who had opened the door to him. Her hair had been expertly returned to its original coal-black colour, pulled back severely off her face and then worked into a thick plait that came to the middle of her shoulder blades. Her brown eyes seemed very large indeed in her long oval face, and she had accentuated her high cheekbones with touches of blusher. Her lips were a bright red that matched the red hunting waistcoat which she wore over a ruffled shirt, which was opened to the swell of her breasts, and black culottes. Her vaguely Spanish-style outfit was completed by calf-length black leather boots. She wore heavy square gold earrings, and a matching choker and bracelet of the same heavy square links. The jewellery — which she knew was guaranteed to cause comment because it was so well-known — had been a present from one of her lovers, an American author, a multi-millionaire who had had every intention of making her wife number eight. Their affair had been spectacular and had ended equally spectacularly, when she had walked out on him during the Academy Award Ceremony. He had won an Oscar for Best Screenplay and during his acceptance speech had said that, "this screen play might have been a lot better and finished a lot sooner if Briony Dalton hadn't been distracting me so often." As the camera had panned to her, picking her out of the audience, she had quite calmly picked up her pocketbook, stood up and walked away, wending her way slowly and graciously through the rows of seats. Someone — Briony later discovered it had been Terri Fierstein — had started to applaud, and as the spotlight and camera remained on Briony she had exited to a sustained round of applause. She couldn't have stolen the screenwriter's thunder so effectively if she had tried.

"You'll knock them dead tonight," Charley said, watching her closely, looking for any signs of nervousness.

"How are things outside?" Briony asked, checking through the contents of her purse for a final time before picking up her black leather jacket and draping it over her shoulders.

"The crowd has been growing all morning," Charley said. "The police put the latest estimates at around two hundred, but that's simply because a busload arrived a few moments ago. But not to worry. They're all out the front. The car's out the back with the engine running, and I've two of my men along for muscle in case we need it."

With a curious sense of unreality, Briony felt herself hustled down the back steps and into a narrow street behind the hotel. Two bulky young men materialised out of the shadows, one taking up a position directly in front of her, the other behind and to her left. The car door swung open as she neared it and she was deftly, though none too gently, manoeuvred inside. The limousine pulled away smoothly, and Charley relaxed, confident that they were invisible behind the smoked-glass windows. "Was all that subterfuge absolutely necessary?" Briony asked coldly.

"My job is to keep you safe. I'm not so sure, if you'd gone out the front door, you'd have escaped quite so easily."

"Come, come, surely you're exaggerating."

Charley leaned forward and tapped the bodyguard in the front passenger seat on the shoulder. The young man passed back a copy of a newspaper. "This evening's paper," Charley murmured. With his slate grey eyes still fixed on her face, he folded it back to the middle pages and then handed it across. There was a large blow-up of the publicity photograph which had appeared for the paperback publication of *Harem* nearly fifteen years ago: she was dressed in a Hollywood version of a harem outfit, veiled head-dress, skimpy bra, bare midriff, diaphanous pants. Alongside it in block type was the single word, 'BLASPHEMY!'

Briony read through the lurid article: in it, an unnamed priest claimed that he had been seduced by Briony Dalton on his altar. Even a cursory examination revealed that the story was an obvious fabrication and was riddled with inconsistencies.

"But this is nonsense," she whispered aghast. "Any right-thinking person could see that."

"I know," Charley said pleasantly, "I was once described in an article as a crook and a charlatan." He sounded so injured by the statement that she had to smile. "So I make it a point of never believing what I read in the newspapers."

"Well, I'm going to sue this newspaper. I'll get my lawyers on to it immediately."

"You'll find they've covered themselves," Charley remarked. "They wouldn't have published an article like this unless they were very sure of their facts or their source."

"Nonsense!" She waved the paper in his face. "These are lies."

Charley O'Neill turned to look at her. "They may be lies, but don't dismiss it as mere nonsense. If this was one of the cheap tabloids you'd know you were dealing with rubbish, and more importantly, the readers would know that they should take it with a grain of salt. But this isn't a rag, this is a reputable newspaper. People believe it. And I guarantee that the newspaper will be able to substantiate all their statements; they'll have sworn affidavits from the subject, probably even pictures."

Briony crumpled the newspaper up into a ball. "But it's just not true. It is all a lie."

"You know that and I know that, but the general public don't know. Someone has waged an extraordinary campaign against you over the past week. You have been branded a pornographer, a hack, a drug addict, a lesbian; you've been called anti-clerical, anti-establishment, an anarchist, a communist and an atheist. This article pulls a lot of those threads together; it's more or less designed to be the final straw. You've made a bad — and powerful — enemy, Briony Dalton, and whoever he is he's going all out to destroy you."

Briony shivered. Charley O'Neill had simply been putting her own vague fears into words.

But who?

It was beginning to drive her crazy. She had made enemies over the years, that was true, but she couldn't think of anyone who would be actually vindictive...

And yet …

Whoever was waging this campaign obviously knew a lot about her and her career. They were adroit at manipulating the press and running a press campaign. They also had access to unpublished material — much of which even she had forgotten about — and which she believed had remained buried in her publishers' files. And that meant someone in publishing …

There was only one person whom Briony could think of who would have the skills to organise an event like this, and who had access to publishers: Catherine Garrett. She straightened in the seat as the idea unfolded. But why, why? Catherine had no reason to love her, but she had never demonstrated any real hatred toward her either. Why?

The reason was obvious. The intense public interest in Briony Dalton would guarantee the success of Catherine's own book!

Simple. So, so simple.

Bitch! Well, by Christ, she would have her revenge. One way or another she was going to have her revenge.

"Is everything all right?" Charley O'Neill enquired.

"Yes, fine. Why?"

"You look … troubled," he suggested. He had seen the look of absolute hatred that had flickered across the woman's face.

"I'm fine. I think I've worked out who's behind this campaign."

Keeping his face and voice carefully neutral, O'Neill asked, "May I ask who?"

"Catherine Garrett," Briony hissed. "She has the motive, the opportunity and the means." She nodded her head decisively. "Yes, it can only be Catherine."

"You could be right," Charley said softly, desperately trying to stop himself laughing in her face. "What are you going to do?" he wondered.

"Play her at her own game!"

When Briony reached the television studio she was met by a tall, thin sad-eyed young woman who introduced herself as one of the show's senior researchers. The woman enthused about Briony's books, claiming that she'd read them all and was dying to read the new one, but since the new book was more than a year old at this stage Briony rather doubted her first statement. She added what an honour it was to have Briony on the show and the fact that they were expecting record viewing figures. The young woman then introduced her to the show's producer and ushered into the small hospitality suite. She refused alcohol, opting instead for mineral water: she needed to be razor sharp to survive tonight's ordeal.

The door opened and a tall blond young man stepped into the room. Briony disliked him on sight. He was too slick, too self-confident and too self-assured for her liking. His outsized Hugo Boss suit gave him a dumpy appearance, and she disliked the current habit in men of wearing their hair back in ponytails.

He came forward, his hand outstretched. His handshake was limp, his flesh damp. "I'm delighted to meet you finally," he gushed. "My name is Marcus Holland; we've spoken on the phone."

Briony started to shake her head. She was sure she'd never encountered the man before ... and then she remembered the journalist who had phoned her over a week ago. Controlling her sudden anger, she smiled at the smooth young man, realising that this was the journalist who had broken the story that she was in Ireland. It might be simplistic to assume this was the man responsible, but he bore a major portion of the blame.

She was therefore unsurprised to find that Holland was in the audience and equally unimpressed when she discovered he had his own weekly television programme. He prattled away, his American accent grating, discussing everything but Briony Dalton and her books, and she knew then — knew instinctively — that he was saving whatever gems of scandal he had for the programme. He was also being so nice to her that she knew he would be an absolute bastard when the show went out.

About ninety minutes before the show went on air, Briony was taken upstairs to make-up. A pretty young woman made her up quickly and efficiently, whilst complimenting her on her hair, her jewellery and her distinctive costume. She said she was a great fan of Briony Dalton's books — and this time Briony believed her — and ended by wishing her luck.

She had a feeling she was going to need it.

The sad-eyed researcher materialised and offered to show her around the studio. Briony followed her through the chaos. With less than an hour before the show went on the air, the studio looked a shambles. Only the two sets were in position, one behind the host and the guests, and the second set was a small stage which would hold the singer and band who would provide the musical intervals during the show. The floor was festooned with wires and cables.

Briony was leaving the set when the door before her opened and she found herself facing a tall, thin, rather severe-looking middle-aged man with hair of such a rich chestnut colour that it had to be dyed.

"And this is our guest of honour," he boomed, stretching out his hand.

Briony automatically reached for it. She waved away the researcher's introductions. "I know Michael Kavanagh," she smiled. "I think all Ireland knows Mr Kavanagh."

Michael Kavanagh had successfully hosted the Weekending programme for twelve of it's fifteen-year run. He was casually dressed in slacks and cardigan, but she knew he would be impeccably dressed for the show later. "We're very honoured to have you with us," His eyes — the same colour as his hair, she noticed — twinkled mischievously. "Are you looking forward to the show?" he asked softly, a slightly foreign lilt to his voice, although Briony was quite sure he was Irish.

"I'm a little nervous," she confessed, surprised to find that it was true.

"Good, that's good. If you had no nerves then I'd be worried." He smiled at her, glancing at his clipboard. "Well, I'd better be getting on. We've less than an hour to showtime." As he turned away, he added, "I can promise you one thing though: it's going to be some show tonight!"

"You'd better believe it," Briony whispered.

Chapter
Twenty-Nine

"Few authors have raised as many hackles as my next guest this evening. She has it all, ladies and gentlemen, charm, intelligence, talent and beauty: the controversial, the outrageous Briony Dalton!"

The strident theme music from the television version of *Harem* swelled as Briony stepped out from behind the set and took the seat next to Michael Kavanagh. The audience applause was decidedly muted, and as she stared out beyond the glare of the lights she noted the grim, unsmiling faces. There were quite a few in clerical garb, she observed. She was surprised to find she was alone on the stage with Kavanagh; she had been expecting a panel. She realised then that the audience had been seeded with people like Holland.

"Briony, it's been a while since we last saw you here in Ireland," Kavanagh began, "what brings you back?"

"It hasn't really been that long, Michael. I usually come home every year," she lied, "although I must admit, it's been over a year now since I was last here." Briony watched Kavanagh carefully. He was a superb interviewer. Behind his avuncular manner and disarming smile lay a predatory mind and he delighted in shit-stirring; she had seen him slide the knife into too many guests and twist it to produce the reaction he wanted. He was sitting across from her on the opposite side of a curved desk; she could see the discreet television monitors set into the panelling. There was a series of tiny file cards set out on the desk directly in front of him: ammunition, she guessed.

"Your visit this time has been surrounded by a certain amount of controversy," Kavanagh said smoothly. "More so than at any other time."

"Certainly there seems to have been an extraordinary campaign mounted against me. I'm not sure of the reasons myself." She continued smiling, watching him intently.

Kavanagh matched her smile, manicured fingers dropping to touch one of the file cards. "There has been a suggestion that this is some publicity stunt for your forthcoming book. You have always thrived on this type of publicity."

"This is not a publicity campaign; it is a smear campaign."

"Are you saying it is a deliberate campaign?" Kavanagh's eyes kept flicking to the monitors mounted into his desk. It enabled him to see the various camera shots of Briony and the audience at the same time. "But who is behind it?"

"I don't know," Briony said evenly. She was surprised at how calm she felt. She realised that for this interview to be successful she had to maintain her composure, no matter what was said, no matter what happened. "However the events of the past week have been too well orchestrated for them to have occurred naturally."

He smiled again. "Surely that's a rather paranoid theory?"

"I think the facts speak for themselves: a series of extremely derogatory articles and statements have appeared in the press over the past few days. A number of quotations from my books — and indeed some that are not from my books — have also appeared in the press. On the way to the studio this evening I read a front-page story about a so-called priest who claimed I had seduced him on the altar of his church in 1965 when I was doing research for *Harem*. In 1965, I was eighteen years old and just about to be married. I wasn't even writing in 1965. And *Harem* didn't appear until 1978, thirteen years later."

"There have been protests outside your hotel," Kavanagh said. He fully expected Briony to answer, but when she said nothing he was caught off-guard. "People obviously object to the types of books you write."

"Certain people object to some of the books I write. Usually a tiny minority, but I don't write for the minority. I am a storyteller. I write entertaining fiction for a mass audience." She was back on safer territory now; she had been over this ground many times before.

Kavanagh grinned. "With a strong erotic — some would say pornographic — content."

"Yes. Sex is part of everyday life. There is sex in my books, but these books are entertainment and the sex, along with the exotic locations, the clothes, the jewels, the perfume, the violence, are all fictions. And most right-thinking people know that and accept it."

"What do you say to people who believe that your books should be banned?"

"They are entitled to their opinions," she stated simply and said nothing further. She knew Kavanagh had expected her to defend her books at greater length or perhaps adopt a stance on the proposed banning of them.

Michael Kavanagh ran his eye down his notes. Usually, once an interview had started, it took on a shape and character of its own and all it needed from him was a gentle nudge when it began to stray. His job, he firmly believed, was to let the guest talk and then ask them inappropriate questions in the appropriate places. But so long as they talked interestingly, it was fine: an interesting and amusing guest made him look good. But so far there had been little interesting about this interview. He moved a card to one side. "Your first major success was *Odalisk* in 1977 and then *Harem* appeared in 1978. Both dealt with the church, and were very explicit in their treatment of sex: there was rape, homosexuality and lesbianism, and some of the settings were in churches or convents. How do you justify that?"

"Have you read either book?" Briony asked.

Kavanagh glanced at his notes. There was nothing on either book. "I would have to say I haven't," he confessed.

"The scenes you refer to, especially the rape scene in *Odalisk* is less than three hundreds words long in a two hundred and fifty thousand word novel. For the mathematicians amongst you, that is point zero zero two per cent of the book. The gentleman who performs the rape — although dressed as a priest — is not actually a priest. *Harem* is about a young girl's emerging sexuality and how she feels compelled to express her love of God in a sexual way. But she is not a nun, she is a novice and eventually leaves the cloister before taking her vows." She turned from Kavanagh to look directly into camera one. "The lesbian scene you refer to, which has also been printed and quoted in the press, does not appear in the published book."

Kavanagh took a deep breath. This was an interviewer's worst nightmare: inaccurate research. He would have someone's head on a stick for this. Changing tack completely, he asked, "Why do you constantly attack the institutions of the church and the role of the family and the place of the woman in present-day society in your books?"

"I think," Briony said, smiling gently, "that you're reading far too much into simple pieces of fiction."

Michael Kavanagh turned from Briony Dalton and faced camera two as the light came on over it. "I'm talking to Briony Dalton, the Queen of the Red Hot Read. I'm Michael Kavanagh; join us after this break."

The audience, led by the floor manager, broke into applause and the show's theme music swelled for a few seconds. All the camera lights went out. The audience began to murmur amongst themselves.

"A good interview so far," Kavanagh said, checking through his notes.

"Yes." Briony sipped water and looked at the audience. She recognised one of the clerics — the craggy wild-haired man in the second row, what was his name? — as being one of her harshest critics. He believed she had used him as the basis for one of her least likeable priests.

Behind him and a little to his left was Marcus Holland, whom she'd met in the hospitality room. So, she'd been right: she'd be getting questions from the floor from "planted" questioners.

She stopped. In the highest tier, at the very back of the room, a ravaged face stared intently at her. He was partially in shadow, but she still recognised him, the same expression, the slight sneer to the lips. It was Niall Moriarty. Suddenly, she felt less confident: what was her ex-husband doing here?

Michael Kavanagh leaned forward. "I'll do a few more questions now and then we'll go to the audience. OK? You're doing great," he added condescendingly, covering her hand with his, squeezing it.

Briony felt a brief swell of anger at his arrogance, and then realised what he was doing — deliberately trying to aggravate her into saying something rash.

The music swelled and the round of applause coincided with the appearance of the light over camera three. "Tonight I'm talking to Briony Dalton, the Queen of the Red Hot Read, one of the top selling authors in the world." He swivelled around to face Briony again, plastic smile fixed to his face. "All your novels deal with Ireland ..." he began, but Briony cut him off.

"My last ten books have been best-sellers; only the first four had an Irish background, the last six and the present novel are not, in any way, shape or form, Irish. They are not set in Ireland and there are no Irish characters in them." She watched him carefully, resisting the temptation to add something else.

"You yourself have always been a controversial figure. You have always flaunted convention, and indeed continue to do so. Would you agree that your sometimes outrageous behaviour has attracted notice?"

A series of photographs began appearing on the audience monitors. They showed Briony at parties, night-clubs, discos, and there was one classic photograph which showed herself and Gabrielle displaying a lot of bare flesh, wearing dresses made of nothing more than pages from her latest book. This photograph remained on the monitor longer than any of the others.

Briony threw back her head and laughed. "Why, Michael, some of those photos are nearly twenty years old. I'm sure you've got photos in your shoe box you're unhappy with."

"This last shot is less than a year old," Kavanagh remarked, unable to conceal the note of triumph in his voice.

"Yes. Isn't it awful? And it was so cold and uncomfortable too. It was a publicity shot for some magazine," she lied, staring him straight in the face. She remembered that night clearly. Gabrielle and herself had done a couple of lines of coke and then cruised the night-clubs in downtown Los Angeles. She had ended up with an out of work actor who had spent the night peeling back the pages of her dress with his teeth. Towards the end of the evening he had vomited down the front of his five hundred dollar shirt and she had walked off in disgust. She had driven with Gabrielle out to the coast and they had made love in the car as the dawn came up behind them and bathed the Pacific in salmon and gold.

"Something you have to remember, Michael, is that writers provide entertainment. And some writers are great performers. Often the most successful writers are great entertainers, though they need not necessarily be good writers. I am not a great writer — nor have I any pretensions to be — but I am a good writer. And," — she pointed to the screen — "I am a good entertainer."

Kavanagh smiled fatuously. He had lost this round. She had manipulated the interview expertly, and he instinctively knew that she was turning the originally hostile audience to her side, appearing as a rather simple, unassuming, reasonable woman. However, he did have an ace up his sleeve. He looked toward the audience.

"Marcus Holland in the audience — Marcus Holland hosts the books programme on our sister channel. Marcus, have you a question for Briony?"

"Good evening, Miss Dalton." His smile was brittle, false. "Your books are not — and I hope you'll not be insulted if I say this — but your books are not very literary."

"I've just said that. They're not supposed to be." Briony was once again back on old ground. This was one of those questions she was almost guaranteed to be asked ... but if nothing else it proved that this Holland person was an amateur. Surely he could have thought of other questions, better questions. "My books are escapist literature, no more and no less. I don't want to be a prize-winning author and sell maybe ten or twenty thousand copies of a book. I want to be a popular author and sell a million or two million."

"But why do people buy your books if they're so bad," he persisted. "I put it to you that it is simply for the explicit sexual content. Your last book, *Pavane*, opens with a sex scene on page one, line one."

"My books are not bad, Mr Holland. The very fact that they sell in such vast quantities is perhaps some indication of their readability, though I will not say quality. I am — and I say this with no sense of false modesty — a very good storyteller. And to say that people buy my books simply for the sexual content is to insult the many millions of people who have bought them world-wide and the many thousands of people here in Ireland who buy my books and push them to number one on the best-seller lists. And, yes, *Pavane* may open with a sex scene, as you so delicately put it, but the next sex scene isn't for another hundred pages."

Realising that Holland was losing the encounter, Kavanagh quickly moved on. "Father Lynch, you have a question?"

The huge bulky man ran his hand back through his wild hair and leaned forward in his seat, impaling Briony with his peculiarly colourless eyes. "Do you call yourself a Christian, Mrs Moriarty."

Briony took a deep breath before answering. Father Patrick Lynch was a dangerous opponent, and they had clashed once publicly many years ago. She had lost that encounter; she was determined not to lose this one. "I was born and raised a Catholic, Father Lynch, and while I no longer follow the Catholic faith I would call myself a Christian. And might I add, Father, I stopped being Mrs Moriarty some years ago." At the back of the audience she saw Niall Moriarty stirring himself.

"The Catholic Church in Ireland does not recognise your divorce," the priest thundered.

"The state does. But we are here to discuss my work, Father, and not my marital status."

The priest smiled, a curious curling of the lips, and nodded slightly. "You profess to being a … Christian then. But surely one who follows the Christian ways would live a Christian life and attest to Christian values. Yet your lifestyle is most assuredly not that of a Christian. Your life-style reeks of Sodom, and your books are cesspits of immorality and vice … " His voice, which had been rising, had now reached pulpit proportions. "You preach corruption, you indoctrinate your readers with the pleasures of the flesh, proclaim the thrills of drug-taking, and show that cunning and thievery are acceptable. You are a symbol of all that is rotten in society!"

There was a momentary silence following the priest's thunderous declamation, and then someone to one side of the audience began to clap. A desultory round of applause followed, though Briony could see that some of the other clerics took no part in it.

"I believe the Father is perhaps over-dramatising the situation," Briony said coolly, meeting the priest's gaze. "My novels are essentially about hope. Good always triumphs. Always. And to recognise the good that exists in our society, we must first appreciate the evil. My books are not like some of the modern novels where the anti-hero is the principal character. In every case in my books the villain receives his come-uppance. I firmly believe that this is another of the factors which has made my novels so successful: they are essentially optimistic books. An American reviewer once likened one to a James Bond movie: a lot of flash, a lot of sex, a lot of violence, a real villain, but in the end the hero gets the girl and saves the day. In my books the hero or the heroine succeeds."

"You advocate drug-taking and casual and often violent sex!" the priest snapped.

"You're making the mistake of confusing me with my characters. Never confuse the writer with the writing. That's rather like mistaking an actor for the role he's playing."

Marcus Holland leaned forward until his face was almost on a level with the priest's in the row in front of him. "A writer writes out of his or her own personal experience," he said quickly, his American accent suddenly obvious. "Have these been your experiences?"

Briony laughed delightedly. "But Mr Holland, how naive! A writer writes because he or she has a story to tell. Their experiences include all they have read or seen, not all they have done. I have never killed anyone, Mr Holland, and yet there are several killings in my books. I have never handled a gun and yet they appear in my novels. I have never flown a plane, and yet one of my heroines pilots a 747." She paused and then added, "For someone who has his own television show devoted to books you are remarkably stupid, Mr Holland."

There was an audible intake of breath and everyone in the audience turned to look at Marcus Holland. Seated beside Briony Dalton, Michael Kavanagh ground his teeth in frustration. He knew what the bitch was doing. He had done it often himself; she had shifted the emphasis away from herself. And no matter what reply Holland gave he was going to end up looking a fool.

"Why ... why ... how ... how dare you!" Holland stuttered.

"Why, Mr Holland, I dare because I have written twenty-five novels. That gives me the right to make a statement about writing and writers. You told me that you have written — what? — two non-fiction books. That doesn't make you a writer, Mr Holland. When you have written twenty-five novels, or fifteen novels, or even five, then you can come and talk to me about my writing. And perhaps I'll listen. And Father Lynch, when you have read even one of my books — and not just dipped into them for the juicy bits — then I'll listen to you!"

"BITCH! THIEVING BITCH!"

The audience turned as one to look at the lurching figure who had appeared at the back of the studio. The seats were tiered and the back row was much higher than the front. Niall Moriarty stood on the top step, squinting uncertainly at Briony Dalton. Neither Marcus Holland nor Michael Kavanagh were surprised. Neither was Briony.

"You stole my book!" Moriarty stumbled down half a dozen steps to stand in the middle of the audience. Camera one moved in for a close-up of his sweating, haggard face and his purple nose. "You stole my book."

"Ladies and gentlemen, I believe this gentleman is Niall Moriarty, Briony Dalton's ex-husband," Kavanagh said eagerly. "Mr Moriarty," he said, not looking at Briony, "are you suggesting that Miss Dalton stole some of your work?"

"Fucking right she did. Stole all my work."

Almost relieved that Moriarty was drunk, Briony rounded on Kavanagh. This time she deliberately allowed her anger to show, but it was carefully controlled, cold and harsh. "Mr Kavanagh, I am surprised — and appalled — by this. I was assured this was a professional show and I consider such a trick worthy of the lowest of the commercial channels." She turned away and faced camera three, speaking directly into it. "My ex-husband was an alcoholic when I married him. I didn't know it then, but over the next hellish years I knew it. I began to write to support my young family because my husband would not and could not work with his sickness."

"Bitch stole my work," Moriarty mumbled drunkenly.

"Niall has always claimed that I stole his work, but such delusions are commonplace with alcoholics. I won't even try to defend myself from that remark, merely to point out that I have written and published many novels since I left him. Niall Moriarty has written and published nothing. And now, after such a shabby trick, I think it is time for me to leave."

Without another word, Briony Dalton stood up, wrenched off the microphone and walked off the set. The applause that exploded into the shocked silence was long and sustained.

Chapter Thirty

"The interview was an outstanding success," Terri Fierstein said to Gabrielle, transferring the call to the speaker on her desk. "I've seen the tape. Briony was cool, calm and collected. When Niall staggered on drunk I thought she was about to lose it, but she was good. It was a pleasure to watch her; it was like watching the old Briony Dalton in action."

"I'm delighted," Gabrielle Royer said. "I was a little apprehensive about it."

"Well so was I, but we had nothing to worry about. Obviously the little holiday she's having is doing her some good." Terri had conveniently forgotten that she had been set against the idea from the very beginning. "There was a great public reaction to the show; the press is off her back and most of the protesters have gone home."

"Most? Do you mean there are still some there?"

"A small hard core. A dozen, Briony said, lead by some fanatical priest called Lynch. She took him down a couple of pegs on the show and obviously this is his way of getting back at her."

"Is she getting any work done?" Gabrielle was sitting at the kitchen table in the apartment on the other side of New York, sorting through the huge pile of mail that had arrived in Briony's absence. Most of it was junk, but everything had to be looked at. Briony delighted in telling the story of how she had very nearly thrown out the first cheque she received for *Odalisk* when it had arrived with her royalty statement because she found the statement to be such incomprehensible rubbish.

"She tells me the work is moving along very nicely. She's achieving more than twice her target wordage every day, so obviously things are looking up. Yes, on reflection I think the holiday idea was superb."

Gabrielle smiled tightly, but said nothing. "Any further word on my own book?"

"I think I'm going to end up putting it to auction."

"Well that's good, isn't it?"

"There are advantages and disadvantages, both for the author and the book. An auction creates a hype that many a book doesn't live up to. If it goes for a high price — and I've no doubt that yours would — then that too creates its own type of pressures on the author and the publisher. Briony is the perfect example of that."

Carrying the portable phone, Gabrielle moved to the sink and began to fill the kettle, looking down across the green expanse of Central Park. Luminously clad joggers flickered through the trees. "How would it put pressures on the publisher?" she wondered.

"Take Park & Park, Briony's American publisher," Terri explained patiently. "They paid two and a half million dollars for the new book, sight unseen. Obviously they will recoup some of that money — or possibly even all of it — through the sale of some of the subsidiary rights, but it was still an enormous strain on their finances. Now Hall's, her English publishers, advanced her one million pounds sterling plus a guaranteed publicity package that is worth another three hundred thousand pounds. Money which I know they didn't have, money which they had to borrow. If Briony's book doesn't work, if she fails to deliver the manuscript, or if the book is late or delayed, or if public reaction is such that the book simply doesn't sell … well then not only will they go bankrupt, but there is also a good chance that Park & Park will also go belly-up."

Gabrielle shook her head in astonishment. "But how can one author decide the fate of an entire publishing house? That's ridiculous." At the back of her mind something clicked. "Are these not important publishers, big publishers?" she asked, turning off the tap, her gaze fixed on the trees opposite, their gentle movement in the breeze almost helping her to concentrate.

"Yes and no. A publisher's importance has nothing to do with size. There are certainly bigger and better publishers now, more successful, more aggressive. But these two — both American and British — are publishers of the old school, and they are particularly well connected. We chose them deliberately because of the opportunity it presented us to see Briony Dalton's name on the same list alongside some of the finest writers of the twentieth century. They both have excellent backlists of top quality authors."

"But you said they had had to borrow to buy Briony's book."

"That's correct."

"But what about this excellent backlist of top quality authors? Why aren't they exploiting those titles ..." She stopped and then added shrewdly. "Perhaps because they haven't the money to exploit them?"

There was a momentary hesitation, and then Terri said reluctantly, "No, they haven't the finances — not at the moment anyway. However, if Briony's book works for them it will give them the funding to begin reprinting some of their out-of-print list."

"Is there no other way they could raise the funds? Sell off some of their authors, something like that?"

"Both publishers are old school, both family-run businesses: that's not how they operate."

"I'm surprised you went to them," Gabrielle said. Something was bubbling up from her subconscious.

"It's true we could have got slightly more from some of the bigger organisations in terms of an advance and an advertising deal, but it was really the image we were after this time. We want to begin selling Briony Dalton as an up-market author with a broader market appeal."

Gabrielle knew shit when she heard it. Briony had no interest in her image; she was only interested in selling books. "Have you ever heard Josef Bach's name mentioned in connection with either of those publishers?" she asked abruptly.

There was a long pause at the other end of the line, and then Terri Fierstein said cautiously. "Be more specific."

"I can't." Gabrielle Royer wandered from the kitchen into the sitting room. She ran her fingers down the spines of the art books on Briony's shelves. "It was just something Mark Cosgrove, Catherine Garrett's boyfriend, said about Catherine selling herself to Bach. I immediately assumed it was Bach who had commissioned Garrett to write the biography. I've been racking my brains trying to come up with a sane reason for him to do so." She waited, expecting a comment, but Terri remained silent. "But now you've said that if *A Woman Scorned* doesn't work then two established publishers will go bankrupt. And it is common knowledge that Josef Bach has bought himself several of the newer publishers over the past few years, but he doesn't have any established authors on his list." She stopped, struggling to tie some of the threads together. "Do you think it's possible that Bach is deliberately attempting to sabotage Briony's attempt to write her book in an effort to bankrupt these two publishers and buy them up cheaply?"

Terri Fierstein laughed delightedly. "You should be writing fiction, my dear. I should think Josef Bach is so wealthy that he could afford to buy either publisher outright, or failing that buy a few top-selling authors for his own publishers. Preventing Briony from writing her book seems extremely far-fetched to say the least."

Having finally expressed the vague thoughts, Gabrielle had to admit they did sound crazy. "You're probably right," she said. "Anyway, I'm doing some further work on Briony's background. I'll be in touch soon."

"I'll keep in touch."

ଔ

Terri Fierstein turned off the speaker phone and picked up her private line. As she dialled the number from memory, she checked her watch. The phone was picked up at the other end, but there was silence broken by the hollow echoing static down the transatlantic line.

"New York," she said quietly.

"Good morning, New York." Josef Bach's voice came through strong and confident. "All is well, I trust?"

"The boyfriend of your tame writer mentioned your name; the girlfriend of my tame writer has made the connection. She's put two and two together and come up with a five."

"Who knows?"

"Just me."

"Not to worry. Be prepared to be surprised."

"I'm always prepared," Terri Fierstein said, but the line had gone dead. She looked at her watch again. The entire call had taken twenty-two seconds.

CB

Gabrielle Royer sat at the polished dining room table, the small Compaq computer before her. She had spent the last ten minutes typing her vague fears on to the screen and had been about to turn off the machine when another thought had struck her.

Who had done the deal for Briony?

Terri Fierstein.

Who had made her sign with — in both cases — small family-run firms, both with strong backlists of respectable authors and neither of them with the money to exploit those authors.

Terri Fierstein.

Furthermore, neither publisher was a "Briony Dalton" publisher: her material was mass-market, popular fiction. Prior to this her books had been published by popular mass-market publishers; why change now?

Maybe she was being paranoid, but as the pieces of the puzzle fell into place, it kept coming back to Terri Fierstein. Had Terri sold Briony out to Josef Bach? And if so, why? Terri had a lot of money tied up in Briony ... or at least she claimed she had. Gabrielle shook her head. She couldn't comprehend it; it didn't make sense.

But should she tell Briony?

Would it be fair to tell her?

Would it be fair not to?

Gabrielle sipped some of the Earl Grey tea she had prepared, grimacing when she discovered it had gone cold. She opened a new file on the computer:

Dearest Briony,

I know this is probably not the time to bring this to your attention. But I have discovered — I think! — the person behind the recent campaign to discredit you. I have listed out some points below which you might consider. Perhaps I'm being crazy: New York does that to you anyway, but I'm not so sure this idea is all that crazy, or at least it's about as crazy as what's been happening to you over the past few days ...

Gabrielle went through the points one by one. Fifteen minutes later, when she was finished, she read through the letter and was surprised to find it actually made sense. It had its own crazy logic, and the facts fitted. But she would let Briony decide. She saved the letter on the machine and then copied it to disc. She decided against e-mailing the message, believing this way more secure. Better still, the would walk over to the Fedex office a couple of blocks away and courier the package to Dublin. She could pick up some salads from the deli on the way back.

&

Josef Bach tapped out the New York number on his secure phone. Its number was unlisted and the buttons in the handset were completely blank, and only Bach knew which button activated which number.

The phone was picked up on the fourth ring and the voice that answered was carefully neutral.

"Yes?"

"I would like you to visit an old friend of mine," he said, speaking in German.

"When?"

"Immediately."

"Where is this friend?" the person on the other end said in English.

Bach gave Briony Dalton's address. "There is a sick young woman staying there. She would probably appreciate a visit from a Good Samaritan."

"How sick is this person?"

"Fatally ill," he muttered, and broke the connection.

ଔ

Workwise, Gabrielle decided, the day was a washout. She had found it impossible to concentrate on writing. Her thoughts were still buzzing around with the idea that Terri was somehow involved with Bach. She had attempted to phone Briony later that day but the phone had been engaged and finally, in an attempt to work off some of the energy surging through her, she had spent an hour in the compact gym that had been set up in the smaller bedroom.

When Gabrielle had first come to work for Briony the older woman had weighed 190 pounds and had taken to wearing long, shapeless dresses to hide her stomach and bottom. She blamed the fact that she was fat on her writer's lifestyle, but Gabrielle had persuaded her that proper exercise would actually help her diet, give her more energy which would allow her to write longer, and make her feel better about herself. After the gym was installed, and following a daily routine of exercise and diet, Briony Dalton weighed 126 pounds, seven pounds more than Gabrielle. Gabrielle had also convinced her to have minimal cosmetic surgery on her double chin, the bags under her eyes and the lines around her eyes and nose. When Briony said that Gabrielle made her feel like a new women — she meant it quite literally.

Gabrielle showered and changed into a comfortable cotton jogging outfit, and then started a light supper with the salads she had picked up earlier. She would shop for groceries tomorrow since it looked as though she was going to be here for another week or so at the very least.

She was sitting down to her tea with Briony's diaries spread out on the table before her when the doorbell chimed. She glanced at the clock: it was close to five. Crossing to the small table beside the door, she flicked on the monitor switch. A small six-square-inch, black-and-white image appeared, briefly whited out and then settled. A uniformed courier smiled at her, holding up an oblong package and a clipboard. He thumbed the speaker. "Recorded delivery. A package for Ms Briony Dalton from …" He consulted the clipboard, "From Park & Park, Publishers."

Gabrielle pressed the door release button. "Top floor, suite one."

Two minutes later there was a knock on the door.

"Hello," Gabrielle said brightly, opening the door.

The delivery man lifted the oblong package. "Goodbye," he murmured. He shot her in the throat with a silenced .22 pistol concealed in the package. The force of the blow punched her back into the room, blood spurting from the destroyed jugular. She was dead before she hit the ground. The delivery man calmly closed the door and then proceeded to ransack the room with methodical thoroughness. He took nothing, but gathered the two television sets, the video recorder, the laptop computer, the three radios and the stereo and piled them up in the centre of the floor. There were a few pieces of jewellery in the bedroom, and these he scattered along the hall.

Standing at the doorway, he looked critically at his handiwork, reading it the way the investigating officer would: there had been a burglary, the thieves were gathering their haul preparing to go when the woman had appeared. Maybe there had been a struggle or maybe she had screamed. They had panicked and shot her, and then fled, dropping the pieces of jewellery on the floor as they left.

This was New York. It was a violent city.

Chapter Thirty-One

The telephone awoke Briony from a deep and dreamless sleep. As she reached for the phone she squinted at the glowing red figures on the digital alarm clock: it read 3:10.

"Yes?" she croaked. "Yes," she said again, her voice stronger this time.

"Briony. It's Terri."

Some vague premonition brought her fully awake. It was ten o'clock, Saturday night, in New York. "What's the matter?"

"You'd better sit down."

"I'm in bed. What's wrong? What's happened?" she demanded.

"Briony," Terri whispered, her voice hissing and sibilant on the line, "I hate having to do this over the phone, but I wanted it to come from me …"

"For Christ's sake, Terri … !

"Gabrielle's dead."

In the long silence that followed the transatlantic line was almost unnaturally clear.

"Gabrielle's dead," Terri repeated. "I'm sorry, Briony. Terribly sorry. I don't know what to say … I don't … " Her voice cracked and she stopped.

"What happened?" Briony asked. There was a noise in her ears, a distant rushing sound, and she was suddenly acutely conscious of herself and her surroundings, the texture of the bedclothes, the faintly stale smell of her own body, the perfume of the flowers on the other side of the room. Her heart began to pound with sudden and ever-increasing speed.

"It looks like she walked in on a burglary in your apartment. All your stuff was in the centre of the floor. She must have screamed or something and they shot her and then fled. Old Mr Peck in the next apartment discovered your door open and peered inside. When he saw Gabrielle's body he called the police. They didn't know where to find you, so they contacted me. I identified the body." There was a long pause and then she said, "Briony ... Briony ... are you still there?"

"Yes, yes, I'm still here. I'll phone you later," she said and hung up.

Briony Dalton lay back on the pillow, arms folded tightly across her body. She felt cold ... cold ... cold and suddenly very afraid. She tried to rationalise her fears and couldn't.

Gabrielle.

Dead.

Gabrielle dead.

So final.

Without closing her eyes she could picture the young woman — young enough to be her daughter — remembering the joy she had brought her. Gabrielle had taught her so many things, but principally she had taught her how to enjoy life to its fullest. When Gabrielle had joined her she had had a desperately poor self-image. She had allowed herself to go to seed, she was overweight, her hair was a mess and she wore shabby shapeless clothes. Gabrielle had changed all that. She had taught her how to respect her body, how to treat it properly. She had weaned her off candy and sugar-laden soft drinks, had taught her the value and joy of exercise. And when she had lost weight and her careworn, rather tired-looking face had been wiped clean with the aid of the cosmetic surgeon's knife, the two women had gone shopping together. Gabrielle had bought her her first pair of silk knickers, convinced her that she didn't need a bra, showed her how comfortable leather could be, how sensuous it felt against the skin. There had been twenty years between the two women, but Gabrielle had erased that gap. Gabrielle had taught her how to be young again. Gabrielle had taught her how to love again.

The first time they had made love had been a revelation, a joy. Briony often said it was one of the most memorable nights of her life. And it was true. It was a memory which she drew upon again and again. It had been so long since she had felt another naked body beside hers, so long since she had been kissed with real passion, so long since she had been so aroused, since she had given herself so freely. And in truth, she realised in that single night, she had never been fully, totally aroused, never received any real pleasure from her husband nor from any of her occasional lovers.

Briony Dalton lay in the bed, her eyes sparkling with unshed tears. Gabrielle Royer had given her so much, but what had she given her in return? The young woman had been so self-contained, so self-confident that she needed nothing. Briony had paid her well — very well indeed — but she had never seemed to need money. She had accompanied Briony everywhere, travelling all over the world with her. Briony had bought her clothes and jewellery, but in truth Gabrielle had never really seemed interested in them. She had accepted them graciously, but Briony had guessed that she would have been equally happy if they hadn't been there. Briony recalled the time she had asked her what she got out of their relationship, and Gabrielle's reply had been the single word, "You." If there had been an ulterior motive in her relationship with the older woman, Briony had never discovered it.

The dawn was grey and gritty on the bedroom window when Briony Dalton decided that she wasn't going to get any sleep. She showered and dressed and then sat in front of her portable computer. She turned it on, looking at the screen for ten minutes before turning it off again. She closed her eyes and sat back into the chair, her thoughts, her emotions confused, upset, turned around. She felt numb. It was shock, she rationalised, but she still thought she should be feeling something: they had been lovers for

Christ's sake. Surely she should be feeling something more?

She was still sitting at the desk when her breakfast arrived at seven thirty. She asked the waiter to leave it on the side table and to place the Do Not Disturb notice on the door as he left.

At twelve noon the breakfast was still sitting untouched when the phone rang. Briony snatched it up, thinking it might be Terri, but instead it turned out to be the hotel porter. "I am sorry for disturbing you, Ms Dalton, but a letter has just arrived by courier service from New York. It is marked urgent."

"Thank you. Please send it right up."

Briony recognised Gabrielle's handwriting immediately. She grabbed the padded envelope from the bellboy and closed the door in his surprised face. Leaning back against the door, she pressed the envelope to her breasts and the tears came then. Slowly, as the racking sobs shook her body, she folded to the floor crying like a child, her knees drawn up to her chest, face resting on her knees, arms wrapped around her legs.

It was later when she came to her senses. The past two hours had gone by in something like a dream, where fragments, images, torn scraps of memory had drifted by like pages from a book. Some she clung to, examining them over and over again, others she let slip away.

On some conscious level she realised what was happening; her unconscious mind was beginning the process that most bereaved people go through, stripping away a layer of memory. The sense of immediacy was being removed, a buffer being inserted between what had been and what might have been. Memories would now never be the same, they would always be tainted, coloured, altered as the unconscious mind sought to protect the bereaved from too much pain.

When Briony Dalton stood up later that afternoon her crying was done. She would weep again, she knew, but it would be more by way of regret than anything else; she didn't think she would weep again with the same passion. The hurt would be there, and she knew it would be there for a long time — after all, they had been closer than most married couples — but it would lessen. The wound would heal, but the scar would always remain.

Carrying the padded envelope to the desk, she sat down and looked at the handwriting, tracing its firm decisive lines — so like Gabby herself — with her fingertip. Finally she tore it open and a computer disc dropped out. Briony parted the envelope, looking inside, but there was nothing else.

She pulled her laptop computer closer and turned it on. It was quite slow to power up, but she found herself tapping her fingers impatiently while it went through its memory test and then scrolled through the files. Briony slipped the disc into the disc drive. There was only one file on it, simply marked LETTER.

Opening the file which, she guessed, must have been written only hours before Gabby's death — had she had some sort of premonition? she wondered briefly — Briony began to read through the text.

Dearest Briony,

I know this is probably not the time to bring this to your attention. But I have discovered — I think! — the person behind the recent campaign to discredit you. I have listed out some points below which you might consider. Perhaps I'm being crazy: New York does that to you anyway, but I'm not so sure this idea is all that crazy, or at least it's about as crazy as what's been happening to you over the past few days ...

1. I met Catherine Garrett: I wanted to see if she would shed any light on your background, and the children's background. She didn't really, but during an argument with her boyfriend he mentioned the name of Josef Bach.

2. *From talking to Terri Fierstein, reading between the lines, Josef Bach has been on the look-out to buy an up-market publishing company with a strong backlist of titles.*

3. *Both Hall's and Park & Park have fine lists he could exploit, and give him credibility.*

4. *Neither company is the type normally associated with a Briony Dalton title.*

5. *Both companies over-extended themselves in their advances and publicity promises to you. Both companies borrowed heavily to finance the deal and if you fail to deliver, or if your book fails to sell, then there is a very good possibility that both companies would go to the wall. They could then be purchased relatively cheaply.*

6. *Terri Fierstein steered you in the direction of these companies and did the deals with them, bypassing better offers from publishers more suited to your titles.*

7. *Someone was orchestrating the press campaign against you: someone with money and information about you, someone who knew you were in Ireland, and, more importantly, where you were in Ireland, someone who had access to unpublished material.*

I sort of spoke to Terri about some of this, but she dismissed it out of hand — but then she would, wouldn't she, if she was involved? Maybe you might ask her yourself why she chose Hall's and Park & Park, instead of one of the big boys.

Now maybe I'm making much of little, in fact I probably am, but I just thought you should know. Call me a fool. But think: what if I'm right? What do we do if I'm right? What can we do against such people?

Anyway, I just had to tell you, it's been driving me crazy all day. I'll express courier this to you now and I'll speak to you tomorrow or the day after and we can discuss it.

All my love,
Gabrielle.

Perhaps if Gabrielle had been alive, Briony would have been inclined to dismiss it. Like most extraordinarily intelligent people, she could draw seemingly limitless conclusions from the most abstract of clues, making much out of nothing.

And yet … and yet … and yet it did have its own crazy internal logic, and what was it Sherlock Holmes said? When you have eliminated the impossible, whatever remains, no matter how improbable, must be the truth.

Briony shook her head savagely. It was crazy to even consider it. What would a multi-billionaire want with a piddling little publishing company like Hall's … but if Hall's was such a piddling little publishing company, what was she doing writing a million pound book for it? And if Hall's was such a piddling company why did Terri practically force her to sign the contract. She remembered now that she had had to ask Terri what they had previously published. But all the major publishers like Warner Books, Macmillan, Penguin and Grafton had been interested in picking up the British rights. Why hadn't it gone to them? And what about Park & Park, her American publishers, who'd given her a two and half million dollar advance, the highest advance ever paid for a single novel? What other big-money book had they published before hers? She'd turned down Tor, Simon & Schuster, Ballantine, Bantam and Random House — all of whom had been interested in *A Woman Scorned*.

Briony read through Gabrielle's letter again. What if there was a grain of truth in it — just a single grain? Then she'd been sold out from the moment she signed that contract in Terri Fierstein's presence eighteen months ago. She leaned back in the chair and closed her eyes, massaging her temples. Was she only imagining it or had there been a sudden flurry of parties and appearances in the months after the signing?

She knew — better than anyone — that her work had been slipping. The stories were no longer coming as easily as they once had, and the sheer physical process of sitting down and writing them had become boring. All the joy had gone out of it. But certainly in the first few months after she had signed for *A Woman Scorned* there had been intense publicity. *Time* magazine had carried a feature on her titled 'The Most Expensive Quarter of A Million Words Ever Written', relating to the size of the book in proportion to the size of the advance. The publicity had generated its own momentum. She had been invited on countless radio and television shows, been interviewed for just about every paper from *The New York Times* to *The National Enquirer*. There had been parties, luncheons, talks and seminars, and when that was done there was damn all time left for writing.

And all because someone had leaked the story of the huge advance.

Part of the deal was that there would be no publicity until the book was actually finished, and then the campaign could begin as the book went through the various editorial stages, so that by the time it was due to hit the shops, it would have generated a huge amount of publicity and word of mouth.

As it was, eighteen months had passed, there was still another six to run before the typescript was to be delivered, and then, although the book could be rushed through in three or four months, all the momentum that had been generated in the beginning was now dissipated. Her advance — while still a record — had been approached on a couple of occasions and very recently a completely unknown author had been paid one and a half million dollars for her first novel.

Briony had always suspected that Terri had leaked the news of the advance to boost her own position. Certainly, following the news, several of the biggest names in the writing business had started to use her as their agent, and having secured an advance of this calibre it gave her the clout to try it again. She had managed to pull off a couple of million dollar advances since then ... and take her usual fifteen percent off the top.

So ... had it been Terri?

When Briony had come to Ireland, someone had leaked that information to the press, but leaving aside Gabby and herself, the only person who had known where she was had been Terri … and Charley O'Neill, of course, and he was Terri's man.

It all came back to Terri.

Her immediate reaction was to phone New York and confront Terri. But supposing — just supposing — it was Terri and she was working with someone else … like Bach, then all she'd be doing would be warning them, letting them know that she was on to their game.

The phone rang, startling her. She had actually decided she wasn't going to answer it, when she impulsively picked it up. She went cold when she heard her agent's voice.

"Briony … it's Terri."

"Hello, Terri."

"How are you feeling?"

"Numb."

"Have you seen a doctor?"

"What for?"

"He might be able to prescribe something."

"No, What's the point? All you do is put off the realisation of what's happened until some later date. I'd rather face up to it now. Tell me what's been going on."

"Not a lot. I've contacted Gabrielle's family. They're flying in today to make the arrangements to ship her body back to Texas. They stress that it will be a family only funeral; I'm sure that particularly applied to you."

"Have the police any further information?"

"Briony, I think you should reconcile yourself to the fact that this is going to end up as just another New York police statistic. The crime will never be solved, unless by accident. These were street punks who were trying to rip off everything movable to sell for dope. I'm telling you this for your own good so you don't build up your hopes."

"I understand."

"Anyway, I phoned you because an NYPD detective, a Morell or a Morelli was looking for you. It's simply routine, I understand, since it happened in your apartment. He wanted to talk to you, and I gave him your number."

"That's fine, Terri," Briony said quickly. "When you last spoke to Gabrielle, how was she?"

"She was fine. In good humour, great humour. I told her I was going to put your biography up for auction — make her some big bucks."

"And that's all?"

"That's all. She was looking forward to forging ahead on the book."

I sort of spoke to Terri about some of this, but she dismissed it out of hand — but then she would, wouldn't she, if she was involved …

Briony read the sentence again as Terri prattled on. "What happens to Gabby's book now?" she asked.

"I don't know. I suppose I'll have a look around to see if I can find anyone to take it up. The advantage we had with Gabrielle was that she knew you so very well." She stopped. "Sorry. I didn't mean … " She sounded flustered. "I'll speak to you later."

Briony sat with the humming phone in her lap for a few moments before replacing it on the cradle. Why had Terri lied? Gabrielle said she had spoken to her about her fears, but why had Terri concealed it?

Unless she had something to hide.

The phone rang again.

"Hello?"

"Ms Dalton, Ms Briony Dalton?"

"Yes."

"This is Detective Andrew Morelli, NYPD. Your agent, Ms Terri Fierstein, gave me this number. I apologise for troubling you."

"She told me you would be phoning, Detective Morelli," Briony said, hardly interested.

"This is just a formality, ma'am. But since the deceased was found in your apartment we need to tie up a few ends."

"I understand."

"You have my condolences, ma'am. This must be a great shock for you." He had said the sentence so often, it sounded as flat and lifeless as the corpses he viewed daily.

"It hasn't really sunk in. What happened, Detective Morelli?"

"The way we see it, ma'am, at least one or possibly two perpetrators entered your apartment … "

"How?" she interrupted.

"Well, it looks like they had a key, because there are no marks on the door and it's a long way up by window. They ransacked the apartment, as is usual, and gathered together all the portable, saleable items in the centre of the floor. That's fairly standard practice. About then Miss Royer entered the apartment. We know she had gone out earlier to post a letter and to buy some groceries. Probably these guys were watching the place and figured she wouldn't be back for the rest of the night. She must have screamed, though none of the neighbours reported hearing a noise, so possibly she simply froze. They shot her. Just once, a single shot in the throat. She felt nothing. There were no other marks on her body," he added tactfully.

"Thank you, detective," Briony whispered, grateful for the courtesy.

"Can I ask you a few questions, ma'am?

"Please go ahead."

"What was your relationship to the deceased?"

"She was my secretary and personal assistant."

"And how long have you known her?"

"A year, give or take a few weeks."

"And you had a good relationship with her?"

"She was twenty years younger than me, detective; after a while I started treating her like a daughter."

"Then she was staying in your apartment with your permission?"

"Most assuredly."

"Had she any enemies that you know of?"

"None."

"Had she received any threatening letters or phone calls?"

"Not to my knowledge. She was a strong-willed, very intelligent woman, detective. I'm sure if she had she would have contacted me."

Should I tell him about Gabrielle's suspicions?

Why? What good would it do? You've not a shred of proof.

"Pardon me, detective?"

"I asked if Miss Royer had any boyfriends?"

"Gabrielle Royer was a lesbian, detective. I was her lover."

There was a pause and then the detective coughed. "Thank you for being so frank with me, ma'am. Could you tell me how long Miss Royer intended staying in New York?"

"A few days, no more. She was doing some research on a book for me. I suppose if she hadn't been there … this wouldn't have happened … " Her voice caught.

"Don't start thinking like that, ma'am. It was an accident, the wrong person in the wrong place at the wrong time. I don't believe it was premeditated in any way; maybe they fired at her to scare her away. We found some jewellery on the floor close to the door which they obviously dropped in their haste." He paused again, then added. "Will you be returning to New York for the funeral, ma'am?"

"The funeral will be in Austin, Texas."

"I thought the lady in question was French … Gabrielle Royer."

"Her mother is French, but her father is an Air Force colonel."

"I see." Paper rustled a continent away. "Well, we'll be doing everything in our power to catch these people."

"But you won't, will you?"

"I beg your pardon, ma'am."

"You won't catch them?"

"I'd hate to have to lie to you."

"I understand. Thank you for phoning." She hung up before he could ask her any more questions. She immediately dialled the desk. "Hold all further calls to my room please."

Briony began to shiver. Suddenly she was very frightened indeed. What if Gabrielle had been right and there was a conspiracy? Didn't that give her death far more sinister overtones?

And was she next?

Chapter Thirty-Two

Briony Dalton walked out of the hotel at six thirty that evening. She took with her only the clothes she was wearing, a small overnight bag and her laptop computer. She was carrying all the money she possessed, which came to around fifteen hundred in Irish pounds, two hundred Sterling, her American Express and Mastercharge cards. As she left the hotel she posted a letter to Terri Fierstein, telling her that she was taking a few days on the Continent. She also left a note for the hotel manager, saying more or less the same thing and asking him to keep the room for her.

She walked down Grafton street, heading for the quays. She had no real direction in mind. All she wanted to do now was get away. To find a place where no one knew her … a place where no one knew where she was. Perhaps she was becoming paranoid, but at the very least she felt she had some justification for it.

She swung around by Trinity College into Westmoreland Street and stopped outside a shipping office. She had thought about taking the boat to Britain; she wouldn't need to use her passport, and there were plenty of places she could hide out in … at least until she could think straight again or the situation had sorted itself out.

Her world was changing, the absolutes disappearing one by one: first Gabby, now Terri, whom she'd known and trusted implicitly for nearly fifteen years. What else could be taken away from her now?

On impulse she crossed the broad bridge and headed down to the quays. There was something she needed to do, something she'd been meaning to do for many, many years, but had always lacked the incentive, the need, the courage to attempt …

ଓଃ

The pub was long gone, overtaken in the development that had swept through this part of the quays. The small cobbled courtyard remained — although incongruously, having been ripped up twenty years previously and replaced with tarmac, the cobbles had only recently been replaced as a 'feature.' The tenements were gone too, replaced by town houses, one and two-bedroom houses costing more than a four-bedroomed house in the suburbs.

The atmosphere was gone too.

Briony remembered the warmth of the original courtyards, the constant hum and buzz of voices, the ever-present smells of food and humanity, washing hanging from the windows, dogs barking, children crying, laughing.

The courtyard was pretty, but cold and cheerless.

She walked to the corner where the pub had once stood, and then turned and looked around. The memories were still surprisingly vivid, some still extraordinarily bitter. She had lived over there with Niall in the first months of their marriage. Her father's pub had been almost directly opposite. The pub had gone, but her father had bought the small house that now stood partially on the site. It was one of the two-bedroomed houses and while Catherine's mother — Briony always thought of her step-mother as Catherine's mother — had been alive it had been gleaming, always freshly painted, the curtains stiff and starched, the pocket handkerchief of a garden always trimmed, the window boxes neat. But Brigid Dalton had died five years previously — neither Briony nor Catherine had attended the funeral — and now neglect showed in the once-pretty house.

The wrought iron gate was rusted, and squealed as she pushed it open. Although it was not yet seven this side of the square was in shadow and there was a light burning behind the drawn curtains in the sitting room.

Briony Dalton stood for a full five minutes before finally plucking up the courage to knock at her father's door.

The curtain twitched and from the corner of her eye she spotted someone peering out. Moments later the hall light snapped on and the flaking front door opened.

With the light behind the figure, it took her several moments before she could actually make out her father's features. He was sixty-five, but looked at least ten years older. Almost completely bald now, his eyes deep-sunk, his cheekbones prominent, his face was an expressionless mask as he looked at her. He was wearing a shapeless cardigan over ancient cords.

"Da?" she said, immediately slipping back into the Dublin expression. "It's me, Da. It's Briony ... Bernadette."

"I know who you are. What do you want?"

His abruptness stopped her cold. "I came to say hello," she whispered. "I wanted to know how you were."

"Why?" The old man's eyes blazed. "You left Ireland fifteen years ago. The first two or three years you sent me a Christmas card, and then there was nothing. I read about you in the papers, I saw you on television. I even went out and bought one of your books ... " He hawked and actually spat at Briony's feet. "That's when I discovered that my daughter had turned into a whore. A pornographer. I'm ashamed of you. You were ashamed of me, of what I was and what I did and where I came from. But I never sullied myself the way you did. You had a talent and you wasted it, pandering to people's basest animal tastes."

Briony started to shake her head, but her father pressed on.

"When people ask me if I'm Briony Dalton's father, I tell them no. I tell them my daughter Bernadette died years ago."

"Da … " There was a burning sensation at the back of her throat, and she found it hard to swallow.

"When poor Brigid died five years gone, you didn't bother your arse even coming to the funeral. A card wouldn't have killed you, a simple bouquet — anything. But no, you were too busy living your lifestyle, making a scandal of yourself. And what are you doing now? Living with some trollop young enough to be your own daughter. I haven't got the education to know what they're calling it these days, but I know it's unnatural and disgusting. You ought to be ashamed of yourself."

"If you'll just listen to me for a moment … "

"Why should I?" His voice was rising to a reedy shriek. "You're a liar, a professional liar, isn't that what you called yourself? But then you've no shame, you've no pride in yourself or your name. When I think of what you did to your children. You should have left them with Niall: he might be a drunkard and a waster, but at least he loved them. And that's more than you ever did!"

Mick Dalton stepped back into the hall and slammed the door in her face.

Briony Dalton turned away, a tight knot in the pit of her stomach that threatened to flood her throat with bile. What he said had hurt deeply … all the more so because it was true.

She walked back up along the quays, wondering what masochistic tendency had made her come here. What right had she to expect anything different from her father? What had she given him out of her success?

The answer to both questions was nothing.

She had lost Gabrielle and now she had finally accepted that she had lost her father.

What had she left?

Only her writing. . . and she wasn't even sure about that. If Terri had her way *A Woman Scorned* would never see print, and Briony Dalton would be finished as a writer.

She stopped suddenly, wind whipping dust into her eyes making them water. That wasn't going to happen. By Christ, she wasn't going to let it happen.

A Woman Scorned would be completed on time — even if she had to kill to do it!

Chapter
Thirty-Three

"She's gone."

Josef Bach swivelled in his high-backed leather chair and looked out across the London skyline. The early morning sun was attempting to burn through the mist and the horizon was grey with rain. It was eight thirty on a Monday morning and the city was at a standstill, the faint cacophony of angry horns barely audible behind the thick glass.

"Be more specific."

At the other end of the line, Marcus Holland shrugged. "O'Neill went to the hotel this morning — you heard about the girlfriend, didn't you?"

"I heard. Tragic."

"Well, I thought I'd find out how she was taking it. But she left last night. Checked out with two small bags. The room is still in her name, though, and she's left most of her clothes, so obviously she'll be back."

"Where has she gone?"

"I haven't been able to find out yet."

"Find out."

"Yes, sir," Marcus Holland said, but he was speaking to a dead phone.

Josef Bach ran his large hands through his snow-white hair. He nodded, his bright blue eyes crinkling in a smile: taking out the girlfriend had been the right decision. The girlfriend's death had been the final straw. The Dalton woman was running. She would never finish the book now.

But …

Josef Bach didn't like loose ends; didn't approve of stray pieces on his chessboard. He wanted to know where Briony Dalton was. Using his private, unmarked telephone he dialled New York, uncaring that it was five hours behind. It rang twenty-two times before it was finally picked up.

"Yes?" a voice whispered.

"Wake up and listen."

Sheets rustled, and when Terri Fierstein spoke again, she was in greater control of herself. "It's three thirty in the morning."

"Your client has gone missing," he said shortly, ignoring her.

"What? What do you mean — missing?"

"She checked out of the hotel last night. Where has she gone?"

"How should … ? I don't know," she said crisply. Bach could hear her breathing deeply in an effort to keep calm. But while she was off-balance, he was in control.

"Find out where she's gone."

"I'll try."

"Don't try. Just do it. There is much at stake here — for both of us, but for you especially." He hung up. He always believed in having the last word in a conversation.

Bach phoned Dublin. It was picked up on the first ring.

"Marcus Holland."

"I think you should take this down," Bach said slowly and distinctly. Holland, recognising the voice, scrabbled for pen and paper.

"An unconfirmed source has indicated that Gabrielle Royer was the innocent victim of an assassination attempt on best selling author, Briony Dalton," Bach continued. "A fundamentalist Christian group opposed to the explicit sex

and abuse of the clergy in her books has claimed
responsibility."

"Has it?" Holland gasped, already seeing the
possibilities of the story.

"It just has. It regrets the killing of the girlfriend,
although she deserved to die as the handmaiden of evil,
and furthermore this group has sworn it will not rest until
it has cleansed this world of Briony Dalton, the Devil's
author. This is an exclusive, use it properly!" he added as
he hung up.

Bach sat back into his chair and steepled his hands
before his face, smiling with genuine good humour. What
would Briony Dalton think when she read that in the
paper?

He picked up the phone: he had one final call to make.

ℭ

"Good morning, *Juffrouw*," the desk clerk said, turning the
red leather bound register to read the name. "Ah, *Juffrouw*
Garrett, we were expecting you. May we welcome you to
Amsterdam and the Amstel Hotel, and hope you enjoy
your stay here?" He reached behind for a key and lifted an
ivory coloured piece of paper. "There was a message for
you, *Juffrouw*."

Catherine followed the page carrying her suitcases past
the marbled statues to the lift, resisting the temptation to
read the note in the lobby. Her curiosity almost overcame
her in the lift, but two American tourists were watching
her intently and it was only as she stepped out of the lift on
the second floor that she realised they had spoken to her
and were obviously expecting an answer. Her room was at
the end of the corridor; it was large and airy and
overlooked *De Magere Brug* to the right. She tipped the
page and locked the door behind him before opening the
single sheet of paper.

Please contact your commissioning editor in London.

Catherine frowned. She didn't have a commissioning editor ... but on the other hand she supposed she did: Josef Bach had commissioned her to write Briony Dalton's biography. He more or less fitted that title. She picked up the phone beside the bed and then immediately put it down again. Better not to phone from the hotel where a record of the number would be kept.

She showered and changed quickly. She had an appointment at noon with a female reporter with NOS, the news channel, who had come strongly recommended by her contact with NTV. Catherine was hoping that with her knowledge of the red-light district and the drug scene in Amsterdam, the woman might be able to help her find Rianne Dalton. If her suppositions were correct, when she found Rianne, she would also find Matt. She checked her diary; she was meeting the reporter in an English pub called the Old Bell on the *Rembrandtsplein*.

She spent ten minutes in the local post office trying to work out the correct change to make the long-distance phone call. When she finally made the connection the line was crystal clear.

"This is Catherine Garrett, I received a message to phone."

At the other end of the line Kaho said crisply, "One moment please."

Josef Bach came on the phone seconds later. "Your stepsister has disappeared," he said without preamble. "She said she was going to the Continent, but that seems unlikely and, as far as we can determine, she didn't actually leave Ireland."

"But why? I thought the press was beginning to turn in her favour following her interview?"

"Her girlfriend was shot during a burglary in her New York apartment. She seems to have taken the news very much to heart. You know her better than anyone: if she was running away, whom would she run to?" Catherine watched the digital display of her money steadily disappearing as she considered. "There's her father," she said finally. "But I don't think she'd go back to him. They weren't on very good terms. He always wanted his daughter to be a writer, but he is a very religious man and he was deeply offended by the type of writing she did. The only other person I can think of is Terri Fierstein. She might know."

"She doesn't. Good luck with your researches." The line went dead.

Catherine replaced the phone and walked out into the bright morning sunshine. Something Bach had said nagged at her. She worried at it for a few moments, before it finally bubbled to the surface: she wondered how Josef Bach knew Terri Fierstein didn't know the whereabouts of Briony. Was there a connection there? Shrugging, she pulled the small map from her bag and wondered where the *Rembrandtsplein* was.

Although Catherine Garrett had never met Annemiek Schaar before, her colleague in NTV had described her perfectly and Catherine knew her the moment the woman stepped into the dim, cool interior of the Old Bell. She half-rose and raised a hand in greeting. The slender blonde woman squinted into the dimness and then deftly manoeuvred her way through the tables.

"Catherine Garrett?" Her English was almost perfect, the t's slightly clipped. When Catherine nodded, the woman extended her hand. "I am delighted to meet you." Her rather plain features brightened when she smiled, and Catherine noticed that her eyes were a bright, metallic grey.

"Thank you for agreeing to meet me," she said, "I do appreciate it."

"I'm delighted to be of help." Annemiek swivelled around in her chair and caught the barman's eye. *"Twee Bols, bevallen."* She turned back to Catherine. "You must drink Bols in Amsterdam; it would be like going to England and not drinking beer."

Catherine smiled. She didn't drink beer in England and hated the gin-like taste of Bols.

"Is this your first visit to Amsterdam?" the woman continued.

"Yes. It is one of those cities I always seem to be passing through or flying over."

"Where are you staying?"

"The Amstel Hotel."

"I know it. It's in the old part of Amsterdam. A delightful spot."

The Bols arrived and they toasted one another.

"Now." Annemiek sat forward, brushing strands of hair off her long, oval face with surprisingly blunt, stubby fingers. "Tell me how I can help you."

"I'm looking for someone," Catherine said, sipping the Bols and hiding her distaste.

"That's a politie — a police — job."

"The young lady in question has made her career in blue movies in the States. She's recently moved to Holland, and I would imagine she will attempt to continue in her chosen profession. It's a place to start."

Annemiek drank some Bols. "Any particular reason why she should have chosen Amsterdam? There are thriving adult movie studios in Germany and Italy."

"Her brother's living here. He's a junkie."

"Amsterdam is junkie heaven. You haven't given me a lot to work on."

"I have her name — both her real and working names — and I have a recent photograph."

"Well, that's some help anyway."

The two women finished their drinks in silence. Finally Catherine said, "You haven't asked me why I'm looking for this girl."

"None of my business, really, is it? It has to be work or research or something." She smiled slightly. "I started working with NOS as a researcher before finally progressing to reporter. I've covered just about every conceivable type of story: there's little that can shock me, or even surprise me now. Although," she added, "having said that, there's always something else, something new."

"But you'll help me look for the girl?"

"Of course. We'll start in the *Zee Dijk*, the red-light district, tonight. Do you think she might be turning tricks?"

"It's certainly possible, though I think it's more likely she'd be working in one of the strip clubs or adult bars."

"Has she a habit?"

"Not to my knowledge."

"Have you seen any of her porno movies?"

"Yes," Catherine murmured.

"Were they straight sex or was there anything kinky?"

"It was all men and women, or men and men and women and women, if that's what you mean."

Annemiek nodded. "No whips, bondage, masks, anything like that?"

"Not in the tape I saw. Why?"

"It just helps narrow it down a little. There are certain clubs which specialise in that type of entertainment, certain cinemas which show bondage movies, and the women who cater to that trade usually hang around outside. It doesn't make our task any harder, but it doesn't make it any easier either."

"Will we find her?"

"It's important, isn't it?" Annemiek said shrewdly. "This is more than business."

Catherine nodded. "It's more than business." She looked into the woman's pale grey eyes. "She's my niece."

Annemiek lowered her eyes. "We will find her. I know someone who might help."

The *Zee Dijk* — the long, narrow street that is Amsterdam's red-light district — is always crowded, but it really only begins to come alive as the light fades, like a slumbering animal grumbling in its sleep and turning over. And when night falls, the beast is wide awake and hungry.

Its very notoriety has made it a tourist attraction. On either side of the street, the women sit behind curtains of beads or gauze or sometimes no curtains, naked, semi-naked, or fully clad. There are sometimes red lights above the doors, or in the rooms, or on the table. Most of the women call out to the passers-by, but others remain silent, watchful, making eye contact with a particular person, enticing him in. Practice has enabled them to tell the casual watchers, the tourists, the rubber-neckers, from the genuine punters. All the women smile, some laugh, but their eyes are dead, completely humourless. Few take any pleasure from their work: for many of them it is precisely that ... just another job. Even with the profusion of venereal diseases and AIDS, there has been no falling off in the numbers of women and girls willing to work in the small windowed rooms or loiter in the street outside, though nowadays few work without first insisting that their clients use a condom. Many of the girls have stopped shooting up heroin, for customers are wary of girls with track marks. Nowadays they smoke the drug — chase the dragon — or inject it between their toes where it's not so noticeable.

With the right contacts and enough money, anything and everything is for sale on the *Zee Dijk*. Everything with a price, that is ... and everything has a price.

Catherine Garrett walked down the *Zee Dijk*, looking around her in absolute astonishment. The completely casual attitude to sex was almost exhilarating in its frankness. Although the porno movie houses and the sex shops were also present, there was none of the seediness she had found in Times Square or Soho. The pavement tiling was broken and Catherine had to watch her footing as she followed Annemiek Schaar along the crowded street. Occasionally Annemiek nodded to one of the working girls, or one of the doormen — usually Surinams or Mollucans, sometimes Turkish — would call out to her.

"You seem to know your way around here," Catherine said.

"We did a programme highlighting some of the problems of the street girls. One of our researchers actually posed as one of the girls and we filmed her over a one-month period. Naturally, we couldn't do that without the other girls knowing, but once we explained what we were doing — and why — they co-operated in every way possible. I got to know some of them very well."

"An interesting idea for a programme," Catherine remarked, looking around her.

Annemiek muttered something noncommittal in Dutch. Touching Catherine's arm, she led her off to the right and down a narrow alley. There was a doorway set into the left hand side of the unnamed alley and Annemiek tapped insistently on it.

"Ja?"

"Annemiek Schaar," she murmured, and turned to Catherine. "Whatever happens, whatever you see, say nothing, do nothing. Don't make judgements."

Catherine nodded.

The door opened and a coal-black face regarded the two women silently for a moment. Someone spoke rapidly from behind the door and the bouncer stepped to one side to allow them to enter. As Catherine walked in behind Annemiek, she looked behind her and found that the man had a twelve-inch bowie knife in his hand. He smiled at her, eyes and white teeth flashing as the knife disappeared into a sheath on his belt.

The man led them down a brightly lit corridor lined with countless thousands of postcards from all across the world. At the end of the corridor there was a metal door with no visible handle. He tapped once on it, said something so quickly that neither woman could hear him and then the door opened silently from within.

In the small dimly light room, a tiny wizened woman no taller than a child stood up to greet them; Annemiek made the introductions. "*Mevrouw*, this is Catherine Garrett, an English lady who is looking for her niece whom she believes may be in Amsterdam."

The tiny woman, her face a mass of deeply-etched wrinkles, her eyes like small black stones, regarded Catherine for a moment before extending her hand. Catherine took it in hers, shaking it slightly; it felt like old, dried parchment. The woman resumed her seat behind a much-battered desk in the centre of the floor. There was only a single seat facing the desk and Annemiek insisted that Catherine take it; she then took up a position behind and to Catherine's right.

Catherine glanced at Annemiek before turning back to the old woman. "*Mevrouw*," she said slowly, wondering if the woman spoke English, "*Mevrouw* — madam — I am looking for my niece. She is twenty-two years old, a wild girl, wilful. I know she made some pornographic movies in America and I believe she has come here. Annemiek said you might know where she was. Or even where I might start to look for her," she added with an attempt at a smile, but the old woman gave nothing back in return.

The woman extended her hand silently. Confused, wondering if she was looking for money, Catherine glanced back over her shoulder at Annemiek.

"A picture," *Mevrouw* snapped in perfect English, "do you have a picture?"

Catherine opened her bag and took out the photograph she had lifted from the video. It was one of those moments when the camera had closed in on Rianne's face, showing in graphic close-up her simulated ecstasy. Immediately afterwards however, there had been a couple of moments when she had simply looked at the camera, her expression blank. They had happened almost too quickly for the eye to see, but Catherine had run the sequence in slow motion, moving it a frame at a time, until she had captured the expression. She had then used a video-grabber to snatch the still image and print it up on a high-definition laser printer.

Mevrouw tilted the photo slightly, squinting at it. "This photograph, " she said finally, "is it old?"

"No, I have reason to believe that it is very recent."

"It is taken from a video," the old woman stated flatly. "Would it be too much to ask if you had the video with you?"

Catherine took a copy of the video from her bag. "Its called *Emergency Ward*. This is a copy so the quality may have suffered."

The old woman waved her tiny knotted hand. "No matter." Although — as far as Catherine could see — she had touched nothing nor pressed anything, the door opened and the man appeared. "Television and video," *Mevrouw* said imperiously.

The man nodded and vanished without a word. When he reappeared a few minutes later, he was pushing a wheeled trolley which held a large twenty-six-inch colour television with a small compact video on a shelf beneath. He plugged in both television and video and took the tape from *Mevrouw*'s tiny delicate fingers to slide it into the machine. He placed a remote control in her hands and then left the room.

The movie began. "Excellent quality," *Mevrouw* remarked. "You obviously took this from a first-generation copy. Cost a few guilder. American production values."

"That's her," Catherine said when the black-haired young woman in the nurse's uniform appeared.

Mevrouw said nothing, but she spent the next five minutes fast-forwarding through the first fifteen minutes of the film, stopping each time to concentrate on Rianne's face, her breasts and her hair. Finally, as yet another doctor was about to enter the Emergency Ward she lifted the remote control and, pointing it at the screen, froze it into immobility

"I believe I know the girl. Be at the entrance to the *Vondelpark* at noon tomorrow. Someone will contact you; they will return this tape as proof of their identity."

Annemiek nodded to Catherine and she stood up and backed towards the door. "Thank you," she said. "Than you very much."

As the door closed behind them, *Mevrouw* turned back to the screen and watched the action with increasing interest.

Chapter Thirty-Four

In the ten minutes they had been waiting at the entrance to the *Vondelpark*, Annemiek Schaar had pointed out four blatant drug buys and Catherine Garrett had seen for herself a young teenage couple helping each other to shoot up.

For some reason — possibly because it was so early in the week — Catherine had expected the place to be almost deserted, but both the park and the cobbled square facing it were thronged with scores of predominantly young people. Many of them were foreigners, and Catherine heard half a dozen European languages and dialects.

"They enjoy the freedom," Annemiek said. "Mostly the freedom to buy and use drugs. If they register as users they are given heroin substitute and clean needles. My television station has highlighted the problem on a number of occasions, and I got to know some of the junkies and pushers reasonably well."

Catherine nodded. "Good documentary material."

The Dutch reporter grimaced. "Frustrating, though. The habitual users have a relatively short life; just because they're here today doesn't necessarily mean they'll be here tomorrow. And even if they are here, there's no guarantee that they'll even remember you. Some of them don't even remember their own names."

At noon all the church bells across the city began to toll and chime, the sound remarkably quaint and incongruous in the otherwise bustling city. It reminded Catherine of Dublin where the bells sounded at twelve and six o'clock every day, reminding the Catholic faithful to pray. She was never conscious of hearing bells in London.

A denim-clad punk approached the two women. He was completely bald and had a skull tattooed over his face. There were numerous tiny rings and beads in his ears, and his jeans had been ripped and slashed to expose much of his skinny body and white legs. His lips were bright red. He stopped before the women, his eyes hard and sharp and desperate. There was a barely perceptible tremble in his finger tips as he raised a video cassette. "This mean anything to you?" he asked in a strong cockney accent.

"From *Mevrouw*," Annemiek said.

The punk smiled, exposing teeth filed to points. "That's right luv." He looked around nervously. "You're to follow me."

"Where?" Catherine asked.

He stared at her for a few seconds before shrugging, "The *Jordaan*," he muttered.

"It used to be a run-down district in the heart of Amsterdam," Annemiek said quietly, as the punk turned and walked away. "But it's been gradually redeveloped and turned around; lots of students have digs there."

The punk hurried ahead, moving with a peculiar hopping, skipping gait, constantly turning his head, sometimes walking backwards to watch the two women.

"He scares me," Catherine murmured.

"Don't worry about him. He's strung out, and we're coming up to fix time. He's probably been promised something when he takes us to our destination. I never have problems with the punks. It's the straight-looking guys that make me nervous." She lifted her hand out of her pocket and showed Catherine a slender black tube. "Mace," she said. "I have found it useful on occasion."

They walked down along the polluted canals deep into the heart of old Amsterdam. The streets were narrow and winding, uneven with cracks and broken paving. The noisy, bustling city gave way to relative silence as they moved into the *Jordaan* district. Occasional radios were playing, but the music sounded distant and although it was now close to twelve thirty in the afternoon, there were surprisingly few people about.

"Most of the students will be in college," Annemiek explained. "The rest are probably sleeping off whatever they drank, smoked, shot up or partied to the night before."

The punk stopped outside a three-storey redbrick building identical to countless others along the narrow street. He leaned back against the wall, one foot propped up against the stonework, nervously tapping his fingernails against the masonry, waiting until Catherine and Annemiek joined him. He handed them the photograph of Rianne Moriarty Catherine had given to *Mevrouw* the previous night. "Top floor, first door on the right at the top of the stairs. You never met me," he said.

"*Nee,*" Annemiek said, "we never met you."

"I was told you would give me one hundred guilders," he said licking his thin red lips, gazing from face to face.

Catherine produced the note and he smiled his thanks in a startling grimace, and then turned and darted down the street.

"In five minutes," Annemiek remarked, "he won't even know his own name."

As they stepped into the darkened hallways, they were both aware of the almost complete silence; no children cried, no radios blared; it was as if the building was empty. The house smelt stale, cooking odours lingering in the air vying with an acrid floral chemical scent which grew stronger as they climbed the narrow staircase. Annemiek lead the way and Catherine noticed that she carried the can of Mace in her hand now, her finger on the button.

The three doors at the top of the stairs were identical. Catherine experienced a momentary spasm of fear as Annemiek tapped lightly on the first. Would she find Rianne, was it this easy?

"*Wie daar?*" The voice was female, and the Dutch was laboured.

"*Een vriend,*" Annemiek said, glancing at Catherine.

"Wie?" The voice was now speaking from the other side of the door.

"Van Mevrouw," Annemiek said. From Madam.

A key turned and a heavy bolt was drawn back. The door rattled back on a safety chain — and Catherine found herself looking into the drawn and haggard face of Rianne Moriarty.

The two women stared at one another for several seconds and then Catherine swallowed hard and whispered, "Do you know me?"

"I know you," Rianne Moriarty said icily, "but I've nothing to say."

"Can I talk to you?"

"No." She went to shut the door, but Catherine stuck her foot in the opening. "I need to talk to you," she said.

"About what?" Rianne demanded belligerently.

Annemiek touched Catherine's forearm. "I'll be waiting down by the canal."

Catherine nodded gratefully and stood back while the Dutch woman squeezed past her and made her way down the narrow staircase. Catherine turned back to Rianne.

"Can I talk to you?" she asked again.

Rianne closed the door and slid back the chain. Catherine heard footsteps moving across a bare wooden floor, but the door didn't re-open. She placed the flat of her hand against the smooth wood and pushed. The door opened silently inwards.

The room was bright and airy, sunlight streaming in through the open windows and the skylight. With the exception of a bed, a sink and a single wooden chair, it was completely empty.

Catherine Garrett turned and closed the door behind her.

Rianne Moriarty was leaning back against the wall with her hands tucked into the pockets of her faded jeans. Her once long luxurious hair had been cropped short in an almost boyish cut. Her black eyes were sunk deep into her face and her cheekbones were prominent. Beneath the cut-off shirt that left her midriff bare, Catherine could see her ribs.

"Its good to see you," she began.

"Let's cut the shit — just what the fuck do you want?"

Taken aback by her vehemence, Catherine felt her anger beginning to bubble to the surface. "I've been looking for you."

"Why?"

Catherine shrugged. "I wanted to talk to you."

"Why now?"

"Maybe I got worried about you; maybe I fell to wondering what my niece and nephew were doing with their lives."

Rianne's eyes were dead in her face. "You don't want to know."

"Maybe I do know," Catherine said softly. She opened her bag and took out the video the punk had returned. She dropped it on the floor and kicked it across the room. It slithered to a stop at Rianne's battered Nike runners. "Maybe I do know," she repeated.

Rianne stooped and lifted the cassette, turning it around, frowning when she saw that there was no label.

"It's something called *Emergency Ward*," Catherine said.

Rianne nodded and tossed it on to the bed.

"I would like to talk to you," Catherine continued. "Maybe we could have a cup of coffee or something. Please," she added, "I've come a long way to find you."

"Yeah," Rianne sighed. She lifted a worn black leather jacket off the end of the bed and walked over to Catherine. Then suddenly — surprisingly — she kissed her on the cheek. "I'm sorry I was … well, you know. It was the shock of seeing you here. It's nice to see a friendly face for a change. God knows I need one."

When Annemiek Schaar had seen Catherine appear with Rianne, she had waved from the distance and wandered off, disappearing into the narrow warren of streets.

Catherine Garrett and Rianne Moriarty strolled down to a small canal-side cafe that served strong Brazilian coffee and tiny sugar pastries. They chose a table close to the canal in the shade of a dying elm and, as Catherine watched, Rianne swiftly ate four of the small cakes.

"When was the last time you ate?" she asked.

"Yesterday, the day before … I don't remember."

"Have you any money?"

Rianne grinned. "I'm stony broke at the moment."

"What do you do for money?"

Rianne's black eyes clouded. "This and that. I get by."

"Are you still making movies?"

Rianne shook her head.

"Why did you leave New York? You seemed to be well set up there."

Rianne shrugged. "The scene is changing; there's more openings for the adult cinema here on the Continent — or so I was told. I've discovered that girls like me — well, we're two a penny … the producers and directors are looking for someone who has a speciality, and I don't mean anything kinky either. Although there's a great market for that too."

"I saw the video. You're very good," Catherine said cautiously. How do you compliment a porno actress on her latest movie?

"It was OK. I enjoyed making it."

"You enjoyed it?" Catherine asked incredulously.

Rianne looked at her. "Yes. It was a good script, a professional crew, and a clean set — no dope, and all the cast had been given a clean bill of health before shooting started. We all had contracts and we were paid. You can't ask for much more than that." She leaned across the table. "It was a job, nothing more, nothing less. The pay was good, the hours were short, the cast was good-looking, and you didn't have to do anything really disgusting. Believe you me, *Emergency Ward* was one of my better movies. You should see some of the early ones!"

"You seem so casual about it."

"It was a job. It's not a particularly difficult way to earn a living."

"Then why throw it up to come here?"

"I told you."

"You didn't tell me the truth?"

Rianne drank her coffee. "Why do you want to know? Why are you even interested?"

"I am your aunt and we did keep in touch once. I thought it would be nice to renew that acquaintance."

"There's more to it than that," Rianne said. "If you've tracked me to New York and then followed me here, you have a very good reason for looking me up."

"I have," Catherine said shortly.

"I'd lay money my mother is involved in this somewhere."

"She is."

Rianne said nothing, but Catherine could actually see the younger woman's shoulders tense.

Catherine attempted a smile. "You know your mother and I are not on the friendliest of terms."

"I knew. So that hasn't changed?"

"It hasn't. She still hates me."

"And I suppose the feeling is mutual?"

Catherine ignored the remark. "I have been approached by a publisher and asked to write your mother's biography."

Rianne became interested suddenly. "Is that why you were looking for me?"

"Yes. I want to include a chapter on you and Matt — only with your permission, of course. I want to tell your stories. I want to show what effect her success has had on the course of your lives."

Rianne began to laugh. The laughter was high-pitched and far too fast, and it quickly dissolved into near hysteria. Catherine reached across and squeezed Rianne's hand so tightly that the sudden pain brought her back to reality.

"What effect her success has had on the course of my life," Rianne repeated mockingly. "Let me tell you what that bitch did to my life — and Matt's, too: she destroyed us. Now print that in your precious book!"

Chapter Thirty-Five

I was seven years old when *Odalisk* came out.

My mother had been writing that book since I was four years old. My brother was eleven. Maybe it was easier for him to understand what she was doing; maybe he was able to comprehend why she sat, day after day, night after night, tapping away on that Remington electric typewriter. God, I hated that typewriter. I could hear it tapping on into the night, sharp, snapping sounds like teeth clicking together that gave me nightmares. Even now the sound can chill me.

We were living in Dublin at this time, in a two-bedroomed house in Cabra, then a suburb of Dublin. We knew that our mother and father had lived in a two-roomed flat across from Granddad's pub, and she was always reminding us that we owed everything to her writing. The house, our clothing, even the food on the table … all of it was paid for by her writing. She was always reminding Dad about that, too, whenever he came home — which wasn't often anyway.

She wasn't a best-selling author then, but she churned out lots of rubbish, westerns, romances, science fiction, horror, even some pornography — although I didn't discover that until much later. She was getting a couple of hundred pounds a book, but she was writing maybe ten or twelve of these pot-boilers a year under a dozen different names, as well as her more legitimate stuff under her own name.

We did all right.

Whenever Dad came home, sometimes for days or weeks at a time, he worked too — odd jobs, this and that, whatever he could turn his hand to. But he so badly wanted to be a writer. And yet he never seemed to be able to make the time to write. Our mother had her times and her place; she wrote in what was called the front parlour, and that room was off-limits to us children and, in most cases, to Dad too.

Sometimes when we got up in the morning you'd hear her infernal typewriter clacking away, and often I fell asleep to the sound. I don't know what type of relationship she had with my father, but it must have been a peculiar one.

I have a vivid memory of seeing my father sitting at the kitchen table with a battered old Royal typewriter — our mother had a new machine — attempting to work on a story or an article while Matt and I listened to the radio or watched the television … and yet he never complained, never shouted or demanded silence.

I remember quite clearly one day sitting watching television singing along to a song when she screamed at me from the other room to *Shut Up*! My father was sitting beside me, but he'd said nothing.

As she was writing her rubbish, she was also working on *Odalisk* — this was to be her big book. Later I realised that it was very carefully tailored to the best-seller market. We saw little of her in the year or so preceding the publication since she was involved in an extraordinary publicity campaign.

I was too young to appreciate what was going on, but I know Matt took some stick at school because of this image she adopted — the vamp, a very blatant sexual image — and I know there were several arguments between my mother and father about her often outrageous public appearances.

When we were growing up, she was always a little apart from us; she was the woman in the sitting room writing stories, and those stories appeared in books, but she never wrote for children and therefore we never read any of her work. So when she started appearing regularly on television and in the newspapers, it was as if we were learning about our mother through that medium. Whatever images and impressions we formed, we formed through them.

Odalisk created a sensation; even as a seven-year-old I knew that. Suddenly we seemed to be getting loads of mail. Usually we got a letter or two a day, but shortly after the publication there were dozens and then hundreds of letters. They were all piled up on the kitchen table and the old metal bin we used for burning rubbish was brought in and put on a newspaper which had been placed on the floor beside the table. My mother would then go through the letters, dividing them up into various piles. Some of the letters went straight into the bin and, as time went on, more and more went into the bin. I remember peering over the edge of the bin one time and seeing that some of the letters had been made up by cutting out letters from newspapers and magazines; others were written in red ink or cut so deeply into the page that they had actually torn through the paper.

These letters were all burnt.

There were phone calls, too.

Most of them came late at night and seemed to last only as long as it took my mother to pick up the phone and put it down again. It became so bad at one stage that a second phone with an unlisted number was installed and the first phone was cut off.

There was some petty vandalism as well; paint daubed on the front of the house, excrement on the steps, slogans on the front gate.

It was about this time that our father left for good. He hadn't been home for weeks, and when he turned up he was filthy and reeking of drink. There was a terrible argument; lots of names were shouted and screamed and she finally threw him out of the house. Physically threw him out.

I was a child; I was seven-years-old. I didn't really understand what was going on and, with a child's natural acceptance of things, I didn't even look for explanations.

Matt did, though. And I'm convinced it was the craziness of that time which is responsible for his state today.

Matt explained it to me later. My mother's books had attacked and threatened all that the Irish Church and State stood for; they were pornographic, often graphically so, and they depicted members of the clergy — or at least people pretending to be priests and nuns — indulging in sexual acts. A lot of people felt threatened by her books; some people even felt they had appeared in them, though thinly disguised. Apparently there were even questions in the Dail, the Irish Parliament, about the books. People were demanding to know why they hadn't been banned and I think the first one was. This was Ireland in the 1960's remember — the Censorship Board still banned unsuitable books.

I don't know why the others weren't banned; perhaps it was felt that that would only give them a certain cult status. But even though they weren't banned, many of the smaller family-run bookshops refused to stock them.

The following year *Harem*, the sequel to *Odalisk* came out. The moment my mother had finished writing *Odalisk* she had gone straight on to the sequel. She had an agent by then, a horrible American woman, Terri Fierstein, and she had done a two-book deal with some English and American publisher … I don't remember who.

And whatever furore *Odalisk* had caused, it was as nothing compared to the outrage *Harem* generated. Years later I read the book, and even I was shocked by some of the scenes in it. It was as if my mother was deliberately writing to offend and cause outrage.

And she succeeded.

We left Ireland the same year, the same month *Harem* was published. I'm not sure if the pressure of living in Dublin finally got to her — I don't think so, I think she's a cold emotionless bitch — but she said she was going to London because that was where her publishers were and that was where the work was.

Money didn't seemed to be a problem in those days. I don't know what advance she got for *Odalisk* or *Harem*, but both books were number one best-sellers on both sides of the Atlantic, and I do know she received some sort of record-breaking advance when she sold four books which were eventually published in two big books called the *Season's Quartet: Spring & Summer, Autumn & Winter*. I haven't read all of them, but I know they were much more international than her first few books, again extremely erotic or pornographic depending on your point of view, violent, arrogant ... and nasty. They weren't nice books. But the money which she got for these gave her — and us — a great amount of financial security. We lived in a lovely house in Hemel Hempstead and suddenly I had friends who would talk to me, children who would play with me. Back in Dublin no one had allowed their children to mix with the Moriarty brats in case they were infected by their mother's ideals, I suppose.

I had friends. But I still had no mother.

I don't know what financial pressures were on her then; I don't think she needed the money. I'm sure she didn't, but she continued to work to her old routine. She was nearly always up before us, and although she now used one of the bedrooms as her study we would still hear tapping away long into the night. She appeared briefly at lunchtime, withdrawn and distant, not at all like the vibrant, animated woman who appeared on television. If the weather was fine she brought out a chair and small table and sat in the sun and wrote. But if she was in the garden, it meant that we couldn't play out there, and even though we now had a large house, we still had to be quiet. I remember one nanny was sacked because she played the radio too loudly.

A housekeeper looked after the day-to-day chores and a nanny looked after us. And that was fine because Matt and I had each other. With no one else to turn to for affection, we had turned to one another.

And then Matt was sent away to a private boarding school. One day he was with me, the next he was gone, and it was left to the current nanny to tell me where he'd gone to. My mother didn't tell me, she was working, too busy to speak to her own daughter, to tell her where her brother had gone.

Suddenly I was alone.

I was ten years old and desperately lonely. I had grown up in a house full of books and papers and I had learned to read at a very early age. I read to escape. I lost myself in a hundred different worlds where everything turned out right by the last chapter. The books taught me everything. They taught me about life and men and relationships. They taught me about sex.

I was reading fiction: I didn't know the lessons and values were false.

Matt ran away from school when he was fifteen. My mother flew into a towering rage … but only because her writing schedule was disturbed. He was picked up a few days later. He was caught stealing fruit from an orchard about eight miles from the school. He had been living rough, scavenging from the bins behind restaurants, stealing milk off doorsteps in the early morning.

He told me it was the happiest week of his life.

Two years later he ran away again. But, because he was still at the same school and they were keeping an eye on him, he was only gone a few hours before they noticed he was missing. The police picked him up the following day.

Again, my mother's writing schedule was disturbed as she had to travel down to the coast to plead that Matt be allowed to remain at the school. As it happened, he wasn't a disruptive influence: he was quiet, reserved, with few friends and, like me, a great reader.

So he was allowed to stay.

The following year, when he was eighteen, he ran away again. And this time he had put some planning into it. He was never caught.

Matt may have been the quiet one, but I wasn't. I was sent away to boarding school when I was twelve … this would have been in 1982. I was expelled the following year: one of the teachers cuffed me for talking in class. I waited until he had walked past me and then I broke a wooden ruler across the back of his head. It very nearly turned into an assault case, but I think my mother paid money to keep it quiet.

I was sent to another boarding school. This was much more interesting because it was mixed. It was a modern school, bright airy classrooms, young teachers, the best equipment. I liked it there, and that's where I had my first sexual experience, with one of the boys from the other dormitory. He was a year older than me but, because of all my reading, I had a much better idea of what to do. It was a funny, sad, encounter, not at all what my voracious reading had led me to expect.

I had my first sexual encounter with a girl then, too. She was much older than me, much more experienced, and she taught me an awful lot about my own body.

And then I was caught in the swimming pool with one of the boys. We had smoked a little grass and things had got out of hand, so we had skipped class, and gone skinny-dipping in the pool. When the headmistress found us we were hard at it.

We were both expelled, although I know he was eventually taken back: people obviously felt I had seduced him … which was perfectly true, of course!

I was then sent to a convent school in northern France. It was almost like a prison. The nearest village was twelve kilometres away, there were no boys … indeed the only other male we saw was the priest who came every Saturday evening to hear confession and then to say Mass on the Sunday morning. On one occasion, I remember making up the most lurid sexual adventure I could think of

— I actually borrowed it from *Harem* — and relating it to him. He listened without changing expression, gave me a moderate penance to say and that was that. Or so I thought. The following day I was taken out of class and brought to the Mother's Superior's office where I was told to sit. I sat there for four days and slept in a small room off the office which was locked at night. When I protested, she used a three foot long bamboo cane on the back of my hands. She never said anything, never gave me a reason … though the priest must have said something to her.

I spent three years in that school. As schools went, it wasn't so bad. It was very international and I learned to speak French — because we had to — but I also learned German, Spanish and some Italian from the other girls there. Like me they were rebels, and the nuns had their hands full keeping us in line.

In 1987 — I was seventeen then — I had had enough. I came home for the holidays and I was the dutiful, obedient daughter. I saw my mother twice that summer: the day I came home, and even then I had to make my own way from Heathrow because she was busy with her publishers, and the following day. She was going off on a country-wide publicity tour, which would also take in Ireland, and there were some American interviews tied up in the deal as well. She left me in the charge of a half-mad, totally deaf housekeeper.

I decided to go looking for Matt. He had written to me once when I was in the previous school giving me an address in Camden Town, and he said that if he was forced to move on he would leave a forwarding address there.

But I wasn't going to do what Matt had done: I wasn't going to leave with nothing.

My mother had left her cheque books and deposit books in the secret drawer of her dressing table. I practised her signature for days until I had it perfect — it was a fairly illegible scrawl, so it was easy to copy — and then I wrote myself some cheques. I made it out for odd sums, odd amounts, so as not to arouse the bank's suspicions, and I always lodged the cheques in my own account in any case, so there was never any question of the banks cashing a cheque for me. I even transferred some of the money directly from her account into mine. I didn't care: I intended to be long gone and far away before my mother found out.

Finally, in the last week of July, I began withdrawing the money I had taken. Again, I took it out in small amounts and at the end of two weeks I had a little over nineteen thousand pounds in cash.

And then I left.

It was only later that I learned what had happened. The housekeeper reported me missing to the police and the police contacted my mother. She had been doing her usual trick, stirring it up all across the country, so there was some speculation that I might have been snatched as a lesson to her, or held for ransom.

Of course it was great publicity.

I went to London to the last address I had for Matt. It was a squat in Camden Town. He was no longer there but one of the guys said he had gone to Amsterdam looking for casual labour. So I followed him. I figured he'd stay close to the British and Irish crowd, so I started to hang around the cafés and restaurants and the parks they hung out in. Finally, just when I was beginning to give it up, I met a girl who'd lived with him briefly. She was a junkie, and from what she said I more or less guessed that he was starting to use then. She said he'd gone to Germany looking for work, so I went there. I tried the same trick of hanging out in the bars where the Irish guys hung out, and then I started following the junkies, seeing where they scored, trying to make contact that way.

I never did find him.

I was beginning to have money problems about then. Nineteen thousand pounds sounds like a lot of money, but I wasn't exactly slumming it. And I was buying drinks for the people I met, trying to get some information.

It took me six months to spend it all. I suddenly found myself in Berlin in January — and I think it must be one of the coldest cities in the world in winter — with no money and nowhere to go.

I was sitting in a pub one night, nursing a drink, trying to make it last because I had no money to buy another one, when a young guy sat down beside me. He was French, though he spoke perfect English. We got talking and he bought me a drink, and then we had another drink and went for a meal — it was only a takeaway, but it tasted like heaven. I went back to his flat with him and stayed the night. He didn't offer to pay, and I didn't ask; I figured he'd already paid.

I told him I had run out of money and was growing desperate because I had to get back to London to my poor sick mother. He told me he had a friend who was looking for models ... well, I had nothing to lose.

So I started modelling. There were nude shots, fairly raunchy stuff, too, for some of the German and Swedish mags. I graduated from singles to couples, sometimes another girl, often another guy or two guys. It was funny; it was so artificial, so cold, so passionless. We were there to do a job; we got paid, we went home. It was easy money.

The next step was into movies. I made a few — straight stuff, nothing kinky — and I discovered that was easy too. It's a crazy, crazy world where you start with the male climax — the money shot, it's called — and then work backwards. I suppose I found it easy because I wasn't using drugs and to me it was a job, nothing more, nothing less. I didn't hang around on the set after my takes, I didn't hang out with any of the other actors or actresses.

Then things started getting a little heavy. I was reading scripts that were getting too weird for my liking. I had a bit of money saved by then, so I went to the States. I had heard of Cutting Edge, seen a few of their movies, and knew of Bernie Cutter through the trade. He had a good reputation, so I decided to take the gamble and go to New York. He'd seen a few of my movies and had been impressed. He was even more impressed when he discovered I didn't use. It was one of his rules; he insisted that none of his boys or girls were users and he also insisted on regular health checks. He looked after his people. Before he took me on I had probably one of the most extensive medical check-ups I've ever undergone. When I passed that, I found I was working for Cutting Edge Movies.

I was happy there. I was well looked after, well paid, the scripts were good and there was nothing kinky in any of the movies ... oh, a bit of bondage maybe, a lot of lesbian action, two men, one girl, or two girls one man, that sort of stuff, but nothing rough.

And then ... and then I got this postcard from Amsterdam.

It was from Matt. He had seen me in a Cutting Edge movie and had written to me care of the studio. And you know, for the first time in my life I felt embarrassed about doing porno movies. The fact that my brother had seen me doing whatever I had been doing ... it gave me a strange, eerie feeling.

We began to correspond regularly. He told me a lot about his life on the road, living rough, using drugs, petty crime, sometimes more serious crime.

And then a couple of weeks ago I got a postcard from him. It just said, *The worst possible news.* He didn't ask me to come, but I knew he needed me. I think even before I met him, I knew what was wrong.

Matt is dying of AIDS.

Chapter Thirty-Six

Scrubbed of all make-up, her hair uncombed, Briony Dalton stayed in an anonymous bed and breakfast in Dun Laoghaire that Sunday night and took the first ferry on the Monday morning to Holyhead. The ferry was packed with holiday-makers and day-trippers to England and she felt safe amongst the numbers.

Perhaps Gabrielle's death had been a tragic accident, but her writer's imagination, used to weaving plots from the flimsiest of threads, drew up a dozen different scenarios of conspiracy and betrayal. When all this was over she was going to write a book about it, she decided. She found herself closely scrutinising the people around her, wondering if any of them was paying her special attention, and she spent most of the trip wandering from deck to deck, attempting to determine if she was being followed.

She was exhausted by the time the ferry docked in Holyhead, but she forced herself to remain awake on the long train journey down to London. She changed from the mainline train to the tube at the first opportunity and then changed tube trains twice more, her exhaustion now adding to her paranoia. When she finally reached the apartment she had bought five years previously she stood for nearly an hour in a phone box across the street watching it. She had only used the apartment when she was forced to stay overnight in London and wanted a place to hide away from the press. Maybe half a dozen people were aware of its existence, and the apartment was registered under the name of Mrs Moriarty.

When she was satisfied that the place wasn't being watched, she used the entrance through the underground garage at the back of the block of apartments. The four-storey late-seventies development was absolutely silent and she met no one as she hurried up the back stairs to her apartment on the second floor. In the few times she had stayed in the place, she had only caught glimpses of her neighbours, and she guessed that many of them, like herself, were using the place as a discreet *pied-à-terre*.

Briony turned the key and pushed the door open.

The apartment smelt musty and close and the blinds were drawn, leaving the sitting room in a hazy twilight. If she was writing this as a piece of fiction, she'd position the attacker in the corner or behind the door …

Taking a deep breath she stepped inside and pushed the door closed behind her. With her heart pounding painfully, she stood with her back to the door, allowing her eyes to adjust, unwilling to turn on the light because the sitting room faced the street. The curtains in her bedroom were open and, staying low and out of the line of the window, she packed a light suitcase with everything she thought she might possibly need from the few bits of clothing she had left in the apartment. She retrieved her spare passport which was in her maiden name, Bernadette Dalton, which she'd wrapped in a plastic bag and buried beneath a hideously spined cactus.

Sitting on the floor below the window, she phoned Heathrow and made her reservation using her American Express card. It was three o'clock. She had booked first class and didn't intend to check in until practically the last moment, so she still had two hours to kill before she started for the airport. She made herself a cup of instant black coffee and then sat beside the window, peering out through the blinds, looking down into the street, desperately attempting to stay awake. She had to be on that flight.

She spotted the car the third time around. It was a deep blue Ford Sierra with distinctive fog lamps mounted on the front. As it drove down the quiet street, it slowed as it passed her building … and then Briony Dalton noticed that the driver did not look in her direction, but rather into the deeply shadowed doorway opposite.

There was a leather and brass-bound naval telescope hanging as an ornament on the wall above the fireplace. Briony unhooked the long tube and pulled it out to its full length and then, moving well back from the window, attempted to focus on the doorway opposite. The glass was murky, slightly distorted, but it was enough for her to make out the shape of a man standing deep in the shadows. A match flared, illuminating a ghostly face for a few moments, and then the light died to a single glowing red ember as he pulled on a cigarette.

Briony Dalton sat back and began to shiver; what she had only imagined before had turned into some sort of reality: she was being watched.

Her first reaction was to flee, grab her small suitcase and go, but that would leave her at the airport far too early and she'd have to hang around for nearly two hours. If there was anyone watching the airport it would give them plenty of time to see her. No, if she stayed in the apartment she was safe. Obviously they didn't know she was here.

Or maybe they did.

But if they knew she was inside why hadn't they done something? But then maybe they weren't going to do anything, maybe they were simply going to watch her...

Were they watching her now?

Stop it!

Briony Dalton did what she always did when she was troubled — she turned to work. She pulled the laptop computer from the case and set it up on the table below the window. Turning off the screen's back lighting, she adjusted the contrast way down until she could barely see the letters on the screen. But she could type by touch and she also had the ability to visualise the page in her head.

With one eye on the street, watching for any unusual activity, Briony Dalton began to capture her emotions — her fear, her confusion, the impotence, the anger — putting them all down on paper, incorporating them into the character of the heroine in *A Woman Scorned*.

She worked steadily for the next hour, then she closed down the computer and picked up the suitcase. She stood behind the hall door, her eye to the fish-eye viewer until she was certain the corridor outside was empty, then she quickly slipped out of the apartment.

Briony left the apartment block the same way she had entered and cut through the complex of apartments that shared the underground carpark to come out on the far side, away from any watchers. A taxi left her at Hyde Park Corner, the nearest tube station, where she took the tube directly to Heathrow.

She was the last person to board the plane for Corfu.

It was only when the plane was in the air, that she finally breathed a sigh of relief and opened the bundle of newspapers — British and Irish — which she had bought.

And the terror returned.

The same story appeared in nearly all the papers, the same picture of Gabrielle and herself, only the tone differed ...

DEATH TO THE PORNOGRAPHER

Lesbian lover of Briony Dalton gunned down in New York

Gabrielle Royer, the private secretary of Briony Dalton, the 'Queen of the Red Hot Read', was gunned down in a mob-like hit in the luxury love nest they shared together in the exclusive East Eighty-fifth Street, just off Park Avenue. A hitherto unknown fundamentalist Christian group calling itself The Warriors of Christ has accepted responsibility, but regretted the killing of Royer, claiming the real target was Briony Dalton.

An unidentified spokesman contacted The New York Times *and spoke to reporters there.*

"We shall expunge this evil person from this world. She is a witch, corrupting the hearts and minds of our children. Our Lord said, 'Suffer not the witch to live.'

Briony Dalton was unavailable for comment, but sources close to her said she was devastated by the death of her lover.

The Irish paper presented very much the same facts, though not quite so luridly.

BRIONY DALTON'S SECRETARY SHOT

Gabrielle Royer, the secretary of the controversial best-selling author Briony Dalton, has been shot dead in their New York apartment. No one has claimed responsibility for the killing yet which police say occurred during a robbery. Unconfirmed sources say that a fundamentalist Christian group claimed they had shot the 25-year-old Frenchwoman by mistake. Their target had been Briony Dalton.

Miss Dalton's latest book, Pavane, *is currently topping best-seller lists on both sides of the Atlantic.*

Briony spent much of the flight in the toilet, vomiting her breakfast.

ങ

"Impossible!" Josef Bach raged, scattering the reports across the room. "Absolutely impossible!"

Kaho faced him impassively. She knew what had aroused him into this state, and she had been with him long enough to know that someone was going to pay.

"Get me Marcus Holland."

Kaho bowed silently and padded from the room. She almost felt sorry for Marcus Holland. But Holland was about to learn a valuable lesson: Bach demanded results, and God help you if you didn't deliver. She made the call from her own office, keeping her voice completely neutral as she spoke to Holland who sounded as if he had just woken up. She glanced at the time on the digital clock on her desk: it was 7:50 a.m. Surely he should be awake by now?

"I have a call for you, Mr Holland."

"Who … what?"

"I have a call for you, Mr Holland," she repeated patiently, "from your new employer."

"Yes … yes. Of course."

Kaho made the connection and then left the line open with the mute button on. She could listen in without Bach knowing. But as an extra precaution she locked the door and turned the volume way down until the voices were little more than reedy whispers.

"Where is she?" Bach demanded without preamble.

"I don't know, sir. She's gone."

"I know that. I want to know where. What about that man you hired? I thought he was supposed to be good."

"Well, so did I. At least he is…"

"Stop your whining. Your report tells me nothing. She went to see her father, so what?"

"She went to see her father almost immediately after checking out of the hotel on Sunday evening. He didn't allow her into the house, and it sounds like they had some sort of argument — or rather he had some sort of argument with her on the steps. The neighbours didn't hear her make any reply. And after that she simply disappeared. I've had men at the airports all day yesterday and last night; they'll remain there until she surfaces. My man is having someone he knows check the reservations. However, we've no way of knowing if she went out by sea, although it is unlikely since she's known not to like travelling by water. We've had people watching her apartment in London since early yesterday morning just in case she slips past us and returns there. She must be still in Ireland. Don't worry, she'll turn up," he added confidently.

"No, Mr Holland, I don't have to worry. You're the one who should worry if she doesn't turn up. Find that woman!" he said simply, the threat implicit in his voice.

Chapter
Thirty-Seven

"Aunt Catherine … "

Although she had been prepared for what she would see, Catherine Garrett still couldn't hide the expression of horror that crossed her face.

Matthew Moriarty turned away, tucking his shaking hands into his pockets. "Yeah, it's a bit surprising, isn't it? Sort of takes your breath away."

"I'm sorry, I …"

"Don't apologise," he said bitterly. "I'm used to it."

Matt Moriarty was twenty-six years old. He looked at least twenty years older. He was skeletal, his parchment skin drawn tight across gaunt features, and his hair was little more than a fuzz, and the effect combined to render his face into an almost skull-like mask, leaving his eyes deep-sunk, dark-rimmed, his cheeks taut hollows, lips drawn back from yellowed teeth in a permanent rictus. He was wearing a grubby long-sleeved shirt and faded jeans that barely clung to his frail form, his skinny arms and bony wrists emphasising his extreme thinness.

Although Rianne had told her that Matt was dying, Catherine realised that the words had not really sunk in. Not until now. Looking at Matt, she wondered how much longer he had.

Matt Moriarty was living on the edge of Amsterdam's Chinatown, at the furthest end of the *Zee Dijk*, in a single shabby room above a porno movie house. Ironically, it had been in this cinema that he had discovered his sister. The room, which looked directly down on to the *Zee Dijk*, held nothing but a bed and a wooden chair. There was a small primus in the centre of the fireplace, a cup, a saucer and a small pot on the floor beside them. The room smelt of sweat, urine and the indefinable odour of sickness.

Matt sat on the edge of the bed, waving Catherine towards the chair. "It's not much but it's home," he said cheerfully and attempted a laugh, which turned into a liquid cough.

She caught a glimpse of his arm as the shirt flapped away, exposing mottled, punctured flesh, ugly red and black weals on the skin.

Rianne took up a position on the window sill, one leg drawn up to her chin, arms wrapped around it, her head resting on her knee, watching her brother intently.

"Rianne said you wanted to speak to me," Matt said. He was hunched over, elbows resting on his knees, fingers laced together.

"Did she explain why?" Catherine asked softly, sitting down in the rickety chair.

Matt glanced at his sister. "She said you were doing some sort of book on our mother."

"A biography, warts and all."

"And we're the warts?"

"You're her disgrace."

He shrugged. "Well, it's not entirely her fault we've ended up the way we have, now is it?" he asked.

Rianne snorted rudely.

"Of course it is!" Catherine exploded. "If she had treated you properly, looked after you, cared for you, things would have been different."

"And was it entirely her fault? What about the other people around us?" Matt said, looking directly into her troubled brown eyes. "What about them; didn't they see the danger signals? Or were they too wrapped up in their own worlds, their own careers, to become involved?"

In the long silence the followed, Catherine answered softly, "I know you're right. Tell me how I can make amends."

"You can't," he said. "And don't get me wrong; I'm not blaming you, I'm not even attempting to excuse our mother. I know what she is, I know what she did. She's become one of the most successful authors in the world — but at what cost?" He shrugged again, bony shoulders protruding from his shirt. "But then maybe she thinks it was worth it. I'm sure if you were to ask her why she did it, why she neglected us, she'd say that she had to work to support a young family. And so she had." He finished, gasping for breath. Perspiration beaded his forehead.

Rianne hopped off the window ledge and made her brother lie down on the bed. His skin had taken on a distinctly yellowish cast. When he caught his breath, he continued, staring blankly at the cracked ceiling. "You know, I sometimes look back and try to work out when our lives stopped being like other children's ... I reckon it was about the time that *Odalisk* was published."

Catherine shook her head. "It was earlier than that," she murmured.

Matt suddenly shivered. "Rianne, please," he whispered, looking towards his sister who was crouched by the side of the bed.

"How long has it been?" she asked, ignoring Catherine.

"Long enough," he muttered.

"Matt ... " she pleaded. "It's only been about four hours."

"Rianne!" The anguish was tangible in his voice.

Rianne Moriarty sighed and then reached in under the pillow and took out a small cloth-wrapped bundle. Laying the bundle down on the pillow, she spread out the contents beside her brother's head: a thin length of leather, a burnt and blackened spoon, a disposable lighter and a twist of silver paper. "You don't have to watch this," she said, glancing sidelong at Catherine.

"Watch what ... what are you going to do?"

"What does it look like?" Rianne said bitterly. "He's hurting. I'm going to shoot him up. Can't do him any more damage, can it?"

Matt smiled at Catherine. "I've got so bad now I can't even shoot up myself." His face was sheened with an oily sweat and his eyes never left his sister's hands as she prepared the needle. She poured a drop of bottled water on to the spoon and then emptied the greyish brown contents of the silver foil into it. Holding the spoon steady in her left hand, she held the lighter beneath it and thumbed it alight. After a few moments the contents dissolved into shivering liquid. Rianne dropped the lighter on to the bed and guided the point of the needle into the liquid, drawing up the fluid in one smooth movement. Dropping the now empty spoon beside the lighter, she held the hypodermic needle aloft and shot off a thin stream of liquid.

"Don't waste it!" Matt gasped. He grabbed his right wrist with his left hand and squeezed hard. The network of veins pumped up on the back of his hand.

Catherine shut her eyes as Rianne efficiently and emotionlessly injected her older brother in the back of his hand. When she opened her eyes again, Rianne was washing out the needle with bottled water, sterilising the point with the lighter flame.

Within moments Matt's whole demeanour had changed. He lay back on the bed, completely relaxed, much of the strain gone from his face, the lines of pain missing. Without the pressure on his skin, the skeletal gauntness had left him, lending him a patina of health. He attempted to focus on his sister as she cleaned the needle, his pupils pin-points. He smiled and it turned into a giggle. "It's sort of like closing the gate after the horse has bolted," he muttered. "Rianne gets me the best junk, good stuff, and none of that methadone shit either. She uses pure water ... " He giggled again. "When I was shooting up in toilets I'd use water from the toilet bowl, or if I was in some alleyway I'd take it from the gutter. And she always cleans the needle after me." He coughed, a deep racking cough that left his lips stained with blood. "If I'd had her with me, I'd never have got this fucking disease."

"How bad is it?" Catherine asked.

He hesitated and then shrugged. "Bad enough. I was diagnosed HIV positive about eighteen months ago … it was confirmed as full blown AIDS about two months ago."

"What happens now?"

His smile stretched the skin on his face, turning it ghastly. "Now I die. Sooner or later, I die."

"What happened, Matt?" she asked, the back of her throat raw and burning, a tightness in her chest that caught at her breathing.

"I'm a user," he said, deliberately misunderstanding her. "I shoot up heroin. I had a girlfriend who was a user too. We shared our needles. Christ, but we shared everything else, why shouldn't we share the needles too? But she'd been selling herself for money to support her habit; stood to reason she'd pick up something, didn't it?

"And then she became pregnant. She said it was mine, but how was I to know? She'd been living with me for about three months at this time, but she could have been screwing around during that time. Probably was. When the baby was born — a girl, the sweetest thing you ever saw with a mop of black hair, so maybe it was mine — well, she had AIDS." His voice was flat, emotionless. "She was dead within a month … I knew then it was only a matter of time before it got me too."

"Why, Matt? What started you on the drugs?"

He attempted to laugh, but another racking cough left him shaking. "I got curious," he said eventually. "Curiosity killed the cat." He chuckled. "I was bored. Lonely. I wanted to see what the fuss was about. I was staying in a squat where folks shot up every day … and oh, the dreams they talked about, the things they'd seen, the emotions they'd felt, and the music … they all spoke about the music." His eyes glazed as he looked back on another time. "I wanted to see those sights, feel those same emotions. I wanted to hear the music." There was a long silence and then his voice changed. "So I started doing a little speed ... and that was fine for a while, but I found I wanted something more. I tried coke, snorting it and then smoking it, and that was great. Suddenly I wasn't living in a rat-infested hole with nothing to look out on but a grey sky and a bleak future. Then I tried heroin." He turned his head to look at Catherine. "Do you know you really have to work at being hooked on heroin? I mean the first time I tried it I was sick, and I mean sick! But the next time it was easier and then the time after that easier still. And it's a really social drug. You can shoot your friends up, they can shoot you up. You can swap needles ... it's even better than sex. I had a habit within two weeks and the rest, as they say, is history." Matt stared at the ceiling, his voice altering again as he reminisced. "Before I started doing the shit seriously I used to be able to get odd jobs, waiting tables, kitchen work, that sort of thing, but the drugs really fucked me up. I lost job after job. I started stealing to support the habit, but you know junkies make lousy thieves. They make good muggers, though. When they need a fix the junk makes them vicious." He stopped, his tongue moving nervously across his lips. "When London grew too uncomfortable for me I moved on. Paris, Berlin, Oslo, Berlin again, finally Amsterdam. I'd like to go back to London," he added, "but I can't travel. I'll die here."

"I can help," Catherine whispered hoarsely.

He rose up on one elbow and glared at her. "Not unless you can work some fucking miracle. There's no cure for this! None."

"There are clinics." Catherine began.

"Yeah and what do they do? Feed you all sorts of experimental shit and swap your blood around. You still die."

"But there must be something I can do!" she said desperately.

"There is," he said, sinking back on to the pillow, his brief outburst having exhausted him. "Tell the truth about us. Tell everyone what happened to Briony Dalton's children."

"Do you hate her?"

He shook his head, a tiny movement on the pillow. "You have to care about someone to end up hating them. I stopped caring about my mother years ago."

♋

Catherine Garrett and Rianne Moriarty walked back along the *Oude Zijds Achterbourgwal*, the canal running roughly parallel to the *Zee Dijk*. Sex clubs, all of them closed and boarded up in the late afternoon, lined the canal, but in the smaller side streets the brothels were open and semi-clad women — most of them of African or Indian extraction — sat in the windows or leaned in the doors touting for business.

"How does he support his habit?" Catherine asked, ignoring a West Indian youth who walked a few steps with them, murmuring "Brown or white, brown or white, mon?"

"Heroin," Rianne said to Catherine's blank look, nodding towards the West Indian. "He's offering you heroin. This is junkie wonderland. You can buy just about anything on the streets. Some dealers have their own pitches, and it's even got racial overtones: white kids sell coke, black kids sell heroin or crack. You put someone like Matt in this environment and it's only a matter of time before he contracts AIDS, shoots himself up with some bad shit or ODs on good shit."

"How does he support his habit?" Catherine repeated, realising Rianne was avoiding the question.

"He doesn't. I do."

"How?" Catherine stopped dead. She knew — and dreaded the answer.

"How the fuck do you think?" Rianne walked on, stopping at the very edge of the canal, staring down into the filthy, polluted water.

"Rianne … " Catherine whispered.

"What else could I do?" she said fiercely into the scummy liquid. "What else could I do? And I couldn't just leave him hurting, could I? He's my brother. I'm all he's got."

Catherine wrapped her arms around Rianne, drawing her close. "Not any more. He's got me. You've got me too."

Chapter Thirty-Eight

Gregory Connors spotted her the moment he came down onto the beach, and he experienced a rare twitch of annoyance. He had had this portion of the coastline to himself for so long now that he had come to regard it as his own. Further down the coast, closer to the village of Moraitika, there had been some tourist development, but usually the tourists never ventured this far up the coast, where the beach — when there was a beach — was rough shingle.

Connors changed direction, determined to get a closer look at this invader; even last year, at the height of the tourist season when every beach on Corfu had been smothered in naked bodies of various hues, this section had been deserted. It was accessible only by boat or a difficult overland trip from Moraitika. And when you finally got there, there was nowhere to stay ... nowhere except ...

A sudden thought struck him and he glanced up at the neat whitewashed villa nestling into the steeply sloping cliffs. When he had first come to the village he had inquired about renting it, but had been told it was owned by an English woman. It had remained empty throughout last season, but this year ... ? He returned his attention to the woman on the beach; was this the mysterious owner?

She was — what — late thirties, early forties, but well-preserved. She obviously took good care of herself, the one-piece, backless swimsuit left that in no doubt. Although she was pale by Corfu standards, she had enough of a colour to indicate that she either visited the sun reasonably regularly or used a sun bed. She'd take a good colour, he decided. She was lying face down on a beach mat, head resting on her arms, a large circular hat on her head hiding her hair and most of her face. There was a pair of Ray Bans on the towel beside her, a bottle of sun lotion, factor ten, and a copy of the new Stephen King novel.

It was the book which took his attention. He was a King fan, and this was one he hadn't seen yet. He turned his head to read the title.

The early morning sun threw his shadow across the woman and she sat up with a scream that froze his blood. There was a long black cylinder in her hand.

"Stay back, stay away from me. This is chemical Mace."

"Whoa, lady. I wasn't going anywhere near you." He stepped back hurriedly, hands at chest level, palms outwards.

"What are you doing here? This is a big beach: what were you doing up here with me?"

Greg Connors tried a smile. He was twenty-eight years old and his boyish smile had walked him out of trouble on more than one occasion. "I'll admit I was curious to see someone here. You're the first tourist this season and I sort of consider the beach mine. And then when I got close … " He shrugged. "I wanted to have a look at the Stephen King book."

"What?" The woman stared at him incredulously.

"It's true." He grinned again. "I'm a very serious King fan. I'm a published author," he added proudly, "and King more or less inspired me to write. I've had three horror novels published. If you read horror, you might have heard of me: Gregory Connors."

The woman looked at him, her face expressionless. She saw a six-foot tall, broad-shouldered young man, mid to late twenties, his skin tanned a deep mahogany colour, and his light brown hair bleached almost blond by the sun. He was wearing Bermuda shorts, wraparound aviator glasses pushed up onto his head, and was carrying a ring binder.

It was the ring binder that convinced her he was telling the truth.

Briony Dalton lowered the can of Mace and attempted a smile. "You'll have to forgive me; I'm a little nervous. A single woman travelling alone can never be too careful." She allowed the sentence to trail away and tilted the large hat back on her head.

"Yeah, yeah, of course. I'm sorry I startled you. I shouldn't have snuck up on you like that. I should have whistled or something."

"I overreacted. I'm sorry." Her smile was wan and pale. "I'm rather jumpy; I really needed this holiday. I suppose I wasn't expecting to find anyone on this beach either; it seemed deserted."

"Are you staying in the villa?" He jerked his head behind him.

"Yes, a … a friend of mine owns it."

"The locals told me it was owned by some famous writer."

"Briony Dalton owns it," she admitted.

"Briony Dalton? *The* Briony Dalton, the writer? You know Briony Dalton?"

"I know Briony."

"Then you must be a writer too," Greg Connors said firmly, sitting down on the shingle.

"How do you know?" she asked.

"A single woman travelling alone, jumpy, reading, living in a writer's house. That's got all the hallmarks of a writer either working on a book, or more than likely taking a break having finished one."

"You've got a writer's imagination." She smiled, and then nodded. "Yes, I'm a writer." Telling him the truth was easier than creating and then continuing with a lie, especially as there was no other life she knew, no other story she could confidently tell him. She leaned forward and stuck out a hand. "Brigid Garrett," she said, using her step-mother's maiden name.

"Gregory Connors, but call me Greg."

"I don't think I've read any of your books, Greg," Briony said.

"Well, I'm not surprised. I haven't really made my break yet."

"You said you write horror. What kind?"

He shrugged and gazed out across the brilliantly blue water. "Well, sort of sex and violence things ... "

"Hump, hack, shag and slash," Briony said.

"What?" he said, looking at her in amazement.

Briony laughed at the expression on his face. "I used to write a schlock horror series many years ago for an American publisher, and that's what he called them: hump, hack, shag and slash novels. Fifty thousand words a novel, five hundred dollars, plus two per cent, per book.

"Brigid Garrett," Greg repeated slowly. "I thought I knew a lot of the horror writers, but that doesn't ring a bell."

Briony pulled her knees up to her chin and wrapped her arms around her shins. "Did you ever read the *Witchfinder* series about a priest called Father Michael Morand?"

"By Ethan Doure! It's a classic series, real pulp gore. And you wrote that?"

"I wrote the first four, up to where Morand is killed off. I refused to bring him back, but the publishers hired some hack to churn out some rubbish and resurrect the character. I never even bothered reading it." She shook her head in astonishment. "Do you know how long it's been since I last even thought about the *Witchfinder* series?"

"But some of them have reappeared in comic book format. Surely your publisher informed you of that?"

"Ethan Doure was a house name. I'm not sure what my rights are."

"I'm just amazed." Connors said. "That series was a great influence on me, and on King, too, I bet." He jabbed a finger at the subtle matt black cover of the new King blockbuster.

Briony picked up the book and tossed it over to him. "Read it, see what you think. I can't seem to concentrate on it yet. I think I probably need a few days to wind down first."

"Oh, I couldn't possibly take it," he said, automatically turning the book over to read the back cover.

"Please. I insist. It'll make up for my overreacting the way I did."

Greg scrambled to his feet. "I'll take good care of it. I'll bring it back in a day or two."

"It's five hundred pages long," she reminded him.

"I'm a fast reader. I'll see you around." He wandered off down the beach, his head already bent to the paperback.

Briony Dalton lay back on the towel, chuckling lightly. Was there no getting away from the monster she'd become? The boy didn't recognise her, but ironically he knew a crappy horror series she'd written while he was probably still in nappies.

And naturally he was a writer. Did the whole world want to write? Oh, if only she'd had a penny for every person who had come up to her and said, "I've always wanted to be a writer," or, "I'm writing a book too," or "How do you become a writer?" And she knew that none of them would ever so much as put pen to paper.

Briony rose on one elbow to watch the young man disappear into the shimmering distance. At least he had had a couple of books published, so he was obviously serious about it. But what was he doing here?

A cold thread of suspicion immediately began to form at the back of her mind: was it more than just coincidence?

Briony Dalton had bought the villa on Corfu as an investment. She had had the idea that she might like to spend a few months every year here, maybe writing, or possibly just relaxing. She had never got around to visiting it. And so, when she decided she needed somewhere to hide out, it had been the obvious choice — perhaps too obvious. She wondered how many people knew she owned this place ...

☙

"I've checked everywhere, contacted all her old friends, phoned every hotel she's used in the past." There was the slightest pause while Terri Fierstein took breath, and then she added, "But I'm afraid I've come up with nothing, absolutely nothing."

Josef Bach ground his teeth in frustration. He needed to know where this woman was. He needed to keep the pressure on her. When he spoke his voice was even, without a trace of emotion. "People do not disappear. That is a myth. When people want to go away for a while they usually go someplace they know. It is a psychological thing. They may have cut themselves off from everything else, but they need to retain some vestige from their past, something to hold on to."

Terri Fierstein listened attentively. This man frightened her ... no, he absolutely terrified her.

"So you're missing something. Check again."

"I've had people visit her homes ... well all except that place on Corfu but she's never been there and she probably wouldn't even know where to find it ... "

"Fax me the address," Bach said and hung up.

☙

"I started out as a librarian in Birmingham," Greg Connors said with a wry smile.

Briony looked across the table, an expression of complete disbelief on her face.

"I know, I know. This is not a Birmingham accent, but I travelled a lot. I spent a lot of time in the States, hitching from coat to coast. I supported myself by doing this and that, mostly that. I've done quite a bit of disc jockeying along the way ... that's principally where the accent comes from. I've picked fruit in Italy, tended a youth hostel in Greece, given walking tours of Paris and Berlin. I was a barman in a gay bar in Berlin for a while."

Briony wondered how much to believe. The story was almost unbelievable, but equally it was almost too fantastic to be made up. If he'd been bullshitting her, he'd have been less inventive.

They were sitting on the patio of her villa, drinking a bottle of the local red wine which he had brought as a peace offering earlier that evening. Her first instinct was to refuse — after all, she didn't know him, she knew nothing about him — but on impulse she invited him to join her in a drink. She had carried two glasses out on to the patio, and then watched while he struggled with the stubborn cork, his embarrassed flush darkening his tan. When he had finally managed to remove the cork, they had toasted each other in the raw young wine while the sun sank down behind the hills beyond the house, casting long shadows out across the beach and over the sea. The breeze had just the touch of a nip in it.

Greg was still wearing only his shorts and was used to the weather, but Briony had overdone the sun and was tender and raw in places. She had liberally coated herself with after-sun lotion and changed her swimsuit for a pair of shorts and a long cotton T-shirt, the cotton delightfully cool against her burns.

"How did you begin writing?" she asked.

"By accident," he said. He reached around behind his back and produced a paperback he had been carrying in the waistband of his shorts. "To replace the King," he explained.

Briony held it up, squinting in the fading light. "*Moonlight*, by Gregory Connors," she read aloud. Opening it, she saw two other titles listed and relaxed a little. So he really was a writer. Since she had met him earlier that day she had half-suspected that he might have been sent to watch the villa, waiting for her to turn up.

"So tell me how you started writing, and how you ended up here," she insisted, watching him intently, aware that her direct stare was disconcerting him.

"I told you: by accident. When I went back to Britain from Berlin I had no money, no job and no prospects. A friend of mine had just sold a piece of science fiction to a British publisher, and he'd got a thousand pound advance for it. I decided I could do it too. I sat down at a typewriter and began to hammer out a storyline for a horror novel. When I had that, I sent out a synopsis and the first publisher I sent it to accepted it and offered me a fifteen hundred pound advance. I told them I'd deliver in six months, but I actually did it in four. I wrote to them immediately with another book, and again they bought it, and on the strength of those two, I sold them *Moonlight*, my biggest book to date." He leaned over and tapped it. "Over one hundred thousand words in that."

Briony grinned. *A Woman Scorned* was to be somewhere around two hundred and fifty thousand words. "You should be very proud."

"I am."

"So now you're doing number four?"

"That's right. It's what I'm doing here. I came by boat."

"Boat ... ?" she asked, astonished.

Greg nodded. "A sailing boat; I'd always wanted a boat. I have a friend who runs a sailing school in Lowestoft and I did a sailing and navigation course with him and then sailed down here, hugging the coastlines of Brittany, and then down along the French, the Spanish and the Portuguese coastlines. I came in through Gibraltar, back up along the Spanish and French coasts, down along the Italian coast until I eventually ended up here ... or rather out there." He gestured towards the darkening sea. "I row out to the boat every day and try to get in a chapter of the book. Sometimes it works, other times it's not so successful. It depends who I meet during the day."

"Do you meet many people during the day?"

"Not many."

Briony sipped the red wine, feeling it harsh against her tongue. She was relaxed and at ease. She hadn't entirely dismissed her doubts about this young man, but he appeared genuine and he did seem to be a writer. "Tell me about your new book," she said. If he was a genuine writer she knew that nothing would give him greater pleasure than to talk about his own work.

"It's my most ambitious work to date. It's a two hundred thousand word family saga with a strong revenge motif."

"Not horror."

He shook his head. "There's a family curse, but that is just the vehicle for moving the story along. But it's not the type of horror I've been writing. I wanted to try something else. I wanted to see if I could do it."

"There is a lot of money in family sagas," she said with a grin.

"I know. Isn't that how Briony Dalton made her fortune? Family sagas with sex and religion. What a recipe for success!"

"You enjoy writing," Briony said, not meaning it as a question.

"Very much," Greg said. "Why? Are there writers who don't?"

"I don't think Briony Dalton does," she murmured.

Greg Connors laughed loudly. "I'm sure you must be wrong. Why, it's given her everything she has, she's devoted her whole life to it. She must enjoy it," he stated emphatically.

She doesn't, Briony said silently, envying him his enthusiasm.

∞

Marcus Holland sat facing Josef Bach, and the young American was terrified. Bach's summons had been imperious and curt.

"Apparently she has a villa on the island of Corfu," the German had begun without preamble. "There is a village called Moraitika about eighteen kilometres south of Corfu town; the villa lies about two kilometres further south. She's never visited it before."

"Then how do we know she's there now?" Marcus Holland said abruptly.

"Don't interrupt me again," Josef Bach hissed. "Listen and then do what you're told."

"Yes, sir," Holland mumbled.

"We contacted the local taverna and ascertained that the villa is currently occupied by an Englishwoman. We don't need enormous IQs to know who that is, do we?" He paused, his fingers meshing together, and smiled coldly at Holland. "Go to Corfu, find this place and frighten her."

"What?"

"You heard me. Frighten her. I don't care what you do. I want her unsettled and confused. I don't want her working on her book."

"Would it not be better to arrange for her to have an accident?" Holland suggested.

Bach looked at him with his cold blue eyes. "That would be too simple: I don't want to kill her, I want to destroy her completely in the eyes of the public."

Chapter Thirty-Nine

Maybe it was something about the young man's enthusiasm, maybe it was the clean sea air, or perhaps it was a combination of both, but Briony Dalton awoke close to five the following morning filled with a burning desire to write.

She showered in tepid water and then, still naked, padded into the kitchen and put the coffee on to percolate. She drank orange juice straight from the carton while she carried her portable computer out on to the veranda and powered it up. By the time she returned to the bedroom for a robe, the coffee was ready. She carried a steaming mug on to the veranda and breathed deeply, tasting the fresh, cool dawn air, sharp with the salt tang of the sea and the rich aroma of coffee. The silence was disturbed only by the distant hiss of the waves on the shore sounding like some primeval creature breathing. She realised that she felt good, she felt relaxed, pleasantly rested, eager to write. Pulling up a wicker chair, she sat down at the humming machine and set to work.

She had prepared the synopsis and worked out the plot of *A Woman Scorned* nearly two years ago now before she had written a single word of the manuscript. It was possible for an author of her calibre to sell a book on the strength of a reasonably detailed letter, and she had heard stories of best-selling authors selling books on the basis of a conversation — though she had never actually done it herself, or knew anyone who had managed to do that. The synopsis was a start, but it was not engraved in stone; in the course of the writing, the book would change. Certain characters would grow, transform, some would begin as minor characters but develop into principal ones in their own right. Her own attitudes, humours, moods and even her state of health would affect how the book came out. She had always hated writing during her period: the writing was always dark, moody, and gloomy then. Now she deliberately tried to work on the darker sections of the novel at those times. The weather, too, affected the book: she hated writing in good weather. It brought back too many memories. Memories of the years she had spent cooped up in the house writing furiously to support the children and the house and her comfortable lifestyle. Winter was best. Then she could wrap herself up all warm and cosy in her study and look down on the rainy streets. Then the writing really flowed.

And of course the major events in her life drifted into her books in one shape or another. Gabrielle's death and her subsequent paranoia had directly translated on to the page as the death of one of the main characters — the pregnant wife of the hero — and the heart-rending scene that followed was, Briony knew, amongst the very best of her writing. She couldn't read over it without experiencing a searing at the back of her throat and feel the tears stinging her eyes. She also knew that she was putting down on paper all those things she should have said to Gabrielle, remembering all those little acts of kindness, the inconsequential arguments; this chapter was her eulogy for the woman she'd loved.

Her own paranoia had cropped up in the book as the fears of one of the younger sons who was involved in drug dealing. The young man knew he was being watched by both his rivals and the police; and, once again, she felt she had captured his mood exactly.

Next to go into the book would be her encounter with Greg Connors.

There were a couple of chapters in the book where the heroine had a brief impassioned affair with her nephew. Briony had originally used her relationship with Gabrielle as the model, where she had tried to capture how the older woman felt about the younger man. But now there was this young man whom she could model the character on and work the situation around.

Not that he attracted her in the slightest.

Although she had only met him the previous day, she had enjoyed her two encounters with him, briefly in the morning and at greater length during the evening. He was fun and he made her laugh. His enthusiasm was infectious. He had a joy for life and living she hadn't come across in a long time. Usually the circles she moved in — especially the party circuit in the States — were filled with handsome, witty young men, well dressed, well perfumed, badly shaven with designer stubble and pony-tails, whose conversation was limited to themselves, their recent successes with members of the opposite — or the same — sex, and the various quantities of medication they had managed to consume and score. These people were bored with life and consequently boring.

But Connors was neither bored nor boring. Briony had asked him the previous night if he ever got bored living what amounted to a hermit's life on a reasonably deserted part of the island.

Greg had laughed. "I'm never bored," he said, sounding almost amazed that she should have asked. "I've my boat, the sun, the sea ... and my writing. What more do I want?"

"But what do you live on?"

"I got a really good advance for my new book." He smiled broadly, and then leaned across the table, adding confidentially, "I was paid seven and half thousand pounds and I managed to get half of it up front." He sat back. "And nearly three and half grand goes a long way on an island like this. If I run short of ready cash, I can always go to the village and sing in one of the local tavernas or wash dishes. That brings in some shillings."

Briony poured herself a cup of coffee and drank it black with no sugar. Later this morning, she promised herself, when the sun came up but before it got too hot she would go for a jog down the beach and swim. But first ...

She looked at the computer, tilting the screen slightly, trying to find the best angle to read it in the strong light.

With the silence only broken by the low humming of the screen and the hiss of the sea, her fingers began to move across the keys, the slight clicking sounds beginning to take up a rhythm that increased slowly but surely.

She rarely worked without her headphones and her classical repertoire of music, but this morning was different and she found she didn't even miss the constant distraction. With her eyes fixed on the sea, thinking of nothing in particular, she began putting together the chapter where the heroine seduces her nephew. Originally she had planned that the seduction would take place in the heroine's apartment on the outskirts of Rome, but that was a little too mundane. She wanted an outdoor lovemaking scene, so how about the Italian Riviera? No, too crowded. She needed a private beach for what she planned. So she'd move her heroine to Portugal, yes, give her an apartment in Portugal, somewhere isolated on the northern coast perhaps and make it out of season. She'd place both of them on the beach in the first light of dawn, when the sky and sea would look just as they were at this moment. She'd have the couple making love in the sand dunes.

Everything she needed to visualise the scene was to hand: the sounds of wind and wave, the sand whispering through the tough marram grass, the water rattling off the rounded stones, the distant booming of the waves in the caves in the cliffs, the tiny tinny cries of the seagulls — and she had thought the morning was silent!

Briony's fingers slowed on the keys as she imagined the couple slipping from their swimming costumes and sinking down on to the sand, arms around one another, mouths locked together … She stopped.

Damnation!

When she was writing a scene like this she would usually turn to her collection of pornographic videos. It would be simply a matter of running one of them — any one, they were all more or less the same — and then transcribing the action on screen to the beach in northern Portugal.

She rested her elbows on the table and cupped her face in her hands. She remembered the last time she had made love to Gabrielle. Funny, she had never thought of it in that way before. They made love very irregularly. It was always just something they did together to please one another, usually after they had done a few lines of coke. Was it only a little over two weeks ago that they'd last made love? Briony Dalton took a deep breath and shook her head. It seemed like a lifetime ago, but it was only eighteen days. That had been the last night of her old life. That had been the last time she had seen Gabrielle alive, too. The following day Gabrielle had gone and Briony had resolved to bring the fight to the enemy — attack, instead of defending.

She had regained much of her old aggressiveness. Paradoxically, Gabrielle's death had made her determined to complete this book as a monument to her, if nothing else. And her determination to succeed had only increased when she had learned that Terri seemed to be involved in the conspiracy to keep her from ever finishing it.

She realised that she was gradually shedding the barriers and defences she had built up around herself over the years. Recently Briony Dalton had needed videos and reference books all around her to write, but the original Briony Dalton had written all her books with the barest of reference materials. Indeed, the first few books were written with only the aid of a dictionary. Nowadays, of course, she didn't even need a dictionary: there was both a dictionary and thesaurus available at the touch of a key on her computer.

All she'd had then was her imagination. That was all she needed. And the new Briony Dalton was going to learn once again to rely on her own imagination.

The morning silence swallowed her sudden laughter. In God's name, surely she could visualise a sex scene … even if it was six thirty in the morning. But it had been a while since she had been with a man, she reminded herself, using it as an excuse. But what about the last time she had made love to Gabrielle?

With her fingers poised over the keys, Briony Dalton closed her eyes and attempted to recapture every detail, every nuance, of her last passionate encounter with Gabrielle Royer.

ભ

Greg Connors lowered the binoculars, feeling both annoyed and ashamed.

When he didn't sleep on his boat he stayed with a Greek family in their tiny farm on the road from Moraitika. In return for help around the farm they gave him food and lodging and taught him Greek. From his bedroom window, he could see the villa below and to his left about a hundred yards away.

He had rolled out of bed immediately upon awakening and leaned against the open window, breathing in the cool morning air, feeling the sweat dry on his body. In the early morning twilight, the lights burning in the villa's windows below were like beacons, and as he watched he saw a shape moving across them. Curiosity made him reach for the binoculars that hung on the end of his bed and focus them on the lighted windows below, confident that he was completely invisible even if anyone did happen to look up.

Brigid Garrett had obviously just risen. She was naked, moving unselfconsciously about the kitchen, drinking orange juice, running one hand through her damp-looking hair. And, although Greg had seen many naked women on the beaches, there was something so completely natural about the way the woman moved, coupled with the realisation that he could see her but she was unaware of him, that he found himself becoming aroused.

She drank orange juice from the carton. Some dribbled down her chin on to her left breast, rolling down the curve to cling to her dark nipple. Unconsciously, she ran her index finger up the sticky liquid and then licked it off.

She moved out of sight and was gone for a couple of minutes before reappearing, this time wearing a white cotton robe.

She picked up a cup of coffee and moved away and then the lights clicked out.

When Greg lowered the binoculars he was so thoroughly aroused that he had to spend five minutes standing with his head pressed against the cold brickwork, afraid to go out in case any of the Greek peasants saw him in his particularly obvious condition.

He tried a laugh and found it was shaky. What was he thinking of? He hadn't been so turned on in a long time … and she was nearly old enough to be his mother, too, for Christ's sake!

Chapter Forty

"I must admit to being a little surprised to see you." Josef Bach moved out from behind the enormous desk, hands clasped behind his back, head thrust forward.

Catherine Garrett was briefly reminded of one of her university lecturers, who adopted the same pose when confronted by a troublesome or giddy class. "I did say I would keep in touch," she said defensively, twisting in the uncomfortable chair to look at Bach as he moved around behind her.

"A letter would have been sufficient. A phone call equally so."

"I didn't want to trust what I have to report to a letter or a phone call."

Bach moved in directly behind her chair, and rested his large hands on either side of her face, forcing her to look straight ahead.

"You're distraught," he murmured. "Tell me what has upset you." Surprisingly sensitive fingers moved up her face, brushing her temples, moving in gentle circles. Catherine closed her eyes and attempted to relax.

"I flew in from Schipol this morning … " she began.

"Ah, you saw the Moriarty children." It was a statement rather than a question.

"I spoke to them both."

"And will they co-operate with your book?"

"They'll co-operate, although to be truthful they didn't really seem interested either way," Catherine said. Something sparked at the back of her mind, and she suddenly tilted her head backwards, looking up at Josef Bach. "You knew Matt has AIDS!" she accused.

Bach made a non-committal face.

"Everything else was in your report. Everything but that. Why didn't you tell me?" she demanded. "Were you keeping it for its shock value?"

"Would it have made any difference if you'd read it in cold print? Would it have prepared you for the shock? But what were your impressions when you discovered that he has AIDS? What were your thoughts, what was your reaction? You're a journalist; you can put those thoughts, those emotions, those reactions to good use in your book."

"Did you know he's dying?" Catherine asked icily.

Bach's fingers stopped their circular motion. He moved around in front of her chair and crouched down so his face was level with hers. His bright blue eyes bored into hers. "How soon?"

Taken aback by his intensity, Catherine shrugged. "Who can tell? He's an addict; he had a girlfriend who was a junkie and a whore, selling herself to pay for her habit. Anyway, she took up with Matt and if he hadn't got the disease before then he got it from her. They shared their needles. That's some special form of loving relationship," she added bitterly, "sharing the same needle, the same dope, the same high. Well, now they're sharing something else. There was a baby," she said softly. "A baby girl. It was born with AIDS."

"Where is the girl now?"

Catherine frowned. Which girl? Did he mean Rianne or the baby or …

"The junkie girlfriend. Did you pursue that line of enquiry?"

"I didn't. I didn't feel it was necessary, nor pertinent to this project."

"He might have told her something," Bach said, his eyes distant, already working out the possibilities of this latest news. "And there was a child too? The child is dead? Briony Dalton's granddaughter dead of AIDS. Excellent!" He rubbed his hands quickly. "You should have attempted to track down the girl."

"For fuck's sake! They were both junkies. They talked about scoring their next hit, nothing else. When you're a junkie your universe contracts to the shit you're pumping into yourself, either the next hit or the last hit. When I asked him her name he had to think about it! He lived with this girl for over a year, she had a child by him, and he actually had to think before he could remember her name!" Catherine was quivering with rage; the intensity of her emotion surprising even herself.

The German seemed taken aback by her vehemence. He reached out and took hold of her arms, squeezing gently. "Calm yourself. I'll get us some coffee."

"I don't want coffee," she snapped, annoyed at her own loss of control, amazed to find tears sparkling in her eyes.

"You haven't met this young man in how many years?" Bach asked, his eyes on her face.

"That's not the point!"

"You feel guilty," Bach stated flatly.

"Yes. Yes, yes, yes!"

"He wasn't your son. She wasn't your daughter."

"Does it matter? They were — they are — my step-sister's children. I am responsible."

"They are not your children," Bach repeated firmly. He stood up and moved across to the desk, leaning back against it, resting on his straight arms, legs crossed at the ankle. "They had a mother."

"They also had me."

"You cannot accept responsibility for everyone. Ultimately, you are only responsible for yourself, to yourself."

"That's shit!"

"No." Josef Back shook his head and moved around the desk to his chair. He sat down in the creaking leather, his hands coming together almost in an attitude of prayer. He stared at Catherine across the tips of his fingers, and when he spoke his voice was soft, little above a whisper.

"My parents were killed during the Allied bombing of Hamburg," he said suddenly. "We were having dinner in the one-roomed flat we lived in. We heard the bombers come over, and then the dull explosions all across the city. When the raid was over, we all blessed ourselves and said a prayer of thanks. We gave thanks too soon. I think it must have been the last bomb left. It exploded in the building right next door to ours. Half of our apartment block was sliced away as neatly as if it had been cut with a knife. One moment I was listening to my mother and father speaking — he was blind, unfit for service — and the next moment they were gone.

"I was nearly twelve years old. I had a younger brother, Max, who was then seven, and a baby sister, Helga, who was five.

"And I accepted responsibility for them.

"What else could I do?

"I could have taken them to relatives of my mother's across the city, or my father had people out in the countryside whom I could have gone to.

"But I didn't.

"We lived in that bombed-out building for nearly two months. Every morning I went out and begged or stole whatever food I could to keep us alive for another day.

"And every day we could hear the Allies approaching. And that terrified us more than anything else, because we had been brought up to believe that they were monsters, inhuman savages. And at night the bombers came.

"We survived there for sixty days ... I know, because I kept a note of each passing day.

"And then my sister became ill, followed, almost immediately, by my brother. They ran temperatures that were so hot I could barely touch them. They vomited and fouled themselves until there was nothing left inside them.

"Later I discovered that they had been drinking the stagnant water in the street ... and it had been fouled with burst waste pipes.

"And they died. They died in agony.

"Because I had accepted responsibility for them.

"If I had taken them out of the city; if I had gone looking for my mother's people or my father's people they might still be alive today. Or maybe not.

"But I swore I would never again accept responsibility for another human being."

Josef Bach blinked and looked at Catherine Garrett, his broad face expressionless. In the same monotone he had delivered the story, he continued, "If you repeat this story — ever! — I will kill you. Do you understand?"

Catherine nodded. "You did what you thought was right. For God's sake, you were twelve years old!"

"You're missing my point. They were my brother and sister, but they weren't my responsibility. Rianne and Matt Moriarty are not your responsibility."

"I should have done something!"

"When?" he demanded. "When Briony Dalton published her first book? Or her second or her third? When she started out publicising herself? When she left her husband? When should you have done something?"

"I don't know ... I don't know ... I don't know," she screamed.

"What are you going to do for them now?" Bach asked, when Catherine had calmed down.

"I offered them money."

"And they didn't take it?" he guessed shrewdly.

"Matt would have. He's still shooting up ... or rather Rianne is injecting him now. He's twenty-six years old. He won't live to see twenty-seven. Rianne refused the money. She's selling herself on the streets to support his habit, trying to get back into porno movies ... "

Bach smiled coldly. "You see, she's accepted responsibility for her brother. We all do it, sooner or later."

"But not you."

"Not now."

There was a long silence. Eventually, Bach said, "Why did you come here today?"

"I ... I don't know. I wanted to know if there was anything you could do."

"Me?" He sounded genuinely puzzled.

"Yes." Catherine frowned. Her reasons for coming to Bach were confused in her own mind. "I thought you might be able to help the children."

"They're not children. They're adults making their own lives, their own decisions. I cannot help them."

"Cannot or will not?" she demanded.

"There is no cure for AIDS. There are drugs which slow down the rapid depletion of the body's reserves but if Matt is as bad as you say he is then he has no reserves to conserve. There are centres which will help him, allow him to die with a certain amount of dignity. But someone like Matt doesn't want to go there. All he wants is more shit to pump into his arm, more dreams.

"And Rianne. What can I do for her? Oh, I suppose I could get her back into the porno movie business. Do you want me to do that? But she will not leave her brother ... not until he's dead," he added grimly.

"There must be something you can do ... your money ... your connections ..."

"There is nothing I want to do," he snapped. "I thought I had explained my position quite clearly. There is nothing I can do," he finished in a softer tone.

"Please ... " she murmured.

"There is nothing I can do," he repeated.

Catherine got up and opened her coat. She was wearing a simple grey tweed suit, cut in a mannish style, double-breasted jacket over trousers. Beneath the jacket she wore a flesh-pink blouse and a blood-red cravat. Through the sheer fabric of the blouse Bach could see her nipples.

Josef Bach stood abruptly. "I paid you a third of your half a million pound advance. You're not short of cash. If you want to do something for them, I'm not stopping you."

"I don't have the resources to pay for the treatment Matt needs." Catherine closed her coat and stood looking at Bach for a few moments.

Josef Bach smiled coldly. "Well, then I suggest you find the resources."

"How?"

Bach shrugged. "You could try publicising the case; some do-gooder bleeding-heart group will get Matt treatment. And I'll tell you what I'll do. Write me an article detailing what you discovered about Matt and Rianne Moriarty. I'll pay you for it … make it an extract from your forthcoming book, first serial rights, something like that. I don't care. Put all your anger and pain into that article, and I'll splash it across every piece of media I've access to. You'll get your publicity for Matt."

"What do you get out of it?" Catherine asked shrewdly.

"When I'm finished, Briony Dalton's name will be shit."

Catherine nodded, satisfied. She turned to leave when she asked, "Why do you hate her?"

Bach seemed surprised. "I don't hate her. I've never even met the woman. This is strictly business!"

Chapter Forty-One

The article was accompanied by an enormous stark photograph of Matt Moriarty staring hollow-eyed at the camera. The camera lighting had emphasised his skull-like appearance, and he was wearing a short-sleeved T-shirt that highlighted the mass of festering sores and livid bruising up and down both arms.

There was a series of small photographs which showed an incredibly squalid room — not the one Matt Moriarty was living in, that having been deemed too clean and neat for the purposes of the article — with a newspaper-covered mattress tossed in one corner, cans of food lying about and stubs of candles stuck on to the rotten floorboards.

A small elongated photograph at the bottom of the page showed a tiny white cross almost lost amidst tall, rank weeds. The name Briony had been airbrushed on to the arms of the cross, making it look as if someone had hand-lettered it.

BRIONY DALTON'S SHAME

This is Briony Dalton's shame.

This is her son, Matthew Moriarty. He is twenty-six years of age, a heroin addict, dying of AIDS. He lives in a single-roomed tenement in Amsterdam, which he knows he will never leave.

Matthew Moriarty spends his day begging on the streets of Amsterdam, hoping to earn enough money to buy a little food and support his habit. Until very recently, when he didn't make enough from begging, he resorted to stealing, snatching purses, or wallets. But now that the killer disease has sapped his strength, he usually end ups eating scraps from the bins behind restaurants or surviving on cans of cat food.

And yet Matthew Moriarty is the son of one of the wealthiest and highest-paid authors in the world, whose sexy novels have made her a millionaire many times over.

'My mother has her own life to lead,' Matthew Moriarty says quietly, with no rancour in his voice. 'And there is no place for me in that life. She didn't abandon me, she just forgot about me.'

But Matthew Moriarty didn't forget his mother.

Six months ago, his long-time girlfriend, Toni, gave birth to their child. But the baby girl was infected with the AIDS virus, and died two days later. The parents were distraught and Toni and Matt split up shortly after that. Toni is also HIV positive.

In a quiet country graveyard on the outskirts of the city is a simple wooden cross marking a tiny grave. Because of Matt's illness, the grave is now no longer as lovingly cared for as it once was. The cross bears the Christian name of the child buried there: Briony.

The child was named after Matt's mother.

Chapter Forty-Two

Marcus Holland was in way over his head. He knew it, and he didn't know what to do about it.

What the fuck was he doing sitting in this filthy bar in a God-forsaken tourist trap in some place called Mort … Mort … Mort-something with Charley O'Neill sitting by his side, drinking warm beer and looking like he owned the place?

This was madness.

Absolute and utter madness.

He was a journalist, a television personality, a book reviewer, an author. He wasn't some sort of heavy, some vague, threatening, comic-book type enforcer.

He knew — in some abstract and almost theoretical way — what Josef Bach was doing. Had done.

First he had lured him with the promise of a job, a plum job. And he had fallen for that.

Then Bach had put him on a retainer to keep him sweet. And he had accepted that.

Now Bach wanted him to do something that was illegal. And Bach knew he would do it … and once he had done that Marcus Holland knew he would have forged the final link in a chain that would bind him inexorably to the German.

But what was even more frightening was that there was nothing he could do about it.

Holland stared into the sour beer. There was a tiny insect crawling across the surface. Of course, he could refuse to do it. He could even threaten to expose Bach, but the German controlled so many papers now that getting the story into print was going to be very difficult. Even assuming it got published, who would believe him? And all that presupposed that he would get away with threatening Bach. He still hadn't forgotten what had happened to Gabrielle Royer: no one was going to tell him that had been an accident!

Marcus Holland glanced sidelong at Charley O'Neill. Bach had insisted he brought him, but Holland couldn't help wondering if the big American had been sent along to keep an eye on things. Certainly, he hadn't looked too surprised when Marcus had offered him the opportunity of a week's holiday on Corfu, along with his usual fee, plus a five thousand pound bonus in return for a little light work.

Bach's instructions had been concise. Frighten Briony Dalton into running; while she was running, she wasn't writing.

Holland had brought along a representative selection of some of the newspapers and magazines which had carried the Matt Moriarty story, including the 'exclusive' interview which Catherine Garrett had obtained from Matt. The story had been bought by one of the English dailies for a much-publicised fee which, the story claimed, was going to be used by Matt Moriarty to pay for his mounting medical expenses. The only medicine Moriarty would be spending the money on would go straight into his arm. Holland had been in the news trade long enough to know a scam when he saw it; the Matt Moriarty story was almost too good to be true; the pictures were a little too harrowing, and the tiny white wooden cross with Briony's name hand-written across it had been the final touch. A nice touch admittedly, but just enough over the top to destroy the story's credibility ... for him, anyway. When he had first read the story, he had wondered if the general public would fall for it.

They had.

Sales of Briony Dalton's books, including *Pavane* which had been number one on the best-seller lists in half a dozen countries, had plummeted and the three Briony Dalton titles which had been riding high in the best-seller lists had dropped off in the past week. The bookshops were already starting to return unsold stock, and the campaign in Ireland, which had almost sputtered to a close when Briony had left the country, had erupted again with renewed fervour, and now like-minded groups in Britain and the Moral Majority in the States were demonstrating against the 'Priestess of Porn'.

Whoever was master-minding this number on Briony Dalton — and he had a feeling it was Bach himself, and not one of his companies — was a real expert. It wasn't so much of a hatchet job as a full meat grinder.

He wondered what the next step would be. If he was handling the campaign, he would give it a couple of weeks for the present story to run its cycle, and then, just when the spotlight was beginning to fall away, he would drop the daughter's story into it for good measure. A twenty-two-year-old porno starlet. Perfect. There were so many angles to the daughter's story which could be exploited, and if he was really lucky she'd be a junkie too … or maybe she'd have a kid dying of some terminal disease, or suffering from some disfigurement, and she was only making the movies to pay for her treatment … or she was being blackmailed into making the movies.

And it was all because her mother abandoned her. He would have worked out something suitably tragic — a teenage pregnancy, a rape — to capture the public imagination, and he was sure Bach would do the same. It would make great copy. And it was another nail in Briony Dalton's coffin.

"It's time." Charley O'Neill finished his drink in one quick swallow and stood, stretching before slapping a wilting straw hat onto his head. He looked every inch the American tourist: bright floral shirt open to the waist, hideous Bermuda shorts, white socks and sandals. There was a camera around his neck. His sun glasses were red-rimmed.

Holland was more conservatively dressed in a white cotton long-sleeved T-shirt and white cotton trousers. His peaked cap was also white. He had dressed with the intention of covering as much flesh as possible; his fair skin and colouring meant that he burnt easily, and already, although they had been less than five hours in the country and he hadn't stood in direct sunshine for more than a few minutes, his skin was beginning to tingle.

They moved out into the small market square facing the taverna. It was close to noon and mostly deserted, the heat having driven all the locals and most of the tourists indoors. Holland hurriedly pulled down the Ray Ban sunglasses, blinking furiously to allow his eyes to adapt after the dimness of the taverna. O'Neill stuck his hands in his pockets and looked around, seemingly unconcerned by the heat and glare.

"What do we do now?" Holland asked.

"We walk!"

The younger man looked. "It's two kilometres."

Charley O'Neill stepped up beside him, so close he could smell the beer off his breath. "So what do you suggest we do — hail a cab and announce to the whole of the island that we're off to see the English lady in the villa?"

"We could hire a car."

"We could also leave our names and addresses with the police. There's too many forms to be filled in when you're hiring a car. Let's try to stay anonymous tourists."

Holland attempted a smile. "You're right. We'll walk."

They had been walking for twenty minutes when Marcus Holland had to sit down and rest. His clothing was plastered to his body, and his leg muscles were trembling with the effort. There was a dull ache in the small of his back and the pressure building above his forehead from the glare of the sun promised to develop into one almighty headache.

In contrast, Charley O'Neill still looked fresh and cool.

"What's your secret?" Holland asked bitterly.

"A six-year stretch in South East Asia. That's the sort of heat and humidity that saps your strength. This," — he stretched both arms wide — "this is gorgeous, dry heat, with just a hint of a sea breeze."

Marcus Holland stood up and turned his face to the breeze. The sweat dried on his body, quickly chilling him.

"Have you a plan?" O'Neill asked as they walked on at a slower place to accommodate Holland.

"No. I was told to frighten the woman away, make her flee the country … do anything to keep her from writing. While she's scared, she's not working."

"No violence?"

"Absolutely not!"

Charley O'Neill nodded. "Pity. It'll also have to be reasonably subtle then, so even if she does go to the police, she'll have no evidence to show them."

"Have you anything in mind?" Holland asked. In Dublin he had been in charge, he had felt in control, he had been the one issuing orders, paying the money. But that control had somehow shifted. O'Neill now knew someone was paying Holland, knew he was only acting as a go-between. And Marcus was completely out of his depth: he was not a man of action, whereas O'Neill was.

"There are lots of ways of scaring the woman. It can be as simple as prowling around the outside of her house at night; it could be as unsubtle as killing a pet, if she has one, and of course threatening phone calls are always useful." He shrugged. "Let's wait and see, get a look at the house first. Something might suggest itself then."

GB

The long, low villa was built into the side of the cliff, its red-tiled roof seeming to slope almost to the ground. There was a veranda, set partially on stilts into the side of the cliff and a narrow, railed staircase led down to the empty beach below. An arrow-straight track led off the road to the villa, and the numerous trees and bushes that had been planted to form a screen had withered into dust. Anyone approaching from the road would be instantly visible.

Charley O'Neill lay in the harsh marram grass, sunglasses pushed back up on to his head, using the camera he carried as a simple telescope. There was a second house, a farm, off to the right, partially hidden behind some trees and wiry bushes. He doubted if it's inhabitants would hear any sounds from the villa.

Turning his attention to the beach, he patiently scanned it in precise military fashion, first dividing it into sectors and then scrutinising each sector.

There!

A flash of colour in the shade of the cliffs. A lightly tanned body, a tiny canary yellow bikini.

O'Neill scrambled back to Holland, who was sitting hunched and miserable in the shade of a thorn bush. "She's at the bottom of the steps leading down from the villa. She's sitting with some sort of black box on her knees ... it looks like one of those portable computer things."

Holland looked up, suddenly interested. "If we could get that it would certainly put a stop to her writing."

Charley O'Neill nodded. "We could do that, certainly. What do you want to do — break it or steal it?"

"Steal it," Holland said decisively. He saw himself handing the portable computer across to Josef Bach. Not only would he have stopped Briony Dalton writing her book, he would have delivered whatever work she had done into Bach's hands. It would be sure to impress Bach. "Steal it," he repeated. "But, let's have a look at the villa first, eh? When do you think it would be safe to break in?"

"Right now," O'Neill grinned. "She's not going to move off the beach in this heat, and it'll take her at least ten minutes to climb up the steps carrying the computer."

"Ten minutes then," Holland muttered. Everything up to now had been within the law, but from here on it became illegal.

Holland had been expecting that they'd have to climb in through a window or pick a lock, but the windows and doors were open, allowing a deliciously cool breeze to circulate through the villa. The rooms were quite stark, walls and ceilings painted white, natural stone floors in the hall and kitchen, smoothly polished wooden boards in the bedrooms. Briony Dalton's few personal possessions were strewn about one of the larger bedrooms, and Charley O'Neill quickly rifled through them while Holland stood by the window watching nervously. There was no money, no passport and no return ticket. The big American moved quickly around the room: there were no pictures on the wall ... which meant ... which meant ...

He found the safe sunk into the floor in a corner beneath a hideous throw rug. It was large and formidable, but not entirely without possibilities. If he had a jack-hammer now ... He grinned at the thought; either that or a stick of dynamite.

"What's so funny?" Holland demanded.

Charley nodded towards the floor. "I was wondering what our mutual employer would say if we asked him for a few sticks of dynamite, or a quarter-pound of plastique."

Marcus Holland knelt on the floor, peering into the large round hole with its metal cap. "It's a floor safe."

"Very good," O'Neill said admiringly.

"Well ... so what?" Holland demanded.

"What would happen — say — if this lady's money, passport and ticket were stolen. Would it inconvenience her?"

"You know it would."

Charley O'Neill tapped the floor safe with his knuckles. "Since there's no money, passport, ticket or jewellery anywhere in the house, it's reasonably safe to assume they're in here."

Holland looked more closely at the safe. "It's got two combination locks."

"Yes, but only the left hand one has been moved off zero. Most people don't bother setting the second lock."

"Could we ask her for the combination?" Holland said, his eyes sparkling. "Threaten her?"

"We could do that, but it lacks subtlety. It's a last resort." O'Neill stared around the room again. "It might be a better idea if this house had a little accident … "

Marcus Holland gazed at him uncomprehendingly.

O'Neill stood up, dusted off his hands and strode into the kitchen. When Holland caught up with him, the American was going through the cupboards, pulling out two plastic bottles of cooking oil and a bottle of red oil suitable for an ornamental oil lamp. O'Neill took one of the bottles of cooking oil, carefully unscrewed the yellow cap and dropped it to the floor. Then he turned the bottle on its side and allowed the thick liquid to pour into a glutinous puddle on the stone floor, ensuring that the sticky oil ran down the wooden cupboard doors.

"We should pour some on the bedclothes," Holland suggested.

"We're not trying to burn the place down."

"But I thought … "

"Subtlety, remember? Throw her off guard, keep her off balance." He smeared the red perfumed lamp oil over the wooden cupboards and spilt it across the plastic worktop. He poured the remainder of the bottle into the puddle of cooking oil on the floor. Taking a disposable lighter from his pocket, he dropped it to the floor, crushing it beneath his heel. He removed the metal pieces and wrapped them in a handkerchief, then traced a line across the stone floor with the lighter fluid into the cooking oil, and then drew a second wet line away from the smaller puddle. Pulling out a matchbook bearing the name of the bar they'd just come from, he struck a light and dropped it to the floor. The line of lighter fluid popped alight, and raced to the larger pool, snapping into flame, then streaking out along the second line into the mixture of cooking and lamp oil. It ignited with a dull thump. Flames danced up along the oil-slicked cabinets, the fire quickly eating it's way through the wooden doors and on to the plastic-coated worktops which immediately began to bubble. Thick, noxious smoke was already wreathing around the room.

Charley O'Neill removed the spent match from the floor with the edge of a spoon. He carefully wrapped it up alongside the pieces of broken lighter, and then looked around the kitchen for a final time. The flames were now licking at the base of the wooden wall cabinets, pale blue and green fires dancing across them like blindly questing fingers. Satisfied, the American backed from the room and closed the door behind him, wiping the handle with his handkerchief. The stone building wouldn't burn down, but it would certainly give Ms Dalton something to think about.

ଓ

Briony Dalton smelt the smoke even from the bottom of the steps. It was sharp, bitter, tainted with plastic and rubber, fouling the fresh air.

She packed up to go home. The smell of burning intensified as she drew closer to the top of the cliff, and Briony could now see tendrils of greyish black smoke drifting out above her head. Frightened, she hurried on upwards, cursing the weight of the computer. When she reached the top step, she stopped, shocked: smoke was pouring from the kitchen windows.

Laying the computer down on the grass, Briony raced towards the house. It was a stone house, it wouldn't burn … it couldn't burn, could it? She ran around to the front of the house to come in by the front door. Hall, sitting room, bedrooms … all seemed fine, although the smell of smoke was everywhere. The kitchen door was closed. Briony touched the handle, and then drew her fingers back with a hiss of pain. The door handle was red hot.

She raced back out of the house and ran around the side — just as one of the kitchen windows exploded outwards. Glass sang past her face, tiny flecks nicking at her hands, her bare arms, the swell of her breasts, stomach and thighs. One piece clipped her forehead, another bit into her cheekbone. But she didn't feel the cuts. She risked a quick glance into the kitchen. The small room was ablaze, the wooden cabinets burning furiously; the wall cabinets in flames, the glasses and jars, the bottles of alcohol and bags of sugar having fed the flames. The fire seemed to be concentrated on this side of the room and, even as she watched, the flames were dying out as there was nothing left to consume.

Briony staggered away from the villa, pain from her cuts beginning to make itself apparent now, her own fear — her absolute terror — replacing the numbness that had seemed to take hold of her when she had seen the smoke and smelt the burning.

It might have been an accident, but she didn't think so.

She thought she would have been able to run, to escape, to hide. But she'd been wrong. They'd found her. She didn't know why they had set fire to the villa … a stone building wouldn't burn. Maybe it was just an attempt to frighten her.

It had succeeded.

ભ

When Greg Connors found her later that day, she was fast asleep, sitting hunched up over her computer, her arms cradled around it, clutching it like a child. Tears had dried in long streaks down her face.

Chapter Forty-Three

She remembered waking briefly, seeing Greg's face inches away from hers, feeling his strong arms around her. There were other brief periods of consciousness when she saw an old woman, face wrinkled like a forgotten apple, bending over her, strong fingers rough against her skin. She became aware, consciously or unconsciously of the odours that surrounded her: sweet-smelling herbs, bitter spices, acrid cheese, the musk of animals.

There was another, brief, curiously reassuring period of lucidity when she opened her eyes and found Greg sitting facing her, arms folded, chin nodding on to his chest, obviously dozing.

When Briony Dalton finally awoke, the sun was streaming in through the open window and Greg Connors had just walked into the room, briskly rubbing at his damp hair. He was naked except for a pair of swimming trunks, and his body glistened with sparkling water droplets. He smelt of sweat and salt.

"You're looking much better," he said, sitting down on a wooden chair.

"I feel much better," she began, but the words were thick and heavy in her mouth. She pushed herself up in the strange bed, pulling the single sheet to her chin, abruptly aware that she was naked and licked dry lips. "Where am I? How long have I been asleep?"

"All in good time. First a little sustenance. Anya!" he called.

The door opened almost immediately and the small, black-shawled women Briony remembered seeing in her dreams appeared in the doorway, carrying a thick earthenware bowl. She handed the bowl to Greg and cocked her head at Briony.

"I think she wants you to drink," Greg smiled, coming over to sit on the edge of the bed and handing the bowl across.

"What's in it?" Briony asked, looking suspiciously at thick, brownish soup.

"I don't know, and I sometimes think it's wiser not to ask. Just drink it. I've eaten and drunk everything she's put in front of me and I've come to no harm."

Briony sipped the steaming liquid, and found it surprisingly pleasant. It was a soup made of some sort of vegetable stock, with strips of what she took to be fish. There was also a curious tartness that bit at the back of her tongue; it might have been herbs, but she rather thought it was sour milk or yoghurt. It warmed her all the way down to her stomach, making it rumble, and she could feel her eyes watering with the spices. But by the time she had finished the bowl she felt alert and alive.

"I came down with a cold a couple of months back," Greg said, watching Briony hungrily finishing it. "Anya poured some of that into me and I was right as rain the following day."

"Well, I'm certainly feeling much better. Now, tell me what happened, how I got here and how long I've been here."

"I brought you here yesterday afternoon, close to this time, in fact; you've slept the clock around."

"There was a fire," Briony said suddenly, sitting forward, the sheet slipping away from her breasts.

Greg studiously kept his eyes on her face. "You had passed out, from shock, I think, or possibly heat prostration when I found you. I suppose you went running around like a mad thing when you saw the fire." He smiled slightly. "But I've got to tell you when I first saw you I thought something serious had happened. Gave me quite a fright. Anyway ... was I relieved when I discovered you were all right."

Briony looked into his bright hazel eyes for long moments and then self-consciously pulled the sheet up to her chin again.

"I can't understand how the fire started," Greg continued as if nothing had happened, aware of her hard stare. "The fire was confined to one side of the kitchen, and yet the cooker is on the other side of the room and there are no gas or electricity lines anywhere near where the fire was fiercest. In fact the only reason the fire raged so fiercely is because it had the wooden cabinets and the foodstuffs to feed off. I called the police. They looked at it, muttered something about careless American tourists and went away, so you're not going to get much help in that direction." He stood up and walked to the window, staring out over the stubbled fields to where the thin blue line of the sea was visible through the trees. "I think you might have an idea who's doing this — would I be right?"

"You might be," Briony said eventually, drawing her knees up to her chin and wrapping her arms around them.

"Do you want to tell me?" He turned from the window and regarded her seriously. "I do want to help."

"I know that, but ..."

"But ..? "

"It could be dangerous."

"I'm intrigued."

"Don't be," she said. "One person has already lost her life because of this."

Greg Connors sat down on the edge of Briony's bed. He reached out and lifted her chin in his hand, tilted her head back so he could look into her deep brown eyes. "I want to help."

"Why?" she asked, genuinely curious.

"Because ... because I like you," he said in a rush.

Briony laughed. "You barely know me."

"How long do you have to know someone before you decide you like them? We've a lot in common, you and I. We're both writers — we've written horror so we know we're kindred spirits — and I reckon we're both hiding out here for a couple of reasons."

"I didn't realise you were hiding on this island."

"Well, maybe hiding is too strong a word. Let's say I'm keeping a low profile. But at least mine isn't a life and death situation as yours is. Tell me about it."

There was never any suggestion that she was going to tell him the truth. She'd lose him and she needed him now; she needed his support, his simple presence around her. Someone out there was trying to frighten — possibly even trying to hurt — her and, being coolly practical about it, having Greg around might help. It certainly wouldn't harm.

"I'm writing a book," she said, "set in Italy about a large Italian family." This much was truth. "I did a couple of years research — on and off — in the villages and towns in the south of Italy, Corsica and Sardinia. I supported myself by doing articles for various newspapers back home; some were light travel pieces — best restaurants, worst bars, good night spots — but there were other, slightly more serious pieces. I wrote about political corruption, scandals in high places, and the Mafia connection." Briony gave her best television interview smile. "And never let anyone tell you that the Mafia, the Family, the Cosa Nostra, does not exist. It is alive and well and living in Italy and New York. I upset the wrong people, and it was suggested to me — none too tactfully, either — that it would be healthier for me to leave Italy."

"What did you do?" Greg asked.

"What could I do? I left. I returned to New York. I did an article for *The New Yorker*, others for *Time* and *Newsweek*, about political corruption and the Mafia influence in the Italian government, and about how many of these Italian families have huge holdings in America."

"What happened?"

"I received a visit from a beautifully dressed, softly spoken young man. He hinted — without actually saying it out loud, of course — that I should desist from my current statements.

"I pointed out to him that I was an author attempting to earn my living by my pen, doing journalistic pieces to keep the bread on the table between books. That's where I made my first mistake: telling him that I was working on a book. He wanted to buy the book from me, even offered to pay me for any future journalistic articles I might care to write. When I refused the money, he grew angry and then finally threatening." She stopped, thinking furiously; the essence of a good lie was to keep it simple, and so far this lie had grown out of all proportion. Most authors make good liars, since most of them spent their entire lives lying for a living. "When he was leaving he told me to say goodbye to my friends. But I laughed at him. Two days later one of my closest friends was killed in what the police thought was a burglary."

Greg stared at Briony in astonishment. "And you think ..."

"She was shot at point blank range by a .22 calibre pistol."

He shook his head. "I don't see the significance."

"Most professional assassins use that calibre gun for a hit, especially if they're going for a head shot. When the small calibre bullet goes into the skull it ricochets around inside, destroying the brain. Also, these smaller weapons are usually lighter and more easily concealed than a big gun. When they're fitted with silencers, they are virtually silent." She smiled crookedly. "I wrote three volumes of the *John Carnage* series, which was about a professional assassin."

"And your friend was shot in this way?"

"Yes."

"And now you think these people may be after you."

"I know it. I don't know how they followed me here, I was very careful. I thought I was safe."

"Well, you're not." He stood up and looked back at the villa. "Have you much stuff down there in the house?"

"Some clothes, bits and pieces. There's a floor safe. I've a passport, some extra cash, travellers cheques and the disks for my computer. The clothes I can do without, but the rest ..."

Greg nodded.

"Why, what are you thinking? What are you going to do?"

"Well, you can't return to the villa now, can you?"

"There are hotels."

"Nonsense." He grinned delightedly. "We'll collect your stuff, and take it out to my boat. You'll be safe there: they'll never even know where to start looking for you."

"But Greg."

"But nothing. Can you think of anything else?"

Briony shook her head, then allowed herself to smile. It was an ideal solution. Undoubtedly whoever had fired the villa would keep watch on the place until she returned and then they would strike again ... and maybe this time they might do more than just frighten her. She didn't even think twice about involving Greg. It wasn't as if she was using the young man. After all, he had suggested it himself, hadn't he?

"You can stay on the boat as long as you like. It's not terribly big, I'm afraid, and it's not terribly comfortable, but it's reasonably dry and it should be safe from the Mafia hit men."

"I can pay," she said quickly.

"I wouldn't hear of it."

"But I know nothing about boats," she protested weakly.

"You don't need to. I'll take care of that end of things." He was prowling around the room like an excited child. "We need to get you moving quickly. Whoever burnt the kitchen has had plenty of time to work out that you've not been around. They may be watching the house at the moment, so I'll scout around first, and then, if it's safe, we'll both go in and clear out your stuff. I'll be happier once you're on the boat."

So will I, Briony Dalton silently agreed.

ભ

Marcus Holland lay in the long grass on the bluff looking down over the villa and dozed in the afternoon heat. His white T-shirt and jeans were soiled with dirt and sweat and the brim on his hat had drooped, a dark moisture stain around the rim. A pair of small green military binoculars lay in his limp fingers.

The dull irritation brought him awake. A strange, insistent ache high on his cheek, burning, stinging. As he drifted back to consciousness, he flicked at the side of his face with his fingers — and white hot pain laced across his flesh. He sat up with a strangled scream, clutching his hand — and found himself looking down the gleaming metallic length of a six-inch diver's knife, the blade wickedly serrated. Rough, callused fingers closed around his throat, forcing his head up, the point of the knife pricking the flesh beneath his chin. He attempted to swallow, but his neck was stretched almost to breaking point.

"Tell me what you're doing?" The voice was British, hard and insistent.

Holland blinked sweat from his eyes and looked away from the mesmerising blade. A blond-haired young man was holding the knife, eyes hidden behind mirrored sun glasses, face an implacable mask.

"Tell me what you're doing." The point of the knife traced a line from cheek to jaw, opening a shallow stinging cut.

Holland choked and the vice-like grip on his throat loosened slightly, but the knife never moved.

"I'm ... I'm a birdwatcher," he whispered.

"You're full of shit. You were watching the villa. You the one who fired it?"

"I don't know what you're talking about …"

"Stand up!"

Holland gazing at him uncomprehendingly. Greg Connors locked his fingers around Holland's throat and hauled him to his feet. The slighter man was now red-faced, gasping, blood welling from the cut and the tiny puncture marks in his throat and chin.

Connors brought his face up close to the American's, smelling his sour sweat and fear. "You get your kicks from terrorising a poor woman, do you? That makes you a big man, eh? You think you've got what it takes … well, take this." Connors suddenly released his grip on Marcus Holland's throat and then struck him in the centre of the chest with the heel of his hand. Holland's arms wind-milled as he sailed backwards over the edge of the incline. He attempted to scream, but his throat was too bruised, his mouth too dry.

The ground dropped sharply downwards from his observation point to the beach. Low scrubs, stunted thorny bushes, twisted trees and marram grass covered a slope of shale, grit and rocks. Holland's body gained momentum as it fell. He stopped rolling after the first few yards and then slid on his chest and stomach in an ever-increasing cloud of dust down the slope to the beach.

Greg Connors stood on the edge of the incline and waited until the dust had settled, coating the unmoving body of the man far below. He didn't think he was dead, not unless he'd been unlucky enough to crack his skull on a rock — and even then, Greg wasn't sure he was going to shed too many tears about that. He rammed the knife back into it's sheath and turned and walked back up through the bushes to the farmhouse.

Briony was waiting by the door for him, sitting in the shade, wearing her bright yellow bikini, sun glasses and a broad straw hat, a splash of colour in the shadows.

"Anyone?" she asked.

"There was no one around," Greg Connors lied. "Let's go and get your stuff now."

૪

Five hundred yards away, Charley O'Neill lowered his binoculars and smiled. Yes, things were working out just fine. He turned his attention to the unmoving bundle on the beach and his smile widened into a grin. Pity about Holland, though. He'd grown rather used to him.

૪

The light was fading as Briony and Greg returned from the villa. Greg had bustled around the bedroom, shoving everything he could find into the single suitcase, while she had worked on the safe in the floor. It had taken her three tries before she had remembered which version of the combination she had set up; was it her birth date in reverse or her New York apartment phone number or the publication date of her first book? It turned out to be Gabrielle's birthday, 2891967.

There was a thousand dollars in American Express travellers cheques, her passport and — most importantly — two copies of her work to date of *A Woman Scorned* on four computer disks. Every evening, when she had completed her work, she copied everything she had written that day on to the disks. It was her insurance. If anything ever happened to the computer, if the hard-disk crashed, or there was an accident and the machine was broken, she could recreate her book with these disks.

"I've got what I was looking for," she said, showing the cheques and passport to Greg, the disks tucked into the back pocket of the jeans she had changed into.

He lifted her bag. "You're all packed here. Let's go."

They had almost reached the farm when they heard the old woman's scream followed, almost immediately, by a long, vituperative string of Greek. Greg dropped the suitcase and dashed the last hundred yards towards the farmhouse, the diver's knife clutched in a white-knuckled grip.

Briony saw him race into the dark doorway and then reappear immediately, flying backwards, followed by a three-legged stool with the metallic glint of the knife buried in it. He sprawled in the dust, clutching at his chest. A figure loomed in the doorway, unmistakably male, tall, broad. Briony squinted, cursing the fading light and her own short-sightedness. There was something about the shape of the person ...

The figure stopped and stared at her before darting away, something bulky on his shoulder.

Greg Connors stumbled to his feet, both hands still clutching the centre of his chest where the stool had struck him. He had a fleeting glimpse of Briony's white face and wide eyes as she raced past into the house.

"Wait!" he shouted, wincing as pain lanced into his bruised ribs. But she ignored him. When he staggered into the room behind her, she was sitting on the bed, her head in her hands, the carrying case for her portable computer cradled in her lap. He knelt on the floor in front of her and attempted to embrace her, expecting to find tears. But when she looked up at him her eyes were bright, her lips fixed in a humourless grin.

"He stole my machine."

"All your work lost?" Greg asked.

"No ... not at all," Briony Dalton said. "I was almost expecting this. And let me tell you, they're going to get one hell of a surprise!"

Chapter Forty-Four

Matt Moriarty was twenty-six years old. And he wasn't going to live to see twenty-seven.

Now there was a thought to wake up to.

Lying in the bed staring at the ceiling, he traced the line of the cracks across the sagging plasterwork.

Walk on a crack, break your mother's back.

He'd never tried crack.

He'd tried just about everything else, though.

Without moving his head, he lifted his right arm and looked at his wrist ... and then remembered that he'd pawned his watch a long time ago. It had been his grandfather's watch, and he had swapped it for a bag of horse; a lifetime of memories in return for thirty minutes of dreams.

It was early. He could tell by the shadows on the wall, the way they crept up the ceiling. The street outside was quiet and the pervasive smells of the canals hadn't ripened to an unbearable level yet. So it was ... seven o'clock, give or take a few minutes. And, after all, he had all the time in the world.

And none.

Time was running out, except in his case it had run out a long time ago and all he was hearing now was the hollow echo as it vanished into the distance. He was living on borrowed time.

He was bathed in sweat; he could smell himself ... and something else too. He sniffed, but his nostrils were clogged with mucus and then he suddenly recognised the odour that caught at the back of his throat. It was ammonia. He had wet himself again. His bladder was letting him down a lot recently; in fact it had become so common that the mornings when he awoke on dry sheets were the exception. He was reverting to his childhood: dribbling, peeing, unable to walk unaccompanied, barely able to eat, to hold a spoon steady and reach his mouth.

Jesus Christ, what a way to live. What a way to die!

Matt Moriarty sat up in bed, slowly, painfully, the room shifting, swimming before him as he straightened. He opened the drawer of the small bedside cabinet, looking for his works. Rianne prepared a needle before she left for the night in case things got too bad in the small hours of the morning. So far he had managed to avoid using it — though actually knowing it was there, ready and waiting for him, was part of the game — but this morning he felt he needed a little jolt to get him started into the day.

There was a wad of money in the drawer, a mixture of Dutch guilder and English pounds. Some of it was the money Catherine Garrett had given him, the rest he had earned — if that was the right word — by posing for photographs for the various British photographers. He smiled, remembering how they had dressed him in suitably dirty and torn T-shirts that exposed his scabbed arms and prominent ribs, and found some tip of a room for him to pose in and then told him how to stand and hold himself while they shot rolls of film.

What a joke — and it had all been at his mother's expense.

He pulled out the money, counting through it. It was disappearing surprisingly quickly — his habit had a voracious appetite. He didn't even want to think about what would happen when it finally vanished ... but maybe he wouldn't have to think that far ahead. When you got the habit, you lived from hit to hit, from day to day, then from hour to hour, and the number of hits you could score in between.

Rianne had wanted him to sign on as a registered user and go on the programme. But he couldn't be bothered with all the formalities, and that methadone really fucked you up. What was the point of filling yourself with that shit? It did nothing for you. And what happened if you came off the junk? What sort of life was there for you? OK, so you were straight — but what about the dreams? Did they just go away because you weren't using? What about the power the drug gave you, that incredible feeling of control? How could you forget about that; how could you give that up?

He'd come too far to give it up now. And at least he had enough money here to keep him happy for a week, maybe a little longer if he started cutting the stuff himself with sugar. He didn't want to think beyond the week.

A wave of disgust suddenly washed over him and he flung the money across the room, then folded forward, clutching his stomach.

Jesus Christ ... what had he become? Twenty-six years old ... twenty-six ... HIV positive ...

"I regret to inform you sir ... ." Big brown eyes staring at him, the result of the blood test in one hand, AIDS literature in the other, the doctor looked like he was about to burst into tears. Well, shit, he didn't have AIDS did he? What had he got to regret?

"I regret to inform you ... "

Regret to inform.

Regret.

Yeah, well he'd a lot of regrets. Like a dead baby; he regretted that. Sometimes when he'd a bad trip he heard that baby crying, screaming somewhere distant, a faint, thin, mewling cry, like a sea gull or a cat ...

Just a little shot to perk him up. He lifted the needle out of the drawer and held it up to the light, looking hard at the almost colourless liquid. It seemed so innocent ... like water, so soft ...

Soft drugs don't lead to hard drugs. Well, shit, of course they don't ... at least not all the time. But you weren't taking the drugs, that's not what you were into, you were chasing the buzz. And the heavier stuff gave you a better buzz. For Christ's sake, you had to really work at being a heroin addict. The first couple of times he tried it — smoking it, chasing the dragon — he puked for hours afterwards. But that was after he'd gotten the buzz. It lasted maybe twenty seconds, but was it good. It was spiritual.

He'd started doing hash, a little grass and then pills. Uppers and downers, bennies, ludes, speed. He'd done speed for a long time, loved the rush, the sharp intensity of the light, the colours, the sounds, staying awake for twenty-four, thirty-six hours at a stretch. Yeah, that'd been good.

And then coke.

Now, coke was something else. Things went better with coke, that's for sure. He'd done that for a long time too. And then, finally, the heavy shit. Just a taster, smoked it first, then did a little muscle popping, injecting into a muscle for the buzz until he wanted something more, something sharper, quicker. He remembered the first time he'd mainlined.

He was fucked.

Right about then, he reckoned.

Matt Moriarty shook his head savagely, the sudden movement hurting him. He'd been fucked a long time sooner, about the time he pulled on his first roach. About the time he walked away from everything. About the time he ran away from school for the last time. About the time he ran away from school for the first time. About the time his mother's book became a best-seller. About the time his mother started writing.

He needed a little push. Just to clear his head …

Crouched over the edge of the bed he worked his left arm to and fro, hand squeezed into a fist. He couldn't find a vein. He couldn't find a fucking vein!

A thin sheen of sweat appeared on his forehead and he was conscious of the dampness beneath his arms. Laying the needle carefully on the bed, he stood up and stripped naked. His body was painfully thin, much of it covered in puckered, bruised and scabbed flesh. The back of his arms, the insides of his legs were virtually useless now. Rianne had managed to find a usable vein on the back of his hands, but he knew he hadn't the dexterity to manage that.

There was the large vein in his penis.

Last resort, some junkies called it. You had to be in a really bad way to use it. Mind you, once you'd fucked up every other bit of your anatomy, you might as well go ahead and complete the job.

Holding his flaccid member in his hand, he lifted the needle. How long had it been since he'd made love to a woman? A year, eighteen months? Never let anyone tell you heroin was good for your sex drive: it certainly fucked you up, that was sure enough, but that was all it did.

The heroin hit his system with a rush, instant, idyllic ecstasy washing over him like a sweet orgasm. His fingers much steadier now, he carefully removed the needle from his penis and lay back on the sodden bed, a smile beginning to twist his thin lips. Yeah, so there were disadvantages to using horse, but there were disadvantages to life itself.

He giggled; he supposed he had his mother to thank for this high. That was about all the fucking bitch had ever done for him.

He traced the cracks in the ceiling again, finding new and exciting patterns in them. The web of life, the woof, the warp. Maybe he should have been a writer; fantasy maybe, science fiction, or pornography. Jesus, if his mother could write then anyone could.

Science fiction. He'd write science fiction. He had a great idea for a plot …

And because he was Briony Dalton's son, he'd have no problems getting it published.

A best-seller. That's what he'd write. A best-seller.

He was aware of his heart beating rapidly, a solid thumping, pounding away with the sudden excitement of the idea. It was so simple, why had he never thought of it before? He'd be a writer, a great writer. He'd use all the dreams the shit had given him over the years in his novels. He'd write science fiction and fantasy ... and maybe horror too. He could use some of the images of the bad trips he'd had for the horror stories. And he'd start this morning.

Yes, yes, yesyesyesyesyesyes ... right now.

He'd need pen, paper ... no a typewriter, or better still a word processor ... but he couldn't type. He'd learn. But why bother? Rianne could type. He could dictate it and she'd type it. He knew someone who'd get him a portable computer cheap ... he had the money. It'd be an investment in his future.

His heart was thundering with the excitement. He hadn't felt this good in days.

If he could write a thousand, no, two thousand words a day, then that was fourteen thousand words a week, then that was fifty-six thousand words a month, then that was a novel every two months, six novels a year.

And his mother was getting millions of dollars a novel. Well, he wouldn't get that, but he'd demand a hundred thousand and he wouldn't take anything less ...

And ... andandandandandand ...

∞

When Rianne Moriarty let herself into the small bare room she wasn't surprised to find her brother lying naked on the bed, a thin trickle of dried blood on his thigh, crusted hard and brown on the stained sheets.

Nor was she surprised when she pressed her fingers to his throat and found no pulse there.

She had known — deep down in that core of her which still recognised truth and fact even when the rest of her didn't want to admit it — she had known that one day she was going to find Matt like this.

The only thing which surprised her was the look of contentment on his face and the smile on his lips.

Matthew Moriarty was happy at last.

Chapter Forty-Five

"So, what really happened to Mr Holland, Kaho?" Josef Bach asked very softly, tossing the hospital report across the enormous desk. Sheets spilled from the manila folder and scattered on the floor. "An accident?"

The Japanese woman ignored the pages and shook her small head, her eyes on the box she was deftly unwrapping. "No, sir, quite the contrary. Mr Holland was careless. He allowed himself to fall asleep and was caught by Miss Dalton's new-found companion. The man pushed Holland off the edge of a cliff."

"How very inventive. What do we know about this companion?"

"Nothing at the moment, but our people are working on it. An impoverished Englishman eking out a living on the island. The islands are full of dropouts." Kaho pulled bubble-wrap from the cardboard box and dropped it on the floor.

"And Mr Holland?"

"Mr Holland suffered extensive injuries. He broke his nose, his jaw, several teeth, both arms, some ribs, and suffered numerous cuts and abrasions as he slid down three hundred feet of very rough terrain. Most of the skin was rubbed off his face, chest, stomach, thighs and buttocks," she added in the same controlled monotone. "You have the Greek hospital report. His medical insurance arranged for him to be flown home. I will get you an updated report as soon as it is ready. However, there is every indication that there will be scars: it is unlikely he will work in television again."

"Oh, dear. And he did so enjoy that life." Bach smiled coldly and then completely dismissed him. "So what have we got here?" he asked as his secretary removed a flat black box from its cardboard wrapping.

"While Mr Holland was sliding down the cliff, his companion, Mr O'Neill, had traced Briony Dalton to a nearby farmhouse. While she and her boyfriend retrieved her clothes from her burnt-out villa he used the opportunity to break into the farmhouse she was staying in and steal her personal computer."

Bach sat forward, looking at the box with renewed interest. "This is it?"

"Yes, sir. Holland must have given O'Neill your name. O'Neill immediately flew to the Rome office and left the machine there with instructions that it was to be brought to your personal attention. They contacted me and I ordered it flown here straightaway."

Bach nodded, impressed. "Pay this O'Neill a ten thousand pound bonus. We can always use someone with initiative and intelligence."

Kaho set the machine down in front of Bach and popped the lid. She moved around to turn on the power and Bach's hands shot out, encircling her waist, moving across her hips. She ignored him as she powered up the machine, continuing as if nothing was happening as his hands moved up beneath the patterned silk of her blouse to her small breasts.

Bach hadn't enjoyed the pleasure of the Japanese woman's company for a long time; perhaps it was time to renew the acquaintance, he mused, and then suddenly all other thoughts were forgotten as the computer blipped, the screen flashed alight and the directory began to scroll upwards.

The secretary's short green lacquered nail shot out and touched the screen. "There. WS is usually used for WordStar. It is one of the earliest word processing packages. I'm surprised Briony Dalton is still using it, but perhaps this was the first program she learned and she simply never bothered to change."

Bach pulled Kaho over until she was sitting on his lap. She could feel him hardening beneath her, even though his eyes were fixed on he screen.

"Where would she have the novel?" Bach demanded.

"It would presumably be in a subdirectory of the WordStar programme," Kaho muttered. She typed CD\WS. The screen cleared to show a different listing. "This is the WordStar file. Here is what we're looking for." There were three subdirectories listed at the top of the page; the first was called WOMSCORN.

"*A Woman Scorned*," Bach murmured, "that's it. That's it! Can you open the file?" Bach rarely used a computer except when he ran business, statistical and financial programs. Word processing was for letter writers and he paid people to do that.

"To open WordStar, you type WS," Kaho said, and pressed the two keys.

A green light which indicated that the machine's hard disk was working came on ... and the screen immediately blanked.

She tried again. Again the hard disk whirred, but the screen remained blank.

Frowning, Kaho typed, DIR/W.

The directory appeared, but spread across the screen now, rather than scrolling upwards. "Look, there it is." she pointed to the command, WS.EXE on the screen. "It should work."

"Try it again," Bach demanded.

Kaho's fingers returned to the keyboard when she abruptly became aware that the hard disk light was flashing furiously as if the disk was working ... but she wasn't using it.

Seconds later the screen cleared, but there was nothing on it, except a C>_ on the top left-hand corner of the screen. She typed DIR.

DIRECTORY NOT FOUND.

Her fingers tapped across the keyboard trying combination after combination but always with the same result. Biting the inside of her cheek to prevent herself from smiling, she turned her head to look at Bach. "There's nothing there; the machine has wiped itself. Everything's gone. The Dalton woman is no fool; she must have had the machine bugged in case it was ever stolen."

Lifting the computer in one hand, she said "This is so much useless plastic."

Chapter Forty-Six

"I thought you'd be devastated by the loss of the machine," Greg said, pulling strongly on the oars of the inflatable rubber dingy. He glanced over his shoulder to where the sailing boat rocked on the gentle evening swell less than a hundred yards away.

Briony Dalton was squatting facing Greg, her arms stretched out to clutch at the handles on either side of the tiny craft. Tilting her head back, she laughed delightedly and when she looked at Greg again her eyes were bright, sparkling. "I had the machine bugged," she said.

"Bugged? Why? How?"

"Like most writers I'm absolutely terrified of someone stealing my work, or even reading it before I'm finished."

"I know what you mean."

"When I bought the portable computer the salesman advised me to insure it against, `high latent shrinkage,' which is Americanese for theft. Losing the machine didn't worry me — losing the material on it did however, or having my manuscript, notes and letters sold to some rag newspaper worried me even more. I became completely paranoid and immediately took the machine to a guy I knew who worked with computers. I asked him to write me a little security device on the hard disk. When you turn on my machine you have to type in "The Book Starts Here," to give you access to the machine. If you just typed in any standard DOS commands or WS, which is the standard way of opening WordStar, the programme I use, the machine actually begins erasing itself. And once it's blanked the machine space is then overwritten, so you cannot undelete and recreate the material."

Greg shook his head. "I don't understand. What do you mean 'overwritten?' I know nothing about computers."

"Well, I'll have to teach you. When you delete something from a computer, it doesn't really go away ... it sort of lingers there, rather like a ghost. With the proper programme, you can undelete it. Even if you completely wiped out all your files it would be possible to bring them back within a matter of minutes with the right programme."

Greg continued rowing, not quite understanding the concept. "But your programme won't allow this to happen."

"No, all the space on the hard disk is overwritten with some sort of computer rubbish. I'm not sure of the details, but it means the material cannot be recreated."

"But what about your book? What are you going to do about that?"

Briony reached into her back pocket and pulled out two of the four disks. "It's here. All I need is another computer, the same word-processing package, and I'm back in business."

"And the people who're chasing you? Will they be back?"

Briony Dalton frowned. "I think so. We've cheated them so far. Now they're going to get mad."

"What can you do to stop them?"

"Publish my book," she said fiercely, her vehemence surprising him.

08

"This is *The Author*, a twenty-one-foot Hublot-designed Club Mousquetaire," Greg Connors said proudly, helping Briony aboard the disconcertingly small boat.

There was a tiny area below decks where Greg tossed the bags; Briony poked her head in. It was so small she could touch each miniature window from the centre of the deck with ease. Sleeping there was going to be a nightmare. And there was no toilet.

"I know it's primitive," Greg continued, sensing her disappointment, "but at least you'll be safe here."

"I know that ... and it's not that I'm ungrateful, but it is true I was expecting something a little bigger."

"With a toilet and a sink, something like that?"

Briony nodded. And then she laughed at his expression. "Don't mind me; I've never sailed ... well, I tell a lie. I did sail once, but it was a round-the-world cruise on the *Queen Elizabeth*."

"I'm not sure that constitutes sailing. The *Queen Elizabeth's* lifeboats are bigger than this," Greg muttered.

Finding her footing on the gently rocking deck, Briony put her hands on his hips and kissed him quickly on the lips. "I'm not ungrateful; truly I'm not." She stepped away and sat down carefully, enjoying the gentle rocking movement of the boat. Overhead the first of the stars were faintly visible through the haze and up and down the coast she could see little patches of lights, where the holiday spots were in full swing and faint, very faint — like the distant buzzing of a fly — they heard music, something dull and throbbing, trembling out over the water.

Greg sat down facing her. The boat was so small that their knees were almost touching. "Now, the way I see it we've two choices. We can remain here — in which case your friends might just catch up with us sooner or later, or we can move on. Have you anything holding you here?"

"Nothing."

"So you've no objection to sailing away with me?" he asked with a grin.

"Will the boat take us? I mean, is it safe for deep-sea, wide-ocean sort of sailing?"

"This is one of the sturdiest small boats in the world," Greg said proudly. "And it isn't one of your fibreglass toys, either." He slapped his hand down on the deck. "This is wood."

"Is that a 'yes'?"

"It's a 'yes'." He lifted his arm, looking at his watch, squinting to read it in the gathering gloom. "We'll remain at anchor overnight, and then in the morning I'll row over for some supplies. Then I'll plot us a course out of here."

"Where are we going?"

"Where do you want to go?"

"Ireland," she said, startling even herself.

"Well," Greg said, "She'd get us there, but how many months have you got to spare?"

"Where's the nearest airport other than Corfu?"

"That would probably be Heraklion, on Crete."

"Could you take me there?" she pleaded.

Greg's teeth flashed in the gloom. "It would be a pleasure." He glanced sidelong at her. "This is like something from a book."

"Well you know what they say about truth being stranger than, et cetera, et cetera ..."

"Maybe you can put this into a book one day," Greg suggested.

Briony grinned. "No one would believe it,"

ଔ

When Briony Dalton first started writing it had been on a Royal typewriter on the kitchen table in the room that doubled as kitchen, dining and sitting room. She had pecked away with two fingers until she had eventually saved enough to go out and learn how to type properly. The courses were expensive even then, but her needs were very simple and she never finished the typing course and she only did it to increase her speed so that she could type as fast as the words spilled out of her. Later, when she had begun regularly selling short stories and articles, she had bought herself a Brother portable typewriter. The difference it made to her life was extraordinary. Now she was no longer stuck to one particular room. She simply picked up the machine, slipped it into its box and off she went. Much of her early work had been written on

Dollymount Strand in Dublin, or in the Phoenix Park sitting with her back to a tree, pecking away, idly watching Matt and Rianne playing in the rolling green parkland before her. They would have been toddlers then.

Surprising that she hadn't thought of the children for so long.

Later, when personal computers became affordable, she had been one of the first writers to begin using one. And if the portable typewriter made a difference to her writing life, then the computer revolutionised that difference. Now she no longer had to type a manuscript three or four times, and in terms of time saved it was worth an awful lot of money to her. Suddenly she was doing two and three and then four short books a year rather than one. She would type the manuscript as normal, only now it was stored on disk, rather than paper. Then she could correct the material on screen, move it, shift it around, edit it, change names, correct spellings, and when everything was finally to her satisfaction she could print it, and it came out in perfectly straight lines with even margins on both sides of the paper, each page automatically numbered. It was wondrous.

But the computer, despite its extraordinary advantages, tied her down to one particular room and at times she felt she was back where she started.

And then the portable computer arrived. Miniaturisation and micro-circuitry had reduced the size of the machines until they could fit into a suitcase. Then laptop machines came along, and they could fit into a briefcase, and recently `notebook computers' were available that weighed around a pound and fitted into a handbag. Suddenly she had her freedom again. Her favourite machine, the big — by portable standards — Hitachi had weighed eleven pounds. The new machines, three times as fast, with twice as much memory, weighed half that.

She had written at least ninety per cent of her work on computers of one type or another, and she had never been far from a machine … until now.

Briony Dalton sat in the bow of the boat with her back to the mainsail, looking out across the placid waters of the bay, with the coasts of Greece and Albania clearly visible. There was a thick loose-leafed copybook in her lap, a soft lead pencil between her teeth.

It had been so long since she had written by hand that she had almost forgotten how.

It was a frustrating experience. Her thoughts raced ahead but she couldn't write that fast, and her writing became progressively more and more illegible as she moved down the page. Because she could only fit six or seven words to a line, she found it impossible to `visualise' a page of the manuscript, the way the words would sit, its shape and style. She also found it impossible to work out how many hand-written pages equalled one page of text.

She flexed her hand, working her stiff fingers. She knew there were still writers who preferred to work with pen and paper, enjoying the visceral experience of putting the words down on the page, the smell of the paper, the odours of ink and pencil. But she wasn't one of them. Writing was a job; maybe it had once been a pleasure, but not now. Now it was something she did ... it was the only thing she did.

She pulled the brim of her hat lower and squinted out across the water. There was a shape, indistinct and ambiguous, disturbing the blinding shimmer on the waves. Blinking hard, aware that her heart was beginning to pound, she stared into the twisting heat waves until she eventually made out Greg Connors pulling strongly in the small inflatable boat, supplies piled high around him. They were going to do a little Mediterranean cruising, sail south for Crete ... and in truth she wasn't entirely sure she was looking forward to it. The boat was so small and she still wasn't entirely comfortable in his presence.

The previous night, Greg had elected to remain on deck and offered her the privacy of the cabin. She hadn't bothered undressing — there didn't seem any point — and although, when she lay down, she'd been quite certain she wasn't going to get to sleep the gentle rocking motion of the boat, the slight slapping of the waves against the wood had conspired to lull her into a deep, dreamless slumber. She had awakened refreshed, ravenous and stiff — incredibly stiff — at dawn this morning.

Greg had helped her up with a broad grin. She was moving like an old woman. "It gets you like that the first time. You should try sleeping on deck, there's a bit more room." He moved around behind her, his strong fingers working at her taut neck muscles while she moved her head to and fro.

"You should have been a masseur," she murmured.

"I was," he said, laughing at the memory, "in Berlin."

"I thought you were a barman in a gay bar," Briony said.

Greg nodded, obviously impressed and rather pleased that she'd remembered. "I was, during the night. But during the day I was a masseur in a proper massage parlour. Nothing seedy," he added quickly, "although some of the customers — women as well as men — certainly thought other things were on the menu. I got a couple of invitations to come and give them private treatment."

"And did you?"

Greg slapped her back. "Maybe I did."

Briony turned quickly. "Men or women?"

"I'm not saying." He winked and gestured to the shore. "I'm going to the village for supplies," he said, and then added diffidently, "I'm afraid I don't have that much money … "

"Of course." Briony ducked back below decks where her suitcase had been stowed. She reappeared with all the Greek money she possessed. "Buy whatever you think we need," she said, pressing it into his hands, momentarily surprised at how rough the flesh of his palms felt.

He saw her surprised look and held up both hands, palms outwards for her to examine. The skin was hard, the flesh of his fingers and around the base of his thumb callused. "Sailor's hands," he said. "I'll be gone most of the morning," he added, shoving the money into the back pocket of his shorts. He hauled in the inflatable dinghy which had been tied up to the stern of the little boat and Briony found herself staring at his naked back, the swell of his muscles clearly delineated beneath the tanned skin, the firm flesh of his buttocks. A wry smile twisted her lips. There was every possibility that she was going to end up in bed with him, she knew, but at least it looked as if she might enjoy it.

Greg climbed gingerly into the rubber craft, squeezing the sides, testing for leaks. Settling himself in the centre he picked up the oars and smiled at Briony. "Cast off, will you?" He fitted the oars in the locks as Briony fumbled with the knots. "What'll you be doing while I'm gone?"

"Writing," she said shortly, finally easing the knot free and tossing the rope into the dingy. As she leaned against the starboard side, smiling, watching him row away, she found herself analysing her cold-blooded assessment of her current situation, slightly shocked by the emotionless way she looked at things, and yet recognising that this wasn't the first time she'd used people to further her own ends.

Like most writers, she was a very independent person, remarkably content with her own company. She lived for so much of the time in her imagination that she often found other people's company intrusive. She had also discovered, down through the years that as she retreated more and more from the real world — and this was especially so when she was writing several books a year or when she became completely wrapped up in a novel — that she found it difficult to relate to the real world and its problems. She started looking at everything in terms of a plot, a storyline. She had also discovered — too late — that life, unlike a novel, doesn't have a nice attractive ending with all the loose ends neatly tied up.

So she watched Greg Connors row away and raised her hand dutifully, because he would expect it. She felt nothing for him, absolutely nothing. She was grateful for what he had done, she appreciated what he was doing and he'd be useful to have around. In return, she would probably teach him a little about the craft of writing — she had a vague idea this was his real reason for helping her — and she'd probably end up sleeping with him … but then again, maybe he'd think she was too old for him. Well, maybe she could teach him something about that too…

∞

Briony caught the rope Greg Connors tossed over and hauledf the dinghy in closer, manoeuvring it alongside *The Author*. She looked at the enormous pile of provisions which took up most of the small inflatable and groaned inwardly; if they were to go into the cabin, it was going to be one tight fit tonight.

"Any strangers in the village?" She asked as Greg handed over the provisions.

"Lots, mostly tourists. But I suppose the people after you could easily disguise themselves as tourists."

It took nearly ten minutes to unload the rubber boat. While Greg was deflating it Briony discovered a two-day-old copy of *The London Times* and a day-old *Le Monde* in the last bag. She scanned them almost hungrily. Newspapers were an essential part of her stock in trade; for her novels to be topical, she had be up to date on what was happening in the world.

The article was at the bottom of the back page of *Le Monde*, and she was suddenly glad of the French lessons Gabrielle had insisted she take. She made her way through it slowly, translating it word for word, her blood chilling with each simple sentence.

AUTHOR'S SON DIES OF DRUG OVERDOSE

Matthew Moriarty, heroin-addicted son of best-selling author, Briony Dalton, has been found dead in his apartment in Amsterdam of a drug overdose. His body was discovered by his sister, Rianne Moriarty. Matthew Moriarty was 26 years old and had been recently diagnosed as an AIDS sufferer. Suicide has not been ruled out.

Briony allowed the paper to fall over the side, the sheets spreading out on the water like leaves before slowly drifting away. She had no tears to shed. She felt nothing. She might as well have been reading about a stranger.

And that very idea terrified her.

Chapter Forty-Seven

"He wouldn't have approved."

Catherine Garrett turned to look at Rianne Moriarty, the only other person present at the funeral service. Even the priest had seemed almost embarrassed saying the Mass for just two people.

"He was an avowed atheist," Rianne continued numbly, gazing at the simple coffin sitting before the plain altar in the tiny church on the outskirts of Amsterdam. "Or maybe he was just a lapsed Catholic — what is it they say: once a Catholic, always a Catholic," she murmured, smiling ruefully. She hadn't been inside a church for years herself, but faced with the reality of Matt's death she had turned to the religion of her childhood and decided to give him a Catholic service. "He played around with a lot of religions," she continued. She was babbling on, she knew it and she knew there was nothing she could do about it. "He became a Buddhist, a Hare Krishna and he even joined some occult witchcraft group in Greece, though he said that was really only for the sex. They weren't real witches, just some left-over hippies living on an island they had claimed as their own, practising free love and smoking dope." She fell silent.

Catherine glanced sidelong at her. Rianne was dressed all in black, her close-cropped hair hidden beneath a simple black scarf. Without make-up, she looked younger than her twenty-two years and Catherine impulsively put her arm around her. Rianne moved into the encircling arm and the tears came then, large and silent. She wept without sobbing, virtually without sound.

She cried for a while and Catherine struggled to keep her own emotions in check. She thought she could imagine what the girl was going through ... and then realised that her imagination didn't even come close. For most of her life Rianne had been alone, had been forced to make her own way in the world, to act and make decisions that demanded a level of maturity far beyond her years. It was only in the past few months that she had finally found a focus, someone to care for, someone to love. Now even that had been taken away from her.

There was a discreet cough and Catherine turned her head to see the dark-suited funeral director waiting in the aisle beside her. Without saying a word he indicated the coffin with his black-gloved hand and stepped away. Catherine nodded gratefully.

Catherine Garrett had come to Amsterdam the moment the news had broken on the wire services. Matt Moriarty's name was still reasonably high profile and most of the newspapers had carried articles of greater or lesser extent on the young man's death, with some of the British tabloids — especially those which had splashed the pictures of his 'living' conditions — making it front page news, accompanied by a stark photograph of the body on the morgue slab. Catherine wondered how Josef Bach had arranged that spectacularly tasteless piece of journalism. And even if he hadn't personally arranged it, it had appeared in one of his newspapers so he was more or less responsible. But she was hardly in a position to apportion guilt: she knew that the money the newspapers had paid Matt for the photographs had paid for the drugs that killed him. And hadn't she therefore, played some part in his death? She too had to bear some of the responsibility.

She had arranged the funeral service which was held after the inquest, where an open verdict had been recorded. Had Matt deliberately taken an overdose knowing he only had weeks at most left to live? Or had it truly been an accident?

Her only consolation was that she was glad he had been spared the worst excesses of the dreadful disease.

From her experience she knew the funeral would be a circus, so she had used her contacts and leaked the news that the funeral would be tomorrow in a nearby church, in order to spare Rianne and herself any further pain and allow them a measure of privacy. Not much of a life, she thought, dead at twenty-six and only two people at the funeral.

Catherine reached over and touched Rianne's hand. They stood up together and followed the two pallbearers, one at either end of the trolley carrying the coffin, down the aisle. Catherine had thought that Rianne would want Matt's body cremated, but she'd been surprised to discover that he and Rianne had talked about his impending death and his last wish was that he wanted to be buried in the family plot in Glasnevin Cemetery in Dublin. He wanted to go home, he told his sister.

The two women watched the coffin being loaded into the hearse and waited until it had pulled away, steel-grey exhaust pluming on the damp morning air. It would be on the evening flight to Heathrow, then transferred to an Aer Lingus flight to Dublin where a Dublin funeral service would take over and complete the arrangements.

Catherine and Rianne watched the car make its slow and sedate way out of the small churchyard and head down the arrow-straight road. The rain which had been promising all morning finally broke, and light drizzle hissed across the tarmac. They climbed into the only other car in the churchyard, an anonymous Volkswagen Passat Catherine had hired at the airport, and sat in silence, as the windscreen gradually misted up.

"It's at times like this that I wished I smoked," Rianne said eventually. Her fingers twisted in her lap. "I need something to do with my hands."

"Have you made any decisions?"

"I don't think there are any decisions for me to make." Rianne shrugged, staring straight ahead, tears sparkling in her eyes. "I was thinking of going back to the States; I'm sure I can get a job in the movie business again."

"Do you want to?" Catherine asked, her voice carefully neutral.

"Do I have a choice?" Rianne said bitterly. "I don't know how to do anything else."

"I need a secretary," Catherine said after the long silence that followed. She turned to look at the younger woman. "You know I'm working on this definitive biography of your mother. I'm going to need a secretary to help me keep on top of the research, the typing, handle the correspondence ... stuff like that."

"Surely you have a secretary?"

"In the office, yes; but this is personal business. You'd be based at the house in Sussex."

"You don't have to do this ... " Rianne began.

"This is not charity. I need a secretary," Catherine said forcefully. "And having someone who knows their way around the Briony Dalton story would be a great advantage. It would make my work so much easier." She paused and said very quietly, "And I would very much like you to do it."

Rianne remained silent. She cranked down the window and cold, damp air wafted into the car. Rain speckled her face. At last she nodded and turned to look at Catherine. "I'd like to do it too. There's nothing left for me here."

Catherine leaned over and kissed her on the forehead. "Thank you."

Rianne reached out and hugged her. "I should be thanking you."

Catherine shook her head and turned away. She started up the car and drove away from the anonymous church.

They drove to the airport in silence. On both stages of the journey, first to London and then to Dublin, they barely spoke to one another, each absorbed in her own thoughts.

ଓ

Rianne was remembering the brother she had only really grown to know in the past few months. A shy, often frightened young man whom she realised had desperately wanted — desperately needed — to be loved. She felt he had initially taken drugs not because they provided an escape — although they did that too — but to belong to a group, to be part of something. Later, when he had been trying out the various religions, she realised that he had been searching for an identity, for a home, for someone to come along and accept him for what he was. His relationships with women were sporadic and short-lived and when, finally, he had taken up with his girlfriend he had imagined that here was the solution to his problems, here at last was someone who would love him for what he was ... but more than anything else, here was someone who would simply love him. He had been overjoyed when he discovered she was pregnant. For the first time in his life he had started to make plans, started to look to his future, to seriously consider giving up the drugs.

He had been devastated when he discovered that his girlfriend loved the drugs more than she loved him. When the baby had died he had attempted suicide — injecting himself with a massive amount of heroin. But the junk had been diluted to such an extent that it had little or no effect on him. The buzz had lasted thirty minutes, the depression and lethargy a lot longer. When he was diagnosed as having AIDS he wasn't even surprised, wasn't even angry; he felt it was justice of a sort.

Matt had been close to suicide when he had made contact with Rianne. But that had been the saving of them both, she was convinced. It had taken her out of the ultimately self-destructive life-style of the porno movies, and it had given him someone to love and someone who loved him.

Their relationship, albeit brief, had been extraordinarily intense; indeed at times they seemed more like husband and wife than brother and sister. Perhaps the fact that they were virtual strangers to one another helped bring them closer together. They could talk about their lives, their pasts, without difficulty, without shame. They both listened, accepted what they had been, what they were now. Neither judged.

In return he, who had so little respect for his own body, had taught her respect for hers. He gave her back her self-respect, returned her confidence, convinced her that people weren't looking at her in the street, talking about her as she walked past. No one knew what she did for a living. No one cared.

"Guys who watch porno movies usually don't look at the women's faces," he had laughed. "And don't forget they wouldn't be used to seeing you with clothes on. I hardly recognised you myself, and I'm your own brother."

There were things she regretted, too.

Regretted not getting in touch with him sooner, regretted allowing him to drift away so easily, regretted not making even greater efforts to find him when she'd first left home. If she had, she was convinced he wouldn't have got into the mess he was in, he wouldn't have been involved with drugs, he wouldn't have contracted AIDS ... and he wouldn't be dead.

And if they'd been together, then she wouldn't have become involved in the porno movie business. Oh, she knew she made light of it to people like Matt and Catherine, but the reality of it was that it was soul-destroying, terrible and terrifying. She'd seen too many girls kill themselves with drugs, shooting up or snorting dope to summon enough courage to go out on the set and allow some guy or group of guys to use their bodies. Suicide was common ... all too common. You had to look very closely to see the scars on her own wrists.

But their lives together could have been so much different. Their lives should have been so much different ... if they'd had a mother who'd given a fuck about them!

Rianne wasn't aware that she was crying until Catherine's hand closed over hers, squeezing tightly. Comfortingly.

"It's her fault, isn't it?" Rianne said, her voice barely above a whisper.

"What? Who?" Catherine asked, taken by surprise. "You mean your mother? Well," she said, shrugging. "If she'd been more interested in her children rather than her precious books, then things would have been different."

"We should have had so much," Rianne said wonderingly.

"You should. You had every advantage. On the surface you had everything going for you. Both of you inherited your mother's imagination and determination — and together that's a lethal combination. You should have achieved so much." The note of sadness in her voice was genuine. She firmly believed that the children's lives had been wasted.

Rianne turned to look at Catherine, hard black eyes blinking quickly. "Is it wrong to want revenge? Is it wrong of me to want to hurt her, to make her pay, to make her feel a little of the pain I'm feeling now?"

"I don't think so."

"I want to make her pay," Rianne hissed. "I never really thought very much about her; I disliked her or dismissed her. But now I hate her. I never thought I could feel this way about another human being. I hate her so badly I want to kill her!"

Catherine's fingers tightened around her hand. "Don't do that. Help me exact a more fitting revenge. Help me destroy her."

Rianne Moriarty nodded fiercely. "I will."

Chapter Forty-Eight

"Do you want to tell me about it?" Greg Connors sat in the stern of the small boat, one arm idly resting on the long rudder bar. He had been watching Brigid Garrett for the past two hours. Although the sea and sky had been spectacular, especially as the late afternoon and early evening light had fallen across the Ionian Sea before finally vanishing into a magnificent sunset, she hadn't moved, hadn't seemed to notice. She had remained on the foredeck, her back to the mainsail, staring out into the middle distance, eyes hooded and vacant behind her sunglasses. There was a copybook in her lap and she held a pencil loosely between her fingers, but he hadn't seen her write a single word all afternoon. She had been almost completely uncommunicative since he had returned with the supplies.

Greg nudged the rudder and the small boat shifted almost imperceptibly, avoiding a long chain of lobster pots.

He frowned, remembering. Everything had been fine until ... until she had dropped the newspaper in the sea! He looked up, understanding beginning to dawn. He'd initially thought the paper had fallen in the sea by accident, but he suddenly wondered if she'd read something there that had frightened or upset her. Had there been something in the paper about her?

He resolved to pick up another copy at the earliest opportunity; if he remembered correctly, it had been a day-old copy of *Le Monde*.

They had spent most of the day tacking to and fro on an errant breeze, gradually working in closer to the Greek shoreline. Greg had consulted his charts and drawn up a route of sorts, which would take them down along the coast of Greece, past Cephalonia and Zanthe, around by Peloponnesus, where they could either swing south to Crete or continue eastwards to the Aegean Islands ... but if they did that there was the very real possibility that they could lose themselves amidst the hundreds of rocks jutting from the sea, or run aground in the treacherous waters.

Before he had hauled up the anchor he had attempted to show her the rudiments of sailing, pointing out the more obvious safety precautions, but she was obviously distracted so he'd finally admitted defeat and left it for another time. She apologised more than once, putting her distraction down to the book gestating in her head. Greg felt he could understand her introspection; he knew when he was writing he sometimes became so absorbed in his fictional world that he often found it difficult to return to the real one. There were moments of disorientation, sometimes even forgetfulness, as the two worlds, one real, the other imaginary, meshed together.

She had helped when he was tacking to catch the wind, following his directions, hauling on the sheets to bring the jib around. He insisted she take a spell on the tiller while he prepared lunch. She attempted to keep the boat on a reasonably straight course, but her mind was elsewhere, the distractions proved too much and the boat kept drifting off course. Following a lunch of cold meats, fruit and salad, she had taken up a position on the foredeck with notebook and pencil and stared into the distance.

"Do you want to tell me about it?" Greg repeated.

The woman turned her head towards him, her face expressionless, her eyes hidden behind large sun glasses. She stared at him for several long moments until he became uncomfortable with her direct gaze, and then she shuddered. He actually saw the tremor run through her body, rippling the muscles of her chest and stomach. The hard lines of her face cracked and relaxed into a smile.

"I'm sorry," she said. "I was miles away."

"I could see that. You had me nervous for a while."

"I'm sorry. I was ... I was remembering. It was long ago and far away ... "

"Good title for a book."

Briony swivelled around from the foredeck. Holding tightly to the stays, she made her way down to sit across from Greg.

"Where do you get your ideas from?" she asked suddenly, disconcerting him.

"What? I don't know. I mean from everything. Videos, books, life. Why?"

"Many of mine come from memories. It can be a single thing — a newspaper article, an image, a fragment of verse, a snatch of a song — but it sparks something deep inside me and I begin to wonder ... I begin to wonder *what if.*" Her voice trailed away into silence.

"And you've been wondering what if," he said.

Briony Dalton nodded. When she took off her sun glasses her eyes were glazed and distant, and Greg Connors knew he had lost her again.

What if ...
What if ...
What if ...

What if she hadn't pursued a career as a writer, where would she be now? What would she be doing?

She would be Bernadette Moriarty, a housewife in a Dublin suburb with a husband and two children. Matt, at twenty-six, would have finished university, maybe have a career of his own, maybe married with his wife already pregnant.

Briony was forty-five; old enough to be a grandmother.

Rianne, at twenty-two, would be still at university, if that's what she wanted to do, or maybe she'd have gone to art college — she was always artistic — perhaps she'd have a boyfriend.

And Niall. What of Niall, her ex-husband?

There had been lots of reasons why they parted; her writing, her success and his jealousy were amongst the principal ones.

But what if they'd stayed together and lived a normal life?

With her help and encouragement, he would probably be a successful writer now ... not as successful as she was, but then his writing had never been as commercial, but he was good. From what she remembered of his work, he had had real talent.

What ever had happened to that talent? Had it really drowned in a bottle?

Maybe they'd have had more children. No reason why they shouldn't. She had never had much time for her children, but then she'd spent every waking hour writing to support them. She wondered now if it had really been necessary; surely she could have written half the amount and still managed to have some sort of life left for herself and her children. Her real success had come early in the children's lives and once the ball had started rolling she found she had to roll with it. The publishers — and the public — kept demanding more and more, and she'd willingly supplied it.

But at what cost?

She shivered, the chill bringing her back to the present, and she realised Greg Connors was watching her intently. He reached out with his right hand, index finger extended, and she flinched when he touched it to her face below her eye. When he lifted his finger, she realised there was moisture on it.

The young man smiled. "I wish I had that vivid an imagination."

"Don't. It's a curse."

"Like prophecy, maybe."

"It is prophecy of a sort. Maybe prophecy is nothing more than a vivid imagination. It's the ability to see what might be or what might have been rather than what is." She glanced at him. "Do you ever regret writing? No, of course you don't," she answered even as he was shaking his head. "But I do. It's given me an awful lot but it's exacted its price, and I sometimes think the price has been too high." She gazed into the placid waters of the Ionian sea and then turned back to Greg, a smile fixed on her lips. "Don't mind me, I tend to get maudlin and upset when I don't do a set number of words a day." She lifted the notebook. "It's been so long since I actually `wrote' as opposed to typed that I fancy I've quite forgotten how."

"I know what you mean. I like to see the words appearing on the page. I can sort of place them on the paper, arrange the sentences and paragraphs."

Briony nodded. "Exactly. I'll tell you what, in the first city we hit, I'm going to buy two laptop computers, one for me, one for you ... I insist," she pressed on as he started to object. "It's the least I can do for all the help you've given me. I'll show you how to use it; it'll unleash your creativity as no other tool can."

"I'm not sure about computers. I've heard a lot of writers don't like them."

"Usually those who haven't tried them. Let me put it to you in very simple terms: by the very fact that you don't have to retype an entire manuscript at least three times ... think of all the time that saves. Time you can use for writing something else. When the typewriter was invented people said it would never catch on. When Mark Twain submitted a typed manuscript — the first such — even the editors said it would never find acceptance with writers. A writer is a craftsman, and like all craftsmen he must use the best tool for the job."

Greg raised both hands in mock surrender. "OK, OK, you've convinced me. You win. After all, you're the expert. You've written a damn sight more than I ever will."

"Oh, that's easy. You can do what I did, Greg," Briony said. "All you have to do is to give up everything and everyone close to you. To dedicate your every waking hour to doing one particular job to the exclusion of everything else. Follow that simple rule and you can be like me. You'll have financial independence and you'll have nothing to show for it. No family, no friends."

Greg reached out and squeezed her shoulder, the bitterness and pain in her voice almost palpable. He had no words for her.

"And you know something? I've no one else to blame but myself," she continued, her voice a hard monotone. "I did it deliberately. I set about achieving that ambition like a general planning some battle campaign."

"Stop it," Greg hissed. "Stop it."

"Every little move worked out in advance ... "

"Stop it," he said more forcefully.

"And it got me exactly what I deserved."

"Stop it." His voice echoed flatly across the water. shocking her into silence. He lashed the tiller and turned to hold Briony, his hands high on her arms close to her shoulders. "Why are you doing this? What's the point? What will it achieve?"

She pulled against him for the moment and then she collapsed into his arms, her head on his shoulder. She lay still, unmoving, and his hands went from her arms to her back, holding her awkwardly, his cheek against her hair. He could feel her breasts through her T-shirt and the soft fabric of the one-piece swimsuit she wore beneath.

"You're right," she said, her voice surprisingly calm. "It'll achieve nothing — but it's good for the soul. Some mental flagellation, eh?" She clutched his arms, fingers high on his biceps. "Will you hold me, Greg? It's been a long time since anyone held me."

She could feel his unease, it was transmitted through his every muscle. The proximity of her body was obviously — very obviously — arousing him. She wondered how long it had been since he had made love. Her mood had changed, suddenly, unpredictably, as it so often did, from deepest depression to elation. She was conscious, too, that she had revealed perhaps a little too much of herself, had shown herself to be weak and afraid. But on reflection maybe that wasn't a bad thing, either: it would make him protective. What she needed to do now was to exert control over him, to bind him to her.

Slowly, deliberately, she raised her face to his and stared deep into his wide hazel eyes. "Hold me, Greg," she murmured, her breath warm on his face, her lips inches from his. It was only natural that he should bring his mouth forward, lips parting, pressing them to hers. She opened her mouth, feeling the pressure of his tongue against her lips, her teeth, moist against her own tongue. His hands were moving against her back beneath the T-shirt, palms flat against the smooth warm flesh, and she could feel him hard and erect as he pressed himself against her.

She pushed him gently away and stood up. Looking down at him, she raised the T-shirt above her head and dropped it on to the deck beside her. Slowly, making him sweat, she reached across with her right hand and slid down the left-hand strap of her swimsuit. She repeated the process with her left hand and then gently eased the slick material down over her small rounded breasts, the flesh startlingly white against her recent tan. She stood watching his face, rocking gently in the boat before she finally pushed the material lower, across her belly, down over her groin. Finally she stepped out of it and stood before him, completely naked.

Greg Connors had seen many naked bodies on the beaches of Greece and Corfu, but none of them had ever aroused him like this.

Resting both hands on her hips, he pulled her forward. His lips trailed across her almost flat stomach, probing her deeply indented navel before moving upwards as he came slowly to his feet, licking her nipples, moistening them, blowing against the responsive flesh.

His own hands were busy with his swimming trunks, pushing them down, allowing his erection to spring free. He pressed himself against her and she reached between their bodies, holding him tightly, squeezing, rubbing him against her tightly cropped pubic hair.

Greg sank to the deck and Briony spread her legs and straddled him. She stood above him for a few seconds before sinking down on to him, guiding him into her in one fluid movement them made that both gasp. Wrapping her arms around his neck, she began to move atop him, deliberately brushing her breasts against his face. His fingers tightened into the soft flesh of her buttocks as he guided her up and down …

On the smooth, placid water, the rocking of the boat grew more and more pronounced until it actually threatened to overturn. Only this threat made them slow their eager thrusting, and then Briony sat on top of Greg, completely unmoving, her lips and tongue busy on his face, her internal muscles spasming, squeezing …

His orgasm caught him by surprise, flinging him backwards as it convulsed through him, almost capsizing the boat in its intensity. Briony's orgasm was seconds later, a deeply satisfying pulsing that coursed through her body in wave after wave of pleasure. She lay forward on to the sweat-sheened young man, fingers coiling in the sparse hair on his chest, resting her head on his shoulder. Her smile was tight and triumphant.

He was hers now. He was bound to her with shackles stronger than any metal.

Chapter Forty-Nine

Later Briony Dalton would remember those days with great affection. A combination of superb weather and a perfect sea, with just enough breeze to make sailing a joy, plain and simple food and their own passion created a mood that both attempted to capture in their writing.

"We're like cannibals," Greg said one day. He was sitting by the rudder, a copybook on his lap, pencil moving easily across the page. Briony was sitting almost directly across from him, his small portable typewriter on her lap, fingers tapping confidently on the keys, having relearned the difference in touch between the computer keyboard and the stronger, firmer touch needed for a typewriter. The busy staccato tapping reminded Briony of how she had written her earlier works.

She glanced up at him, her fingers still moving across the keys, unconscious mind transcribing the words and phrases in her head down on to the page, a tiny portion of her consciousness directed to him. "What do you mean 'cannibals?'"

"It has occurred to me that a strong, handsome, twenty-eight-year-old blond-haired young man is probably making an appearance in your book."

"Don't forget virile," she smiled.

"I wasn't. But am I right?"

Briony stopped typing and looked down at the page in the machine. "Strong, handsome blond-haired, hazel-eyed and virile. Perfect in every way."

Greg held up his copybook. "And what have we here? A vibrant dark-haired, dark-eyed pretty woman, mysterious, passionate, compelling."

Briony laughed. "Doesn't sound like anyone I know."

Greg closed his book and looked seriously at Briony. "You know about writers. Tell me, do they always cannibalise from their experience?"

"Absolutely! You take from your experience and from everyone else's. Why?"

He frowned, looking out to sea. "I don't know. It just … it just doesn't seem right. I mean, I think the last week has been amongst the happiest in my life, and yet now I find I'm putting it down on paper, using it. It sorts of cheapens the experience."

Briony shook her head firmly. "Nonsense. You're simply enriching your writing. Think of it as sharing your pleasurable experiences with your reader." She lowered the arm on the typewriter on her lap and then locked the carriage. Resting her elbows on the machine, she put her chin in her cupped palms. "Tell me about your book."

Greg suddenly looked embarrassed, and Briony had to laugh. She'd been living in complete intimacy with this man, they had made love so often over the week that she had lost count … and now here he was turning all shy on her. "If you don't want to show it to me that's OK," she said quickly. "I know some writers don't like other people to see their work in progress or even talk about it. I used to be like that. Now I sometimes find that if you talk about it — vaguely, of course — to other people, they might pass a comment or make a suggestion which sparks something in your own head. But please don't let me force you."

"No, no, it's not that," he said. "It's just …" he shrugged helplessly.

"I know. It's your child. I understand fully."

"No, I'd like you to read it … nothing would give me greater pleasure."

Briony leaned over and rested her hand on his knee. "Greg, Greg sweetheart … I'm a writer. I know what you do, what you feel."

He stood up and disappeared below deck, reappearing a few moments later with a large cardboard box brimming with typed sheets held together with paperclips. Without saying a word he handed her the box and sat down facing her.

The manuscript had been stored face down, with the last pages going in on top. Briony turned over the page and found it was typed in single space. The number on the bottom of the page was four hundred and eighty. She did a quickly calculation in her head. There were approximately four hundred words to a page of single-spaced typed work, which meant … one hundred and ninety-two thousand words, give or take a couple of thousand. "How long is the book?"

"Two hundred thousand words."

"So you're in the home stretch now," Briony murmured, not looking at him.

"Yes … but how did you know?"

She winked at him. "Trick of the trade. What have you got left to do? A couple of chapters?"

He nodded. "Three. Maybe four. I haven't quite got the ending worked out yet."

"Tell me about it," she said absently. She put the portable typewriter down on the deck and turned the box upside down so the manuscript was the right side up.

"It's a big family saga. It's about this family, part-English, part-French, who are cursed, and how, just when they seem to achieve everything they want — fame or fortune, good marriage, children — tragedy strikes."

Briony nodded, encouraging him to go on.

"So on the one hand you have the contemporary story about the youngest female in the line who is just about to make an excellent marriage to a handsome man of a good family. Interspersed with this are the historical family bits about the various tragedies which have befallen her predecessors. I wrote these chapters separately and I'll insert them as necessary, but in reverse order, so you'll first get the mother's story, then the grandmother's, the great-grandmother's and so on. Until at the very end we have the however-many greats back into the past to where the family are cursed."

"And how was it cursed?" Briony wondered him. The idea was fascinating, and she could see endless possibilities with it.

"Aren't you going to read it?" he teased.

"I'll read it. But tell me how the family was cursed."

"One of the female ancestors of this woman — and the curse is carried in the female line — stole the husband of another woman, a local wise woman, a witch. The woman who has been scorned curses the entire female line so they will never achieve happiness and their heart's desire until they have spurned the thing they love the most. So the only way for the curse to be lifted is for the soon-to-be-married young woman to give up her fiancée'. Now, will she or won't she?" He shrugged. "Even I don't know yet."

"What about a title?"

"I haven't really got one. I originally thought of calling it *Fortune and Despair* now the working title is *The Curse*, but that won't do. It's too horrorish."

Briony gazed at him, eyes sparkling. "Call it *A Woman Scorned*, since that's where the central idea for the book stems from."

Greg Connors looked like he'd been struck. "*A Woman Scorned. A Woman Scorned*," he repeated softly, and then he jumped up and kissed Briony on both cheeks. "It's brilliant, I mean really brilliant. What a title! You were right; it was worthwhile talking to someone else about my book. *A Woman Scorned*. What a great title … "

∞

Briony Dalton read until the light faded to a soft grey and then vanished. The book was a first draft so obviously the inconsistencies were still present — one character had three different nicknames, and whilst the hero was right-handed through most of the book he became obviously left-handed later. There were spelling mistakes and typos everywhere.

But the story was brilliant.

Briony felt a brief pang of jealousy. The boy was good, damn good. The story had power and pace, fairly dragged you screaming through the novel; indeed, in terms of construction and plotting, it was not unlike her own work except that she would have had more sex in it, but that was easily remedied.

With proper marketing and publicity it would be a bestseller. Let him keep the title, it fitted the book. It was going to cause quite a stir in the bookshops though, having two books in the same genre with the same title on the shelves. But there was no comparison between the two. His was just so ... so good. It needed work, but she didn't mind helping him; he had — amongst other things — saved her life.

Realising that Greg was staring anxiously at her, she straightened, her face unsmiling. In the twilight she could just about make out his expression. "You want me to give you an honest review?"

"Yes, yes, of course."

"I've only read about a third of it to date, so I can only comment on the portion I've read."

"Of course."

"Well ... well," her face broke into a broad smile. It's bloody brilliant, absolutely marvellous. A real winner."

"You really think so?"

"I'm sure of it."

"And now it has a great title," he added, obviously relieved.

"The title will help. A good catchy title always works."

"But is there anything wrong with it?"

Briony shook her head. "Nothing wrong with it," she said. "It needs some work ... "

"It is only a first draft."

"I know that. It's very tight, very good. Whatever revisions you have to do will be minor."

"I always find working on the second and final drafts the hardest part of writing," Greg said.

"I know what you mean ... but I'll tell you what. Let me do the final revisions for you. I've told you, there's no major re-writing to be done. All I'd be doing is tidying it up."

He looked at her in astonishment. "But ... I mean, what about your own writing? Why?" he asked.

Briony returned the bundle of manuscript to its box and then slid over beside Greg. Placing both hands on his shoulders, she stared into his eyes. "I want to do this. You did something for me ... did it without asking, did it selflessly. You uprooted from your idyllic life-style, you even put yourself in danger for me. I can offer you money, but that would be an insult to both of us, and I'm not going to do that. What I can offer you is the advantage of over twenty years as a professional writer. What you've done is written a good book, a fine book, a great book — that's the talent — but what I can do is to polish it professionally for you — that's an acquired skill. It's my gift to you; my way of saying thank you." She kissed him gently on the lips. "What do you say?"

"I say thank you."

&

There is something almost primeval about sitting on a boat at night with the only light coming from the heavens, reflecting hazily back off the water.

They had dropped anchor in a tiny natural bay off an unnamed island which was in total darkness. Greg had sat on the foredeck long into the night, the gentle rocking of the boat on the swell lulling him, relaxing him. He could hear Brigid moving around below decks before settling herself into one of the tiny berths. There really was only space for one in comfort below decks, and — except on those occasions when they made love — he preferred sleeping up on deck. At night the temperature fell sharply, but his sleeping bag was well-insulated and he enjoyed lying looking up at the stars, feeling the wind on his face, sensing the presence of the sea around him. It was easy to imagine how man must have felt on those first great voyages of discovery.

He found it gave him time to think.

He could almost feel the conscious portion of his brain closing down, allowing his unconscious to bubble to the surface. His thoughts were vague and confused for a while, chaotic, abstract fragments, before they finally settled and fixed on the woman, Brigid Garrett.

He had been amused and then flattered at the attention she had paid to his book. He wondered why he had shown it to her; he had never done that before, not even when he'd been in long-term relationships. One of his girlfriends had once accused him of paying more attention to his book than he did to her: it was an accusation he could not deny. So why had he shown Brigid the manuscript?

A Woman Scorned.

It was a good title, indeed an excellent title for the book, and it captured the essence of the story perfectly. And yet he couldn't help feeling he'd heard that title before … and that was entirely possible. There was no copyright on titles. But he could always check up on it in the nearest English language library. All he had to do was to look it up in *Books in Print*, an enormous four volume reference book, now thankfully on microfiche, that listed all the books currently in print under either the author's name or the title.

A Woman Scorned.

Who was Brigid Garrett? There was something about her … something he couldn't quite put his finger on. She was fascinating, completely charming, knowledgeable, cultured — and frightened. It was obvious in the way she looked, a certain nervousness, jumpiness, and on a couple of occasions he had heard her cry out in her sleep. He had also realised that there were certain things — and he hadn't quite worked out the combination yet — that she wouldn't talk about. Her past, for example; he reckoned she was only telling him what she wanted him to know. She grew vague and evasive when he asked her about her family. He guessed she was in her early to mid-forties, but he was useless at judging ages, and she could easily have been older. She'd been married and divorced, and he thought there'd been children, but she never spoke about them. She spoke about her writing, but not about specific books, although she seemed to have written a lot under a variety of pseudonyms. She wouldn't admit to anything bearing her own name and yet she said she had published fairly recently ... which made Greg suspect that Brigid Garrett was not her real name. She never spoke in detail about what she was currently working on and she was careful not to leave any of her manuscript lying around.

If he hadn't seen the fire for himself, caught the guy spying on her and then been belted by the big guy who'd stolen her computer, he was sure he'd have found her story about being chased by Mafia hoods a bit too novelish, something like a plot lifted from her own books. And then there was that business of the computer: was it natural to bug your own machine? It wasn't the sort of thing a sane person would do. But then, whoever said that writers were sane people? Was he sane? Was it sanity to ride to the rescue of a woman he knew nothing about, a woman nearly old enough to be his mother? It was even more insane to sail away with her. Maybe the men chasing her had been police, maybe the fire in the villa had been accidental, maybe he was helping a dangerous criminal to escape.

But he liked her.

She had taught him a lot about women, even more about himself. He had never before encountered an older woman to whom he could honestly relate. Maybe it had nothing to do with that: maybe it was simply because she was another writer, and understood him.

And he could learn a lot from her. She'd taught him how to make love Oh, he'd made love to women before, but he'd never before had a woman who'd taken the time to tell him what she wanted, how she wanted him to move, where to touch, when to stop and wait. She took great joy and pleasure in lovemaking and he found that in giving her satisfaction, he was satisfying himself immeasurably.

A shooting star flickered across the sky, and Greg Connors made a wish.

He wished for a future for himself and the woman known as Brigid Garrett.

Deep down he didn't think there could be.

ᲒᲖ

Briony was awake and already reading through the bundle of manuscript by the time Greg awoke. Rolling over on his belly he looked at Briony hunched over beside the tiller, pencil in her hand, making notes as she read through page after page with extraordinary swiftness. She was more than halfway through the bulky manuscript.

"Well?" he asked, startling her.

She blinked at him for a few moments before answering. "It's brilliant. Quite brilliant. When this is finished, I'm going to make you a bestseller."

"Why?" Greg asked.

"Because I want to."

"Is there a catch?"

"No catch," she smiled.

"What do you need to make this a best-seller?" he grinned.

She took the question seriously. "I need a computer with the WordStar word-processing package, and a printer. And we're not going to get them here." She leaned forward, her eyes hard and challenging, the authority in her voice unmistakable. "I will do a deal with you. Sail to Crete as planned, then sell your boat and fly with me to Ireland. I have a house in the west. It's wild and isolated, and we can work in peace. I'll buy myself a computer, and I will make your book a best-seller. Do we have a deal?"

"Do I have a choice?"

"There are a few occasions in every lifetime when someone or something comes along that can change the entire course of your life. It happened to me very early in my career; it is happening to you right now … "

Chapter Fifty

As the Rolls Royce Silver Shadow turned off the motorway on to the minor road, the phone trilled and then the fax began to buzz. Josef Bach opened his eyes and read the printout from his London office. It was coded at one end and then decoded by his own fax, but even so he insisted that all messages should be discreet.

Whereabouts of lost luggage still a mystery. Identity of last flight companion now known. Details to follow.

He tore off the two-line message and fed it into the shredder attached to the side of the fax. He had hired Charley O'Neill through an intermediary to trace the whereabouts of Briony Dalton and to discover the identity of the man who had disposed of Marcus Holland so adroitly. It was as if the woman had simply vanished off the face of the earth and yet the airport and ports were watched and he'd given instructions that no one even vaguely resembling her was to be allowed to leave the island. Despite this, and the money he had spent with the proper officials, she had slipped away.

The capable Mr O'Neill had apparently identified the man who had assisted Dalton, but even he hadn't managed to trace her so far. Where was she? Where would she run to? And to whom? He had thought he had covered every eventuality, but bitter experience had taught him that it was impossible to prepare for the variable factor, the wild card. Dalton was predictable to a degree, but the man who had helped her on Corfu was the enigma.

So where was she? She'd obviously gone somewhere with the man. And why?

Bach looked through the windows, his eyes glazing, not even seeing his own reflection in the glass. The situation with the woman was becoming increasingly annoying. What had started out as an irritation had become a positive nuisance. He was reluctant to resort to the New York solution, but if needs must …

What was really annoying him was that it was now taking up far too much of his time, and that he most certainly could not allow. Too many things were happening, too many deals were coming together, and all of them needed his full and undivided attention. He had acquired holdings in the burgeoning Russian markets, including several ailing publishers, all of whom were ripe for reorganisation along profitable lines. Once he had tapped into that enormous market, where the demand for western literature was at a premium, he was going to need a backlist of authors whose works could be translated and published with the minimum of delay and without the necessity of negotiating expensive contracts. Enormous print runs could be produced in Russia at a fraction of the European costs, and it would be theoretically possible for him to sell an average paperback at the same price as a daily newspaper. He wouldn't sell them so cheaply of course – there was far too much money to be made — but he fully intended to launch a paperback list at prices that would undercut every other publisher in the East. When he had established that market, he could expand his other commercial interests in Russia, moving from books into magazines — women's mags, specialist and hobby interests, soft and hard-core pornography — where the profits were enormous. Right now he needed both of Briony Dalton's publishers more than ever for their extensive backlist of respectable and well-known authors. Bach would not – could not — allow them to reap the profits of Briony Dalton's new best-seller. That money would help refinance the publishing houses he had spent months undermining. Josef Bach's huge hands closed into white-knuckled fists. She was not going to finish that book

… even if he had to break the rule of a lifetime and take care of her personally.

☙

"There's a rather tasty looking motor coming down the lane."

Rianne Moriarty was standing pressed up against the French windows looking down over the rain-slicked patio, wistfully thinking of somewhere sunny — anywhere sunny would do. The Downs were practically invisible beneath a blanket of mist and rain, the sky the colour of stone. On days like this it was easy to believe that the sun would never shine again.

"What sort of car?" Catherine asked, coming in from the study, carrying a pile of scrapbooks bulging with newspaper clippings.

"Rolls Royce Silver Shadow," she said absently, then whispered, "Shit!" She turned to look at Catherine. Her eyes were wide, astonished. "It's turning in here."

Catherine put down the scrapbooks, feeling a cold chill run up her body. The phone rang. Rianne reached for it, but Catherine snapped, "Leave it … leave it," then added in a gentler voice, "I know who it is." With her eyes fixed on the younger woman's startled face, Catherine picked up the phone and said, "Hello, Josef." Peering through the window she could see him holding the receiver in the car.

"What a surprising person you are, Catherine Garrett. Am I welcome in your house?"

"You are always welcome in my house," she said stiffly, already beginning to wonder what she was going to say to Josef about Rianne and vice versa.

"I was in the area and I thought I'd drop in and visit," he continued, as the car turned majestically to bring the passenger side as close to the front door as possible.

Catherine didn't believe him for a moment. Bach was the sort of man who was never "just in the area." She hung up and said to a bemused Rianne, "Do you know the name Josef Bach?"

"Everyone knows the name of Josef Bach ... but you don't mean that was ..." She turned to look out the window.

"The same. Please be nice to him. And be careful of him."

"But ... hang on a sec," Rianne said as Catherine walked past her, heading for the door. "How do you know him? What's he doing here?"

"I've worked for him on and off over the years. He's also my publisher. He commissioned the book on your mother." She caught the blank look on Rianne's face before she opened the door just as Bach stepped out of the car under the shelter of the umbrella held by the uniformed chauffeur.

The big man strode in, brushing silver water droplets from the shoulders of his white suit. He went straight through the hall and into the sitting room where he immediately settled into the large leather armchair before the fire. Putting both hands on the head of his carved walking stick, he rested his head on his hands and regarded Catherine solemnly. Her eyes flickered madly to the right, and Josef turned his head slowly to find the slim figure of a young woman standing in the doorway.

There was something familiar about her, he thought, something about the shape of her eyes, her cheekbones...

Catherine moved to stand beside the woman, placing her hand on her shoulder. "Rianne, I'd like you to meet the famous Josef Bach ... Herr Bach, this is Rianne Moriarty."

Bach came smoothly to his feet, a smile twisting his lips, his bright blue eyes sparkling. Briony Dalton's daughter. And here with Catherine Garrett! He was assessing the possibilities and potential of the situation even as he took her hand and bent over it in a slight bow.

"Delighted to meet you, my dear."

Overawed by the sheer presence of the man, Rianne smiled. "It's a pleasure to meet you, Herr Bach. I've certainly heard a lot about you." She glanced at Catherine. "Am I to understand that you commissioned the book Catherine is writing about my mother?"

"That is correct," he said easily, straightening to his full height, meeting her gaze steadily. "Why?"

"No, no reason. It's just that she never said. I'm a bit surprised."

"But why, my dear? Your mother is newsworthy — indeed, she has gone out of her way to make herself newsworthy. She is a personality, and there is always a market for personality biographies."

"No, it's not that. I suppose I'm just surprised to find you taking such a personal interest in it."

"I take a personal interest in all my projects," he said, finally releasing her hand. "It is one of the reasons for my success."

"Of course." Rianne again glanced at Catherine, who was standing nervously to one side. "Would you like some tea, sir?"

"That would be delightful, and please, my dear, only my employees call me " sir". I am Josef."

Rianne smiled, completely captivated by his old world charm. "Yes sir … Josef."

Bach waited until she had left the room and then he turned to Catherine, the smile fading from his thin lips. "What is she doing here?" he said, striding across the room to stand before the French windows.

"After her brother's death she had nowhere else to go, except back on the streets or into porno movies. I asked her to come with me and work as a technical advisor on the book."

Bach stared out towards the rain-sodden Downs, considering, and then he finally nodded. "I think that is an excellent choice. You've done well. What does she know about the type of book you're writing."

"She doesn't. She thinks it's a straightforward biography. She didn't even know I was working for you until a few moments ago."

Bach nodded again. "Excellent. We can use her name as part of the advertising campaign: written with the assistance of ... or the co-operation of ... something like that."

"What brings you here?" Catherine asked, after Bach had fallen silent for several seconds.

He looked over his shoulder at the kitchen door, lips curled in a half-smile. "I'm actually looking for the girl's mother."

"I thought you'd found her on Corfu."

"We did and then lost her again. She had help, some local she'd picked up, I presume. I'll have details later on. Have you any idea where she might have gone?"

"You're keeping an eye on all her properties?"

"Yes, in London, New York and Corfu. I've got people at her houses and the airports. Is there anywhere she might have favoured for holidays, somewhere from her past maybe?"

"Not that I know of."

"Is there anything you can think of that might be useful? I need to know where she is and what she's doing."

Catherine started to shake her head.

"Had she a favourite resort, hotel, beach?"

"I grew up with her; until she was married we went everywhere together. We holidayed in Ireland every year, always in the south or west of the country, but to be truthful I don't even remember where. She never went away with her husband, so there's no point in asking him. Terri Fierstein might know. When Briony started to make real money, she took quite a lot of time off, wrote her books in some exotic locations while the children were in boarding schools. I suppose she could have gone back to one or other of those."

"It's enough to be going on with ... aaah, tea." He turned as Rianne Moriarty came back into the room, Catherine's best tea service balanced precariously on a silver tray. He took the tray from Rianne's hands and put it down on the small side table. "Allow me," he murmured, pouring tea for the three of them, looking from Catherine to Rianne. "Milk and sugar?"

"Milk," Catherine said.

"Yes, please." Rianne smiled at the German. "Two sugars."

"Now tell me, my dear ... what's a pretty girl like you doing cooped up in an isolated spot like this, eh? You should be out enjoying yourself, seeing a little of life."

"I'm taking a brief break with my aunt."

"And what do you do at present?"

"Well, I'm temporarily between jobs. I am working with Catherine as a researcher and assistant."

Bach looked shocked. "Why, what a waste! With your features you should model. Have you ever considered modelling?"

"I've done a little modelling," Rianne admitted.

"Why, perfect, perfect. I knew it. I knew it. Don't you think she has the most perfect features, the most perfect face?" he asked Catherine and then continued without waiting for an answer: "Your boyfriend must count himself a very lucky man indeed."

"I don't have a boyfriend ... at the moment," Rianne said, almost shyly.

"Why, my dear, you are wasting yourself down here. You should be in the city where there is life and energy and people of your own age for you to mix with and relate to."

"Rianne is essential to my work here," Catherine said quickly.

"Of course, of course she is, but I'm sure if there was anything essential you could always contact her. And surely she can only help you with the early chapters on her mother's life? Have you not completed those yet?"

"I'm about a third of the way into the book," she began, but Bach wasn't listening. He was nodding to himself, as if reaching a decision. "You still have your London apartment, do you not?"

"Yes," Catherine said reluctantly; Josef Bach knew damn well she still had the London apartment.

"Why don't you allow Rianne to spend a few days there, and in the meantime I'll see if I can swing a few modelling contracts for her. Eh?" He looked from Catherine to Rianne, smiling broadly. "Is there a problem?" he asked, seeing her expression change.

Rianne shrugged. "I suppose I should tell you now, before you go to any trouble on my behalf … I have appeared in a few adult movies, pornographic movies. People like me don't do modelling … well, legitimate modelling, that is."

"Nonsense," he said quickly and then stopped. "But I do see the problem; it changes the market somewhat. Have you any objections to appearing nude?"

"None."

"Would you have any objections to appearing in one of the adult magazines?"

"Doing what?" she asked suspiciously.

"Nude modelling. I am talking about the quality magazines, along the lines of *Penthouse*, *Men Only* and *Playboy*. The pay is excellent. And there's no shame in it. Many of the girls who appear in the glossy pages go on to movies."

"I could do that. I'd like to do it," Rianne said.

"I see a whole new career opening up for you, my dear." He looked at Catherine, lips curled in a smile. "Between us, you and I, we can make this young lady a celebrity!"

తి

Catherine stood in the door and watched the Rolls Royce disappear through the swirling mist into the rain-drenched evening. She had just realised that Bach hadn't told her a reason for his visit — the real reason. If he'd wanted to ask her about Briony's whereabouts, all he had to do was to lift a phone. Obviously Rianne's presence here had completely thrown him. And why had he offered to help her? Josef Bach never did anything without a reason. It had to be connected with the book. But where was the advantage in it for him? He'd already got enough mileage out of poor Matt's death to destroy Briony; surely he could leave the daughter alone.

"What's wrong?"

Catherine turned to find Rianne standing behind her. She shook her head. "There's nothing wrong … I just think you should be wary of Herr Bach and his offers."

Rianne placed the palm of her hand against Catherine's face. "Don't worry, I know the signs, I've met the type before. Mind you, `I can get you a job as a nude model' is a new chat-up line. Usually it's, `I'm a movie producer, I can get you into movies.'"

"But Bach is different; he really can deliver."

"I know that, and it's what makes his offer so intriguing. So, he'll get his jollies looking at me naked … I guarantee you now that he'll want to be on the set during shooting. And then he'll expect a little repayment. I know the type, I've met them before. I can handle them."

"You might be able to handle them, Rianne," Catherine said seriously, "but you have never met anyone like Josef Bach before!"

Chapter Fifty-One

By faking her own orgasm, Briony quickly brought Greg to his own shuddering release, and then held him in the warm aftermath, until he fell asleep. When his breathing was deep and regular, she gently eased her way out from beneath him and slid out of the narrow bed. Wrapping a dressing gown around her naked body, she padded barefoot through the small cottage and stepped out on to the patio. In the distance, close enough to be clearly audible but invisible because the ground sloped up towards the dunes, the Atlantic pounded against a rocky beach.

Briony Dalton had been surprised at how accustomed she had become to the sound of the sea during those few idyllic days on the Ionian. The constant murmuring reminded her of the throbbing of a slow, powerful heart. Similarly, she missed the gentle, rhythmic swelling of the sea and during the flight back from Heraklion to Dublin — although flying had never previously bothered her — she had been abruptly terrified by the absence of movement beneath her body.

"It's primeval," Greg had explained. "I once heard it described as like being back in the womb: the pounding of the sea sounds like the beating of a mother's heart, the sensation of movement is similar to what a baby experiences. Sailing appeals to some people on a deep instinctual level. It terrifies others." He shrugged. "Maybe they had a bad birthing experience."

She had reached over and rested her fingers on the back of his head. "Do you regret coming with me?"

In reply he had simply kissed her.

She had thought that, when it came down to it, Greg might have balked at leaving Greece, but she had sensed no reluctance on his part. He had had no trouble selling his boat in Crete to a British maritime agent who rented similar boats to tourists throughout the season. They had taken the first available flight to Ireland.

Dublin had been cold and damp after the dry heat of the Mediterranean and on the taxi ride from the airport to the Westbury Hotel in the heart of Dublin they had huddled together until the taxi had heated up. Greg had remained in the taxi making small talk with the driver while Briony had run into the hotel. He was just beginning to become concerned at the amount of time she was spending — and the amount on the meter — when she surprised him by reappearing with numerous suitcases and bags of belongings. She said nothing to Greg and he didn't ask, and on the drive back to the airport she had been quiet and withdrawn.

When Briony had returned to the hotel to claim her belongings and settle her bill, she been surprised to find that Gabrielle's belongings — including her small Compaq laptop computer — had been sent from New York to her last known address, which had happened to be the hotel. The clothes, the papers, the few pieces of jewellery — many of which Briony had given her — had brought back memories which were now bitter-sweet, tainted by her death. She had run her fingers over the small computer. If she believed in omens she'd have been inclined to think that this was a good one. Her machine had been stolen … but Gabby's had returned. And, with the exception of the work Briony had done since Gabby had gone to New York, it contained the complete manuscript of *A Woman Scorned*.

She looked at the dead woman's belongings neatly parcelled and piled up in a corner of her room. Picking up the computer, she squeezed it fiercely. She was going to finish the book. And if not for her sake, then for Gabrielle's.

She carried the machine over to the table and opened the lid. Without bothering to plug it in, she turned it on, confident that there would still be a charge in the batteries. With her fingers clumsy on the small keys, she had called up the word processor and opened the directory containing *A Woman Scorned*. She had created a new file entitled 'Dedication' and typed the single line, 'This is for Gabrielle's sake'. She had saved the file and closed down the machine, packed up her belongings and had them brought out into the waiting taxi and piled them into the boot. But she had carried the computer herself.

From Dublin Airport they had taken a flight to Knock International Airport in the West of Ireland. There they had hired a car under Greg's name and driven out along the lonely coastal roads, travelling a few miles past the village of Carraroe to the tiny whitewashed cottage that Briony had purchased on a whim many years ago. Usually a local agent in Galway let it out during the summer months, but this summer — long before everything had started to go awry — she had written with instructions that the cottage was not to be let this year. She had had a vague intention of bringing Gabrielle to this place where they could spend a peaceful few days away from everyone and everything.

But that was not to be.

She regretted Gabrielle hadn't seen this place. She knew the younger woman would have loved the wild and rugged landscape, the air so clean you could taste it, with only the wind, the Atlantic and the countless sea birds for company.

Bringing Greg here wasn't quite the same thing even though he loved it. It reminded him of the Scottish islands, and he'd been captivated when he discovered that the natives here still spoke Irish, a language very similar to Scots Gallic.

He was happy here.

Briony Dalton wasn't.

She walked out into the night and climbed the slight rise to look down over the beach. The white caps of the breakers were just visible in the distance. She wondered if she ought to tell Greg her true identity; she wondered how he would react. Naturally, he'd be upset, angry, hurt too, when he discovered that she had been lying to him. Mind you, she was aware that he wasn't being entirely honest with her either. From bits and pieces he had let slip, from clues in his writing, she guessed that his desire to go to Corfu hadn't been entirely to do with his writing. Of course, the main difference was that she was consciously and deliberately using him; he too was using her, but not with the same cold-blooded deliberation.

Maybe when her work on his book was complete she could tell him the truth. At least he'd be able to see how selflessly she'd given of her time to help shape his masterpiece.

And it was a masterpiece ... well, maybe masterpiece was too strong a word. There was very little in popular literature that could truly be called a masterpiece, however frequently the word was bandied around. But Greg's book was good, damn good. She had written enough best-sellers and read even more to know the elements.

And she was jealous.

She nodded, finally admitting it to herself. The book was good; properly marketed it would be an enormous success. She was jealous. She was envious of his talent. Maybe she ought to be able to pass on her mantle as a best-selling author graciously, but she found she didn't have it in her. The more books he sold, the fewer she'd sell. The mathematics were very simple. Bookshops could only stock so many titles and after a while certain authors became passé; how many best-selling writers had she read in her youth who were rarely — if ever — read now?

Greg Connors was of the next generation of writers. His style was excellent and his story had pace, great colour and flair. It was the type of book that would appeal to the younger generation, the television, pop video generation, where the images were presented in the same way, flashy, lurid, immediate.

Her style of presentation had originated many years previously, when people still read, when time could be spent with the reader developing a story, when characters could be rounded out, motives, emotions and reactions explored. There was no time spent in Greg's book — it was immediate. And if her own writing lacked anything it was that — immediacy. She used tricks like explicit sex to shock and stop her reader; Greg used the sex — which was no less explicit — as part of the story. He was comfortable writing the sex scenes and they were more or less flawless, seamlessly woven into the story. She had always been uncomfortable writing the sex scenes and she felt it showed.

Yes, she was jealous, but it was a good enough story to deserve the best editing it could get, and she was going to do it for him. It shouldn't really hurt her own schedule. She would spend the morning working on his book — it would help put her into a writing mood in any case — and then spend the afternoon and evenings on her own. She smiled into the night; she'd be working on two books, but with only one title: *A Woman Scorned*.

Chapter Fifty-Two

The small Japanese woman who had introduced herself as Kaho Tomita escorted Rianne Moriarty along what seemed like miles of plush carpeted hallways. Although Rianne had been careful to dress fashionably yet conservatively, instinctively guessing that was how Josef Bach preferred his women, she still felt shabby standing alongside the elegantly dressed, exquisitely coiffured, beautifully made-up Japanese woman.

Kaho, her face impassive as usual, thought that Bach's taste in women was becoming progressively stranger; there was an Oriental saying that went, `Older men prefer sweet young tea.' Most men had neither the money nor the opportunity to realise their fantasies: Bach had both.

And this one was young enough. This one was Briony's Dalton's daughter. Early twenties, she imagined, pretty, though not beautiful, but with a fine bone structure. Only her eyes let her down: they were like dead stones in her face. Young certainly, innocent, definitely not. It showed in those eyes, the set of her shoulders, her walk. Her every gesture was withdrawn, defensive. Her eyes were constantly moving, checking everything, and when she smiled it was a professional thing, a twisting of her lips with no real warmth in it. As she led the young woman towards Bach's door, Kaho was saddened to see one so young reduced to such a state of distrust. She wondered at the circumstances that had made her this way.

"Miss Rianne Moriarty," Kaho said, standing to one side, allowing Rianne to precede her into the room.

"Thank you, Kaho. Coffee, please … no, tea, and Miss Moriarty takes hers with milk rather than lemon." He came around the huge slab of his desk, arms outstretched, beaming. "Why, my dear, you look stunning," he enthused.

"Thank you … Josef."

"Excellent, excellent." He led her to a chair and held it while she sank down into it. "How good of you to come," he continued, perching himself on the edge of the desk.

"How could I refuse your invitation?"

Bach's Rolls Royce had arrived at the door at nine o'clock to take Rianne to London, Bach's secretary having made the arrangements the night before, phrasing the invitation in such a manner that a refusal was simply unimaginable. Rianne didn't know what Bach was doing, what game he was playing, but she could read his desire in his body language and posturing. He was interested in her, that much was certain; she also guessed that someone of his great wealth would have been able to thoroughly check through her background, and that meant he had probably seen one or more of her movies. Many men were fascinated with porno actresses … and a surprising number of women, too, as she'd discovered through the years. She bit back a smile; despite Catherine's warnings, despite Bach's great wealth, he was just another man.

"I have made some enquiries since our brief encounter last week and, as I'm sure Kaho explained to you, there is the possibility of work for you — today — if you so desire."

"I'm intrigued."

There was a tap on the door and the Japanese secretary entered. She put the tray down on the desk to the left of Bach and looked at him for a moment in a silent question. He shook his head and she bowed, first to Bach and then to Rianne, before gliding silently from the room.

"She is very elegant," Rianne said, her eyes on Bach's face. She wondered if the woman was his mistress, and then decided that she probably wasn't. Someone like Bach would not mix business with pleasure.

"She is elegant," he agreed, pouring the tea, "but you are beautiful."

Colour touched her cheeks, surprising her, and she lowered her eyes, "Thank you," she murmured. He was good, she had to admit that.

Josef Bach passed her tea and then added milk for her. "Now," he continued, suddenly all business, "you know the magazine *Mate*?"

Rianne nodded. *Mate* was one of the top-selling of the current crop of men's magazines, having attained the popularity and prominence that *Playboy* had enjoyed during its heyday. Top photographers, journalists, columnists and authors all had their work published in *Mate*. It was part of the Bach publishing empire.

"The editor is currently looking for a model — a new, young, vibrant, attractive model — for next month's centre-page spread. The entire magazine will be devoted to emerging talent." He was watching her face carefully. "I would like you to test for the part. You know what an appearance in *Mate* could do for your career, don't you?"

Rianne did. Two of *Mate's* centrefolds had gone on to be Bond girls, whilst another had appeared as the leading actress in a series of cult horror movies which had achieved far greater success on video than they had in the cinema.

And if Rianne Moriarty had a dream — inasmuch as she could have a dream, it was to be an actress, a legitimate actress.

"They will be testing this afternoon," Bach said. "Prospective models will be expected to complete a nude set. You know, of course, that elasticated underwear marks are unsightly, so you have plenty of time to remove them and allow the marks to vanish."

"I partially guessed this was what you had in mind," Rianne said, biting the inside of her cheeks to stop herself from laughing in his face. He was so transparent. All men were so transparent! "So I decided not to wear any this morning."

Bach swallowed hard. He had a sudden image — lifted from one of the two dozen or so of her pornographic videos he'd seen — of the young woman naked in the chair before him. He turned away from her and went to stand before the glass wall, staring out over the city of London while he attempted to regain his composure.

Rianne lifted her cup to hide the smile that curled her lips.

He gazed at her reflection in the glass; so young, so innocent-looking … but looks could be so deceiving. He had seen her perform with three men, with other women, singly and in groups. What was it about her that intrigued him? It was very easy to say he was using her as just another way to get to Briony Dalton, insurance, a card held in reserve. But Josef Bach was convinced he owed some his success to the fact that he always tried to be honest with himself. And if he was being honest with himself now he would admit that there was something about this young woman which attracted him. She was pretty, but not beautiful, and with his wealth he could have any number of beautiful women. He glanced over his shoulder. She raised her eyes and he looked quickly away. There was something about her eyes — so big, so wide, so dark, so lost. Her eyes fascinated him. When he was looking at her videos, watching her performing the most obscene acts, he had concentrated on her face, her eyes, running the video again and again, pausing, rewinding, freezing the picture to study her face, her eyes, eventually recognising what had caught his attention: her eyes had retained the look of absolute detachment, of complete innocence, throughout the action. They reminded him of someone …

"Tell me about your modelling experience," he said suddenly.

Holding her cup and saucer like a lady, Rianne spoke in a cool, detached voice, aware of the effect she was having on him, enjoying the power. "I started with straightforward nude modelling for porn mags — posing either singly or in a group, and from there progressed to `action shots' with men or women, or multiples of both. There's nothing real in it, it's all posed," she added. "Around about then we started to see magazines appearing which were nothing more than stills from the movies, where the photos are usually shot during the filming of a feature. Suddenly the magazine market faded and I found myself going for longer and longer periods without work. The next logical step was for me to go into movies." She smiled, realising that Bach was watching her intently. "It was a job, nothing more. It paid the rent, kept me fed." She lifted her head, staring into his reflected eyes, her tone challenging, direct. "I did what I had to do to survive."

The words — so familiar — chilled him. Bach turned from the window. He knew who she reminded him of now. She reminded him of himself. And yet she also reminded him — in some strange and obscure way, because they weren't alike in any way — of Sophie, the young woman who had found him in the rubble of post-war Germany. He had been twelve but looked older; she had been sixteen and looked a lot older. They had fallen in together as they had made their way out of the city. They had both lost family in the bombing, both lost siblings to hunger and disease, both were orphans. In the months that followed they shared many things. She taught him how to live, how to fend for himself, how to recognise the danger signals in animals and men, how to read the emotions in a man's eyes, in a woman's smile. She taught him how to lie and cheat and steal — all in the name of survival. These were the lessons he had taken into business.

And when he had caught her selling herself to the advancing British and American troops, she had simply said, "I did what I had to do to survive." And he found he hadn't got it in his heart to condemn her. He hadn't that right.

He had woken up one morning in a barn close to the edge of the Black Forest and she'd been missing. He had spent the next three days frantically searching for her, but to no avail. He had been devastated, and in those days he realised that he had actually loved her ... although they had never made love. That was one lesson she hadn't taught him. He was convinced that she was still alive; dead bodies were plentiful, and if anything had happened to her he was convinced he would have found the corpse, and he swore that one day he would find her. But it wasn't until he had achieved his success and wealth that he had been able to pursue that particular quest.

The private detective agencies he had hired, first in Germany and then in the States where the search had taken them, had cost him a small fortune, but — even though his meanness was legendary he didn't begrudge a penny of it. He needed to know. He didn't need to know what happened to her, he simply needed to know that she was all right. And there was one — just one — question he needed to ask.

The detectives had found her finally in a small town in the mid-west, a grandmother now, having married an American serviceman and returned with him to a gentler life in America. Bach had flown to the States and then sat for two days watching the house, looking at her coming and going, afraid — literally afraid — to approach her.

Finally, unable to bear it any longer, he had walked across the dusty, red-sanded street, pushed open the white-painted gate in the picket fencing and strode up to the woman sitting in the rocking chair on the shaded veranda. The white-haired, blue-eyed woman was still the Sophie he knew, although he guessed he had changed out of all recognition.

"Hello, Sophie, it's been a long time." He spoke in German. She had stared at him for a long time before answering. Then she smiled, and her eyes misted.

"Josef? It is you?" Her German — thought she hadn't used it in nearly fifty years — was still perfect.

"Tell me why, Sophie?"

"How did you find me?" she asked, not answering his question.

"I've been looking for you."

"For all this time?"

"For all this time. Just tell me why, Sophie? Tell me why you ran away and said nothing. I searched for you. I nearly went out of my mind with worry. I thought you were dead ... I didn't know what to think. Just tell me why."

The white-haired grandmother stared at him, face tightening in a mask he remembered from so long ago. "I did what I had to do," she said firmly, and turned her face away from him.

Josef Bach had nodded and left.

And now he had seen the same look of absolute determination in Rianne Moriarty's face.

Turning from the window, Josef Bach smiled brightly. "Come, let's see about making you a star."

α

They had flown by helicopter across London, the flight both thrilling and terrifying Rianne, who had never flown in a helicopter before. "It's the only way to beat the traffic," Bach had laughed as she clutched his hand tightly.

The photographer's studio was on the south side of the river, but Rianne, completely disorientated by the flight, couldn't identify the exact location, although she knew they had flown high over Waterloo Bridge, Bach had pointed out the National Theatre and she had seen Waterloo Station off to her right.

The realisation that Bach was serious actually sunk in when she arrived at the studio. She had seen countless photographers' studios before, in London and New York and later in Amsterdam, usually shabby bed-sits with a single camera set up on a tripod. Some were genuine, others were men just getting off on taking pictures of nude women.

This studio was different.

It was situated in one wing of an enormous Georgian house on the outskirts of London, which was set in its own grounds with a small stream bisecting part of the estate.

"I own the house and the estate," Bach explained as the pilot brought the helicopter down for a landing on the helipad at the back of the house. "Most of my magazines are put together here — everything is on hand, editorial, typesetting, colour separation, that sort of thing — and it seemed only logical to establish the photographer's studio to complete the package." He helped her down on to the tarmac and, heads ducked low beneath the whipping blades, they hurried across to the paved pathway. Behind them the pilot powered his machine down. Rianne linked her arm through Bach's as they climbed a score of steps from one level to another in the landscaped gardens. "I have arranged for you to be photographed by Michelle Seigner, one of *Mate's* top photographers. I fully anticipate that you will be next month's centrefold." He said it in such a way that Rianne *knew* she would be next month's centre-fold.

"Well, I wouldn't be so sure. I'm not exactly pretty, my hair's too short, my breasts are too small."

Bach shook his head. "No, no, no. That look — the gamin, the boy — is in now, and you know yourself what a good photographer can do to ensure that the camera flatters the model. And you will have the advantage of the best make-up artists and stylists," he added with a smile.

"I really don't know what to say. You're being very kind, Josef."

"Thank me when you have the contract."

"Can you tell me why you're doing this for a girl you've barely met?" she asked quietly, glancing away but watching him out of the corner of her eye.

They walked in silence until finally Bach said, "I could lie to you and tell you that there was no commercial reason behind it — because there is, of course. You have a look about you, an aura, that is very rare. Once a photographer has captured that image it can be used to sell magazines, clothes, perfume."

"But you don't need the money."

"No, it's not just the money. It's something else, something quite indefinable, its something to do with the fact that you are unique, something to do with the fact that many, many people looked at you, photographers, directors, producers, cameramen, but none recognised your potential. But I saw that potential. I discovered you. Me! That is my kick, my thrill. That is what I get out of it. Oh, I will exploit that potential, make no mistake about it. I will splash your face across every magazine and newspaper in the world. I am going to make your name a household one, Rianne Moriarty. Do not doubt it."

"Why?" Rianne asked.

"Because I want to. Because I can," he said fervently, and Rianne, walking by his side, felt that the latter answer was closer to the truth. But she also realised Bach would want to be paid, sooner or later, and the only negotiable coin she had was her body. But if he came through with his promises ... well, she had known girls who had sold themselves for less ... hell, she had sold herself only recently to make enough money to keep her brother in junk, so she had no great scruples about that.

She was also aware that there were other reasons, deeper, possibly darker reasons, behind Bach's treatment of her. Rianne Moriarty might be many things, she might be whore or porno starlet, but she was no fool. One of the reasons she had survived in a business which took souls and then lives at a relatively early age was because she always knew when to get out, when to stay ahead. Josef Bach had employed Catherine Garrett to write a biography — warts and all — of Briony Dalton because Catherine, as well as being her step-sister, loathed Briony. And now the same Josef Bach was busily cultivating Briony Dalton's daughter. He had something up his sleeve ...

All she had to do was to wait, take what he gave her and see what transpired ... and then get out while she was still ahead. She'd played this game before — never for such high stakes, it was true — but she'd always won. She'd win again.

Chapter Fifty-Three

The moment she heard the wailing crackle of static down the line Terri Fierstein knew who was calling. She sat up in bed, looking at the clock — it was a little after three in the morning — and wondering how to play this.

"Briony … what a delight!" She shook her partner Charles awake and mimed wheels turning. He hopped from the bed, padded into the room Terri used as an office and touched the record button on the small tape-recorder affixed to the phone. It was a device Terri had often found useful. "How are you?" crackled over the small speaker.

"I'm fine, thank you," Briony said crisply, the echoing line not disguising the coldness in her voice.

"Where are you? I've been going frantic trying to make contact."

"I'm on holiday," Briony said. "I want to know something," she said slowly and distinctly. "What will happen if I fail to deliver *A Woman Scorned*?"

"Well, you won't do that, will you?"

"Answer the question."

"As I've already told you, your financial position at the moment is precarious … "

"Make it simple and short. This call is costing me a fortune."

"I can phone you back," Terri said immediately, eager to have Briony's number at least.

"Answer the question," Briony snapped.

"It will be financial ruin for you. You will lose everything. I've done the best I can over the past few months, selling subsidiary rights, translations of the older works, serialisations in magazines, but it's still not enough.

You have to deliver the book. How close to completion is it?"

"It's not."

"Aaah." Terri's thin lips twisted in a bitter smile; Bach would be pleased.

"What will happen to the publishers?"

"Hall's, the British publishers, will probably go into liquidation, Park & Park the Americans, might weather the storm … but it's unlikely."

"If anything were to happen to me, what then?"

"I'm not sure what you mean."

"Are the publishers not covered against a loss of this type, have they no insurance or something like that?"

Terri looked at Charles and frowned, wondering where this was leading. "No insurance is possible," she said slowly. "They pays their money and they takes their chance. If you don't deliver, they would have to attempt to claim the money back from you by the legal process. The problem is that you don't have it." She stopped and added, "But I've already told you all this. Why the sudden interest now? You knew this was the case from the very beginning."

"I just wanted to get it straight in my own mind," Briony said, and Terri could detect the weariness in her voice.

"Look, come back to New York. I'll get you a secretary, a team of secretaries, maybe a ghost writer or something like. You spin out the plot for him or her, and they can fill it in. It's been done before."

"No," Briony said firmly.

"If you don't deliver this book, you will never be published again. You know that, don't you?"

"I know," Briony Dalton said and hung up.

Terri Fierstein looked at the buzzing instrument and then carefully replaced it on its cradle. In the office the voice-activated tape recorder turned itself off. Terri turned to Charles. "Well, what do you make of that?"

If Terri were to admit the truth, she was a little worried about Briony Dalton. But even Briony, who had achieved her every success through tremendous hard work and determination, was nothing compared to Josef Bach. She might be worried about Briony, but she was terrified of Bach. She hadn't wanted to betray Briony ... she had made Briony, and in return Briony had been responsible for much of Terri's own success. It was assumed — not always correctly, of course — that top-name authors went to top-name agents. Being Briony's agent had been a superb advertisement for her agency.

But it was a business arrangement, she had to keep reminding herself of that. It was a business arrangement, nothing more. And Bach's terms were better, much better.

Also, while she might be frightened of what Briony would do if she discovered the truth, she knew she was not in actual danger of her life.

She wasn't so sure she could say the same about Bach.

☙

Briony Dalton wrapped her arms across her chest and walked to the kitchen window. She stared out over the low stone walls and across the countless scrubby fields, each one squared off with the mortarless, flat stone walls that were a feature of the West of Ireland landscape. Even though it was still early morning, the sky was cloudless, the blue washed a pale azure, the light dazzling. She pushed open the window and turned her head slightly, listening, but there wasn't a sound across the empty landscape, even the distant ever-present rumble of the sea having diminished, become such a part of her unconscious that she no longer heard it.

She wasn't sure why she had phoned Terri Fierstein. She had known about the necessity of finishing *A Woman Scorned*. She knew it meant financial ruin if she didn't — not only for herself, but also for the publishers involved — knew also that finding a publisher for her next book would be well-nigh impossible. She had known all this.

She just needed to hear it said one more time.

She popped her head into the bedroom. Greg was still asleep, sprawled diagonally, arms and legs akimbo — he slept like a child — on the bed that was neither a single nor a double and which was as hard as a rock. He had been up into the early hours of the morning working on the last couple of chapters of his book. A dozen sheets of single-spaced-typed paper sat beside his typewriter; she would eventually copy the pages on to the computer and edit them.

Briony gently closed the door behind her and walked out into the early morning. The air was sweet, rich with the sea and the land: she knew now what poets had said about drinking the air like wine. It was heady stuff. She had thrown a heavy Aran cardigan around her neck, leaving the sleeves dangling down over her shoulders. Holding the sleeves tightly, she strode to the beach, consciously thinking of nothing, allowing the memories to crowd in, to jostle and push and then pop up one by one for inspection before disappearing, leaving her calm and totally relaxed.

Memories.

Memories of the time she had bought this cardigan. She'd been with Gabrielle in Dublin … and it seemed like an eternity ago.

Had she loved the woman? She had her doubts now. She used to think they had been good for one another … but, well, she wasn't so certain about that either. Certainly, in the early stages, Gabrielle had been magnificent. But as the time had gone by when their relationship had changed and they had become lovers … well, she had found herself with precious little time for writing.

Memories.

Gabrielle had introduced her to so many new things, sex with a woman, and grass and speed and coke. And it had all happened around the same time … No, the same night.

She padded on to the beach and walked to the water's edge, watching the waves run in then slow down, hissing across the sand, sizzling almost, just brushing the edge of her trainers.

Memories.

It had happened the same night. A party in Bel Air in the home of some oriental martial arts film star who was in the process of being `made' in the States. Briony had suffered through one of his movies and decided that Bruce Lee he wasn't. It was one of those parties where one was seen to go and went to be seen. There were lots of people, lots of drink, lots of drugs. The drugs were lying around quite openly in bowls, on trays or in little bags like sweets. Gabrielle had fished out two bags of brownish-white powder and dragged Briony off, giggling, to one of the mansion's twenty-seven bedrooms.

They were both drunk, Briony remembered, but not that drunk. She knew what had been happening, knew what was going to happen. And she had allowed it to happen because she had been curious and intrigued.

What would it be like to snort coke?

What would it be like to make love to another woman?

The woman on the beach at the edge of the Atlantic found she was suddenly shocked. Shocked with herself, shocked with her attitude. Had she become so bored with life that she needed the drugs and the sex for excitement?

Memories.

She remembered when she'd been writing so intensively in Dublin before she'd got her big break. She didn't drink, rarely ate red meat — because she'd read that the body used up valuable energy digesting it — and she'd lived a completely celibate life.

She had firmly believed then that the sex act and the creative urge — writing, painting, sculpting — were one and the same thing. They sprang from the same source, the same well. But one could not have both. She remembered how, following a night of lovemaking with Gabrielle, she would be exhausted, physically and mentally, unable to write or even think about writing the following day. Staring at the heaving sea, she smiled, remembering.

Memories.

The woman had been half her age and endlessly energetic, so inventive, so demanding. Lovemaking with Gabrielle was an intense experience, and she never failed to reach orgasm time and again, long intense waves of pleasure.

Unconsciously glancing back over her shoulder to where the whitewashed cottage was hidden by the dunes, she realised that sex with Greg was different. He was a gentler lover, and although he tried to bring her to orgasm every time he failed more often than not because he was simply trying too hard. Sometimes she faked orgasm to please him. But that wasn't to say she didn't enjoy their lovemaking. It simply wasn't as demanding ... and she was able to write the following day.

She'd enjoyed the times with Gabrielle — well, most of them anyway. It had been a crazy time. But there was no such thing as something for nothing. She'd had her fun and now she was paying for it. The wages of sin. By rights she should have finished her book and been well into the next one whereas she was less than a quarter of the way through.

She looked into the future, but found it bleak and desolate. Unless she finished the book there was no future.

What was she going to do?

In God's name, what was she going to do?

The woman pulled the cardigan off her shoulders and wept into the soft, fragrant wool.

Chapter Fifty-Four

By the time Catherine Garrett had written nearly sixty thousand words of the biography, she realised that she was not cut out to be a writer. She was bored. It was one thing to do a series of reviews or articles every week and quite another to sit down day after day, night after night, and churn out word after word on a subject she had discovered she absolutely loathed.

Best of friends, worst of enemies.

Like most best friends, when Briony and Catherine had parted, there had been a lot of bitterness. They had known each other too well, known the weak spots, the vulnerable places.

They knew how to hurt one another.

Catherine's intense dislike of Briony had always bordered on loathing and disgust; she found her contemptible, a sham, and yet Catherine was powerless to do anything about it. She had thought that writing the book would be easy and, in a roundabout way, possibly even a way for her to exorcise her feelings about Briony. It hadn't. The deeper she looked into the woman's life, the more disgusted and enraged she became. Everything about her, her whole life, her success, the casual way she had destroyed her children's lives was founded on a lie. A whole series of lies.

And there was nothing she could do about it.

When it came down to it, all she had was hearsay, libels, slanders, third-party rumours and stories. Catherine knew she couldn't use any of it — there was no way she was going to give Briony Dalton the satisfaction of suing her … not that Bach's lawyers would allow that to happen in the first place. Before this book went to print it would be vetted by a highly paid team of lawyers.

Briony Dalton was completely amoral; she had destroyed everything in her lust for success.

Even herself.

Catherine flexed her fingers, hearing the knuckles crack. She had to give the writer credit for one thing, though: to be able to sit for hours hammering out words was quite an accomplishment.

03

Briony Dalton sat across the table from him and watched him write.

He reminded her so much of herself. Writing solidly, hour after hour, page after page, chasing the story to its very end with only the vaguest idea how it was going to turn out, as fascinated with the story as the eventual reader.

She remembered the time she'd been able to do that. Now she was lucky if she managed to get in an hour without interruption.

And usually the interruptions were of her own making. Oh yes, be a writer, make your own schedule, work your own timetable. Bullshit! It was a job, and if it was to be successful you worked it like a job. Either that or it was a passion … an all-consuming passion. She didn't think there was a middle ground.

In the beginning it had been her all-consuming passion, occupying her every waking hour, but later … later it too often, too quickly, became a chore.

But right now Greg was at the passionate — or the obsessional — stage.

He looked up and caught her watching him.

"Penny for them," he grinned.

"Nothing. Just thinking."

"Happy thoughts?"

"Some."

"What were you thinking about?" He pushed the typewriter away and rested his arms on the table, leaning forward on them.

"I was thinking about you."

"Me?"

"Tell me what writing means to you," she said suddenly, surprising him.

"It's … it's … it's what I do," he said finally. "It means everything to me. Surely it means the same to you?"

Briony Dalton smiled sadly. "Not any more, I'm afraid. What would happen if you couldn't write?" she persisted.

Greg looked past her, his eyes distant. "I don't know. There's nothing else I want to do … not now, not when I know I can write." His large hazel eyes focused on her face. "I'd be devastated for a while, I guess, then I'd move onto something else."

Briony Dalton nodded.

"What would happen to you?" he asked.

"I don't know," she said truthfully. "But I've nothing else to move onto," she finally admitted.

Chapter Fifty-Five

Rianne Moriarty ground her teeth in frustration as there was yet another delay in shooting. The young man who did the make-up hurried across, a heavy dressing gown thrown over his arm. Rianne gladly allowed him to drape it round her shoulders and hugged it to her body. A modelling assignment in the giant caves in Dachstein in Austria sounded fabulous. The enormous primeval caves with their spectacular growths of soaring stalagmites and giant, drooping stalactites was breath- taking ... but when you were standing there more or less stark naked the only thing which took your breath away was the cold. It was bloody freezing.

"What is it this time?" she muttered, her teeth chattering.

The young man smiled sympathetically. He nodded to where Josef Bach, swathed in a three-quarter-length leather coat, was chatting to a burly balding man in a shabby anorak. "Some friend of Herr Bach's. We thought he was just another voyeur and security tried to eject him, but he made such a fuss that Herr Bach himself went to investigate." He glanced over his shoulder. "I don't believe they've ever met, but they seem to know one another." He turned back to her, looking critically at her hair and make-up, and touched a tentative finger to his lips. "A little more gloss ... and we'll have to take the shine off your breasts, otherwise they'll positively glow when the flash hits them."

"Whatever you have to do, Tony," she said tiredly. She'd been standing here in these freezing caves with an Arctic wind whistling around her for the past two hours and so far they'd only managed to shoot about four rolls of film whilst she posed and pouted against the enchanting backdrop and straddled stalagmites. There was an interruption every ten minutes: the light wasn't right, the film was wrong, the pose had to be just so, there were too many people in the caves, there were shadows on the wall, there were reflections off her skin, her goose-bumps were visible. She'd made full-length porno features in less time.

And with every interruption her make-up had to be fixed, her hair had to be combed — including her pubic hair, for Christ's sake! — her costume, neo-baroque-cavegirl, had to be adjusted to show more of this, less of that. The only thing they had stopped doing was rubbing ice cubes to her nipples to make them stand out. This whole bloody cave was one giant ice cube.

Maybe she'd be the star Josef Bach promised, but she'd be a star with pneumonia.

Clutching the dressing gown tightly closed she strode across to where Bach was talking to the big man. Her cardboard and fur cavegirl booties did nothing to keep out the chill.

" ... the West of Ireland," the big man was saying in a New York accent, the caves catching and throwing his voice, "with the same guy from Corfu." He turned as Rianne approached, a big, bulky man into his fifties, a hard face, cold grey eyes. She knew the type. She'd often seen them hanging around the porno movie circuit, and in her experience they were always working for someone else, always looking after someone else's interests.

Bach turned to her, his bright blue eyes sparkling with good humour. "Ah, Rianne, my dear, you must be cold and tired with all this waiting?" He made no attempt to introduce her to the American.

Rianne stuck her hand out to the American, simultaneously allowing the dressing gown to part in the centre. "I'm Rianne Moriarty." She frowned. "Haven't we met before somewhere? New York, perhaps?"

Caught off guard, disconcerted by her nakedness, the man accepted her hand and shook his head. "I don't think so, pretty lady. I haven't been back to the States since before you were born."

"I'm sure we've met …" Rianne began, but Bach interrupted her, inclining his head, his eyes looking past her. "They're looking for you. We'll go as soon as they finish this set," he added, glancing at his watch, "I've a meeting in Milan this evening."

Rianne smiled at both men and turned away, wondering why the American hadn't given his name. And why had Josef used her name? Since she'd won the contract for the centre-page shoot — which had come as no surprise since she was Bach's protégée and Bach owned the magazine — she'd starting using her stage name Ryan once again. But Bach had almost deliberately called her Rianne, as if he was warning his companion… She glanced over her shoulder and saw Bach returning his cheque book to his pocket; the big American was folding away a slip of cream-coloured paper.

Rianne smiled broadly. She knew how to get the man's name …

Cß

Charley O'Neill walked away from Josef Bach with a cheque for fifty thousand pounds in his pocket. He had been surprised when Bach had gravely thanked him for the information and taken out his chequebook, but it was only with the greatest of difficulty that he had been able to contain his elation when he'd seen the size of the cheque the German had written. He'd have been happy with a tenth of the figure.

And Charley had no doubt but that there would be plenty more where that came from. As Bach had passed across the cheque, he had shaken Charley's hand and told him there was always room in his organisation for men of proven ability … and Charley had obviously proven his ability by finding Briony Dalton.

He had discovered her whereabouts completely by accident. Following the debacle in Corfu — although he had recovered the woman's portable computer and been paid for that, so it hadn't been entirely wasted — Charley O'Neill had returned to Ireland, imagining that his work was done. With Holland out of the way for a long time, he didn't think he'd be seeing any work from that quarter again. But his professional curiosity had been piqued. He had begun to investigate Briony Dalton on his own time. A phone call to a contact in New York got him her IRS records for the past ten years, and then, with the dogged persistence which made him such a successful private investigator, he had begun to fine-comb through the records. He wasn't sure what he was looking for, but he knew he'd recognise it when he saw it. And he found it remarkably quickly.

Eight years ago, Briony Dalton's solicitor had issued a cheque for twenty thousand Irish pounds to a building contractor in Galway in the west of Ireland. And in that year's IRS return there was another property assigned to her, a summer residence, current estimated value twenty thousand pounds Irish.

As simple as that.

A call to the builder in Galway elicited the address in Carraroe, and then a phone call to a colleague in Galway and a cheque for one hundred Irish pounds, had bought him the information that a wealthy woman — the local people said she was either an artist or writer and her son, also a writer — had taken up residence in the cottage at very short notice.

O'Neill had actually picked up the phone to call Bach's London office when he decided this sort of news was better brought in person.

Finding Bach had been more difficult than finding Briony Dalton. And once he'd found him actually getting close to him had proved almost impossible.

But perseverance had paid off, and now, taking all his expenses, including his time, air fare and fees to colleagues, he had made about forty-nine thousand pounds profit. And that's what he liked to show on a deal: a healthy profit.

Once he'd completed stage two he was sure there'd be a bonus. Bach's instructions had been explicit: he wanted O'Neill to ensure that Briony Dalton was denied the pleasure of working on her new book. Bach had been quite diplomatic about it. He wanted her to have some time to recover from her accident. And Charley O'Neill knew exactly what kind of accident.

ॐ

Josef Bach could be a fine and sensitive lover. Rianne had found he took his time — though that might have been a factor of his age — and he was always solicitous, checking to see if he was hurting or pressing too hard, pushing too roughly. Indeed, for such a high-powered businessman, he was remarkably gentle. In Rianne's experience, people like him tended to be exactly the same in bed, aggressive, rough, uncaring and unthinking.

But today as the plane curved south across the edge of Switzerland into northern Italy, Rianne sensed that he was preoccupied, that he was making love to her as a matter of course, as if to prove to himself that he could. He orgasmed quickly — though he usually attempted to bring her to orgasm first with his fingers and lips — and then quickly fell into a deep and, if his twitches and jerks were anything to judge by, a troubled sleep.

Lifting the sleeping man's hand from her breast, Rianne had slid out of the bed and then stood for a moment while the plane banked. She smiled suddenly: she wondered if she now qualified for membership of the mile-high club. Making love in a plane was an extraordinary experience, the thrumming of the powerful engines trembling up through the floors and walls, vibrating the bed, intensifying the pleasure.

Josef Bach was, by nature, a meticulously neat man and his clothes had been folded across the edge of the double bed which opened out across the floor of the 747. Rianne went though his clothes with quick efficiency, finding his chequebook in the right-hand inside pocket. The stub was made out to Charley O'Neill, which left her no wiser than before, but at least she had a name to work with. She wondered if Catherine knew.

ભ

Catherine Garrett had started with the children's stories, devoting two separate chapters, one each to Rianne and Matt from the time they ran away from school and left their mother. There was a third chapter which detailed their reunion and which ended with Matt's death. In the book Catherine called it an overdose, but privately she had other ideas.

She then began to work backwards, writing up the notes she had prepared from her conversation with Gabrielle Royer. Gabrielle's reply to Catherine's blunt question, "Are you lovers?" had elicited an unequivocal, "Yes. But only I am the lesbian; Briony is simply lonely."

Now she found she was twisting every phrase, altering and arranging every sentence, to present Briony Dalton as an evil woman.

Catherine Garrett stopped, looking at the words glowing green on her computer screen. Evil. It was a strong, emotional, emotive word. It was easy to say that certain people were evil, murderers, rapists, drug-pushers, these were evil people. But surely it was pushing things too far to suggest the same about a writer?

Briony Dalton was a liar and a thief. She had destroyed her husband's life, devastated her children's lives, had been responsible for the degradation of her daughter, ultimately responsible for the death of her son. Was it not the ultimate evil to wreck the hopes and futures of the young?

She had been going to call the book *Lies* … maybe. *This Evil Woman, A Biography of Briony Dalton* would be a better title.

ଓ

Every evening, Greg would read the 'Afters' version of *A Woman Scorned*. The version he gave to Brigid was the 'Befores.' The difference between the two — his original and her edited version — was astounding.

Greg had never really had the advantage of a proper editor. His previous books had been short, tightly written, rigidly plotted and required little editorial work. But this new book was truly different.

Because Briony hadn't bought a printer to hook up to the computer, he had to be content to read it on the screen, scrolling up screen after screen of the glowing words. It was practically the only thing he knew how to make the computer do having failed miserably to grasp even the rudiments of operating it. Anyway, he liked the solid, almost reassuring tapping of the typewriter and the steady mound of paper that marked the passage of days and work completed.

While he wrote the final chapters she worked on the revised portion. She had actually suggested three alternative endings and they had talked through each one before finally settling upon the classical grand denouement.

Many times when he read through what she had done he could find little or no change between his original text and her version. Occasionally there might be a word changed, a phrase inserted or shifted around, the punctuation tidied up, making sentences shorter, or longer, adding commas and full stops. But there were also plenty of cases where she had completely rewritten his deathless prose, removing huge chunks of text, simplifying it, cutting away his extraneous padding. She ran paragraphs together, took sections from one chapter and inserted them into another, all the while honing and refining the story, taking it — a good tale, workmanlike, exciting, fast-paced, romantic — and turning it into something else.

She was making it into a best-seller.

It was like learning to write again.

og

As she read through the novel, she tried to imagine how she would write it. Often Greg surprised her by using the same ideas she would have used, but equally, he often took the story along lines so totally dissimilar from what she'd been expecting that its sheer brilliance took her breath away.

His imagination and audacity left her speechless.

Briony had set up the word-processing programme on two separate directories on the tiny machine's hard disk. She did all her work on one of the directories and then copied it to the second directory for Greg to read through at his leisure.

She had 'hidden' her working directory, tucking it away behind a false name and allowing access to it only by the use of a three-digit code number. She showed Greg how to turn on the machine and taught him how to read a directory, pointing out the word-processing programme and then wrote a file on the machine which meant that all he had to do was to type GREG and the machine automatically opened up the directory where his reading copy of *A Woman Scorned* was kept. She showed him how to open the files and close them when he was finished, and then how to shut down the machine. She showed him nothing else.

The book she had originally been writing, the first *A Woman Scorned*, lay neglected in a subdirectory. She hadn't done any work on it for weeks and, indeed, now found herself substituting names and characters from that book into Greg's story, taking elements of the plot from hers and weaving them amongst his. She knew she was destroying her own book in the process, but she didn't regret it; she knew she would never get to finish that book.

Chapter Fifty-Six

It was Greg's suggestion.

Or so she would console herself.

They had made love long into the night. Greg was a caring and gentle lover, and she was eager to feel his arms around her, his breath on her body, eager to feel him inside her. In his arms she found it easy to forget the past, easier still not to think about the future. Perhaps that was the great secret of lovemaking — one lived only for that timeless, immortal moment. She had surrendered to his attentions, allowing him to do all the work, content to lie back and feel his hands and lips, his tongue rove over her body.

Greg crouched above the woman, his lips moving down along the line of her throat across her breasts, moistening the nipples, sliding down her belly, his breath hot against her navel. He had made love to her so often now that he knew how to arouse her, how to please her, where to touch, to kiss, to lick. He knew this body … but he didn't know the woman. Who was this fascinating, mysterious woman who had come out of nowhere and proceeded to completely change his life? And his work.

And a writer's work was his life.

He had broken all the rules with her, allowed her access to his work, allowed her to share it with him, allowed her to see that secret part of him.

He had lived with this book for so long now that it was a part of him. Other writers had told him that their work became closer to them than family, the characters sometimes more real, the subject more interesting than cold reality. He knew what they meant now. The great attraction of writing is the power; the power to completely control the characters and situations, the opportunity to play God. Greg had tried drugs; he found writing more addictive. He had always disbelieved those writers who claimed that sharing writing with a loved one — the sharing of something so deeply personal — brought the couple closer together. Until he had met Brigid Garrett. Until he had seen what she had done to his novel, until he had watched fascinated, as she proceeded to rewrite his text with such obvious care and devotion until it had become in itself almost an act of love. He had never felt so close to a person before, had never given so much of himself so freely or so openly. The book was part of him, it was the best he could do, but she was improving it, strengthening it.

The bond that had grown up between them had deepened and was then reinforced as they continued to share the creative process by discussing the novel, deciding how it would go, talking through various characters, determining how they would act and react.

They had come to know one another through the book and their writings. Now they made love effortlessly, as if they had known one another all their lives. He found himself emulating the way one of the characters in the book made love — was that life imitating art? — and then he realised that Brigid had adopted the positions and characteristics of the female protagonist in the novel. They had shared their fantasies on paper; now they were simply sharing that fantasy.

He moved up her body and lifted his face to hers, his lips brushing across her cheekbones, the line of her jaw, finally coming to rest on her lips. She raised her legs and as he slid into her, her ankles locked across the small of his back. They lay together, unmoving.

"Thank you," he murmured.

"For what?"

"For everything. For you. For the book."

"We're not finished yet," she smiled.

"One last chapter. One more day's work."

"Maybe two day's work. It's an important chapter." Her fingers tightened on his upper arms as she felt the muscles in her stomach begin to contract. "Have you decided how it's going to end?"

"I think we'll go for the all-out, over-the-top ending."

"Bodies everywhere."

"Yeah. What do you think?"

"We need to keep one alive ... for the sequel," she added, catching his surprised look. "Never burn your bridges."

"Bit of a cop-out though."

"Not if your readers think the character is dead!"

"Brilliant," he gasped.

Their bodies had found an easy rhythm seemingly of their own accord. His flesh was sheened with sweat, the muscles in his groin were beginning to pulsate. He could feel her moist flesh closing over him, holding him tightly, the trembling in her stomach and thighs. Their hearts were pounding in unison.

"This is really your book, you know that. Your name should be on the cover," he whispered. And then his orgasm took him and he threw his head back, eyes squeezed shut, teeth clenched.

He didn't see the look in Briony Dalton eyes.

ॐ

Your name should be on the cover ...
Your name should be on the cover ...
Your name should be on the cover ...

Briony Dalton awoke in the still quiet hours before the dawn. She had no conscious recollection of having fallen asleep. She remembered Greg's orgasm; she had been close to orgasm herself at that point, but his words had chilled her and the moment had passed, and she had ended up faking her orgasm to please him. He had fallen asleep moments later, still inside her, still wrapped in her legs and arms.

Now, four hours later, her legs were bruised and numb and she felt raw and tender after their coupling.

Your name should be on the cover ...
Your name should be on the cover ...
Your name should be on the cover ...

The sentence had raced around her dreams through the night, echoing and re-echoing like some Alpine yodel. What was startling was that she thought he was right, he was merely echoing her own thoughts over the past few days: her name *should* be on the cover. She'd put a lot of work into it, in many respects it was her book. It had been knitted so seamlessly together that she now found it difficult to point out the pieces which were hers and which were his.

It read like a Briony Dalton novel.

Granted, it didn't read like a recent Briony Dalton novel, but it was vintage Briony Dalton; it had the power and energy of her earlier books, especially *Odalisk* and *Harem*.

She smiled bitterly at the cracks in the ceiling. There never would be another Briony Dalton title. She wasn't going to finish *A Woman Scorned* and when she didn't deliver there was going to be hell to pay. And that was a pity, because she had come close to rediscovering her love for writing in the past few weeks. Greg's enthusiasm was infectious.

The thought crept in like the tide on the beach, slowly, steadily, inexorably, and perhaps, like the tide, it had always been there and she had simply refused to accept it. What frightened her, what truly terrified her, was the ease with which she accepted it.

The book was hers. Even Greg said so. The style was hers, much of the writing was hers, even the title, for Christ's sake, was hers.

Greg was young, immensely talented. He could write another book; Jesus, in *A Woman Scorned* alone he had ideas for half a dozen more. His whole life, his future and the future of an entire publishing house weren't dependent on him delivering his next novel. Hers was.

So why not take it?

Just take it.

It existed on the small portable Compaq; it existed on disk. And it existed in Greg's typewritten sheets of the first draft.

Briony Dalton slid from the warm bed and walked naked into the sitting room. Acting swiftly, knowing that if she stopped to analyse her actions she wouldn't go through with it, she gathered up the typewritten pages and returned them to their cardboard box along with the spiral-bound notebook Greg had used to keep track of his characters and situations. She turned and padded into the kitchen.

Carrying the box under one arm, she hurried from the cottage, terrified now that Greg would wake. Picking her way across the rocky beach to the sandy strip at the water's edge, she stood for a dozen heartbeats, feeling her skin pucker in the chill, her nipples hardening, gooseflesh rising along her arms, her groin, damp after lovemaking, now cold and uncomfortable.

This was her last chance to change her mind ... but the decision had already been made.

Kneeling on the cold, damp sand, she scooped a hole deep enough to hold the box of paper and the notebook. Then, she piled several stones on top of the box to stop the paper flying away in the light breeze. She had brought firelighters, lamp oil and matches from the kitchen.

It took seconds to bring the oil-doused paper to a blaze. Fed by the firelighters, the flames ate through the cardboard box full of paper, cinders spiralling heavenwards, gossamer leaves of blackened charred paper gusting off into the night. The fire burned for five minutes, bathing Briony in a warm yellow light, sending shadows dancing across her naked skin, turning her eyes to flat metallic coins, turning her tears to beads of liquid gold.

When the fire died down, she broke up the ashes with a stick and then covered in the hole, burying the remains. As she walked away, the tide was already smoothing the sand clean.

Briony Dalton's latest novel *A Woman Scorned* was complete, apart from the last chapter. It would be finished three months ahead of schedule.

୦୨

By the time Greg Connors awoke, the women he knew as Brigid Garrett had been gone for nearly three hours. He wasn't unduly worried; she often went for long walks along the beach or across the wild countryside.

He had actually finished breakfast before he noticed that the small computer was missing. Maybe she'd taken it with her; the battery-powered machine was designed to be used practically anywhere.

He was searching for his notebook to check a character description when he discovered that it too was missing ... as was the box of his original manuscript.

Aware that his heart was beginning to pound, abruptly conscious of the stillness in the cottage, he walked into the bedroom and looked around. It took him a few moments before he realised what was troubling him: everything of hers was missing. There were no clothes scattered about, no make-up on the dressing table, no magazines on the floor. The bathroom had been stripped of all of her cosmetics, her deodorant, her razor, toothbrush, toothpaste, even her towel. It was as if she'd never been in the cottage with him.

Everything was gone.

His manuscript. His notes. His work.

All gone.

Chapter Fifty Seven

"Miss Dalton, this is an honour."

Nigel Hall, managing director of Hall's publishing company, came around his desk to shake hands with Briony Dalton. Neither was quite what the other expected, but she was better at hiding her surprise than he was. Hall was a young man, in his late twenties or early thirties, though already balding, his class and schooling clearly identified in his speech and accent and his manner of dress. He was the third generation to work within the family-run firm, which had once been one of the premier publishers in the world though it had now fallen on poorer days. The publishing house, behind Fleet Street, had a quaintly old fashioned feel to it, dark wood and small windows, a clanking metal lift and ornate clocks on every floor that she was quite sure were all running slowly. In keeping with the atmosphere of the publishing house, Briony had been expecting the managing director to be much older, complete with wing collar, velvet tie and fob watch.

Nigel Hall had been expecting someone younger, slimmer, certainly someone better dressed and, if her publicity photographs were anything to go by, beautifully coiffured, manicured and made-up. Instead he found he was staring at this rather ordinary middle-aged woman, her skin deeply tanned, though dry and wrinkled, her black hair showing grey roots. She was wearing faded jeans, with the knees worn threadbare, trainers with no socks and a baggy man's jumper. He had heard that she had a reputation for being hard-headed and ruthless, but what he saw was a slightly eccentric looking woman. Maybe this was the real Briony Dalton, and the other was an image created specifically for the media. He knew authors who did that.

Nigel Hall had made numerous attempts to meet with the woman when his company had surprisingly secured the rights to her latest book. Luncheon appointments had been made — and broken — dinners had been arranged, only to be cancelled at the last moment, phone calls never materialised, faxes never arrived. Eventually Terri Fierstein's excuses became so flimsy that he decided that Briony Dalton simply didn't want to meet him and put it down to author ego or arrogance. The two were often indistinguishable.

The young man looked at the woman expectantly, noting that she was carrying no luggage, no obvious manuscript except a slender purse-like case. And yet when she'd phoned from Heathrow she said she wanted to deliver the completed manuscript of *A Woman Scorned* in person.

Waiting until Briony had settled into a sighing leather chair, Nigel moved back around behind his scarred wooden desk. "I am delighted to meet you finally," he said, smiling easily.

Briony nodded. "There was little point in seeing you until I had the book in hand." She paused and added, "I know we were supposed to meet, but I'm one of those authors who believes that everything I have to say is contained in the book."

"I quite understand," Hall lied. "I will admit to being somewhat surprised to see you here. Terri Fierstein phoned me intimating that there were some problems with the book, and as recently as two weeks ago she suggested that the manuscript might not be completed in time." He attempted a laugh that was a trifle too shrill for comfort. "You can imagine our fright. We had an emergency meeting of the board and all that. My head was rather on the chopping block."

Briony nodded seriously. "I know you personally authorised the one million sterling advance for this book; that's why I came here the moment I finished it."

The truth was that she had come to Hall's because she wanted to unload the manuscript before Greg tumbled to the truth and the shit hit the fan. She needed to establish her ownership of the book. Copies of the disks were already on the way to her lawyers in New York by express courier. That would enable copyright to be established.

"When did you finish?" Hall asked pleasantly, trying to conceal his astonishment at this unconventional approach.

"On the flight to London. I completed work on the final draft of the last chapter somewhere over Wales."

"I had thought you were bringing the manuscript with you," Nigel Hall said. This was most irregular. Did her agent know what was going on? He would have expected Briony to have delivered the book to Terri Fierstein, and then she, in turn, would pass it on to him.

"Oh, but I did." Briony reached into her pocket and took out a small three-and-a-half-inch disk.

Nigel Hall was unable to conceal his surprise. "That's it?"

"All of it." Briony held the disk between thumb and forefinger. "I presume you will need a hard copy, so I'll need access to a printer and a computer."

"Of course." He came around the desk and stood behind her chair as she stood. "You will pardon my surprise ... Though I am delighted too, of course."

"I never print up a copy of the final manuscript until all the book is finished," Briony said, deliberately misunderstanding him, "but unfortunately my printer went on the fizz at the very last moment."

"Not to worry." Hall led her down a flight of stairs into an enormous room that had obviously once been divided up into a series of offices, but which had been recently remodelled into one large open-plan office. "All our editorial work is carried out here," he explained. "Our art department is on the floor below, with administration on the floor above. We are one of the few independent, family-run businesses actually left in the publishing world."

"You must find it difficult to compete," Briony murmured, looking around the room, abruptly realising just how badly Terri Fierstein had advised her. This place wasn't a publishing house: it was a joke!

"It's difficult. Our books sell, but slowly, and nowadays it's tough getting shelf space in the shops and wholesalers. We have an excellent backlist of authors we published many years ago, if only we had the cash to exploit it. We have a huge occult backlist, for example, and that's quite the growth market at the moment, and we have a series of literary biographies that have never been surpassed, but again we haven't had the money to reprint and reissue them. That's why your book is so important to us, Miss Dalton." He glanced over his shoulder at her and she could see the look of desperation in his eyes. "I know I really shouldn't be telling you this, but we've gambled everything on this book. We know it is a guaranteed best-seller, and the revenue will enable us to reprint and re-establish our backlist. Within eighteen months, twenty-four at the latest, we could be major players in the publishing world again. So you can imagine how we felt when your agent said that you might not deliver."

"What would have happened?" Briony asked innocently, smiling to take the sting from her words.

Hall shrugged. "We've had some buy-up offers in the past which we'd managed to resist. In order to raise the money to pay your advance, we haven't been able to buy our usual quota of books in the past year so we've had nothing new on our lists. Our revenue from new titles has dropped ... If you'd let us down ... " He shrugged again. "We would have gone to the wall. Someone would have bought us up and exploited the backlist which my father and grandfather spent their lives acquiring."

"But I didn't let you down," Briony said softly.

"I should have known better than to have had any doubts. Your reputation is that of one of the most professional authors in the world." He stopped and indicated a series of computer terminals. "Laser printer," he said, pointing to the large photocopier type machine.

"I know," Briony muttered. She sat down at the nearest terminal, finding the screen absolutely enormous after the tiny one she'd been used to over the past weeks. She inserted the small disk, and logged on to the master drive, searching for the WordStar programme. Nigel Hall watched her call it up, still trying to reconcile this rather dishevelled women with the cool beauty he had seen interviewed. Indeed, when she'd first walked into his office he had thought it might have been some sort of joke.

"Is the printer on?" she asked.

He checked the glowing panel of lights. "It's on."

"How many copies do you want?"

"Four."

"I'll make it six, then, if you don't mind. I would like two for myself," she said, hitting the print key, then sitting back into the chair, her arms folded across her chest. "Here is your book, Mr Hall ... "

At twelve pages a minute, *A Woman Scorned* began to shunt from the smoothly cycling, virtually silent laser printer. Briony swivelled around to face Hall. "How soon do we see *A Woman Scorned* in print?"

"We'll liaise with Park & Park the American publishers, but we both want to publish as quickly as possible. It will go straight to a copy editor and then to the typesetter. When you've corrected the proofs, it will go on to the printer. It's now the first of May. You should see simultaneous American and British hardback publication towards the middle of August, sooner if we can make it. If we're going to make it *the* big summer book we have to get it out as soon as possible."

"And the pre-publicity?"

"Most of that is already in place." He smiled nervously. "You caused us a few problems, though. Because we had no manuscript to work from, we ran a teaser campaign around you, using the title, and praying that you wouldn't change it." He rubbed his hands quickly together. "But now that we have the book, we can really go to town."

"How about a shot of me presenting the manuscript to you? 'The Million Pound Book', something like that?" she suggested.

"Excellent. We should do that soon."

"We should do it today," Briony said immediately. "Strike while the iron is hot. Let people know the manuscript has been delivered and that is it wonderful. Believe me," she added with a wry smile. "It is wonderful." She glanced at her watch. It was just before eleven. *A Woman Scorned* was over a thousand pages in manuscript so at twelve pages a minute they'd have a printed copy in about an hour and a half. She needed to get to her London apartment, change, have her hair done, be made up, manicured. "I'll be back here around three o'clock. Have the photographers here. That way we should make the evening papers."

"We'll try and work in some television as well," Hall said excitedly.

"Contact the book trade press," she added, "*The Bookseller* and *Publishing News*."

"I'll get our publicity department on to it right away."

"Now, I'll need to use your phone," Briony said. She put the original copies of the discs into her pocket. "You wouldn't happen to know any reputable personal security firms, would you? If I'm going to go back into the news in a big way the whole anti-Briony-Dalton circus will start again. You saw what happened in Dublin. It'll mean I'll attract the attention of every nut and crackpot in the country."

Nigel Hall nodded. "I know just the firm, run by the father of a chap I went to Oxford with." He grinned. "We wouldn't want anything to happen to you just now, would we?"

CB

Greg Connors was numb, totally, completely and absolutely numb. As the morning had drifted on towards noon, his moods had alternated between rage and despondency, touched with confusion and a terrible fear. He hoped, prayed even, that she'd just gone into Galway for something ... but if that was the case then where was his manuscript? Where was her laptop computer? Where were her clothes? Was it a joke? It was ... that's what it was! A joke. She was probably hiding on the beach or in the caves, watching him, waiting on him, and ...

But Greg Connors knew that this was no joke.

The woman was gone.

And he didn't even know her name. Who was Brigid Garrett? As recently as a couple of days ago, he'd gone into Galway, the nearest city, and spent a morning in the library, ostensibly doing research for a new book but in reality checking through *Books in Print*, the massive four-volume reference book that listed all the books currently in print by title and author. There had been no Brigid Garrett listed. He had then gone through the four-volume American equivalent, but with no success. Although he knew it was going to be a waste of time, he visited the big bookshop in the heart of Galway and asked one of the assistants to check Garrett on the microfiche listing of *Books in Print* which was updated every month, unlike the books themselves which only appeared once a year. Nothing. Brigid Garrett did not exist. Or if she did, she wrote under a different name ... but hadn't she already told him that? But why didn't she use her real name with him? When he'd come back from the city his curiosity had been roused to such a pitch that he had waited until she had gone walking on the beach that evening and then searched through her few meagre belongings, but there was nothing, no clue to her identity. He couldn't even find her passport, although at the airport he had thought he'd heard the clerk refer to her as Mrs Moriarty. Who was Mrs Moriarty? Where was Brigid Garrett?

Greg Connors hung around the cottage for the rest of the morning, almost afraid to leave in case Brigid returned and everything was explained. For a while he had entertained the fantasy that she'd gone into Galway to have the manuscript printed up — she'd certainly talked about it — but then why had she taken his original typewritten version? Why had she taken her clothes? He'd spent about an hour going around the small cottage looking for something — anything — that would indicate she'd be coming back. He couldn't even find a single thing that would indicate that she'd been there in the first place! The inescapable conclusion that he was left with was that she was gone for good and had taken his book with him. She had stolen his book. And that book had been his life, had meant more to him than life. It had been part of him for so long now, such an integral part that he felt almost incomplete. She hadn't just stolen his work, she had taken a little of his soul.

Some time in the early afternoon he made himself a sandwich and ate for the sake of eating, and then walked down to the deserted beach. There was a storm coming up, dark clouds massing on the horizon, the wind coming in off the Atlantic cold, sharp and damp with the promise of rain. Overhead gulls wheeled and circled and the seals that inhabited the caves up the coast were clustered around the rocks. He took a grim pleasure from the changing weather: it matched his mood exactly.

Connors was turning back to the cottage when he heard the car on the road. They were so far off the beaten track that cars were unusual here and the few they had encountered had been tourists who had taken the wrong turning on the way to Inishbofin. Shading his eyes against the glare he squinted up to the road and saw a steel-grey Saab pull in to the verge, grey dust swirling up around it. A dark figure climbed out of the car, and Greg saw the early afternoon light glint off glass as the figure looked at him through binoculars. Smiling he turned away; he was becoming completely paranoid. The tourist was simply looking at the seals in the caves behind him, or at the storm gathering on the horizon.

If Brigid hadn't returned in the next couple of hours — say, by six — he'd head into the nearby village and report the matter to the police. He wasn't sure what they'd do; he wasn't sure what they *could* do. Another thought struck him which stopped him cold. He had better report the matter to his publishers. They were going be looking for a manuscript very soon, a manuscript he no longer had.

When Greg came up off the beach he found the Saab parked in front of the cottage. He stopped.

Maybe Brigid had returned.

The car was empty and there seemed to be no one around, but ...

The blow took him across the back of the knees, driving him forward and down. Leather-gloved hands wrapped around his head, wrenching it to one side until he could feel the strain on his neck and spine. "Where is she?" The accent was American.

"I — I — I don't ... "

"Don't tell me you don't know," the man said.

"She's gone! Went this morning. Cleaned everything out. Stole my book!" Greg spat. The grip didn't loosen around his neck and he knew how little it would take to snap his spine. "Check for yourself. The bitch's gone. Everything's gone."

He was pushed down on to the sandy gravel. "Stay there; don't move." Greg could see boots — like working men's boots, thick-soled, with steel toecaps — move past his head. The man walked away a dozen steps and then he stopped. "And don't even think about running," he warned. Greg remained still on the ground, arms outstretched. This was one of the men from Corfu, he realised, one of the men who had been chasing Brigid. Somehow they had managed to trace her here. He stopped; did that not give credence to her story about the Mafia? Did that not mean that she was telling the truth? Had she somehow known this man was coming and had fled? Too many questions. The boots returned into his line of vision.

"Get up."

Greg Connors climbed slowly to his feet. His neck felt stiff, his throat strained and sore and it hurt when he swallowed. He was about to lash out at his attacker, but when he saw the tall, bulky man he quickly changed his mind. The American's eyes were flat, completely devoid of all humanity. This man would hurt him and think nothing of it. "Where's she gone?"

"I wish I knew," Greg said, wincing as his throat protested. He nodded towards the cottage. "Can we go inside? I need a drink."

The big man stepped back. Greg walked a few paces ahead of the American. "Do you want to tell me what you want her for?" he asked.

"Just business."

"The same business as on Corfu?"

"The same."

There was a half-empty bottle of Jameson Irish whiskey in the kitchen. Greg dropped two dusty glasses on to the kitchen table and filled a jug of water. He sat down and poured them both a large measure of the amber liquid. The American sat down opposite him, his enormous hands swallowing the glass. He drank his whiskey neat; Greg added water to his. "I was told you were Mafia hit-men."

The American laughed aloud. "You've been reading too many books. I'm no Mafia shooter."

"I don't suppose you want to give me your name?" Greg asked.

The American grinned, his smile gap-toothed and innocent. "I don't. But you're Gregory Connors, twenty-eight years old, a novelist of sorts, currently working on your fourth book. You met the woman on Corfu where, for some reason known to yourself, you decided to *protect* her. Is that the right word?" he asked with a smile. "You sailed from Corfu to Crete where you sold your boat and immediately flew to Dublin. You've been living here for the past two weeks."

"I'm impressed," Greg said. "You're either police or a private detective."

"Private. You said the woman had taken something of yours," the American leaned across the table and pressed on. "Would you like to tell me what it was?"

Greg stared into the man's cold, slate-grey eyes. At this moment, he hated Brigid Garrett enough to hope this man caught up with her. "She stole the manuscript of my new book," he said. "She was working on it with me, changing it, correcting it. When I woke up this morning, I discovered that she was gone. It wasn't until a little later that I discovered my book was missing too, including my notes. Everything."

"What sort of book is this?"

"It's romantic fiction. Sort of a love story with dark overtones," Greg said with an attempt at a smile. He watched the big man closely, suddenly realising that here were some of the answers to his questions.

"How big is the book?"

"About a quarter of a million words."

"And it was complete when she took it?"

"There was some work to be done on the last chapter but, yes, it was essentially complete."

The American came quickly to his feet, and Greg shied away from him. But the man marched straight out of the door and down to his car. He pulled open the door and then perched, half-in, half-out of the car and picked up a slender phone. He dialled what was obviously an overseas number by the amount of digits. Greg watched as he spoke for less than a minute, and when he hung up he sat into the car and pulled the door closed behind him.

"Wait!" Greg ran up to the car. "Wait! What's happening? What's going on?"

"You better be telling the truth, son," the American threatened balefully, "because if you're not I'm going to hunt you down and kill you."

"It's the truth, I swear it."

"Stay here, someone will be in touch tomorrow." The American revved the engine.

"But who was she? Who was the women?"

"Why? Didn't she tell you? What name did she use?" the big man asked.

"She told me her name was Brigid Garrett."

The American put the car in gear and eased away, gravel and sand crunching beneath the tyres.

"Who was she? I have to know!"

The American glanced through the window and smiled. "The woman was Briony Dalton!"

Chapter Fifty-Eight

Kaho Tomita replaced the phone and allowed herself a brief smile of pleasure. Herr Josef Bach had been outfoxed, and the very rarity of the occurrence made it an occasion for celebration.

Kaho had never met the big American, Charley O'Neill, though from the physical description in his file and from the sound of his voice she knew she would not like him. She had been perfectly polite and distant on the phone — she knew all calls to Bach's London headquarters were recorded — and the smile had only come when she had replaced the receiver.

She knew the game her German employer was playing with Briony Dalton, though she didn't know to what end. She had seen him play similar games with other people, making or breaking them to his will and to some secret design of his own. He had some obscure and arcane master plan he was pursuing.

And now it looked as if it had all been for nothing.

Bach had spent an enormous amount of money, time and effort trying to prevent this poor woman from finishing her book, and he had very nearly succeeded. But now it seemed as if she had stolen another author's book and passed it off as her own, effectively taking the wind from Bach's sails.

She loved the irony of it … and she was going to enjoy telling him.

It was nice to see Bach come out on the wrong side of something for a change. However, he rarely remained on the wrong side for very long. As she dialled his Hong Kong number, she realised this game wasn't over yet; it was rather like tennis and at the moment Briony Dalton had the advantage. But that would not last for too long.

ભ

Josef Bach put down the phone and turned back to the room, face impassive, arms folded across his chest, only the sudden appearance of the veins at the side of his neck betraying his annoyance.

Rianne Dalton was lying naked on an enormous bed that had once belonged to the Empress of China. The bed was swathed in a coverlet of crimson silk embroidered with an exquisitely detailed imperial dragon. Against the red, Rianne's skin glowed with a faintly pink luminescence. Michelle Seigner had been called back to photograph 'not only the face, but the body of the decade' as *Playboy* had so succinctly put it. Michelle Seigner had done the original photography for Rianne's first test, and the two women had worked remarkably well together.

The strobing of the flash gun blasted through the room at regular intervals accompanied by the whirring of the camera's motor drive, and he could hear Michelle's soft French-American accent keeping up a constant patter as she urged Rianne into a series of erotic poses on the bed, an obviously phallic Samurai sword clutched in both hands. But for once Bach's eyes were not on the young woman. All he could see was the mocking smile on Briony Dalton's lips.

So she had delivered her book — or at least the book she claimed was hers. He supposed his actions had forced her to steal the manuscript, and what he had to decide now was how to use that information. He could certainly bankroll Connors in a lawsuit, but contesting her ownership of the manuscript and it's authenticity was probably fruitless — it would mean presenting her with a load of free publicity and who were the public going to believe, a multi-million-copy best-selling writer or some poor hack? Personally, he had no doubt that the work was the hack's, but if the man was stupid enough to have placed himself in a position where it was possible for her to walk away with it then he deserved just about everything he got.

How was he going to handle this? It was a delicate situation, a very delicate situation. It needed careful consideration.

Five minutes later he picked up the phone and dialled the Sussex number.

ભ

Catherine Garrett replaced the phone before Bach had finished speaking. She sat quite still, staring at the instrument for a full three minutes while acid flooded her system and bile gathered at the back of her throat. Finally, she ran into the bathroom and knelt on the floor, arms wrapped around the toilet bowl, as she vomited.

The bitch! The bitch! The bitch. The bitch had done it.
Again!

Throwing back her head, she screamed aloud.

ભ

The transformation was absolutely astonishing.

Nigel Hall found it difficult to reconcile the rather shabby and certainly ordinary woman who had delivered the manuscript earlier that day with the stunning beauty who stood before him now.

"Don't look so surprised, Mr Hall," she said. "We all have our public and our private faces. You've seen both of mine."

"Forgive me, ma'am. It's just … "

Briony Dalton had had her hair styled and coloured. Then, professionally made up, most of the lines and wrinkles had vanished leaving her looking at least ten years younger, while her chipped and ragged nails had been manicured and buffed to repair the damage of the past weeks. For the photo-shoot she had chosen a simple

Dior creation in dark grey over a high-collared Cossack style blouse. The effect was elegant and restrained.

She picked up the manuscript, grunting at the weight.

"I've read some of it," Hall said.

Briony looked at him keenly.

"It's very good," he said, almost shyly. "I mean, I've read all your books; and this reads like pure Briony Dalton, but … better, almost like your earlier works."

"So it's better than my last book?" she asked with a smile.

"Oh yes, much. This will be your masterpiece. I'll wager that this is the book you will be remembered for."

"Good. I think so too." Briony linked her arm through his. "Now, come along and let's have our photograph taken. I want to get this monster off my hands."

�☙

… And finally on tonight's news, one of the most expensive books ever commissioned, Briony Dalton's A Woman Scorned, *was delivered by its author today, ahead of schedule.*

American publishers Park & Park paid two and half million dollars for American hard and paperback rights to Miss Dalton's new book on the basis of a single-page letter. British publishers, Hall's, then paid one million pounds sterling for the British hardback and paperback rights. No one knows what A Woman Scorned *will net for Briony Dalton. Estimates range from between five and ten million dollars. Well, you don't have to write too many of them in a year. This is Ruth Shern for ABC News …*

ᚼ

Terri Fierstein turned off the television set and stared at the darkened screen. Charles moved uneasily in the bed beside her, tossing in a troubled sleep.

So Briony had — by some miracle — delivered the book. Well, God help her.

What was going to happen now?

Terri thought of Gabrielle Royer, and she was suddenly terribly afraid for Briony Dalton. Chilled, she sank back onto the soft bed and hugged her lover close, but could draw neither heat nor comfort from his body.

Chapter Fifty-Nine

"Do you want to tell me who sent you?" Greg Connors asked coldly. "I presume you and that goon yesterday are working for one and the same person?"

Catherine Garrett ignored him. She wandered through the small cottage, peering into all the rooms, lingering longest in the bedroom, before she returned to the kitchen where Greg was sitting at the kitchen table, an almost empty whiskey bottle and a glass before him. She wondered how much he had drunk; he neither looked nor sounded drunk. She sat down facing him, stared into his moist hazel eyes ... and revised her opinion of how much alcohol he had consumed.

"I know you're hurt and angry," she said, "however, I think you should concentrate your anger in the right direction. I didn't take your book. I'm here to help you if I can."

Colour flushed his cheeks and Greg opened his mouth to reply and then visibly mastered his anger. Resting his forearms on the table, he slumped forward, reached for the whiskey glass and finished it in one quick swallow. "You'll forgive me," he said tiredly. "I spoke to my publishers about an hour ago. They want a detailed letter explaining precisely what has happened and what exactly I'm accusing Briony Dalton of. My editor — a woman I've worked with for the past few years — sounded almost like a stranger." He raised his eyes and gazed at Catherine. "They don't believe me," he whispered, as if sharing some deep secret. "They don't believe me. They think ... " He shook his head angrily. "I don't know what they think."

"They're going to be looking for proof," Catherine said quietly.

"But they have the proof ... the synopsis I sent!"

Catherine looked up quickly. "That might be just what we're looking for. How detailed was it?"

"Detailed enough."

"How detailed."

Greg thought about it and then shrugged. "Well, not very I suppose. Brigid or Briony or whatever the fuck her name is, made a lot of suggestions when I was writing it, and then she changed it even further. I doubt if the finished book matched the original synopsis too closely."

The woman shook her head quickly. "So what you are saying is that you have no proof."

"None."

"They will think you are lying. They'll think you could not write the book they commissioned you to write. They'll think that you're using this way to get out of your contract and gain a little free publicity into the bargain." Catherine Garrett spelled it out slowly and distinctly, pulling all Greg's fears out into the open, forcing him to accept them for the first time.

He propped his elbows on the table and buried his head in his hands.

"My name is Catherine Garrett ... " she began.

Greg looked up suddenly. "She said her name was Brigid Garrett," he said, his tone accusatory.

"That was my mother's name. Briony Dalton's step-mother."

Greg Connors frowned, completely confused now. Catherine held up her hand. "Go and make us both some tea and I will explain everything." She wanted him moving, doing something — anything — to take his mind off his present problem and to stop him drinking. She knew what he was thinking: Briony Dalton was too big a name for a complete outsider to go up against; and it didn't look like his own publisher would back him in the contest.

"My name is Catherine Garrett," she repeated as he started to fill the kettle. "I am Briony Dalton's step-sister."

"Catherine Garrett ... I know you," Greg said turning suddenly, water splashing down his jeans and onto his shoes. "You've got that book programme on the BBC. You do all those book reviews?" he said excitedly. "Do you believe me?" he asked. "Do you believe she stole my book?"

"I believe you," Catherine said. "In fact, I *know* she took your book and all we have to do is to prove it. Because if we can prove she stole a struggling author's work, then she is destroyed: she will never write again. You will be able to live on the proceeds of the court case for the rest of your life, the royalties will be transferred to you and every publisher will beat a path to your door for your next book. You will be able to name your own price." Catherine dangled the bait, following Bach's instructions. She knew in reality that things would work out very differently. "Now I want you to tell me everything you know about this woman, everything you did, everything she said. Tell me about you, tell me about the book."

Greg Connors began to fill the kettle again. "There's not an awful lot to tell," he conceded. "I'm a writer. I've had three books published and I was working on my fourth." He glanced back over his shoulder. "I never told Brigid ... Briony this, but I had some trouble with the law in England and decided to lie low in Corfu for a bit. I didn't think I'd get in to any trouble there."

"What sort of trouble with the law?"

"Do you have to know? Is it necessary?"

"Do you want me to help you?"

He stared out of the window at the distant grey line of the sea. "I'd been involved in the drug scene way back before I started writing. I was bored, I'd nothing else to do, I started using and then I began dealing, not much, just enough to support my habit. I was picked up a couple of times by the police, but I never did any time though I spent a while in detox. Then I began writing, and that got my head sorted out. I didn't have to smoke shit to give me weird dreams. I was having them on my own with no help, and getting paid for them.

He sat down facing her, hands folded in front of him. "Anyway, there was this girl I was involved with. She was a junkie, but she'd been using a long time before I knew her. We sort of drifted apart and I hadn't seen her for about two years when she suddenly started calling around. The shit had fucked her up and she was in a bad way, so I gave her some cash, some food and she crashed in my place. She slept during the day and went out at night. I thought she was hooking to support her habit, but I never asked and she never told me. But we weren't sleeping together," he added hastily, "she was a friend, that's all."

"And you weren't going to risk sleeping with a junkie prostitute anyway," Catherine said shrewdly.

Greg coloured and Catherine realised she'd hit close to the mark.

"Anyway ... anyway, she OD'd on some bad shit or something, and she turned up dead in the Underground. The police knew she and I had been going together so they came round and hauled me in, accusing me of selling her the shit and pimping for her. They accused me of living off her immoral earning. They were under a bit of pressure, they needed to be seen to be doing something. And I wasn't the only junkie or pusher who got leaned upon, but I was leaned upon the hardest. Finally, when they let me go because they could pin nothing on me, I decided I needed a holiday. The only problem was that they'd warned me to stay around, but I knew what would happen then: every time some junkie OD'd or some bad shit hit the streets or the Bill needed to up their arrest record I'd get rousted.

"I sailed down to the Med and ended up anchored off Corfu. I met Brig ... Briony there. We got talking about books." He grunted a laugh. "She even told me she wrote a few books, horror mainly. She told me she was writing this book about an Italian family and that she'd researched it in Italy or Corsica or somewhere and the local Mafia were upset about it. She said she'd been threatened in New York by the same people so she'd fled to Corfu for a bit of peace while she wrote her book.

"And when these two guys turn up and begin hassling her ... well, what was I to do but believe her? They attempted to burn her villa down, they ransacked her house.

"So we fled in my boat, sailed to Crete and came from there to Ireland. Meanwhile, she had read my book and began working on it. She said she was doing it as a way of thanking me for all I'd done for her."

"That doesn't sound like Briony." She paused and glanced at the notes she had scribbled on the back of a postcard of the West of Ireland. "Did she ever mention her son? I wonder if she knows he's dead?"

"How did he die?" Greg asked.

"He had AIDS. He had been given only weeks to live. He died from a drug overdose." She spoke each sentence separately. "I believe it was self-inflicted. He was twenty-six years old."

"She never mentioned any family," Greg said finally, the realisation that Briony's son was only two years younger then himself — and dead — beginning to sink in. "I got the impression she was a spinster."

"She never had much time for her children," Catherine said.

"Children? There's more than one?"

"There's a girl, Rianne. She's twenty-two."

"She never said," he murmured. He looked across the table at Catherine and frowned. "How can you live with someone for weeks and not mention that you've children, or not let it slip out in some away?"

"If you don't think about your children, don't care about them, then I suppose it's easy. She didn't really know her children," Catherine explained. "They both left home in their teens, having been virtually abandoned by their mother while she pursued her writing career. They were left to fend for themselves, and they ended up on the streets in one way or another. Matt became a junkie, Rianne supported himself by working in porno movies."

"Jesus Christ!" Greg said feelingly. "What sort of person allows that to happen to their children?"

"The same sort of person who steals your work and then passes it off as her own." Catherine reached into her bag and slid across the copies of *The Guardian*, *The Mail* and *The Mirror* which she'd picked up in the airport. Folding back *The Mirror*, she pushed it across the table towards him.

It took the young man a few moments to recognise the woman in the garishly coloured photograph. It was of a mature, elegant woman, smiling at the camera holding a thick bundle of manuscript.

THE ONE MILLION POUND BOOK

Superseller Briony Dalton dropped a £1,000,000 book on her publisher's desk today. Coming in at close to one thousand typed pages and weighing just under eight pounds, this steamy blockbuster by the Queen of the Red Hot Read is a guaranteed best-seller.

And at £1,000 a page, it had better be!

The picture in *The Mail* showed Briony Dalton handing the book across to Nigel Hall, two uniformed security guards standing self-consciously in the background.

The Guardian showed the picture of Briony holding the manuscript and smiling at the camera, and had a caption which ran, 'The Most Expensive Book in the World'.

Greg stared at Catherine. "This is my book?" he asked hoarsely.

Catherine kept her face impassive. "This is *A Woman Scorned*."

"*A Woman Scorned*!" he said. "That was my title!"

"No, that is the title of the book she was commissioned to write about eighteen months ago. She was paid two and a half million dollars for the American rights, one million pounds for the British rights. When the subsidiary rights, including the movie rights, have been sold, it is estimated it will make her upwards of ten million dollars." She was watching him closely as she gave him the figures, pushing them home, giving him time to think about them. "What did you get for your book? A few grand perhaps?"

Greg nodded. He was unable to speak; his throat was on fire and he felt he was going to vomit.

"There were a lot of questions hanging over this latest book of hers," Catherine continued. "It was felt she wasn't going to be able to finish it. Briony Dalton had taken to living a very rich life-style which left little time for writing. But it was a bit of a Catch-22 situation. She needed the money from her writing to fund her life-style, but the same life-style didn't allow her to write. So she initially came to Ireland and then later moved on to Corfu in an attempt to find time to finish her novel.

"And she desperately needed to finish it. The amount of money involved must have put enormous pressures on her, and she was also heavily in debt. The first portion of her advances had been squandered; she needed the monies due on delivery and publication of the book to clear her debts.

"Meeting you was just a coincidence — but what a coincidence! You must have seemed like the answer to her prayers. A writer — and a bloody good writer too. The publishers are claiming the new book is the best Briony Dalton yet.

"How ... how long was she planning this?" Greg whispered.

"Almost from the beginning, I'd say," Catherine said maliciously, "certainly from the moment she first read your manuscript and discovered that it was good."

"Is there anything I can do?"

"You can go to the press and your publishers."

"They won't believe me."

"They won't," she agreed.

"Then what can I do? I've lost everything. The fucking bitch has destroyed me!"

Catherine took his anger and worked on it, manoeuvring him exactly where she wanted him. "You can take your revenge," she said, smiling.

"How the fuck am I going to do that?"

"That's why I'm here."

"What's it to do with you?" he demanded.

Catherine grimaced. "You and I have something in common," she said quietly. "Briony Dalton once hurt me as badly as she's hurt you. I know what you're going through."

"I doubt it," Greg snapped. "I doubt that very much!"

Catherine leaned across the table and grabbed his forearms with both hands, the nails digging into his flesh. "Oh, but I do," she hissed vehemently. "You see, Briony Dalton stole my first — and only — book!"

Chapter Sixty

That was the summer of 1966.

Briony had married Niall Moriarty in 1965, and I knew it wasn't going to last. Briony was too independent, Niall was too weak. They'd been married, oh, about three months or so when she became pregnant. I'm sure it was an accident; I don't think Briony ever wanted children.

Apparently she told Niall she was pregnant on the same night he told her he'd quit his job because he'd had a novel accepted by some British publisher. He'd given up a full-time pensionable job on the basis of one novel, but for him it meant that he was finally on his way to being a writer.

What he didn't know, of course, was that Briony had been selling magazine articles and short stories with surprising regularity. So, there they were: a few months married, her pregnant and him out of a job. It's not quite so dramatic as it seems. Her father owned a very successful pub, and they'd never have been short of money. I'm sure if Niall had wanted a job he would have got one in the pub, even though Mick — her father and my step-father — didn't totally approve of Niall.

But Niall Moriarty wanted to be a writer. It was his dream, his fantasy.

I don't think Briony ever *wanted* to be a writer, not in the same way that Niall did. With her it was a simple matter of economics. She needed the money and was too proud to ask her father, too ashamed to let him know the mess she'd got herself into. I believe Niall wrote simply to see his name in print. He was an 'author', Briony was a 'writer'.

So she began to write, and write openly now. Heretofore, it had been done in secret, without Niall's knowledge. I remember that initially he was amused, contemptuous, patronising and then angry ... especially when he discovered that she was selling just about everything she wrote.

But here the differences between them became apparent.

Niall Moriarty approached his work like a dilettante. He rose late in the morning, found a hundred excuses not to go to the typewriter, and when he finally sat down, he'd type maybe half a dozen lines and then stop — his muse having deserted him.

Briony began writing the moment she finished breakfast. She'd work solidly until eleven, stop for a cup of tea, write until one, stop till two, and then write until six. That was her routine and, barring interruptions, it never varied. She was writing for all of the Irish and most of the British magazines, selling features, articles, letters to those columns which paid, short stories, competitions, slogans ... everything.

I remember one particular week when she sold practically everything she'd written in the previous two weeks and won a short story competition. Her earnings for that week alone were nearly five hundred pounds ... and in 1966 that was a sizeable sum of money.

And Niall's envy knew no bounds.

He tried to dismiss what she was doing — and failed. He castigated her style of writing, her grammar, her syntax, her subject matter, told her she was writing shit. She agreed with everything he said, and simply reminded him that it paid.

He then changed tack. He began to interrupt her at every opportunity, shouting, whistling, singing, asking her questions, talking to her ... but Briony was used to working with the noise of the radio and the sounds of children playing directly outside her window. She had the facility to tune out the outside world and concentrate with total absorption on what she was doing. Nowadays she writes to the sound of music through headphones.

Then one day he hit her.

And she walked out.

This was early in the summer of '66. I can remember it so clearly: it was the year I first went to the States, the year Briony Dalton's first book appeared, in December.

I was living in a flat in Glasnevin, which is on the north side of Dublin. There's a huge graveyard there — the old-fashioned type with enormous, ornate stones complete with a fake round tower — where most of the leaders of the 1916 Rising are buried. My flat actually overlooked the graveyard and at night I'd sit at my window and look out over the standing stones and imagine all sort of things.

It was creepy and eerie and strange and wonderful, and quiet. A sense of calm, of serenity, hangs over the graveyard and Briony had fallen in love with it the moment she'd first visited me there. It was only later that she discovered she couldn't work there. And yet on the surface it should have been the perfect writer's study. It had everything going for it. The flat was lovely, bright and airy, it got the sun in the morning and in the evening there were no noisy neighbours, no children, no dogs.

It was close to two o'clock in the morning when she arrived at my flat. I didn't need to be told that something was wrong. Briony and I were closer than sisters then, and she'd already spoken to me about Niall's treatment of her. She was wearing a headscarf pulled forward over her face. As she stepped past me into the room I caught sight of the shadow on her cheek, and when she pulled off the scarf I saw the bruising around the side of her face and her eye. It seemed that Niall had come back to the flat drunk that night and found her writing. There had been an argument, he'd started shouting, and eventually snatched what she'd written, torn it in half and tossed it on to the fire. She grabbed for the paper and he hit her across the side of the face.

She was six or seven months pregnant at the time.

When he had staggered off to bed and fallen into a drunken slumber, she'd simply packed a bag and left. She walked across the city to my flat, even though her father only lived across the square from her.

I was concerned — naturally — but I could do very little for her and in Ireland in the 1960s there were few options left open to her. Divorce was unobtainable, legal separation virtually unheard of, and annulment unlikely now that she was pregnant.

And anyway that year, 1966, was a very exciting one for me. I was twenty years old and studying journalism. I'd been given the opportunity to go to Boston on a student exchange scheme, and there was also the possibility of working on *The Boston Globe*.

And, like many journalists, I was working on a book.

I suppose many of us who go into journalism do so because we want to be writers and decide that this is the way to learn the craft. It's not really true of course, though some of the finest writers have started out as journalists, and certainly the journalistic experience is invaluable material for any would-be writer.

So, I'd written a light romantic story called *The Song of Summer* about a young woman coming of age in Dublin during the period of the First World War and the 1916 Easter Rising. It was a period of history which fascinated me and my mother's father — my grandfather — had fought in the Rising and had been killed in the Civil War in 1922. I'd been working on the book on and off for the best part of a year and before I left for the States I'd finished the first two drafts. I never published that book.

Briony Dalton — Bernadette Moriarty as she was then — stole it.

I don't know what happened. I can only guess at the sequence of events.

Briony couldn't work in my flat — she admitted that much to me in the second of the two letters she sent me. It was too quiet, too peaceful, she was too used to noise. But she was stuck: she couldn't go home to Niall, she didn't want to go back to her father, and she needed money especially now that the baby was coming ...

But she couldn't write.

She found my manuscript.

It was eighty thousand words of a fairly polished second draft. It still needed some work, but not much, and I anticipated finishing it off when I returned to Dublin, and maybe submitting it to one of the English publishers. I remember that Penguin published several Irish authors at the time, and they were the obvious choice.

So Briony Dalton took *The Song of Summer*, rewrote it, added raunchy sex — by 1960s standards — a few titillating scenes of sadism and created the evil, debauched priest who was to become something of her trademark. It became not so much a novel of a young woman coming of age in a time of change but rather a young woman being abused and enjoying it. She submitted it as *Summer's Song*. It was accepted and published in 1967. It was extraordinarily popular in Britain, sold in America in both hardback and paperback and it was banned in Ireland ... which only added to its popularity.

And it was my book.

She stole my book and had it published as her own.

The first I knew of it was when I was passing a bookstore in Boston. They had a window full of the 'The Novel of our Time, *Summer's Song* by B. Dalton,' which was the penname she used for her fictional pieces. I can remember standing before that window for several minutes just staring at it ... and being pleased for my half-sister. I was surprised that she hadn't told me, but she was often secretive about her writing.

And wasn't it a coincidence that she'd used a similar title to mine? Well, hardly a coincidence ... we were so alike in so many respects.

I remember buying the book and telling the sales clerk that B. Dalton was my step-sister. He had looked shocked and said that he thought B. Dalton was a man.

The bookstore was only a couple of blocks from the *Globe* offices and I waited until I was back at my desk before I opened it.

I knew then that something was dreadfully wrong.

The first words of my book were, "In the time of war, she lost her innocence..."

In Briony's book the first words were, "She lost her innocence in the time of war..."

I read through the book with a growing sense of *déjà-vu*. I was reading my own book. Oh, certainly, words and phrases had been changed around, small scenes had been added, but it was still my book.

I phoned her — and it was hideously expensive then. I demanded to know what was going on. She said she didn't know what I was talking about.

When I said that *Summer's Song* was *The Song of Summer* she laughed at me, said she'd never heard of *The Song of Summer*. She said she had thought I'd be glad of her success instead of jealous, and then hung up.

What could I do?

I was too far from home to take any sort of realistic action, and who was going to believe me in any case? She had the reputation and the background as a writer by this stage; she had a list of articles and stories to her credit. I had nothing.

It cost me a hundred dollars for a lawyer to tell me that I had no case unless I could back up my story with notes, references, or preferably a copy of the manuscript ... which I couldn't, of course, because everything was back in Dublin.

When I finally returned to Dublin, I discovered that Briony was back with her husband and that all my notes, my reference books, the copybooks with scribbles, the scraps of paper, were gone.

She stole my book. Briony Dalton's whole career is founded on a huge lie.

And now she's stolen yours ... she has re-established her foundering career with another huge lie.

Chapter Sixty-One

As soon as she stepped out of the building the press swarmed around her. Briony Dalton bit back a smile; it reminded her of old times.

"Miss Dalton, can you tell us how difficult it was to write *A Woman Scorned*?"

"What special pressures were placed upon you by the enormous advance?"

"You wrote part of this book in Ireland. Is it true that you returned to Dublin for your inspiration?"

"There have been rumours circulating in the publishing world that you wouldn't be able to complete *A Woman Scorned*. Are you aware of the tremendous difficulties that would been placed on your British and American publishers?"

"Miss Dalton, we understand that the publishing trade is now seriously reviewing the payment of enormous advances to authors such as yourself? Would you care to comment?

"Did the stories in the press about your family, and especially the death of your son, affect your writing?"

"Gentlemen, gentlemen, please ... and ladies too." Briony Dalton smiled her charming smile and turned to stand with her back to the television centre, instinctively taking the higher step which would give her the advantage of height. She took a deep breath before replying; the trick now was to answer all the questions she had been asked without allowing them to put any further questions to her.

"Ladies and gentlemen, I should begin by saying that *A Woman Scorned* was my most difficult book to write, and it is also, as you will find out soon, the best piece of work

I've produced. I'm delighted with it. Naturally the payment of the large advance placed pressures upon me to finish, but I would have given the same attention to the novel if I'd only been paid two hundred and fifty dollars rather than two and a half million. Yes, I was aware that if I didn't deliver it would have placed my publishers in a very difficult position. *That* placed far greater pressure on me than the money. Whenever I felt myself slowing down on the book, or I felt disinclined to write, I would remind myself of all the people depending on me, and that would give me the energy and enthusiasm to forge ahead. I should add that I have never failed to deliver a book, and the recent speculation has absolutely no basis in fact and had been generated — I'm sorry to say — by the press.

"I went back to Ireland to visit my father and for a holiday; naturally I did a little work there, but then again I'm always working, always writing, no matter where I go. I travelled extensively while I was writing the book, but it was principally written in New York, Dublin, Corfu and finished in Galway in the West of Ireland.

"I think there will always be authors who will be paid huge advances, and I don't think that's wrong. The labourer is worthy of his hire, as the Good Book says. And so long as care is taken that the big advances are given to those books worthy of them, then I really don't see any problem.

"And finally, ladies and gentlemen, I don't read the gutter press who will rake up any filth and exploit any tragedy to sell copies." She smiled again. "Nor do I answer questions from them. Good day."

Chapter Sixty-Two

"I loved her, you see."

"And you thought she loved you in return." Catherine Garrett shook her head, smiling ruefully. She stopped to stare out across the waves towards the cloud-covered smudges that were the Aran Islands. Behind the islands, grey-white clouds laced through with shafts of white sunlight delineated the horizon.

"I thought she loved me," Greg whispered.

"Briony Dalton loves no one. I'm not even sure if she likes herself." Catherine shivered suddenly, and pulled her coat tightly closed, turning away from the slate coloured sea. The afternoon had turned cold and the rain that had been threatening since lunchtime was spitting down out over the sea, rolling slowly inland.

"Do you hate her?" Greg asked, falling into step beside her.

"Yes … no … I don't know." She smiled at his expression. "I used to think I simply hated her, loathed her, despised her. And then I started to work on this biography of her. Suddenly I found I was actually pitying her … even beginning to understand her. But even though it's been twenty-five years since Briony Dalton stole my work, that particular memory above all the others remains fresh and bitter."

"But did you never tell anyone?"

"You're the first."

"Why did you tell me?"

"Because you know what I'm talking about. You can share the feeling, the loss."

She wondered why she had told Greg. Perhaps it was hard to explain to someone other than a writer what it was like to have one's work stolen; she had once dramatically likened it to being raped, and on reflection she didn't think the analogy was that far off the mark. It had been her first book — and it was such a tentative fragile thing — with so much of herself in it. Even the heroine was based on herself. She had used it as a vehicle to explore her own thoughts and emotions, to set them solidly down on paper. She liked to think that it was a good book — a sensitive book. It was an insult to have it so crudely tarted up with gratuitous sex and explicit violence, to destroy the very core of the novel. The final insult, of course, was to have it achieve such a commercial success because she couldn't help but wonder if her own novel — the original one — would have achieved that level of success? She didn't think so.

She could understand how Briony had come to steal it. She could rationalise that … for Christ's sake, she might have co-authored it, anything … all Briony had to do was to ask. But she couldn't forgive the way she had befouled it. She couldn't forgive the way Briony had denied it was Catherine's. All the feelings that had lain dormant — the betrayal, the anger, the jealousy — had come to the surface again.

In 1967 she had neither the power nor the ability to harm Briony Dalton.

Now she had.

"Tell me what to do," Greg said as they trudged down the beach.

I wish I knew, Catherine thought, but aloud she said, "First things first. I think you should fly to London and speak to your editor in person, explaining the story in full. I will accompany you if you wish. Perhaps she will give some credence to your story if she sees that someone like myself has taken it seriously. Then the next step is to see a solicitor and then possibly the press, although the solicitor will advise us about that."

"I can't afford any of that," Greg said in alarm. "I don't even have the money to pay back the advance on my own book."

"I'll take care of the expenses," Catherine said firmly.

"Why?" Greg asked. "The last person to offer to do something for nothing for me was Briony Dalton."

Catherine smiled at his cynicism. "Because you and I share something in common. And because I'm writing the unauthorised biography of Briony Dalton, and her treatment of you will make a fitting final chapter."

Greg Connors stopped on the edge of the track leading up to the cottage. "I think you really do hate her," he said almost wonderingly.

Catherine Garrett turned to face him. "Don't you?"

He considered for a moment and then he slowly nodded his head, "Yes … yes, I do. She's taken everything I had." He reached out and grabbed her arm. "What do we do now?"

"We'll go and see your editor first thing Monday morning, but right now I suggest we find shelter from the storm." Even as she spoke, rain spattered the ground around their feet, dappling the sand. They ran for the cottage as the storm raced up the beach, churning the sand to mud:

∞

Jean Packard had been an editor for nearly ten years and had been in the publishing business for nearly twice that. She had worked at various jobs in the industry before ending up as a secretary in Gordon Books and had then gradually worked her way up through the system, surviving numerous take-overs and management buy-outs. She had been the editorial director there for the past five years and had been responsible for the huge growth and diversification of its list, making it one of the most popular and successful of the mass-market paperback publishers.

A small, crimson-haired, ruddy-cheeked Scotswoman, good-humoured, even-tempered and incredibly patient, she was generally well liked by both her staff and authors and she enjoyed the reputation of being fair but firm. Now her good humour, her even temper and especially her patience were being put to their ultimate test. In her ten years as an editor she had heard some pretty wild stories to account for the non-delivery of a manuscript — "The dog ate it," was still her favourite — but this ... this outrageous accusation by Gregory Connors was just incredible.

"Greg," she said carefully, looking up from her notepad, "Greg, these ... these accusations are very serious indeed." It was far too early on a Monday morning for this.

"But they're true!" Greg insisted for the third time, his voice cracking. He was almost crying with frustration and he could feel the anger bubbling in his stomach, scorching the back of his throat. He turned to Catherine Garrett. "Please, can you try to convince her?"

Catherine smiled at Jean Packard. The two women had met on several occasions in the past at parties or launches, and their dislike had been immediate and mutual. Packard had written to her once when she had thought Catherine had unfairly slated one of her authors. Catherine hadn't replied to that letter in person, though she had used it on her television programme.

"We have thoroughly investigated Mr Connors' story," Catherine said, "and all the facts bear it out. We have witnesses to testify that they met in Corfu and spent some time in one another's company before they went sailing together. We have the airline receipts that prove the couple flew to Dublin together, and we have people who will swear they both stayed at the cottage in the West of Ireland."

Jean Packard held up both hands. "Miss Garrett, I am not disputing the fact that Mr Connors met Miss Dalton. I am quite prepared to believe that. I am simply questioning the story Mr Connors has told me about Briony Dalton stealing his manuscript."

"You don't believe me!" he accused.

"I just wonder why an author of Briony Dalton's calibre would want to steal your manuscript," she said firmly, her soft lowland Scots accent turning hard and clipped. She looked at Catherine, her thin lips settling into a straight line. "And unfortunately Miss Garrett's presence here lends neither credence nor weight to your story. Her dislike of Miss Dalton is well known, and her recent articles about her in the press were ... well, reprehensible to say the least."

"I was merely reporting the truth," Catherine said defensively.

"Of course you were. Now the situation is this," the woman pressed on ignoring her, "Gordon Books will not support you in your claim if you go to the press with this story ... we cannot, at least not without sufficient proof. Do you have any proof?" she asked, "notes ... disks ... early portions of the manuscript."

"She stole my notes, she stole everything," Greg howled.

"Somehow that answer does not surprise me," the woman said almost wearily.

"Surely you have Mr Connors' synopsis of the novel he intended to write," Catherine interrupted.

"I have." Packard slid it across her desk with the tips of her fingers. "Unfortunately it was less than detailed. A slip on our part, but then Greg had written for us in the past and when he outlined this project we were sufficiently confident in him to commission it upon this basis. So what we have here is a short letter."

She read it to them:

"A family-saga type book recounting the fortunes of a family cursed by ill-fortune and how, whenever success is within their grasp, tragedy strikes. The total length should run to around 200,000 words. Unfortunately I have no title at present, but possibly Fortune and Despair.*"*

Jean Packard glanced up from the letter, looking at Catherine now. "It's not a particularly spectacular idea, I'll agree, but I thought it would make a good mid-list title. I can show you a hundred books, no, five hundred books, that would fit that description. And the title we have here is *Fortune and Despair*, which doesn't even come close to *A Woman Scorned*."

She turned away from Catherine and spoke directly to Greg, her green eyes now hard, challenging. Her accent was bitter. "I think you met this woman on your holidays, and I think you had a holiday romance with her. You were smitten with her, but perhaps she was not so smitten with you, eh? You were fascinated with this wealthy author, the epitome of what you'd like to be. And suddenly the holiday is over, she's gone, and she doesn't want to see you any more and you're angry. And maybe you do see an idea of yours in *A Woman Scorned*; she'd be a poor writer if something of her encounter with you didn't appear in her work in progress.

"So what do you do? You try to gain a little of her limelight, and I can even understand that. Sometimes we all like to bask in someone else's reflected glory.

"And you haven't got your manuscript, you lost it, maybe you never wrote it, maybe you couldn't … after all, you'd only written horror prior to this. It would have been quite a change for you. So you thought up a story … you're a writer, a professional liar — and that's a compliment, by the way. You tell me that Briony Dalton stole your manuscript." She stopped before she added, "And that's when you went too far!"

Greg had been shaking his head as Jean had been speaking, but she pressed on, ignoring him.

"You see, I've been doing this job for too long, I've heard every excuse, every permutation, every lie. I know when an author is telling me the truth, and when they're bullshitting me ... and right now you're bullshitting me!"

Greg lurched to his feet, but the woman continued forcefully.

"If you continue with this accusation Gordon Books will do two things: expect delivery of a manuscript from you or a refund of the advance we paid you under clause sixteen of your contract. And I think I should tell you that we would not be interested in looking at any further proposals from you ... nor, I think, would any other publisher in London." Her cold green eyes moved past Greg to Catherine. "Perhaps you might advise Mr Connors about the inadvisability of pursuing this matter ... especially if he intends to continue his career as a writer." She buzzed for her secretary. "Mr Connors and Miss Garrett are leaving now, would you show them out?"

∞

"You tried," Catherine said softly, watching Greg pace around the hotel room, thin-lipped, white-faced.

He stopped with his back to her and stared out the window looking across Hyde Park, his head bent, shoulders trembling.

"What am I going to do?" he whispered. "What can I do?"

Catherine came up behind him and spun him around to face her. She stared up into his hazel eyes. "You've got two choices: you can fight, or you can give up. If you give up, she wins ... again. You do the work and she claims the credit. She did it to me and now she's doing it to you, and God alone knows how many others she's done it to. I know her ex-husband always claimed that she stole his work too."

"But if I contest this I'll probably lose anyway, and I'll never be published again!" he protested. "You heard what Packard said."

"She is one editor in one publishing house, but you're forgetting that I've got a little power myself. Why don't you let me see what I can do? Maybe my television studio would be prepared to do an exposé, and I know I can definitely sell the story to one of the papers I work for."

Greg nodded. "And what does that get us?"

"Exposure. It puts your name up there as a writer. High-profile authors get high-profile advances," she reminded him. "Controversial authors get equally controversial advances." She squeezed his forearms tightly. "I'm going to make you a controversial, high-profile author." Catherine rose on her toes and kissed him lightly on the lips. "Now, go to bed and get some rest. You've had an exhausting few days. Let me do some checking around for you, and we'll discuss it later."

Greg pressed the palms of his hands to his temples. "I can't even think straight at the moment. She's only had it three days, but already I'm beginning to feel as if I never wrote the book in the first place. All I think about is that … that woman stealing it. It's over a year's work!"

"I think that's the least of your worries," Catherine said softly, twisting the knife, "I'm just a little afraid that she may have destroyed your livelihood into the bargain." She urged him towards the bedroom. "I'll be back this evening."

As she was leaving she palmed the plastic electronic key for the door.

Catherine looked at her watch as she strode down the corridor. She would give him plenty of time: time to think and brood, time for the anger to turn to something else, something colder, harder.

And then all he'd need would be a nudge in the right direction.

She looked at her watch again, cynically plotting her moves. She had time to get her hair done and do a little shopping. And she needed some new underwear.

Chapter Sixty-Three

It was good to be back in New York.

Briony Dalton loved the city, loved the buzz, the excitement, the sheer pace. And after her extended holiday she decided she needed to party, to do a little shopping, to unwind. She was hot stuff now, she'd be on every socialite and would-be socialite's party list, and already she'd started turning down radio and TV interviews. She didn't want to waste herself on the local shows. When she went on TV to promote *A Woman Scorned* she'd do it coast to coast.

Briony stepped out of the lift and strode down the corridor, ignoring the man who followed her. Having lived for too many years in New York, her keys were already in her hand as she neared the door to her apartment. The large man in the double-breasted suit who had been following her touched her arm as she put the key in the lock. "Allow me, ma'am." She stepped back and he preceded her into the apartment. He was part of the two-man personal security team she had picked up in London courtesy of Nigel Hall. The publicity for the Million Pound Book had been splashed across most of the newspapers and Briony had expressed very real fears for her safety in the wake of the publicity. Hall's were paying for the bodyguards, to 'protect our investment'. It had all the hallmarks of a Dalton publicity stunt, but privately Briony was worried because Gabrielle's killer had never been caught and the two men who had been following her in Corfu were still at large.

The bodyguard appeared in the open doorway before her. "All clear."

It was three months to the day since she had last stood in the apartment. A lot had happened in those three months, and the apartment reflected those changes. The rooms had been completely redecorated in her absence, and the smell of paint and new carpets was heavy in the air. The colours were cold, pale blues and greens, lending it a detached, almost clinical feel. It looked like an upmarket doctor's waiting room.

But Gabrielle Royer had been killed in this room.

Briony walked around the apartment looking into the various rooms, the thought niggling at the back of her mind.

Gabrielle Royer had been killed here.

Why didn't she feel … feel something.

She had thought about selling the apartment when she'd heard about Gabrielle's death, but she'd decided to wait before making any decisions. As time went by, common sense had prevailed, and she realised she probably wouldn't find another apartment that suited her needs so easily. In fact, she probably wouldn't be able to find an apartment in this part of the city.

Initially, she'd been inclined to think that Gabrielle's death had been part of some organised campaign against her but, with the passage of time and especially now with the pressure of the book off her, she was beginning to think that perhaps she had been … . well, not imagining, but certainly over-emphasising some of the events. She'd been subjected to newspaper campaigns before — why should this one have been any different? And what was so unusual about someone writing a biography of her? After all, she was famous, and who would be the most obvious choice to write the book but her step-sister?

Briony Dalton stopped in the hallway. It had been painted in a two-tone colour scheme, dark blue coming up from the floor to about waist level then gradually fading into a paler blue that continually lightened as it neared the ceiling. The ceiling had been stippled with a swirling blue and white motif, and her immediate impression was that she was under water.

She stood in the centre of the narrow hallway and looked around. Writers are gifted — or cursed — with a vivid imagination, and Briony Dalton could clearly see the apartment door opening and Gabrielle — dear, sweet Gabrielle — stepping into the room, her mouth and eyes opening wide in surprise. The young woman turned to look into the sitting room. The portable contents of the apartment had been piled up in the centre of the floor.

A shadowy figure stepped out from around the corner, a gun in his hand. Briony saw his finger whiten on the trigger, and the blinding flash of light and the pain ...

"Miss Dalton ... Miss Dalton ... ?"

Briony blinked and found the bodyguard standing before her, blue eyes fixed on her face. "Is everything all right, Miss Dalton?"

She took a deep breath and attempted a smile. "Yes, yes, Ken." She indicated the hall. "My secretary was shot just here. The police said she interrupted a burglary."

"It's a rough city," the big man said softly, smiling to take the callousness from the statement. He'd been baby-sitting this woman for over a week now, and so far it had been a doddle. The ones who were rich but not especially famous, but who thought they were, were always the easiest. They could be a pain in the ass if they suspected everyone who even came close to them, but so far this one was working out OK. Maybe she had a legitimate beef. She had a bit of a reputation, and she'd been in all the papers because she'd been paid millions of dollars just for writing a book for Christ's sake! In this city there were people who'd cut your throat for a dollar bill. "Was there a police investigation?" he asked. "Show an interest in the client's problems," he'd been told.

"Yes, a detective ... a detective Andrew Morelli. I don't know the precinct."

"Not to worry. I'll have someone from the office look into it."

"Why? You don't think there could be some connection to me, do you?" she asked quickly.

"It's just routine."

"At the time some extremist moral majority group claimed that they had killed Gabrielle, mistaking her for me."

"They're opportunists, ma'am, looking for cheap headlines. I don't think you've anything to worry about; it was probably nothing more than some kid looking for disposable items for cash to support a habit. When he saw your secretary, he panicked." He shrugged. "It happens."

Briony dug her hands into the pockets of her Gaultier jacket, tugging it out of shape. "I suppose you think I'm a foolish woman looking for protection?" she asked wryly.

"On the contrary, ma'am. You're one of the wealthiest authors in the world: I'm surprised you haven't got more protection."

"Authors aren't like pop stars, they don't have hoards of screaming fans, they don't get mobbed … well, most of them don't," she amended.

"What are your plans for today, ma'am?"

"I'm staying in. I've got a lot of catching up to do. There's a mountain of mail to answer, for starters."

"Not writing your next book?"

"No, I generally take a couple of weeks off between books."

The bodyguard laughed and wandered off, and moments later Briony heard the muted buzz of the television in the kitchen. She turned into the sitting room, smiling broadly. The last time she'd been in this room she'd been desperately trying to work out how she was going to finish her book. Now, three months later, the book was actually finished — ahead of schedule, too — and she felt a little at a loss. She should be doing something, she should be writing.

She thought of Greg Connors as she sat down at her desk. Technically she supposed she had taken his book, but then where had his book ended and her input begun?

The two had been stitched so closely together that drawing a dividing line between them would have been virtually impossible. No, *A Woman Scorned* was *her* book from the title to the grand and bloody finale.

And Greg Connors should have been honoured to have been given the opportunity to work with someone like her. He had probably learned more about the craft of writing in the few weeks they'd been together than in all his previous books. No, on mature reflection she didn't feel in the least guilty about what she'd done to him.

Briony shuffled the enormous mound of mail into an orderly bundle and quickly sorted through it, disposing of the circulars, brochures and catalogues straight into the bin. She was left with half a dozen letters. Turning over the first, she recognised the distinctly quaint, slightly ragged elite typeface on the envelope: it was from Terri Fierstein. She hesitated for a moment before opening the letter. She had already decided she wanted to finish with Terri. She'd get herself a new agent: there should be no problem now with *A Woman Scorned* destined to become a major worldwide best-seller. She should be able to negotiate a very favourable contract with one of the new generation of agents who were more clued into the movie business, the whole multi-media genre. She was about to toss the letter aside and forward it to her lawyers, but her curiosity got the better of her and she tore it open.

Dear Briony

Delighted you finished A Woman Scorned *on time. You know I never had any doubts about you. I'm surprised that you chose to deliver it personally to the British publisher instead of passing it on to me to give to Park & Park, but the resultant publicity was excellent.*

Perhaps you would phone me at your earliest convenience.

I'm sure you have an idea for a new book — perhaps a sequel to A Woman Scorned?

Yours, Terri

Briony reached for the phone. She'd talk to her lawyer now about terminating her contract with Terri Fierstein. And then she stopped. How politic would it be to cut off all contact with Terri now? Would it not be better to retain it for the moment, and use the woman as she had used Briony? After all, the woman did have a vested interest in the book's success and, no matter what happened, Terri was still entitled to her fifteen per cent commission.

But if she didn't make the break with Terri, it meant that she would get the proofs of the book first and Briony didn't want that. She didn't want Terri to have any further contact with the book. If she could only wait until it was in print, then she could ditch Terri without a second thought. She knew Hall's intended to rush into print to cash in on the publicity. Their publicity department was already working on a campaign that would feed the newspapers regular stories about Briony Dalton and the Million Pound Book until it actually hit the shelves.

Briony shook her head. She needed advice and there was no one left in her world to give it to her.

ଔ

Less than a mile away a long black limousine nosed its way through Times Square. Daylight robbed this part of the city of the tawdry glamour it assumed at night and much of the buzz, along with most of the inhabitants, was missing but there was still enough action to keep the tourists and those who preyed upon them interested.

Josef Bach sat in the back of the car and stared out through the heavily tinted windows, not really taking in the street scene. There was an open suitcase on the swing table before him containing the most recent reports on the Dalton case, and reading through them he realised he had committed a cardinal error. He had underestimated the woman and then compounded the mistake by leaving the job to fools. He hadn't been cheated often, and the sour taste rankled.

So the book was delivered and the publicity campaign was underway. He hadn't been able to stop her writing the book and he hadn't been able to prevent her delivering it, and removing her from the picture at this stage would be counter-productive.

They had tried blackening her name and that hadn't worked either, although there had been a time, when the son had died, when he had felt that public opinion was swinging against her. He had been close to destroying her then.

He moved the sheets of paper on his lap, looking at the vast sums of money that both Park & Park and Hall's were expending on advertising. If the book were to flop, then although Briony Dalton would probably remain unhurt, the publishers would still go to the wall. The irony of it was that he couldn't allow anything to happen to her now: if she were to have a fatal accident for example, then the book's success was guaranteed as the posthumous work of the best-selling author.

There were a couple of alternatives still open to him. He could screw up the publishers' schedules by delaying delivery of the paper to the printers, since he owned both the paper makers and the hauliers, and that would mean the book would be late into the shops. But no matter how late it was it would still be a success. It would always be a success so long as it was Briony Dalton's. No, the way to make the book fail was still through the woman; the public would have to be turned off her, she would have to disgust them to such an extent that her book would be unsaleable. There had to be some secret in her past or present that would destroy her ... and if there wasn't then he'd create one.

Josef Bach's bright blue eyes narrowed as he stared out into the shabby streets at the hookers, the junkies and the pimps, the down-and-outs clustered in the doorways. And then he looked at the expressions on the faces of the tourists — disgust, amusement, curiosity, horror. He needed something that would induce similar expressions of disgust and horror in Briony Dalton's readers.

What could she do?
What would he do?

༄

Rianne Moriarty had never been a whore … well, she had,
but only when she was desperate. She had appeared in
porno movies, done nude modelling, danced topless,
danced naked, but she had never lived off any man.

Until now.

Rianne sank up to her chin in the Jacuzzi's bubbling,
buzzing hot water and closed her eyes, wrinkling her nose
as the water splashed up it.

Now she was Josef Bach's whore. And she wasn't sure
how she had ended up in this situation. No, that was a lie,
she did know and she'd gone into it with eyes wide open.
He'd been using her, just as she'd been using him.

Bach represented money and power and both
represented opportunity … the opportunity for someone
like herself, even with her chequered background, to create
a new life, a life of her own. Bach knew which strings to
pull. He'd mentioned movies often enough, which were
her dream although she knew there were few openings in
the legitimate cinema for someone with her background on
the porno circuit.

He'd got her some good contracts, she appeared nude
in all the best men's mags, and she had more money now
than she knew what to do with … or at least technically
she had earned herself quite a lot of money, but Bach had it
tied up in some fund which only he had access to and
doled it out like pocket money.

And lately the offers of work had not exactly been
flooding in. She supposed there was only so much nude
work you could do, and once you'd gone the rounds of the
magazines the only way to go was down. You started out
in all the best mags, but you generally only appeared in
them once and there were few second chances. When
you'd exhausted the first run mags, you moved

downmarket and maybe you did raunchier sets for them, and then the next phase was soft core and then into hard core and once you started on that slide there was no way off it. And she'd already been down that road once.

So what was she going to do? What could she do?

She stayed with Bach, she slept with him, she accompanied him when he wanted to be seen out with someone pretty — and she had to admit that the cosmetics and stylists had brought out a beauty in her that she never knew existed. When she was with Bach she always dressed conservatively, and she never gave interviews.

And he paid her.

Oh, nothing so crass as money, but there were little presents, jewellery, clothes, shoes. But she knew she was being paid for her services ... just like any other hooker.

She simply couldn't work out why.

Josef Bach was one of the wealthiest men in the world. He could have his pick of women: why, then, should he pick someone like her, with her background?

Rianne dipped her head beneath the water, counted to three and then came spluttering to the surface. Her gut feeling was that she was being primed for something. She wished she knew what.

Chapter Sixty-Four

Greg Connors gradually surfaced from a deep sleep in which he dreamt he was making love to Briony Dalton. It took him long moments before he realised that the breasts pressing against his back, the hand splayed across his stomach, were real.

He came fully awake with a shriek, but Catherine Garrett's voice came out of the darkness. "It's only me."

He turned around in the bed, facing her, aware that his body had reacted in his sleep and that he was fully aroused. "What ... what time is it?" he asked inanely, and then said. "How did you get in here?"

"It's a little after midnight, and I came in through the door using your key. You were still out for the count and there was nothing on TV, so I thought I'd catch a nap."

Greg leaned up on his elbow. He could just about make out the shape of the woman in the darkness. "And do you usually just slip into the nearest bed?"

"Depends who's in it," she said coyly.

"There's no answer to that." He flopped down on the pillow and slid his hands behind his head. Catherine moved over alongside him, pressing her breasts against his chest, drawing her left leg up along his thigh.

"I didn't want to disturb you. You were obviously exhausted."

He nodded in the darkness. "I was. I don't think I realised quite how much. It's been a crazy few days. I'd some weird dreams," he admitted. "Mind you, none of them were as weird as when I woke up."

Catherine had been rubbing her hand up and down his stomach as he spoke and then she suddenly climbed astride him, drawing the blankets around her shoulders. She leaned forward, her arms straight down on either side of his head, strands of her chestnut hair tickling his face.

"I thought it was every man's fantasy to wake up to find a woman making love to him."

"You weren't making love to me," he reminded her.

Catherine moved up on his thighs and then slid down forcefully on to him, smoothly impaling herself on him. "And now?" she whispered.

"This is fantasy."

His hands traced the length of her body, pausing to cup her breasts, to trace the nipples before moving upwards along the line of her throat, across her strong jawline. Her tongue rasped against his fingers and she swallowed his thumb deep into her mouth, sucking on it in time to the movements of her body. Her short, blunt nails bit into his shoulders and she moved up and down on him, spreading her legs wider to receive him deep inside.

They made love easily and in virtual silence. She took the lead and he seemed content to allow her to do all the work. His orgasm took him quickly, spasming through his body with enough force to lift him off the bed, almost dislodging Catherine. She cried out in simulated orgasm, her fingers clenching and unclenching on his chest, and then she dropped forward, almost crouching on top of him, her head on his chest. Beneath her ear, she could hear the rapid pounding of his heart beginning to slow down and his heavy breathing slowly returning to normal.

When his breathing had deepened even further, assuming a steady regularity that she judged was close to sleep, she began to speak to him, keeping her voice low and level, driving home her facts in simple sentences, judging his responses by the beat of his heart beneath her head. She had spent most of the afternoon rehearsing the speech.

"I did my best for you today, Greg. I spoke to just about every editor I knew. They all said the same. Briony Dalton has told them that you were a holiday romance who got jealous. She's portrayed you as an envious, petty-minded lout who thought he could grab a little of a great author's limelight. No one will touch your story. Even the tabloids need proof. None of the television or radio stations are interested in recording an interview.

"And no one is ever going to publish you again.

"No publisher is interested in even looking at any submissions from you. No one wants anything further to do with you. She's destroyed you, Greg. She's destroyed your livelihood. You'll never write again. Briony Dalton has destroyed you."

The slow, steady throb of his heart increased and she could almost feel the adrenaline surging through his veins. The muscles in his stomach contracted; his hands, resting lightly on her back, closed into fists and the muscles in his cheeks and jaws worked, tightening into knots.

When he spoke his voice was choked with emotion. "The bitch ... fucking bitch ... fucking bitch. I'll fucking kill her!"

In the darkness, Catherine Garrett's triumphant smile was invisible.

Chapter Sixty-Five

"Rianne!"

Catherine stood in the doorway of her Sussex cottage, looking in amazement at the creature who bore only the vaguest resemblance to the young woman who had last walked through it.

Rianne Moriarty threw her arms around Catherine's neck and hugged her close. "Bach's with me," she murmured, and then her eyes widened as the tall, handsome young man stepped into the hallway behind the older woman.

Catherine glanced back over her shoulder. "Rianne, I'd like you to meet a friend of mind, Gregory Connors; Greg this is Rianne Moriarty, Briony's Dalton's daughter," she added, her eyes flashing the warning. Over the past month Greg had become increasingly incensed with Briony Dalton and the pre-publication furore that had grown up about *A Woman Scorned*. She didn't know how he was going to react to Rianne.

Rianne was shaking hands with Greg — and wondering why Catherine had mentioned her mother's name — when Josef Bach stepped up to the door, his presence filling it. His hard blue eyes flowed past Catherine and settled on Greg, and then he looked at Rianne. The young woman had lived with him long enough now to understand the unspoken signal, and she turned without a word and picked her way across the sodden ground back towards the Rolls Royce, her high heels sinking deep into the mud; two thousand dollar high-heels shoes were not designed for muddy English summers, she decided, sliding into the warm leather seats and pulling off the soiled shoes. She bent her head to the task of wiping away the worst of the mud with a tissue, but her eyes were fixed on the scene taking place at door of the cottage. She watched Catherine make the introductions and Bach shake hands with Connors.

What the hell was going on here? Who was this Greg Connors, and why had Catherine pointedly told him who she was? It was a warning, she decided. And it also meant that Catherine hadn't been expecting the visit from Bach, otherwise she would have forewarned Greg. Rianne watched the door close on the trio and wondered about the young man, tall, handsome, and much younger than Catherine. What was the relationship there: friend, lover, assistant? Another pawn in one of Bach's games ... like herself? She had become convinced she was just another piece waiting to be moved when the time was right. But Bach was so devious that not only did his left hand not know what his right was doing, but the fingers on each hand seemed to be working independently of one another.

Rianne hadn't been aware that they were going to visit Catherine in Sussex until shortly after their flight had taken off from Kennedy. They had spent most of the past month in America, where she had done a centre-page spread for the *Playboy* Christmas Special; she was amused and awed when she learned that she had been paid more for that two-day shoot than she had earned in a year of making movies.

She had seen a lot of her mother on television in the States. The woman had run the gamut of guest spots on all the big-name shows, and was now beginning to appear on the independent and cable channels. The questions were always the same; with the professional interviewers it wasn't so obvious that they were reading from a prepared list ...

"When did you start writing?"

"How many books have you written to date?"

"Tell us about *A Woman Scorned* ..."

"How long did it take you to write it?"

"What does it feel like to be paid millions of dollars to write a book?"

"How much will you get for the sequel?"

With the amateurs, some of them were actually straining forward to read the auto-cue. Briony had been unusually reticent during her interviews, restrained and controlled, and Rianne had been surprised that she hadn't seen her mother on *Coast-to-Coast* or *Good Morning, America* or *Larry King* ... until she realised that these would probably wait until the book itself was published. A series of teaser ads had appeared in the newspapers and magazines, and some of the larger billboards now ran the single lurid line of blood-red type against a solid black background:

'Who is *A Woman Scorned*?'

The book was going to be enormous.

'Bigger than the Bible', Rianne had read in *Newsweek*, when they'd run it as their cover story, showing two books side by side, the Bible and a dummy copy of *A Woman Scorned*. It went to on to say that there was every possibility that *A Woman Scorned* would finally nudge the Bible from it's number-one-best-selling-book-in-the-world perch. The initial print run was of one million copies, and already the pre-publication sales came close to eight hundred thousand copies across America.

Rianne had sat down with her calculator and worked out that if the entire one million copies of *A Woman Scorned* sold out in hardback at $29.95, and if her mother's royalty was ten per cent, although it was probably closer to fifteen, then she stood to make — at the very least — $2,990,000 and she'd been paid $2,500,000 as an advance. So she'd earn back her advance on the first print run. The pundits were estimating that she would earn around ten million dollars from this book alone, and that was before the movie rights had been sold.

And just where did Bach fit into all of this?

Rianne Moriarty might be many things — whore, porno-starlet — but she wasn't stupid. She knew Bach had an interest in Briony Dalton, she'd just never been able to figure out what or how. He'd commissioned the biography Catherine was writing — or rather one of his companies had, because he rarely did anything without distancing himself with layers and shields — and while there was nothing unusual in a publisher commissioning a biography of a celebrity, what was unusual was the publisher taking a personal interest in the author and the subject.

Rianne Dalton scratched on the glass that separated her from the chauffeur. He was sitting well back in his seat, cap pulled down over his face, breathing evenly. He didn't move. With infinite care, Rianne pressed down the handle, cracking the door open a fraction. She slid her feet into her ruined shoes and looked at the cottage again. The only room big enough to hold a conference of any sort was Catherine's study at the back of the house …

∞

"You know me," Josef Bach stated flatly.

The two men were sitting facing one another on either side of the fire. Catherine was standing behind Greg's chair, her arms draped over his shoulders. "You're Josef Bach," Greg said, looking up at Catherine. She shook her head slightly, but he couldn't work out whether she was warning him to say nothing or not to ask any of the score of questions that had come to mind.

"Did you know I commissioned Catherine to write the definitive biography of Briony Dalton?"

"I knew she was working on the book; I didn't know you had commissioned it."

"She has told me the extraordinary story of your experiences with Briony Dalton," Bach continued relentlessly, staring hard at Greg. "Is it true?" he asked.

Greg felt Catherine's hand tighten on his shoulder and he controlled his temper with difficulty. The rage that had built up in him over the past weeks — carefully nurtured by Catherine — now threatened to boil over at the very mention of Dalton's name. He took a deep breath, calming himself, and said simply, "She stole my work."

"She has effectively done more than that," Bach said mildly, leaning back into the chair and crossing his legs, resting his hands on his knees. "She has put the story around the publishing trade that you are a liar, a jealous holiday romance who attempted to cash in on her name. She has effectively ensured that you will never be published again."

"So I've been told. So what do I do? Do I grin and bear it? Do I say nothing? What choice do I have?"

Bach looked at him, smiling benevolently. "I'm about to give you a choice. Catherine believes you, and she's convinced me that you are innocent. Now, you know she is nearing the end of her book. I would like your permission to go public with your story."

Greg stared at him blankly. "But we've no proof," he said desperately, "and without proof she'll probably sue me on top of everything else. If we'd proof I'd do it."

"Assuming you had the proof, would you be prepared to stand the resultant publicity and the possible court case?"

"I would."

"What proof would you need?" Bach asked.

"My original manuscript," Greg Connors said.

"Well, I cannot give you that. But do you think you could recreate your manuscript from this?" He passed across a heavy padded jiffy bag. When Greg tore it open he discovered a three-inch-thick bundle of printed pages. "It's the proofs of *A Woman Scorned*," he said in astonishment. "But however did you get it?"

But Josef Bach just shook his head, smiling gently. "Don't ask me," he said. "Now, Briony Dalton will be receiving a copy of these proofs in about four hours. She will then have two weeks to read through them and make whatever corrections she feels necessary before returning them to the publishers. I feel sure she will endeavour to do this as quickly as possible. She is due money on the publication of the book and she is desperately short of cash at the moment." He paused and the smile on his thin lips turned cold and unpleasant. "However, I am not so confident that Briony Dalton will be able to correct these proofs within the two weeks allotted to her: my crystal ball has prophesied that she is due for a stressful time."

Greg looked at him, unsure whether the man was joking or not. Bach's eyes were flat, expressionless. "What I want to know from you, Gregory Connors, is whether you will be able to retype your manuscript from these proofs in two weeks?"

The young man thumbed through the loose pages. "Well, yes and no. I mean, I can recognise some of the bits I wrote, but Briony rewrote much of it and, to be honest, I cannot tell where my bits end and hers begin."

"Let me rephrase it," Bach said patiently. "Retype your manuscript from these proofs, and I really don't care how close to the original it will be. Copy this, but make some minor changes in it, make it a little cruder if you can, a little less polished. I want your version to seem like a second or third draft." He looked sharply at Greg. "Will you do that? Are you prepared to do it?"

Connors nodded. "I can do it. I just don't see where this is leading."

Bach held up a hand, silencing him. "Catherine will include the story of how Briony Dalton stole your work in the last chapter of her book. We will go to press immediately the book is finished and launch it in a blaze of publicity and controversy. Naturally, Briony Dalton will refute your claims and there will be a court case, which she will fully expect to win. Our ace will be that we can bring in a copy of your manuscript ... which you had written and copyrighted weeks before she registered hers!

"Briony Dalton will be ruined. You will be able to do to her what she has done to you ... with one lovely little addendum: all the monies which she will earn from *A Woman Scorned* will go to you."

Greg stared at him in astonishment. He turned to look up at Catherine and then back to the imposing figure in white. "Let me get this right," he whispered, "it's just … I don't know. I can't see…" He took a deep breath to calm himself. "You're giving me the opportunity to make a sort of copy of these proofs, which you will somehow get registered as predating Briony Dalton's book. You will then force her into a court battle to prove the ownership of the book, and she will lose."

"I guarantee it."

"Her name will be mud in the literary world," Greg continued softly, speaking aloud, working through the ramifications, "and I will earn the millions that are now due to her."

"It is your book she's earning the money on," Catherine reminded him.

Greg nodded, and then he suddenly looked at Bach. "Why?" he asked. "What do you get out of this?"

"I ensure that my own book is a phenomenal bestseller." Bach shrugged. "And it will give me a great deal of satisfaction to see someone like Dalton get her just deserts. I'm wealthy enough not to care about money, but that wasn't always the case. There was a time when I had nothing, a time when everything I owned or cared for was stolen away." He reached out and Catherine came around the chair to take his hand. "And Catherine is a friend. She asked me to help you." He smiled broadly. "Now I don't think I'm asking you to do anything to Briony Dalton that she hasn't already done to you, but I'll not force you into doing anything that is against your conscience, so think about it."

Greg grinned wolfishly. "That bitch stole my work without a second thought; she didn't care what the consequences would be for me." His fingers tightened on the proofs. "I don't have to think about it."

Confused and troubled, Rianne Dalton moved away from the window and walked back to the car. She had heard enough to know that something very bad was going on, something involving her mother and Aunt Catherine.

And she hadn't got a clue what she was going to do about it.

Chapter Sixty-Six

The page proofs of *A Woman Scorned* had arrived.

Briony Dalton had been writing for twenty-five years and she'd never seen book proofs arrive so quickly. She had delivered the manuscript just over a month ago: usually it would take anywhere from six to nine months for the proofs to arrive. Obviously both her American and British publishers had a very good reason — or several million very good reasons — to rush it through and reap the rewards of the high-profile publicity she was currently enjoying.

The front door buzzer had gone about an hour earlier. When she'd thumbed on the small black-and-white monitor she had been shocked to discover Charles Beaumont Lesalles, Terri Fierstein's personal assistant, on the step looking up at the camera. He was holding a cardboard box in his hand.

"What do you want?" she demanded rudely, wondering if he would speak.

On the tiny TV monitor, he silently held up the parcel.

"What is it?" she asked.

For thirty agonising seconds, the man struggled to speak and he managed a few words before his crippling stammer caught up with him. "*A Woman Scorned* proofs … f-f-f-from … P-P-P-Pa-a-a-rk."

Briony released the door lock, and it opened downstairs in absolute silence and swung gently inwards.

Briony was fuming with rage as Charles came up in the elevator. She was principally annoyed at her own stupidity, annoyed that Terri should have seen the proofs before she had, annoyed that she hadn't cancelled her contract with Terri when she'd thought about it. Too late now; but she was going to instruct her lawyer to terminate her contract with her agent immediately.

Briony opened the door and waited for Lesalles to arrive. She watched him step out of the lift and walk down the corridor, and she couldn't help wondering how Terri Fierstein had ended up with someone as effeminate as Charles Beaumont Lesalles. There was no question who wore the trousers in their relationship ... but maybe that's what she liked: her ex-husbands had all been achievers in their own right; she claimed that they had smothered her creativity.

When Lesalles had neared the door, Briony held out her hand for the box, unwilling to allow him into the apartment. He stopped about two feet away from her, gave her the box and then he said suddenly, racing his stammer, "Don't blame Terri, it wasn't all her fault." He turned and hurried away before she could ask any questions, leaving her standing in the doorway with the box in her hands.

Briony stepped back into the room and closed the door behind her, carefully locking it with the new deadbolt she'd had installed. She'd dismissed the security people a few days previously; the lack of privacy was beginning to get to her and although the two men who'd been assigned to her — Ken One and Ken Two, she'd called them — had been souls of discretion, she had always known they were there. They made her feel like a virtual prisoner in her own apartment. They had been very gracious when she had told them that she was dispensing with their services. They had thanked her and she had presented them both with engraved gold fountain pens, but the following morning their boss had been on the line. He had been charming and in what sounded like a delightful parody of an upper-class British accent had pointed out the numerous dangers inherent in being a celebrity in New York; leaving aside the very real possibility of a crank taking a shot at her, there was also the danger of kidnap, and very few millionaires were as accessible as she was and it was unfortunate that she had had her face in the newspaper so very frequently recently, rendering her very high profile, and...

Briony had cut him short by the simple expedient of hanging up on him. She knew he was only telling her all this to frighten her — and he had succeeded. That same day she had gone out and bought herself a can of chemical Mace and had applied for a licence to carry a gun. Maybe she was overreacting, but better she overreacted than not react at all and end up suddenly and possibly terminally surprised.

But now with the two guards gone, the apartment felt empty and she was more than a little on edge, more than a little frightened, and she realised that she was no longer comfortable there. Maybe she would sell it, after all, and move out to California. It was no safer on the West Coast but at least the weather was better there.

Briony put the proofs down on the table and then went around the room gathering up her coloured pens, sliding Handel's *Sonatas for Flute and Harpsichord* into the CD player before putting the kettle on to boil.

This was the final stage of writing a book. The first stage, when the book was coming out of her unconscious on to the screen was exciting, while the second stage, making the corrections, stitching the book tightly together, was tedious and boring, then this final stage was often a mixture of the two: exciting because she would usually have forgotten much of what she'd written, and frustrating because, although she could make corrections, it was neither advisable nor cost-effective to do any major revisions to the text, and that often meant allowing sections to stand that needed to be rewritten. She found it intensely frustrating.

Was this book going to be any different, she wondered, as she prepared the large pot of tea. Probably not, she decided. Here she was, less then five weeks after completing and delivering it, with it back in her lap again, so was it any wonder that she was beginning to become bored with it? But Greg would probably enjoy it.

She was putting the cup and saucer, milk jug and sugar bowl on to the tray alongside the teapot when she realised that this was only the second time since she'd delivered the manuscript that she'd consciously thought of the book in connection with Greg. She wondered where he was now and what he thought of her. And she wondered if he still thought of the book as his. Well, it wasn't, not any more it wasn't. He had had a creative input, certainly, but she had shaped it, she had crafted it, honed it, made it what it was. Certain paragraphs, individual lines were his — although she couldn't put her hand on her heart and say that this was his, that was hers — but the book now read like vintage Briony Dalton. It *was* vintage Briony Dalton.

And she had no regrets.

Briony Dalton sat down at the large table with the tea tray to her left and placed the proofs on the table directly in front of her. Two elastic bands held the bulk of them together and thirty-page sections had been stapled together. She immediately turned to the last page, checking the page number, wondering how big the book had turned out to be — five hundred and twenty-eight pages. That would look respectable on the bookshop shelves and especially impressive in hardback, although the price of that size book was going to hurt.

She went back to the beginning and turned over the title page to look at the dedication.

For Gabrielle ... a woman scorned indeed ...

Pouring herself a cup of tea, she stared at page one and began to read slowly and carefully. Two coloured pens were used for correcting proofs, a red pen to highlight mistakes made by the printer and a black pen for alterations made by the author or editor. Briony usually read aloud for this final stage of correction; she had discovered that if she could read without stumbling or faltering then everything was fine, but if she stumbled then the text needed to be re-jigged. Usually she would pick up the typos, dropped letters and spelling errors on this preliminary reading, but in any case she would quickly re-read the proofs a second time before returning them.

She worked on through the afternoon drinking cup after cup of tea, even after it had gone cold. The book was good — no, it was better than good, it was bloody marvellous. And for a book that had been typeset so quickly it was remarkably free of errors. After a while she found she was reading it for enjoyment and although she knew what was coming next, she still found herself turning the pages, fascinated by the way the story twisted and turned. The characters were so real!

And as she was reading through it an idea began to formulate for a sequel. From experience she knew that the best thing to do was to leave the idea alone, let it ferment in the back of her mind so that it would abruptly pop fully formed and complete into her consciousness.

The original idea for *A Woman Scorned* had been concocted from half a dozen sources. All of Briony Dalton's books were commercial, deliberately so. Before she had set out to write this book she had read through the best-seller lists for the previous three years, examined what her closest rivals were doing and had finally opted for the traditional family saga, only coming at it from a different angle.

But it wasn't worth the telephone figure advances she had been paid. Just about every writer working in the same field had tackled similar themes with varying degrees of success.

However, this book, this version of *A Woman Scorned*, was a best-seller. It transcended the family saga genre; she had taken Greg's horror story and woven it into the family saga, creating something very new and exciting. And there was the opportunity for a sequel … in fact, there were opportunities for a series of novels written around either the contemporary or the historical characters in the book. But she knew she'd only be able to write one sequel to the novel; writers of her calibre rarely wrote long series, they were expected to move on … but then again, Briony Dalton set the trends, she didn't follow them. Maybe she could do a series. This book would set trends.

In growing excitement, she began to jot down notes for two different series, one a historical trilogy based on the background given in *A Woman Scorned*, the second for two contemporary sequels to the present book. There was a lot of research involved, and she'd need a research assistant for that, and a secretary. She stopped, pen poised above the page as another thought struck her: should she try for a two-book deal, or just sell a single book? If she got two and a half million dollars for one book, would she get five million for two? She didn't think so. But then again, she might. Briony Dalton was hot stuff at the moment. She certainly wouldn't get that sort of money if she went back to Hall's or Park & Park. Next time, she was going to a big publisher. The biggest.

She'd need an agent. It would have to be someone who handled all the major names ... unfortunately Terri Fierstein handled all the major names. But she'd never use Terri again; Briony felt the woman had betrayed her; she'd never be able to trust her again. Anyway, what was the name of that agency in New York, the big one ... it was world famous?

She was reaching for the current edition of the *Writers & Artists Yearbook*, which listed, amongst other things, publishers and agents across the world, when she smelt a sharp bitter odour. It tickled her sinuses and caught at the back of her throat. Briony raised her head, turning it from side to side, sniffing. The air in the apartment was dry and smelt faintly of the decorators and a herbal air freshener which was secreted around the apartment and which she'd been unable to find so far.

The smell brought her to her feet and, still sniffing, she walked around the apartment, trying to track down the smell. It got stronger as she approached the hall, and then she suddenly recognised the odour: it was petrol.

Frightened now, she hurried out into the hallway and stopped. The smell here was almost overpowering. She had taken a step towards the door when her leather-soled slipper trod in liquid. She looked down at the carpet, but it was dark blue and showed nothing. She knelt and touched it, discovering to her horror that it was sodden. Bringing her fingertips to her face, she caught the bitter stench of petrol. The carpet was soaked in petrol. She was still crouching when she looked at the door. Unlike many American apartments, it had a mail box. The flap was partially open and there was a slender flesh-coloured tube sticking through the letter box leading down on to the carpet. As she watched, colourless liquid dribbled from the tube.

She was opening her mouth to scream, when the letter box snapped up and two dark eyes regarded her malevolently. She heard a scratch and light flared around the eyes, turning them yellow and metallic.

Briony Dalton was moving even as the blazing book of matches was dropped in through the letter box. She had almost reached the door at the end of the hall when the petrol ignited with a dull roar, the force of the blast lifting her up, slamming her into the door. As she lay dazed on the floor she watched the flames dance towards her, the pale blue fire mesmerising and beautiful, melting the carpet pile, releasing a thick noxious pall of smoke into the air.

She was aware of pain in her back, across her shoulders and in her head and, almost abstractly, she wondered which would get her first, the fumes or the flames …

Chapter Sixty-Seven

Briony Dalton came awake with a scream that brought the nurse to her side. She sat bolt upright, wide-eyed and shivering, even though she was covered in a light sheen of sweat.

"You're fine, Miss Dalton, you're fine," the tall Hispanic nurse soothed her. "Everything's going to be all right."

"The fire!"

"The sprinkler system in your apartment put it out," the nurse said softly, pushing her back down on to the pillows. "You're fine except for a little smoke inhalation." The nurse turned, abruptly aware of the man looking into the room. "I'm sorry sir, this is a restricted area."

"I heard the scream." He dug in his pocket and showed her his shield. "Detective Morelli. I'd like a few words with Miss Dalton if she's awake."

"Miss Dalton cannot see anyone at the moment."

The detective smiled, flashing extraordinarily white teeth. "I'm sorry ma'am, but I've some questions that won't wait."

"I'll speak to the detective, nurse," Briony said hoarsely from the bed.

"You should get some rest," the nurse advised. Seeing the obstinate look in Briony's eyes, she turned to glare at the detective. "Five minutes."

He smiled and stepped aside, allowing her to leave the room, then showed Briony his shield. "Detective Andrew Morelli, NYPD," he introduced himself, dragging up a chair and straddling it.

Briony stared at the man. He was tall, dark, obviously Italian with his black eyes and jet-black hair, and he had eyebrows that met in a straight line over his nose. She was sure she'd never met him and yet the name sounded familiar.

"I spoke to you some time ago when your secretary, Miss Gabrielle Royer, was shot," he said, gently reminding her of the last time they'd spoken.

Briony nodded slowly, recalling the detective who'd phoned her in Dublin.

"I know you've had a very frightening and traumatic experience, ma'am," he continued, "but I want you to think very carefully and then tell me in your own words exactly what happened."

"Then you didn't catch him?" she whispered.

"No ma'am, we did not."

Briony eased herself up the bed, and the detective immediately jumped up to shift the pillows behind her shoulders. He poured her a drink of water and she sipped it gratefully. She realised she was wearing an absolutely hideous night-dress — obviously hospital issue — and she pulled the sheets to her chin. "Lesalles brought over the proofs of my new book …"

"Who is this Lesalles, ma'am?"

"Charles Beaumont Lesalles," she explained. "He is the personal secretary of my ex-agent, Terri Fierstein."

"How long is ex?" he wondered aloud.

"As soon as I get out of here."

"Do you want to tell me why?"

"Personal reasons."

Morelli scribbled in his small notebook with a tiny pen that Briony found almost feminine. She noticed that he had elegant hands, long-fingered, beautifully manicured.

"And then?"

"I'd been working on the book for a while when I noticed the smell."

"Have you any idea when this was exactly? How long had you been working?"

She shook her head. "When I'm working on a book, I tend to lose track of time. It was a couple of hours, certainly, two, three, something like that. Anyway, I went to investigate the smell. I couldn't identify it at first — you know when you smell or hear or see something out of place or context, you can't put a name to it immediately."

The detective nodded patiently.

"The smell was strongest in the hall," she said, closing her eyes, remembering. "I walked towards the door and the carpet squelched underfoot. I bent down to touch it and I knew then it was petrol. When I looked at the door I could see that the letterbox was open and that there was a thin tube sticking through it."

He glanced down at his notebook. "You saw a tube sticking through the mail slot." He prompted. " What then? I take it gasoline was coming in through the tube?"

"Yes. I could see it spilling on to the carpet."

"And then what?"

"The letterbox flap opened …and someone looked in at me," she said very softly, shuddering at the memory.

"The person looking through the mailbox, could you tell if it was male or female?" Morelli said, keeping her moving, unwilling to allow her to dwell on any particular event.

"Male," she said immediately, and then considered. "Yes, definitely male."

"And then what happened?"

"I saw the eyes crinkle …" She stared at Morelli, "You know, like when someone smiles? And then this blazing matchbook came in through the letterbox. I think I was running then. I heard a bang and I was thrown against the wall. I remember lying on the floor watching the flames eat their way through the carpet towards me." She stopped and then shook her head. "I don't remember anything else." She gazed around the room. "How long have I been here?"

Morelli checked his watch. "This is Saturday the sixth of June. You came in twenty-four hours ago. The sprinkler system in your hall kicked in and took care of the fire. Lucky for you it is one of the new heat-sensitive types that only reacts to the hot spots, otherwise the water would have done more damage than the flames. One of your neighbours smelt the smoke and came to investigate; he found that the carpet on the outside of your door was burning and that your door handle was red hot to the touch. He phoned the fire department and ambulance. We were called in when the fire chief suspected arson, and I was alerted because I had handled Miss Royer's case."

Briony looked up suddenly. "You don't think there's a connection, do you?"

Detective Morelli stood and pushed the chair back to the window. "Someone tried to kill you yesterday, Miss Dalton," he said very quietly. "In the light of this we have re-opened the investigation into the death of your secretary. I'll be straight with you, ma'am. Maybe the same person who killed her is now out for you. Maybe he was out for you then and got her instead. We'll be assigning someone to stay with you for a while."

"I had hired bodyguards in London and they came over with me to New York. I only let them go a couple of days ago."

"I'd have no objections if you were to hire them again. I would suggest that whoever did this has been watching you, waiting for a chance to get you alone."

"Will he try again?"

"I'd be lying if I said he wouldn't."

"When …when Gabby was shot I read a report that some fundamentalist Christian group had shot her, mistaking her for me."

"That was newspaper nonsense. A couple of crazy people claimed responsibility for the shooting, but that's not so unusual. We investigated them, but nothing came of it." He had turned towards the door when he stopped and turned back to look at her, head tilted to one side, straight eyebrows raised quizzically. The entire move was so smooth that she thought he must have practised it. "Have you any idea who might be interested in doing this?"

Briony started to shake her head, and then she smiled ruefully. "I'm sure you're aware of my reputation, Detective Morelli. My books attract a lot of interest ...some fanatic maybe, some religious nut," she suggested.

"Maybe," he agreed. "Anyway, there will be a man on the door and we'll work out something whenever the docs let you go. In the meantime, if there's anything you think of, no matter how trivial or unimportant, the officer on the door can get in touch with me at any time."

"Thank you ... and detective," she added as he pulled open the door, "thank you for being so frank with me."

"I always think its best to be open up front," he said, and stepped out of the room.

Briony Dalton sank back on to the pillows, numb with shock and horror. Someone had tried to kill her.

And had tried before.

And Gabrielle had died because of it. He had obviously gone to her apartment with the intention of killing her, discovered Gabrielle there and killed her, either accidentally, or mistakenly, thinking she was Briony. She shook her head: it didn't make sense. None of this made sense. She was a writer, nothing more, nothing less; how had she ended up in this situation? It was beginning to sound like the plot of a novel. Except that this was real.

A killer had struck at her twice and had failed. What about the third time?

She was surprised she didn't feel more frightened. Her only regret — and it was surprisingly brief — was at Gabrielle's needless death. But she had already grieved for Gabrielle and the young woman was fading in her memory, like a character in a novel she had written a long time ago. What she needed to do now was to employ bodyguards, maybe move to the West Coast ... although, no, that wasn't really practical at the moment, she needed to be close to the publishers during the book's production.

So, she was stuck in New York, stuck with the situation — so why not make him work for her? Fuck him! He had frightened her — truly terrified her: she knew she was going to see those eyes staring in through the mail slot for a long time. He probably thought he'd frightened her off: he was about to find out how wrong he was.

She was swinging her legs out of bed when the door opened and a doctor and nurse entered.

"Miss Dalton, what are you doing?" the nurse demanded.

"Discharging myself," she said, assuming her imperious voice, the voice which needed real wealth to give it the proper tone of authority.

"You cannot." the doctor began.

"When I want a doctor's opinion I'll pay for it! Now bring me my clothes, please. Immediately," she snapped, when they both stood staring at her.

"Miss Dalton, this is most irregular." The doctor looked at the nurse for assistance.

"If you do not bring me my clothes immediately, I shall file a suit against both of you and the hospital for unlawful detention."

The nurse retreated, and when she returned a uniformed police officer was by her side. "Miss Dalton, I really don't think you should leave here at the moment," he said.

"Find your Detective Morelli and tell him I'm leaving. If you want to keep me here, arrest me."

The officer looked at her for a moment and then shrugged and backed from the room, hands raised in front of him. "Keep your hair on, lady. I'll see about getting you a ride home."

"I can take a cab!" She glared at the doctor and nurse. "I would like to dress." They left the room without a word. She was over-reacting, she knew, but — Christ Almighty! — someone had tried to kill her and she wasn't lying around in a hospital bed waiting for him to try again. She was entitled to be freaked out.

The trick now was to capitalise on the event, buy herself some newspaper column inches, some air time, lure this guy out into the open and then let the police take care of the situation, or better still, let her bodyguards take care of it a little more permanently.

She pulled on her jeans and struggled into the stained, smoky sweatshirt. There was only one shoe, and she remembered the other burning on the carpet, so she tossed it into the trash and opened the door. The police officer immediately put his arm across the entrance. "I've just got my orders, lady. You're to stay until Detective Morelli gets here."

"I'll sue," she fumed.

"Yeah, sure lady. Listen, I'm just doing my job and you're not making it any easier. Stay in the room for another ten minutes and talk to the detective, eh?"

Briony attempted to push past him.

"You've just committed an assault, lady," he said with a smile.

"I'll scream."

He shrugged. "So scream."

Briony had actually opened her mouth to scream when she spotted the tall dark-haired figure of Andrew Morelli striding down the corridor. He grabbed her arm and manoeuvred her back into the hospital room, closing the door behind him with his foot and standing with his back to it, arms folded across his chest.

"So what brought this on? Ten minutes ago you were lying in that bed without a bother. Now I hear you're acting like a crazy person."

"Maybe it only just sunk in that someone's tried to kill me, and I suppose people do one of two things when that happens: they either curl up or they fight. I'm a fighter. Now, if you want to do something for me, then get me a ride back to my apartment. There's a few things I want to pick up."

"You can't stay in your apartment, there's no door on it," Morelli said patiently. "What are you going to do?"

"I'm going to phone my publishers. I'm their greatest asset right now; let them find somewhere to put me up."

Morelli stepped away from the door and opened it. "Did they really pay you two and a half million dollars for a book?"

"They did," she said, challenging him with her stare. "Why?"

"Did they know how much trouble they were buying?" he asked. "Did you?" He turned away before Briony could reply.

Chapter Sixty-Eight

ATTEMPT ON AUTHOR'S LIFE

Best-selling author Briony Dalton barely escaped with her life today when the maniac who has been stalking her for the past few months struck again, fire-bombing her apartment. Only the sophisticated security devices in the multi-millionairess' apartment saved her.

Miss Dalton is now under police protection and was unavailable for comment.

RED HOT AUTHOR GETS RED HOT PRESENT

The Queen of the Red Hot Read, Briony Dalton, lived up to her name today when her exclusive New York apartment was fire-bombed.

Three months ago, Briony Dalton's secretary and lover was murdered in the same apartment. It was suggested that she had been the victim of a burglary, although a fundamentalist Christian organisation admitted responsibility, claiming that Briony Dalton herself was the target. The police have re-opened that line of enquiry.

The terror of the celebrity killer has gripped New York notables once again and security has doubled around the stars' homes.

Briony Dalton is now in hiding and was unavailable for comment, but friends close to her reported that she was unworried by the attack and was currently working on the proofs of her latest blockbuster, A Woman Scorned, *due for publication later this month.*

Chapter Sixty-Nine

"Looks like someone else is going to do your job for you," Catherine remarked, pushing the newspaper across the table to Greg. "Where were you last night?" she asked archly.

"You know damn well where I was," he said, his mouth full of toast. "Why, have you forgotten already what we were doing last night?"

Catherine frowned. "Vaguely. And then again it might have been a dream."

"It wasn't a dream," Greg laughed. "I've got the scratches to prove it."

The previous night he had been working on his manuscript of *A Woman Scorned* when Catherine had crept up behind him and covered his eyes with her hands. He'd been quiet and irritable all day and had brusquely dismissed her ... until he felt her naked breasts against the back of his head. They had spent the rest of the night making love and he had awoken early, relaxed and refreshed.

Greg tapped the newspaper with his hand. "What do you make of it?"

"Could be a publicity stunt, of course, but I'm inclined to think it's genuine. I wonder who's behind it, though."

"A religious fanatic?" he said.

"Could be. Maybe another author she's ripped off," she said seriously.

"That's not even funny."

"It wasn't meant to be." Catherine leaned across the table, taking his hands in hers. "She stole my book from me nearly twenty-five years before she stole yours. Do you think she hasn't done it in the meantime?"

"Are you suggesting that all her work is stolen?"

"No, don't be so silly. I'm merely suggesting that you and I are probably not the only ones. I would imagine when my biography of her appears there are going to be a couple of people who will sit up and say, 'Yes, she did that to me too.'"

Greg read through the newspaper article again. "It says here that someone fire-bombed her apartment. That's some serious shit!"

Catherine reached over and snatched the paper from his hands, tossing it aside. "A couple of weeks ago you'd have done the same, but what's happened? You've had time to think about it, and you've gone soft. Maybe that's what happens to all the people she's stolen work from. After a while, they say, 'Well, what the hell? Fuck it, it's not worth the effort. Let her keep the book, it won't do her any good!' And do you know something? that's exactly what I said. I was convinced she'd never have any luck with the money she earned from it. God, providence, the wheel of karma would see to that. You see, I was young then, I imagined there was some sort of justice in the world. Well, let me tell you something, Gregory Connors, that's just so much bullshit. The only justice in this world is the justice you make yourself." She was almost shouting now, deliberately using her anger, directing it at Greg, attempting to anger him in turn. "Her career was founded on the book she stole from me and now, when her career was flagging, it's been relaunched by your book. Your book. She gets a few million and you get zilch."

"You don't need to tell me," Greg snapped. "I know that, I'm very well aware of it. That's why I'm sitting here day after day retyping my manuscript and changing it — fucking changing it — so it won't look like hers ... which is really mine anyway. I've told you I'll bring Briony Dalton down, and I will. And maybe last week I would have resorted to murder, but that was then and this is now. I'm willing to try this stunt of Bach's, and if it fails, well then,

I'll try something else. I don't know what that something else is, but it won't be murder. It's only a fucking novel, for Christ's sake!"

"It was your life," Catherine reminded him viciously. "Your future. She's taken both."

૦8

Usually she was a late riser, but this morning Rianne awoke before Bach, alert and refreshed, and that in itself was unusual: she was a night person, her body clock having adjusted to too many years working at night, sleeping by day.

Rianne had gone to bed early the previous night. She'd been feeling tired and irritable after a day spent shooting a fashion spread on the Champs Elysée with the Eiffel Tower as a backdrop. She'd been part of a group of a dozen girls, all of them professional models, and she'd been uncomfortable and felt out of place right from the beginning. She knew that no amount of make-up, no matter how cleverly it was applied, would make her look anything like any of the professional models. She was only there because Josef's money and power opened a lot of doors. Between shoots the models had mingled together chatting animatedly, pointedly ignoring Rianne, falling silent when she approached, then giggling and laughing when she turned away. She knew she would never be one of them; she had broken the cardinal rule of the professional model: she had appeared fully nude. Although the models had said nothing, they had still managed to make her feel like dirt. She took some consolation from the fact that she was earning three times what they were for the day's shoot.

Bach had been distracted all day. She knew he was in the process of closing a deal with the Russians; it was obviously important enough to involve him personally, and the figures were evidently big enough to frighten even him. Other than that, however, she had no idea what it was. As she'd been leaving the château on the outskirts of

Paris in the still darkness before the dawn, her limousine had passed a fleet of five gleaming black Citröens, each one bearing CD plates and flying a small Russian flag. When the day's shoot finished in the early afternoon, she had decided to return to the chateau immediately rather than spend time shopping as Josef had suggested. The five Citröens were still there, neatly parked outside the main entrance to the château, dark-suited chauffeurs lounging around the ornamental fountain. She had gone in through the back entrance, showered and changed in her bedroom and then taken a stroll around the beautifully kept lawns in an attempt to unwind. Although the gardens seemed deserted, she knew that her every move was being monitored by the cameras and microphones hidden amongst the trees and bushes. Bach was incredibly security conscious, but he had the wealth to ensure that it did not intrude too conspicuously into his life.

Rianne enjoyed the walk. It was rare for her to have time for herself, time to be herself and not put on a front or a face. She fell to wondering what it would be like to be ordinary. She found herself thinking of her contemporaries, the girls she had gone to school with in England and France. Where were they now? What had they achieved with their lives? What had she achieved with hers?

She was twenty-two years old. She had done things which many other women would never dream of doing, seen things that no person should have to witness, gone to places that those girls could never even conceive of, never comprehend.

At twenty-two the girls she'd gone to school with would more than likely be working, maybe engaged, maybe married with children. And happy? Yes, possibly … probably. She found it difficult to conceive what the life of an ordinary woman of her age would be like. She'd lived in the shadows for so long now it had become part of her. She was twenty-two; by rights her life should be starting, there should be great possibilities ahead of her. But in the twilight world of the porno-movie circuit, twenty-two was getting on a bit; you no longer got star billing or first run movies and now the same rule applied to the modelling business. The women were getting younger and younger; she still had a couple of working years left, but she was aware she was being eased out by virtue of her age. All the fashion models she had worked with today had been aged eighteen and nineteen. A handful of models continued working in to their forties and fifties, but they were beautiful women, and Rianne had known for a long time that she would never be called beautiful.

When the shadows began to dip across the lawns the sprinkler system came to life, hissing across the gardens, creating dozens of tiny rainbows in the last of the sunlight. She turned back to the château. The cars were still there, so she had ordered a light salad to be sent to her room and avoided the main halls and stairs in case she met Bach or any of his guests. She was in no mood for entertaining. She showered again and changed into pink satin pyjamas and then lay on the bed watching satellite television, flicking between the channels, stopping only briefly when she picked up a Swedish or Danish porno channel, watching it critically for five minutes, noting the old tricks and the complete absence of expression or interest in the women's eyes. She finally settled on the children's channel, watching an endless series of cartoons until she fell asleep around nine.

She was vaguely aware of Bach coming into the room much later, turning off the television and pulling the covers up over her before climbing into bed beside her. She heard him sigh tiredly and he made no attempt to touch her; within minutes his breathing had deepened to sleep.

She was awake at six, bright and alert.

She sat up in bed, looking out at the cloudless blue skies, and decided that she couldn't possibly go back to sleep. Bach was lying curled on the opposite side of the bed, the silk sheets bunched into his fists as if he'd grappled with them through the night. Sliding silently out of bed, she showered briefly and dressed in a livid pink tracksuit she'd worn for an advertisement a few weeks back. Her metabolism was such that she didn't have to diet to keep her weight down, but she had been promising herself that she'd begin a regular regime of exercise. She'd start this morning; she'd jog around the grounds and enjoy the morning into the bargain.

Within five minutes, however, she decided she wasn't fit enough to jog. There was a stitch in her side and she had a feeling she was going to be sick. This was obviously something one built up to. She was bent double, hands on knees, staring at the gravel through tear-filled eyes, when she heard someone else crunching along the pathway towards her. Rubbing the palm of her hand into her eyes, she saw a tiny pair of bright yellow jogging shoes appear topped by perfectly white socks and slender, beautifully tanned legs.

"Kaho!" Rianne said in surprise, straightening slowly, pressing her hands into the small of her back.

"Miss Rianne." The Japanese woman didn't bow as she usually did, but regarded Rianne quizzically. Kaho was dressed in a white singlet and shorts, and a white headband kept her thick black hair from her eyes. She pressed the button on the chronometer on her wrist, pausing it.

"I didn't know you were over," Rianne continued. She rather liked this seemingly shy, often sad-looking Oriental woman who rarely demonstrated the enormous power she wielded within Bach's organisation. She wondered how old the woman was: somewhere between thirty and fifty, she guessed, though a twenty-year-old would have been proud of the lean body she possessed.

"Some details to be attended to," Kaho said, and then deftly changed the subject. "You are up early."

"I can remember days when I used to be going to bed at this time." Rianne breathed deeply, savouring the damp fresh morning air. "Party all night, sleep all day. What a waste."

"It is the best part of the day," Kaho murmured, "quiet, serene, still. Except in Tokyo," she added with a smile, "where it is never quiet and where serenity and stillness are found only within oneself." She smiled again, as if she were enjoying some secret joke. "I didn't know you jogged."

"I don't. And I've just discovered I can't. It's something I've always wanted to do, but could never find the time. I used to think you just climbed into a tracksuit and a pair of running shoes and off you went." She took another deep breath. "I think I'll just practice walking."

"Discipline," the Japanese woman said firmly. "Like every sport, every field of study, discipline is foremost. Come, run with me for a while." She set off with an easy regular stride, Rianne falling into rhythm beside her. "Begin easy," the woman continued, "begin by alternately walking and jogging, then gradually increase the jogging element of your exercise. And it must be regular. There is no point in killing yourself one day and doing nothing the next; that achieves nothing."

Rianne nodded, unwilling to waste any of her precious breath on an answer. She admired the way the Japanese woman could jog and continue to speak so calmly and evenly.

They had now run down along the gravelled path, swinging around close to the artificial lakes. The ornamental dolphins with their stone cherubim riders were forever frozen in the act of spitting water in high arcs, creating a delightful hissing in the quiet morning air. Kaho led the way around the fountains and into the box-hedge maze that bordered the artificial lakes. She suddenly stopped and looked at Rianne, smiling strangely. When she spoke her voice had lost much of its American-Oriental sing-song intonation and her accent was now clipped and precise, almost British.

"This is one of the few places in the château and grounds which isn't under constant supervision. The noise of the water in the fountains drowns out the microphones and the constant moistness in the air takes care of the cameras."

Rianne was staring at her blankly and Kaho laughed at her astonishment.

"Why so surprised? None of us is quite what we seem, are we?"

Rianne attempted a smile. "We all have our secrets."

Kaho took her hand and led her deep into the heart of the maze, moving confidently through the confusing walls of hedging. "I usually spend about twelve minutes in here," she said, checking the chronometer on her wrist. She pointed to an opening in the hedge. "It actually only takes me three minutes to get from one side to the other."

"What do you do with the other nine minutes?" Rianne wondered.

Kaho sank on to the soft turf. "Josef Bach owns me — just like he owns you — but the nine minutes I steal from him every day mean more to me than all the money he can offer."

Rianne sat down beside her. "What do you do when you're not here in Paris? How do you manage to steal your nine minutes then?"

"Lots of little ways."

"What did you mean when you said Bach owned you?" Rianne said softly, nervously plucking strands of grass.

"I also said he owned you," Kaho reminded her slyly.

"I know you did, but I know he owns me. I always thought you were nothing more than an employee."

"You're never just an employee with Bach. He likes to know everything about everyone. He likes to pretend he's God. Sometimes he even likes to act God." She paused before adding, "Which is exactly what he's doing to your mother."

Rianne looked at her sharply. "What is he doing to my mother?"

"Simply put, he's destroying her because she's the key that could topple two publishing companies which Bach wants. Once he possesses these, he can use them to exploit the Eastern Bloc countries while simultaneously flooding the western markets with cut-price books. It's an enormously grandiose scheme, and if it works it will make him without doubt the richest man in the world … and you can imagine he's not going to let anyone or anything stand in his way." Kaho glanced at her watch and stood up, pressing her small hands into her back. "Remember, Bach does nothing without reason … and that especially relates to you."

"I know he's cultivated me for a reason," Rianne murmured. "I just don't know the reason. But what's yours? Why are you telling me this? What's to stop me telling Bach everything you've said to me? You know I've no love for my mother."

"You are Briony Dalton's daughter. Flesh of her flesh, blood of her blood. Are you going to stand there and let him destroy her? Do you hate her so much? And before you answer, think." Her large dark eyes bored into Rianne's. "Can you say you hate her? Maybe once you did, but such grand emotions cannot be sustained. I don't think you hate her any more. I think you dislike yourself and what you've become far more. You could be reconciled if you wanted to be. But, leaving that aside, consider this: Josef Bach is hell-bent on your mother's destruction. He's tried subtle methods, he's tried straightforward bribery, corruption, and threats — the Bach trinity — and even that's failed. Your mother's been blessed with extraordinary good fortune … so Bach will be forced to play his ace card. And that's you!" She checked her watch a final time. "Come on, let's go."

Rianne grabbed her arm, turning her around. "Hang on. You can't leave it like that. You never answered my question. Why are you telling me this?"

"Because I've watched him do it too often to too many people without saying or doing anything. After a while you don't even think about it, you accept it as *normal*. Maybe I just got tired of accepting things like that as normal, maybe I just got tired of Herr Bach. When you've that much money, that much power, you stop being human." She turned away, heading towards the opening in the hedge.

Rianne raced after her. "You can't just walk away like that, you've got to be more specific."

"Read this morning's papers," Kaho said bitterly. She smiled at Rianne and jogged out of the maze, eleven minutes and forty seconds after she'd jogged in. Rianne Moriarty followed more slowly.

Chapter Seventy

Constance Park's husband had founded Park & Park Publishing in the midst of the Depression. With capital inherited from his father he had set about achieving a life-long ambition and founded his own publishing company virtually on the eve of the Wall Street crash. Overnight he had seen his personal fortune, which was close to two million dollars, wiped out.

And so they had been faced with a choice.

Sell the house or sell the business.

"Constance, we have a problem," was how Howard had so neatly put it. "Either we keep the house, which has neither growth nor earnings potential, or we keep the business, which has."

She remembered her reply to him as if it had been yesterday and the older she got the closer those balmy yesterdays seemed. "Howard, my dear, I've never really liked this house anyway."

They had sold they house — at a fraction of it's true value too — indeed, they had sold everything they possessed and lived over the offices of Park & Park Publishing, running the business themselves. Howard had some experience but she had none, other than her good sense. While her husband dealt with the finances she performed the duties of editorial director. She personally read through every manuscript that passed across her desk; she never knew what she was looking for, but she always recognised worth when she found it. Constance Park like to think that she had good taste and she bought only what she liked. When many other publishers were not accepting submissions from untried authors, Park & Park had staunchly defended the unknown author and it's yearly publication *Tabula Rasa* showcased the best of the writers they had discovered that year. Writers who first appeared in *Tabula Rasa* later achieved international prominence and recognition. They included three Pulitzer Prize winners, two Booker Prize winners and a Nobel Prize for Literature.

Howard Park's policy at that time was not to offer the author an advance — simply because the money wasn't there — but to publish the book and pay the author a slightly higher royalty than he would normally receive. He guaranteed immediate payment, not waiting until the end of the year to render accounts, which was the norm. The deal was intriguing enough to attract some of the very best of the new wave of American and European writers and as the list built, Park & Park's archives slowly became a treasure trove of the early writings of some of today's contemporary masters. The collection of manuscripts and letters alone were of inestimable value. Due to financial constraints, however, much of this vast collection of extraordinary material had never been published.

Howard Park had died in the late 1970's, happy that he had achieved a little of what he'd set out to do fifty years previously. Park & Park would never be a big press, never be a popular press, but it had never sold out on the principles he had laid down in the dark days of the Depression. It had treated its authors well and respected the estates of those who were dead. It published quality, and had a very solid and enviable reputation in that field.

Constance Park observed a proper period of mourning for her late husband. She then set about revitalising the press, moved it away from its staid and often academic leaning, dragging it screaming into the late twentieth century. She commissioned books and bought in others which Howard Park would never have even considered suitable for the exclusive Park & Park list. She began a campaign of reprinting and reissuing some of their earliest material in handsome facsimile editions.

In less than two years, Park & Park went from a forty thousand dollar profit, to a trading profit of close to one and a half million dollars.

But they still needed the big book, one that would bring the publishers into the public eye, put them in the big league, bring the name of Park & Park to international prominence. That had always been her dream, but she knew Howard would never agree, knew also that he would be terribly disappointed if she even suggested it. Constance was sure that the way to attract manuscripts was to market and sell an international best-seller.

A Woman Scorned was to be that best-seller.

She still wasn't sure how she'd got the book. It was a combination of extraordinary circumstances, a dash of good luck and two and a half million dollars, of course. She'd mortgaged just about everything she owned to buy the book, including the business, her house and most of her stocks and shares. If it failed, she was ruined — but, thank God, at least Howard wouldn't be around to see it. He had never believed in gambling, which was one of the reasons he had only ever enjoyed a moderate success. But if the book was successful, and she'd every reason to believe it would be, then her fortune and the security of Park & Park was assured.

Constance Park rarely felt her age. She would be eighty-two next birthday. She looked and felt about sixty-five, but in the last few months she had felt every one of her eighty-odd years, especially when rumours began to circulate amongst the book world and publishing trade that Briony Dalton was not going to finish the book. Her own enquiries had only confirmed the rumours: the Dalton woman was a washout, spending her time partying and enjoying the company of younger men and women. It was no wonder the book was not going to be finished. Briony Dalton simply had no time to write. She'd gone to Ireland to write her book, and then that campaign against her had started. Constance had been sure then that whatever future there had been for a Briony Dalton product had gone down the toilet. Someone out there didn't like the Queen of the Red Hot Read, and they were determined to destroy her public image.

Except that they went a little too far.

The dividing line between being in and out of favour with the public is a very fine one. And by portraying Briony Dalton as being *too* bad, public favour had turned in the opposite direction. Things began looking up. And the situation improved dramatically when Briony Dalton delivered the book. It was a bonus to discover that it was magnificent — a best-seller and no mistake — and the publicity campaign was already rolling. Suddenly everything was back on schedule.

Until the fire.

Someone — a psycho, a nut, a fanatic — had tried to kill Briony Dalton. Her secretary had been killed in the same apartment: obviously the two events were connected. Paradoxically, if anything happened to Briony Dalton it wouldn't actually hurt the sales of the book, but they would be infinitely higher if Briony were available to talk about it and promote it. And, of course, the publicity had done absolutely no harm to the book. The only thing worse than being talked about was not being talked about, she thought, paraphrasing Oscar Wilde. Anything and everything that kept Briony Dalton's name before the public until publication was good for business.

However, it was important to keep the woman safe. Why not hide her away someplace, someplace isolated but not so isolated that it was completely out of touch. And what better place than Constance Park's own home in upstate New York, deep in the heart of the country yet with every convenience, and with the advantage of being set within enclosed grounds that already boasted an elaborate security system?

Surprisingly Briony Dalton had agreed to come to the house.

Constance Park had been prepared to dislike her. She had heard stories of the author's excesses and had read accounts of her outrageous demands and her prima donna attitude, but surprisingly Briony had turned out to be a quiet, rather reserved woman who kept to her room and worked on the proofs of the book. She breakfasted at seven and began work shortly afterwards, emerging at noon for lunch and a stroll around the grounds. She returned to her room around two thirty and remained there until dinner at eight.

After a while, Constance Park arrived at the conclusion that the woman was genuinely frightened. It showed in the way she walked, the way she moved, her shoulders hunched as if she was expecting a blow, the way she started at every sound. Constance had watched her walk around the grounds; she took a different path every day and she moved quickly, taking the exercise almost as a duty.

She had been in the house for the best part of a week now and so far Briony's conversations with her had been brief almost to the point of rudeness. This morning, however, although she looked tired, her eyes deeply shadowed and red-rimmed, she seemed more relaxed.

"You didn't sleep well, my dear," the older woman said quietly, looking over her paper at Briony.

"I didn't sleep at all last night," she admitted with a smile. "But I finished proof reading *A Woman Scorned*."

Constance put down the paper and folded her hands together on the table before her. "Excellent. Are there many corrections to be made?"

Briony shrugged as she buttered her toast. "Surprisingly few. There's the odd line of text missing here and there, and there's a consistent misspelling of the main character's name. But in view of the speed with which it was set, I'm very pleased."

"I'm delighted. You know how much this book means to us. We are determined to make it a success."

"What about the jacket?"

"They arrive this morning by courier. We've commissioned six different treatments and we can make our choice from them or, indeed, if we don't like them we'll commission another six."

"Do we have the time to do that?" Briony asked.

Constance sighed. "Not really; it would be lovely to capitalise on all the publicity you're generating." She smiled ruefully. "An assassination attempt is the ultimate newspaper hype." She paused and said casually, "Have you any idea who might be out to get you?"

Briony shook her head. "Some nut I should think. I know a lot of people dislike me and my style of writing. But I didn't think anyone hated me enough to try and kill me. But I suppose there are fanatics in every walk of life. Who would have thought that someone would want to kill a pop star?"

"Do you feel safe here?"

"Yes, yes I do. You have a gorgeous home, and I don't think I've properly thanked you for allowing me to stay here. I know I've been a bit … distant, the past few days."

Constance waved aside the apology. "I know what writers are like, my dear."

"It only happens when I'm working on proofs. I find I need to give them my total concentration. And I suppose I've been a little … well, frightened isn't too strong a word. I've been frightened — *terrified* — that someone will have another go at me. You know the police no longer think that the death of my secretary was the result of a random burglary?"

"I do, but you are safe here. We're four miles from the nearest main road, the estate is completely surrounded by a ten-foot-high wall which is topped by electrified wire. And as well as the usual security arrangements, we've brought in six men from an agency in New York."

"I've seen them around the grounds," Briony murmured, looking over Constance's shoulder through the deep bay window as a guard in a tan uniform strolled past. There was a rifle slung on his shoulder. "They must be costing you a fortune."

"All good publicity, my dear. *People* magazine are going to do a photo shoot of the house and the guards. It won't appear until you've left here, of course, so there's no need to worry."

Briony sipped her coffee. "I'm sure some people think I engineered the fire."

"I haven't heard that, but it is the sort of thing Briony Dalton would do, isn't it?" she asked with a cheeky grin.

Briony found herself warming to this energetic lady. "She might have done once upon a time when she was young and foolish. But not now, I think. She's got sensible in her old age."

"She's lost none of her fire, though."

"Oh, she has," Briony said tiredly.

They finished breakfast in silence. When Briony patted her lips with her napkin and was about to stand up, Constance Park asked, "What about the next Briony Dalton book? Have you given any thought to it?"

Briony smiled. "Yes. Yes and no. The ideas began to come as I was correcting this one, fragments of plots, the obvious sequel, that sort of thing, but then I fell to thinking, wouldn't it be nice to finish with this one?. Maybe retire with what it will make me. I'm forty-six next birthday, why am I giving myself this grief?"

"You're a writer," the older woman reminded her gently. "You write. Didn't you once say somewhere in an interview that you were 'a writer, simply a writer, not an author, just a writer'? If you gave it up, what would you do?"

Briony shrugged. "Enjoy myself, I suppose."

"What were you doing before you wrote *A Woman Scorned*?" Constance asked. "But before you answer, think about it and then tell me which you enjoyed more, the partying or the actual writing of the book."

"I hated writing the book," Briony said, surprising herself, "but then I hated the false world of the parties and the dinners too. I suppose Gabrielle — my dead secretary — was responsible in a roundabout way for bringing me into that scene. I haven't been to one since she ... since she died. I've got the invitations — more than I can handle since all the furore about the book started — but I found I didn't want to go."

"And if you gave up writing, and you no longer went to parties, no longer had that life-style, what would you do then?"

Briony stared at her for a few moment, and then a smile crept across her lips. "I'd get very bored, very quickly."

"And then?"

"And then I'd start to write again."

"Give me the option on your next book."

"We'll see," Briony said warily.

Chapter Seventy-One

"Unprecedented sales," Catherine read slowly. She put down the magazine and picked up another. "A runaway best-seller." Josef Bach pushed a third across his desk towards her. "Likely to be the best-seller of the twentieth century." She read the headline and glanced up. "That's a little over the top, isn't it?"

Josef Bach stared at her with his cold, hard eyes, his thin lips drawn into a straight line. There was no trace now of the genial German or the affable country gentleman. This was the face of the real Bach, the ruthless businessman.

"Such was the hype surrounding this book that queues began to form outside bookshops before they opened in London today. It's the sort of thing which hasn't happened since readers were waiting for the new Sherlock Holmes from the *Strand* magazine or the first publication of the Morton book." His voice was clipped, measured, barely the trace of an accent audible. "Pre-publication demand in the States was so high that the initial print run of one million copies has been doubled. And this is for the hardback, remember, at twenty-nine dollars and ninety-five cents ... "

"Jesus Christ!" Greg Connors said feelingly. He was sitting beside Catherine, clearly in awe of Bach, frightened by his cold temper. He'd been doodling on a pad, and had begun to work out the figures even as Bach spoke. The totals made him forget his fear of the German. "That's ... that means she earns ... "

Josef Bach nodded coolly. "Even at the minimum royalty rate of ten per cent that comes to six million dollars. However, she would have escalating clauses built in so on the initial print run of two million copies Briony Dalton stands to make between eight and ten million dollars. That's in the States alone. And then, of course, there's the paperback sales; they should make whatever she earns out of the hardback seem like small change, and of course let us not forget the movies rights, the translation rights, the magazine serialisation rights, the television series rights, the goddam *Readers Digest Condensed Book* rights. We are no longer talking millions, we are talking tens of millions ... and all of it earned on *your* book, Mr Connors."

Greg swallowed hard and looked down at the paper again, squeezing his pen so tightly that he was afraid he would break it.

"Now there's nothing we can do about that," Bach continued, regaining his composure, as the door opened and Kaho entered carrying a tray laden with tea and coffee pots, milk, cream, brown and white sugar and three cups. He ignored her as she poured coffee for Catherine and himself, tea for Greg. "I understand the biography is finished?"

Catherine lifted a box off the floor and slid it across the marble-topped table towards Bach. "Two hundred thousand words, give or take a few. It's right up to date and includes a separate section devoted to how she came to write — or, rather, not write — *A Woman Scorned*, the massive hype surrounding the book and its extraordinary success right up to publication date." Bach opened the box, took out the spiral-bound manuscript and began flicking through it.

"It tells how she met Greg on Corfu and stole his book," Catherine continued. "There is then a separate chapter which is in the form of an interview with Greg ... page five twenty-two, I think," she added as Bach began to thumb through the pages in search of the relevant chapter. "In the appendix I have included a sample chapter from

Greg's manuscript, showing the differences between it and Briony Dalton's published book. In a second appendix, which I haven't prepared yet, I would like to include a statement from Greg sworn before the appropriate authority that the book is his. I also want to include a copy of the letter which he's sent out to the Society of Authors, *The Bookseller* magazine, *The Author* magazine, *Publisher's Weekly*, the Publishers' Association, and the Booksellers' Association."

"You say you would like to," Bach said smoothly. "Why haven't you?"

Catherine smiled icily, and for a single moment her expression was identical to Bach's. "Because I want to make sure that the existence of Greg's manuscript pre-dates Briony's."

Bach pressed the hidden switch in the arm of his chair. The door at the far end of the room opened almost immediately and Kaho reappeared. "Bring me the Townsend file," he snapped.

The small woman bowed, her face impassive, and backed from the room. When she closed the door, however, the mask faltered for a moment and something like fear flickered behind her coal-black eyes. She wondered why Bach hadn't buzzed her on the intercom … unless, of course, he'd realised that she'd kept the channel open so she could eavesdrop on the conversation. But no, if he even suspected that he would have reacted immediately … especially when it involved something so sensitive.

Her electronically coded identification pass opened both her office door and the filing cabinet. She pulled out the Townsend file, holding it almost distastefully in her slender fingers. If Townsend was involved in this, then it had to be not only shady but probably downright illegal. Kaho didn't know the full story; she had the impression that Bach had something on the young barrister, but she knew for a fact that when Bach needed a piece of legal paper, usually for a nefarious purpose, then Richard Townsend supplied it.

Kaho carried the file into Bach's office and placed it on the desk at his right hand. She took a step back and waited until he dismissed her with an imperious wave. She walked slowly from the room, turned at the doors with great dignity and bowed, even though no one was looking in her direction, but, as soon as the doors had closed behind her, she raced for her desk. Her own office door was locked behind her and the only one who could get to her was Bach, and she would hear him coming; she'd certainly have long enough to kill the intercom and return to her glowing computer screen.

Bach's voice was coming in loud and clear on the intercom. She turned the volume down until it was little more than a whisper.

Josef Bach passed across a sheaf of papers to Greg. "Here we have a deposition from Richard Townsend, barrister, swearing that you deposited a rough first draft of an unnamed book that will bear a remarkable similarity to *A Woman Scorned*." Bach looked up at Greg. "I'm afraid you're going to have to re-write your book again, young man, but making it a little cruder this time, a lot less polished. We need it to seem like a first draft. Spill coffee on it, crease it, bundle it up … whatever. Oh, and we'll need it within the next ten days. I also want you to deposit copies of the manuscripts of your other three books with him, and if you have any drafts of them give him those also." His eyes were glittering with malice. "What we're doing here is establishing that you always sent copies of your manuscripts to your legal advisor. It wouldn't do if he only had a copy of this book." Bach glanced at his notes again and lifted another page. "This is a copy of his letter to you confirming receipt of the final draft of *Fortune and Despair* … that was what you intended calling your book, wasn't it?" He handed the letter to Catherine, who read through it briefly and then passed it to Greg. "As you will no doubt notice it's dated Thursday, the sixteenth of April, which is about when you were sailing off the Ionian coast with Briony Dalton. You had obviously sent it to him just before you left Corfu. The parcel will be wrapped in Greek paper and will have Greek stamps on it."

"You're going to a lot of trouble," Greg murmured.

"There's a lot at stake here." Bach smiled. "By the way," he added, "you are suing Briony Dalton for sixty million dollars. You are also suing both the American and British publishers, the largest American bookselling chain and two of the big British wholesalers."

"I am?" Greg whispered.

"You are."

"And when do I actually do this?"

"When you sign these." Bach slid across a series of letters which Greg had `sent' to Richard Townsend. They were in sequence, outlining the case, explaining what had happened, detailing his relationship with Briony Dalton, telling how she had stolen his book. Townsend's replies, confirming that Greg Connors had lodged copies of the manuscript with him and that he would begin to institute proceedings against the author and publisher, were already signed.

Bach waited until Greg had signed the letters and then passed across a copy of a press release. "This goes out in half an hour. That's when the fun and games start."

Greg picked up the page.

Author Gregory Connors (28) has instituted legal proceedings against best-selling author Briony Dalton. In an astonishing claim, Connors, who has already published three books, maintains that Briony Dalton, whom he met on holiday on the island of Corfu, stole his book, Fortune and Despair *and passed it off as her own work,* A Woman Scorned.

But what is even more extraordinary is that Gregory Connors claims he deposited copies of his manuscripts with his solicitors prior to the publication of Briony Dalton's best-seller, and that he can prove his claims.

Experts who have examined Connors' original manuscript and Briony Dalton's book have no doubts that it is the same book.

"What happens now," Greg asked, unable to prevent the broad smile crossing his face.

"Now we make you rich and famous," Bach said.

ɷ

The only light in the room was the amber illumination from the glowing computer screen. It washed over Kaho's face, robbing it of all its soft lines, lending it a demonic cast. In contrast Rianne Moriarty's face looked almost innocent, virtually blank of any expression. Two tall glasses of orange juice on the table were blood red in the light.

"Your mother will lose everything," Kaho finished, "she will never write again. There might even be criminal charges."

"Why are you telling me this?" Rianne asked.

"Don't you want to know?"

"No ... yes ... I don't know."

"Do you hate your mother?" Kaho asked suddenly.

Rianne stared at her in surprise, thought about it and then slowly shook her head. "I don't know," she said finally. "She was never much of a mother to us."

"But she provided for you; kept a roof over your heads, ensured you had food, clothing, good schools."

"Yes. But there was no love."

"And would you rather have been loved, but lived in a hovel, gone hungry and worn rags? Would that have been all right?" Kaho's smile turned bitter. "Love is a luxury sometimes; a luxury the poor can afford to do without." She closed her eyes a moment and visibly controlled her temper, and then she said, "You told me you did what you had to do to survive. Your mother did the same. When your drunken father gave up a good job, who paid the rent, who paid for the food, who worked all the hours in a day to keep you and your brother together? Does that not count for something? Do you not feel you owe her something? Are you going to stand by and allow Bach to destroy her?"

Rianne said nothing.

"Perhaps you need a more personal motive? A little self-interest, perhaps? Why has Bach kept you around? Why has he made you a star? I know you've often wondered. Have you ever wondered why he has always presented you as Ryan Divine? Could it possibly be something to do with the fact that it allows him deniability? He can always say he didn't know who you were. He can always claim you fooled him. Tricked him. Deliberately got close to him. For what ... to do what?" She leaned forward, "You're his insurance. If anything goes wrong with the current plan and he's exposed in any way, all he has to do is to expose you. You've obviously been sent to spy on him by your mother. Possibly you even intended to attack or injure him!"

"That's ridiculous!"

"No, not ridiculous. It's the way he works."

"What do you want me to do?"

"I don't want you do to anything. I'm merely telling you what I know. After that what you do with it is entirely your own affair."

"What do you suggest I do? Should I tell my mother what's happening?"

Kaho glanced at her watch. "Oh, I fancy she already knows what's happening. I'm merely telling you to follow your conscience."

"I don't have a conscience," Rianne said with an attempt at a smile. "It was a luxury my previous employments did not allow me to have."

"Then do what you have to do to survive," Kaho said firmly. "If Bach pulls your mother down he's not going to need you; if he doesn't manage with this attempt he'll use you for whatever nefarious plan he has in mind. Either way you lose."

"Story of my life," Rianne said bitterly.

ଔ

Catherine Garrett stood naked at her bedroom window, staring out across the rolling Downs. She'd worked towards this moment for so long now; surely she should be feeling something more. Where was the euphoria — shit, where was the satisfaction? She had destroyed Briony Dalton, as she'd sworn she'd do over twenty-five years ago. She realised now that everything, the choices she'd made, both personal and career, had been directed towards this single aim. Was it right to carry a grudge thirty years? Was it even sane?

Greg came up behind her and wrapped his arms around her waist, bringing his hands up to cup her breasts. "What are you thinking?" he murmured.

"Wondering why I don't feel ... something else, something more."

"I understand. I swore I'd get even with her, you told me why I had to get even with her for my own sake, for my self-esteem, for my career. And now — beyond all my wildest thoughts — it's happening, and as well as getting my own back I'm going to be rich. But why don't I feel more?"

"Bach," Catherine said softly.

"Bach," Greg nodded.

The German had manipulated them. Each of them had been working towards achieving their own goals — which in a way they had, but their plans were secondary to Bach's. And now it looked as if he too was about to achieve his plan. They had been used; however, the fact that it had made them wealthy made it a little easier to bear. Money buys a lot of things, including principles and conscience.

ଔ

Usually the Napoleon brandy was reserved for special —
very special — occasions. Josef had drunk some when he'd
made his first million, then again when he'd reached ten
million, again when his personal assets reached fifty
million. He allowed himself a glass of the incredibly rare
liquid when he closed a major deal, or pulled off an
extraordinary coup.

But whatever coup he would pull off in the future,
whatever stroke he'd manage, none would ever match this
one. It was possibly the most complex deal he'd ever
undertaken, even though it concerned just one person. Like
all economists, his theories were concerned with the herd,
not with the mavericks. Briony Dalton was definitely a
maverick, maybe all artists were. However, this deal was
also entirely memorable in the amount of the return.
Initially, in return for a ten million dollar investment, he'd
recoup — within the first trading year — close to one
hundred million dollars. Beyond that the projections grew
a little hazy and the figures became nonsensical. Out of the
profit the Russian venture would bring he would then be
able to finance his publishing and communications empire
in the west.

And the pen was truly mightier than the sword;
nowadays, power was no longer measured in armaments
— although he had interests in those companies also — but
rather in communications and information. Whoever
controlled the flow of information controlled the free
world. And it was a very small step from controlling the
flow of information and its output to controlling — even
generating — the news and the information itself.

In a way he felt almost sorry for Briony Dalton. She'd
been the wrong person in the wrong place at the wrong
time.

But in life there were winners and losers.

Josef Bach threw back the brandy. And he'd always
been a winner.

Chapter
Seventy-Two

SCANDAL ROCKS BOOK WORLD

The book and publishing world has been shaken by an extraordinary scandal.

Previously unknown author, Gregory Connors (28), claims that Briony Dalton stole his book Fortune and Despair *and passed it off as her own book,* A Woman Scorned.

The blond haired brown-eyed writer claims he met the international author on holiday in Corfu, where they enjoyed a brief holiday romance. But the romance was to turn sour when Briony Dalton left with a copy of his manuscript.

Solicitors acting on behalf of Gregory Connors are suing Briony Dalton and her publishers for the full profits of A Woman Scorned *and substantial damages.*

A WOMAN SCORNED IS MINE, CLAIMS HORROR WRITER

Horror writer Gregory Connors (28) claims that Briony Dalton has stolen his magnum opus, Fortune and Despair *and passed it off as her book,* A Woman Scorned.

And he can prove it, too.

Solicitors acting on his behalf have begun proceedings against Briony Dalton, her publishers and distributors. A settlement could run into millions.

Briony Dalton was unavailable for comment, but a spokesperson for the American publishers of A Woman Scorned *has dismissed the allegations as absolutely nonsensical.*

Nigel Hall, Managing Director of Hall's, the British publishers, said that he was astonished at the claim, adding that to the many millions of Briony Dalton fans A Woman Scorned *was classic Dalton, with all the elements they would have come to expect.*

Sales of A Woman Scorned, *in Britain and America, have now topped two and three-quarter million copies, with many bookshops sold out of the steamy family saga.*

LIES

The Biography of Briony Dalton

By
Catherine Garrett

The shocking biography of one of the most successful novelists of all time, including exclusive interviews with the children she forgot and her jilted lover, Gregory Connors, allegedly the real author of A Woman Scorned.

Available from all good bookshops now.

Chapter
Seventy-Three

She walked in the grounds just before dawn, the trees damp and dripping with a heavy night's dew, the ground sodden beneath her feet. The silence was absolute, broken only by her passage through the trees and bushes, her own breathing. The throbbing of her heartbeat was loud in her ears.

Briony Dalton decided she liked Constance Park's house, liked the solitude, the peace, the fresh, clean air and the isolation. Especially the isolation and the security. She'd never really lived in the country before; she was a city girl, born and bred, the buzz, the taste, the smells, the hum of city life was part of her. She suddenly remembered the summer she'd stayed in Catherine's flat overlooking the cemetery in Dublin: it had been so quiet then she thought she was going to go crazy. She turned up the fur collar of her coat and shivered. She'd been convinced that things were moving around the graveyard at night. She had a particularly vivid memory of sitting before the bedroom window with the lights off, watching the shadows creep and twist and turn across the graveyard. Christ ... maybe she should be writing horror! A horror story about trees which came alive. Only she'd write it and Greg Connors would steal it, and then the circle would be complete.

Gregory Connors.

A bitter smile twisted her lips: funny how the mind played tricks on you. He was the reason she was out here so early in the morning. She had some basic decisions to make, but so far she'd successfully skirted around the subject ... only to find that it had crept up on her.

Briony found a tree stump beside the small pool that Constance called a lake and sat down on it, resting her elbows on her knees, cupping her chin in her hands, staring out across the still, flat water, a gauzy blanket of mist hanging over it, wisps of thicker fog rising upwards into the overhanging trees.

Decision time.

Nigel Hall was flying in from London later in the morning, along with his solicitor, for a meeting with Constance Park and her lawyer. A meeting had been scheduled for three in the afternoon. Constance Park hadn't been particularly forthcoming; she'd merely said that they wanted to talk to Briony and formulate a plan of campaign. Suing Greg Connors was not enough; not only would they need to destroy his credibility and his story, but they would need to get at his backers. Catherine Garrett was an obvious target — but they might have to go after the publishers of Catherine's book and the distributors; unfortunately they were the same British and American distributors who were handling Briony's book.

Anyway, everything would be sorted out later today. The old woman had stared Briony straight in the eye as she'd said it, but the writer had caught the merest hint of menace in her voice. Briony felt her heart beginning to stutter and she immediately breathed deeply, savouring the fresh damp air, concentrating on the still waters, attempting to quell the rising panic attack.

Decision time.

Briony dug the toe of her boot in the mulch and turned up a stone. She tossed the stone out across the waters watching it hit with a dull plop and then sink without trace, oily ripples spreading lazily outwards, disappearing surprisingly quickly.

Decision time.

She realised that all she was doing was delaying the inevitable, that point when she was going to have to work out her stratagem for the coming afternoon and, really, her choices were quite simple. She could admit to having stolen Greg's book, or she could categorically deny it.

Admitting it was tantamount to committing suicide. Her personal fortune — which, prior to the publication of *A Woman Scorned* had been negligible, though it was now substantial — would vanish completely along with her various assets, the houses, the antiques, the paintings. Both Park & Park and Hall's would be forced into bankruptcy with the attendant job losses and both Nigel and Constance stood to lose their personal fortunes. And even leaving all that aside, what was she going to do when all that was said and done? Who'd publish her? How would she — how *could* she — survive?

So she'd deny it. That was easier; she would stick to her original story — the best lies were always based upon a kernel of truth. She had met Greg Connors on holiday, they talked about books, they had a brief holiday fling, which ended when she returned to Ireland to finish her book. He wasn't happy with that, he wanted more, wanted her to progress his writing career, started suggesting that they would collaborate together. Eventually, she was forced to refuse any further communication from him, she didn't return his calls, nor answer his letters. Obviously these outrageous claims were his way of getting revenge.

Hold on.

Greg was supposed to have copies of earlier manuscript versions of *A Woman Scorned*. How had he got these? He'd never mentioned earlier manuscripts; she had been quite convinced that there were no earlier versions of the book. When she left him in Galway, she was convinced that she taken everything on the book that he possessed: notes, journals, copy books, rough drafts.

Briony looked deep into the water, allowing her thoughts to drift. If this were a novel how would she solve the problem? She tossed another stone into the water, following the circles to their limits, watching as they were absorbed into the leaf-strewn liquid … and a slow smile spread across her face as an idea formed, bubbling to the surface of her consciousness. She nodded slowly. She didn't examine the idea, simply let it lie there. When she wanted it she knew it would come fully formed.

Now, what else? Greg was supposed to have lodged copies of his manuscripts with some high-class London solicitor, and had letters from him to that effect.

A couple of things didn't add up there. Usually authors sent a copy of their manuscript in the registered post to themselves. As the date was clearly marked on the package, the registration was a record that on that date this particular manuscript was in existence. So if there were ever any copyright problems the parcel could be brought into court unopened as some sort of proof. So why had Greg bothered sending his manuscripts to his barrister Townsend?

And how could a three-book author, who'd received the lordly sum of seven and a half grand for his new horror novel — while on the run from the police, she suddenly remembered — afford such a high-class legal adviser? Why hadn't the same high-class legal adviser sorted out his problem with the law?

No, something didn't add up. Who was bankrolling this operation. And why? If she didn't know any better, she'd assume this was a continuation of the campaign being waged against her.

Which brought the wheel right around again. Who was backing Gregory Connors? Catherine Garrett? Possibly. Probably.

Best of friends, worst of enemies. Wasn't that how it went?

She'd been so close to Catherine. Catherine was a year and a month older than her, but they had shared everything. She remembered when her father remarried, one of his fears was that Briony wouldn't get on with Catherine, but his fears had been groundless. Whenever she had a secret to share she told Catherine, whenever she was in trouble she told Catherine, and when she needed a place to go to when she left Niall, she'd gone to Catherine for help and advice.

And how had Briony repaid that great friendship, the love that had existed between the two of them? She'd stolen her work, taken a little piece of her life without a second thought. Without a regret.

And now she'd done the same with Greg.

Only this time things weren't going to work out quite so smoothly. Whoever was backing him was powerful and wealthy. And not really concerned if they had to destroy the lives of her publishers and the hundreds of people working for them just to get her.

She stood up, brushing off the seat of her trousers, suddenly feeling chilled. She dug her hands into her pockets and turned back towards the house. It was difficult to even comprehend such hatred.

Should she be feeling some remorse for what she'd done? Was there something wrong with her because she didn't — or couldn't — feel that emotion? She'd taken Catherine's manuscript all those years ago as if it had been a gift from God. It had launched her writing career. And now, when she'd been in desperate trouble, when it looked as if she was going to lose everything, she'd met up with Greg and his manuscript. Another gift from God. Let's face it: his book hadn't been that good in any case. She'd taken his framework and fleshed it out, making it into something very special. Why, reviewers were calling it 'classic Briony Dalton.' She grinned; it made her feel as if she were a hundred and two.

In both cases she'd been the right person in the right place at the right time. She'd always said that success in life was all about seizing opportunities. Well, by God, Greg's manuscript had been an opportunity which she'd seized in both hands and run all the way with it.

And there was no way she was going to let a no-account horror writer claim the credit for her book, yes *her* book. *A Woman Scorned* was her book. He was going to have a very hard job proving otherwise.

CB

"They have a very strong case," Nigel Hall's lawyer said, looking at Briony over the rim of his glasses, eyes pale grey and watery. He was a grey, unremarkable man with a serpent's steady gaze in a three-piece suit, and she hadn't even bothered to remember his name.

"They claim they have proof," Constance Park's lawyer added, smiling genially, his eyes almost disappearing behind the rolls of fat. He was an enormously stout man with a strong Southern accent. He wore a light linen suit and, with the exception of his eyes — which were equally cold and calculating — he was the complete opposite of the English lawyer.

Briony Dalton's lips turned up in a polite facsimile of a smile. She was dressed severely in a tweed suit over a stone-coloured blouse, an ornate Celtic-style brooch on her left lapel matching her earrings. Her hair was pulled back off her face and she wore the minimum of make-up. She had deliberately accentuated her age, portraying an image of solid respectability. Not the sort of person who would stoop to stealing someone else's book; not the sort of person who needed to.

They were sitting in Constance Park's dining room with it's huge bay windows looking out over the woodland. Briony had deliberately chosen a seat with its back to the window so her face would be more or less in shadow. Constance and her lawyer sat on her right side, while Nigel Hall and the small reptilian Englishman sat on her left. The smoothly polished table was covered with legal documents and photocopies of letters; both men, she noted, had copies of the English and American editions of *A Woman Scorned*.

"Do we know who is backing Mr Connors?" Briony asked, ignoring the implied questions.

"Not yet," the Englishman said. "All correspondence has come through Richard Townsend."

"Tell me about this Townsend," Briony said, fixing him with her dark, intense stare. "What sort of man is he?"

The Englishman gave a tiny movement that might have been a shrug. "Young, ambitious." He made the two words sound like crimes in themselves.

"I believe there have been questions asked about his professional conduct," Briony said, working a hunch. She knew absolutely nothing about Townsend.

The watery eyes blinked rapidly. "Well, yes; the Bar Council has had occasion to reprimand him for his, ahem, his eagerness."

"And is he expensive?"

"His fees would be commensurate with his talent, his experience."

"Is he expensive?" Briony repeated firmly.

"His charges would be of the type likely to ensure that his clients came from the wealthier classes." He frowned. "But I really don't see the point."

The American lawyer leaned forward. "I think the little lady is wondering how this Gregory Connors, who's never held down a real job in his life, came to afford someone like your Townsend."

"Exactly," Briony favoured him with a smile.

The big American consulted a maroon, leather-covered notebook. "Says here," he drawled, "that he's living with the lady writer, Catherine Garrett, the one who did that biography of you. Nasty biography," he added, letting her know that he'd read it.

"She's my step-sister. There's no love lost between us. Over the years she has frequently attacked me in the press; that will be a matter of record. She has always been jealous of my success and has used every opportunity to vilify me. Again, all of this is a matter of record. Possibly the success of *A Woman Scorned* has unhinged her and made her concoct this scheme with her boyfriend."

The small Englishman licked his lips with a grey tongue. "Tell us about your relationship with Mr Connors," he suggested smoothly.

Briony turned to stare at him, waiting until she saw the first beads of sweat appear on his lined forehead. She spoke slowly and distinctly, choosing her words with care. "I met him on holiday. I was lonely, upset after the death of my secretary. I suppose I was looking for companionship. We were both writers — or at least he claimed he was. What would be more natural than we should have ended up together for a couple of weeks?"

Constance Park raised her head. "Was he working on a book then?"

"He told me he was, but I never saw any of it."

"Were you working on yours?"

"I was. I'd sit on the beach every morning or on the veranda of my villa with my portable computer and try and hammer out a chapter a day."

"And Connors was aware of this?" Constance pressed.

Briony bit the inside of her cheek to prevent herself from smiling. "He was. He was fascinated by the computer; said he was going to get one for himself for his own writing." She allowed herself a tight, bitter smile. "I even showed him how to use my machine." She looked from face to face, gauging their reactions. Constance and Nigel desperately wanted to believe her; she thought, and the American lawyer was reasonably well disposed towards her, while the Englishman simply didn't care. "As you know my villa was fire-bombed while I was on Corfu, and shortly after that my portable computer was stolen. Greg told me the two men who bombed my villa did it, but I never saw those men and I never saw my computer again."

"What was on the computer?" Nigel Hall asked, barely able to suppress his sudden excitement. He could see where this was leading.

"The first and second drafts of *A Woman Scorned*," Briony said very quietly.

"Is there any record of any of this happening?" the American lawyer asked, looking at his English counterpart. Both men had pens in their hands now.

"I reported the theft of the computer some time in April, when we reached Crete. My insurance company would have a record of it, I'm sure."

"Let me get this right, Miss Dalton," the English solicitor said slowly, "because this — very obviously — could have a major bearing on our case." He glanced down at the notes he'd been taking as she'd spoken. "You write all your books on a computer?" He glanced up and she nodded impatiently. "Your computer, bearing the notes and earlier versions of *A Woman Scorned*, was stolen, and Mr Connors was present when this occurred?"

She nodded again. "He claimed he saw it happen. I used him as a witness on the insurance claim."

"Would it be possible for him to create bogus versions of your book in various rough, unfinished states if he possessed this computer?"

"Of course."

"And how were you able to continue with your final version of the book?"

"I had a copy on disk."

"I see," he murmured, and then said to the American, "There is certainly room for thought here; we can now dispute Connors' contention that the book is his."

"There is still the matter of the legal papers," the American reminded him, ignoring everyone else in the room.

"I'll have someone in London look into it." He looked at Constance Park and Nigel Hall. "I'm delighted we've had the opportunity to discuss this. I'm certainly happier now than I was coming here and, on balance, I'd say we have a good case. Everything is on our side. We have an author with a track record as opposed to a hack; and we can successfully demolish the previous versions of the manuscript. That was worrying me," he added with a smile. He shuffled his papers together and stood up.

Nigel Hall came around the table and, grabbing Briony's hand, shook it quickly and then kissed her on the cheek. "You must forgive us for being so cautious, such nonsense, of course, but you don't know how much is at stake here."

"I do," she said. "And look on the bright side: think of all the free publicity."

Constance Park also came around the table to stand before Briony. The old woman's grey eyes bored into Briony's, making her own assessment, reaching her own conclusions. Briony attempted a laugh. "You do believe me, don't you?"

"I have to," Constance said softly. "I've no choice."

Chapter
Seventy-Four

Josef Bach rolled over in the bed and propped himself up on his elbow, gazed down at the woman beside him. Asleep, with the tension gone from her shoulders and neck, her forehead smooth, her skin relaxed, lips slightly parted, Rianne Moriarty seemed almost like a child. She wasn't beautiful, but she had character and intelligence, and it showed in her eyes, her expression, her carriage. She appeared to know instinctively when he wanted her around, and again when she wasn't needed. She was also able to sense his moods during lovemaking, being submissive when he felt dominant and dominant in turn when he simply felt like lying there.

He'd broken a rule with her — he seemed to be losing all his old values — he had allowed her to stay far too long with him, allowed her to get too close to him. He didn't love her — God forbid! — but he did feel something for her, a fondness, the same sort of feeling you'd have for a pet.

It would be a shame to have to destroy her.

Bach swung his legs out of bed and padded naked into the bathroom. One wall of the long broad bathroom was entirely glass and he stopped to admire himself in the mirror. He patted his flat, hard stomach and then ran his hands through his shock of snow-white hair, pulling it back off his high forehead. He thought he looked good, felt good too for a man of his age. He stepped into the shower and turned the water on as hot as he could bear. Resting the palms of his hands against the cold marble walls of the shower cubicle, he bent his head beneath the water. He squeezed his eyes shut as the drumming sound completely enfolded him. This was one of the few times in the course of a day that he would be alone, guaranteed no interruptions, no calls, no demands made on him, no decisions to be made. He simply allowed himself time to think.

The situation with Dalton had got out of control.

And now he was beginning to feel just a little too exposed for comfort. Usually when he operated he did it alone, or passed on orders through layers of subordinates so if there was any heat they would take the blame. But this situation was unique and too many people had come to learn of his personal involvement with the Briony Dalton situation.

Greg Connors and Catherine Garrett.

These two knew more than anyone else; these two could do him the most damage. They had outlived their usefulness. The Garrett woman had written her book, Connors had substantiated her claims; that ball was up and running and it would be interesting to see where it dropped. Unfortunately, while it was still running, the level of publicity it was generating for the book was phenomenal, and suddenly both companies, Hall's and Park & Park, were showing short-term profits that effectively made a takeover difficult, if not down-right impossible. But he still needed the companies. He had made commitments both in time and money to his Russian contacts; he'd signed contracts and was already owner and part-owner of half a dozen Russian publishing houses. These contracts would need to be serviced, money would have to be found to pay off the contracts, and then he'd have to find something for the companies to start publishing to begin recouping the money he'd spent. He needed Hall's and Park & Park more than ever now.

He turned the water from scalding to chill and stood gasping with the shock to his system. He was going to give himself a heart attack one of these days with that trick.

He still had Rianne Moriarty: that was a card he hadn't used yet.

He flipped the water back to hot, feeling it score its way down his back. He'd picked her up as insurance with no real plan in mind. He had thought that someone with her sordid background should prove useful, indeed would prove useful if had been trying to blackmail someone who was clean and upstanding with a reputation to preserve. Unfortunately Briony Dalton was neither clean nor upstanding and had no reputation to preserve. However, the girl remained an option. He could give her up to the press: "Best-selling author's daughter in porno movie scandal ... "

Bach shook his head. That would probably only sell more books. Rianne could have an accident ... but that, too, got him nowhere. He tilted his head to one side, considering. Briony Dalton could have an accident but, again, that got him nowhere.

So.

So back to basics then. When he was in Germany during the war, life had been hard but simple. He had to find enough food to survive. End of story. He often applied the same process to business. State your objective and then achieve it.

Destroy Briony Dalton.

No.

Destroy Briony Dalton's publishers; destroying Briony Dalton was a secondary but necessary part of that process. The huge profits they had made out of *A Woman Scorned* had to be wiped out. So they were back to Gregory Connors suing her for theft, breach of copyright, plagiarism, whatever.

Bach soaped himself thoughtfully, the scent of lavender heavy and cloying in the warm moist air.

Assume Briony Dalton was guilty of having stolen Connors book — and to be perfectly honest he hadn't actually thought about it, nor did he care one way or another — and assume she felt things were moving against her. What would she do?

If she were guilty, she'd strike at Connors.

How?

Josef Bach stopped suddenly, the smile lighting up his face. He took a deep breath and began to hum softly to himself.

Simple, neat and so, so dramatic.

There was a shape on the other side of the steamed-up glass, and then Rianne Moriarty peered in over the top of the shower stall. Without a word Bach opened the door and she slipped inside. She gasped with the sting of the hot water. Bach turned it down a few notches and drew Rianne in under the shower, pressing his lips to hers, holding tightly to her forearms, the wiry grey hair across his chest rasping against her nipples, the touch like a caress, arousing her. The water ran against their faces, plastering Rianne's short dark hair against her head. She raised her hands, pushing it back off her face, blinking water from her eyes. "You're in good form this morning."

"Aaah yes," he mumbled, drawing the back of his hand across his lips. He threw his head back, shaking water from his mane of snow-white hair. "There has been a particular business problem bothering me recently."

"I'd noticed you were a little distracted lately. That's why I kept out of your way. I knew when you had sorted it out you would be back to your old self again."

"Well, I think I may have sorted it out, as you put it." Bach kissed her again, running his hands down her back, tracing her spine. He was aroused now, his erection hard against her thigh, but he wouldn't make love to her, not now. That was another habit of a lifetime. He'd discovered early on in his career that if he lost that sexual tension, that important energy in the morning, then he'd feel tired and listless for the rest of the day. No, far better to keep the tension, feel the energy pulse through his veins. But that didn't mean that he couldn't indulge himself a little.

He brought his hands around, across the woman's flat belly and up to cup her breasts.

"You know me," he said suddenly, surprising her.

Rianne looked at him, puzzled.

"You know my moods, my humours, don't you?"

She nodded. "I think I do, but then I don't really know you at all. I only see what you want me to see."

"And you're clever too," Bach continued, his thumbs flat against her nipples, feeling them harden beneath his blunt fingers. "There are people who think they know me because they know an aspect of me."

Rianne looked up into the man's cold blue eyes. "I don't think anyone could ever know you. I'm not even sure if you know yourself."

Bach's hands now moved up to caress the column of Rianne's throat. "Do you love me, Rianne Moriarty?" he asked quietly, his voice barely audible above the thunder of the water in the enclosed space.

Rianne stared into his eyes, seeing something there, something she didn't think she had ever seen before, a wanting, a needing, perhaps even a fear. What answer did he want to hear: a lie or the truth? Finally, she settled for the truth.

"I … I think I'm too frightened of you to allow myself to love you."

Bach pushed her away, holding her at arm's length, while he snapped off the water. In the sudden silence every sound seemed magnified, his rasping breath thunderous.

"Why do you fear me?" he asked, sounding genuinely puzzled. "What have I ever done to warrant such fear?"

Rianne tried a smile. Maybe she should have lied to him, told him she doted on him, maybe that was what he wanted to hear. "You've been nothing but kindness itself to me. I could never even begin to thank you for all you've done. You've give me life and hope when I had none. You've given me a future. But is there any future for us together? A long-term future. Do I feature in your plans?" she wondered.

Josef Bach drew her cold, damp body close to his and hugged her. "Oh, Rianne! Did you think I was just going to throw you out like some old piece of clothing, eh? Stupid girl. You're special, very special. I've spent a fortune giving you a career; I have invested in you, if you want to call it that. Do you think I'd do all that and then simply let you go?"

"I don't … I'm not sure what I thought," Rianne said, genuinely puzzled now.

He could feel himself hardening again, feel the strength flowing through him. "Rest assured: you feature in my future plans. Prominently!"

Bach reached over and turned the water on full blast, the sound thunderous, the needle spray thrumming against their skins.

And Bach, his head resting against Rianne's, nodded slightly. Yes, yes, yes. She really did feature in his future plans.

Briony Dalton *would* strike at Gregory Connors … using the daughter she'd planted in Bach's employ as her tool!

Chapter
Seventy-Five

Briony Dalton sat down at the portable computer and opened the lid, bringing up the screen. She was reaching around behind it to turn on the power when there was a knock on her door.

"It's open," she called. She pressed the switch and there was an ascending whine as the machine powered up and the screen flickered to life.

"I didn't mean to disturb you," Constance Park said, standing in the doorway.

"Come in. You haven't disturbed me. I was just … " Briony smiled. "I was just sitting here looking out the window at the trees, dripping in the rain, looking sad and neglected, when I had the idea for a book." She shook her head. "And people ask me where I get my ideas from. If I told them the truth, they'd think I was mad."

"No, they wouldn't. They'd just say you were a writer," Constance said, coming in and closing the door. She crossed the room and sank down into an easy chair almost directly behind Briony. "Work away, don't let me disturb you. Tell me about this idea."

Briony turned back to the computer and waved her arms vaguely. "I haven't sorted it out in my own mind yet, but it'll be something to do with a patch of land, a couple of acres, a field or something. I'll tell the story of that land down through the ages and the various families who have lived there. A big historical novel. I haven't done a big historical novel for a while." She stopped, and then said slowly, "Maybe the heroine could be reincarnated each time. No," She shook her head. "Too clichéd. Anyway, I'll see what comes out." She glanced over her shoulder at Constance. "The new Briony Dalton novel will have to be something spectacular to keep up with *A Woman Scorned*."

"I'm sure you could put your name to the New York telephone directory and it would sell," Constance said, her voice sounding tired.

Briony turned to look at her. Usually the old lady was a bundle of energy and enthusiasm. "Are you all right?"

"I'm a little weary," Constance admitted. "It's been rather hectic over the past few months, and now there's this court case. What a hornet's nest that's stirred up. There is a lot of media interest and they've practically besieged our offices. I've told them you are resting and I don't know where you are. There's been a lot of enquiries about your next book from various publishers, looking for the rights or the option. You'll have to think about an agent now. You know you can have your pick."

"I know."

"We've even started getting letters in the office from the public looking for the sequel. Have you given that any thought?"

"Some. I've a couple of ideas for two different sequels — a historical series relating some of the background, and a contemporary sequel which more or less continues the story. The historical series runs to at least three volumes; the contemporary novel comes out at one very big book or possibly two."

"Both of those sound excellent ideas. I would suggest the contemporary novel first. Make it one large book, roughly the same size as the present novel. We could try and schedule it for hardback publication at the same time as the paperback of *A Woman Scorned* comes out. You will, of course, give me the first option on your next book, won't you? Oh, and you did steal that book from that boy, didn't you?"

It took a few moments to sink in, and Briony Dalton fixed her face in a mask of indignation … which faltered before the old woman's implacable stare. "I ... I must say I'm surprised at you ... as if I would ... I mean, the very thought of it ... it's just preposterous!" she blustered.

"No, not so preposterous," Constance Park said softly. "Let me tell you what I think," she said, watching Briony closely. "But first let me tell you what I know. I know Briony Dalton was having trouble with her new book, all the trade knew that. There was some speculation that if she didn't deliver then Park & Park and Hall's in Britain would go up for sale. We've had a couple of approaches in the past and the wolves would come around again. Oh, don't look so surprised, my dear. I know we're small — and that's why I'm surprised we even got your book in the first place — but we have a superb backlist of authors. They were nothing when they initially signed with us all those years ago, but now some of them are household names. Someone with money could exploit those names and their works and make themselves a fortune. I am very aware of that, because I wanted to do it myself!"

"So what happens?

"Briony Dalton is under serious pressure to finish her book, but there are constant interruptions so she runs away to Ireland, but that's not much better because there are still interruptions. Why, it's almost as if someone had organised a campaign again her, each move designed to prevent her working on her book and finishing on time." Constance Park nodded, no trace of a smile on her face now. "I've been watching your career closely over the past year and a half, Briony Dalton. I've a good idea what you went through; and if it's any consolation I went through it with you. I felt every delay, I shared your frustration, your anguish. I had as much to lose as you did.

"I think your secretary was killed on purpose. But I don't think the attack was aimed at you; at that stage it was no secret that you were in Dublin. I think your secretary was killed as a way of unsettling you even further.

"So you went off to Corfu and you met a handsome young writer. But you didn't use your real name. Why? I suppose because you were simply frightened. You were lonely, scared and alone, he was young, handsome and available. And then he helped you and of course you felt grateful; what should be more natural than you should want to help him in turn, in the only way you knew how: by working on his book for him?"

Briony opened her mouth to speak, but the old woman forged ahead, ignoring her. The menace in her voice was almost palpable.

"At what point did you start thinking of it as yours, Briony? When did that writer's mind of yours begin working out all the possibilities? You had in your hand a completed manuscript, close enough to the outline of your own book, certainly close enough to be passed off as your own with a bit of work. It would solve all your problems, wouldn't it? And who were people going to believe — you or some unknown writer?

"The only problem was that the people who wanted to prevent you writing the book in the first place would be none too pleased to suddenly find you with the book already complete. So they picked up Gregory Connors and backed him in his claim, maybe even encouraged him to make the claim in the first place. He was introduced to Catherine Garrett, who no doubt tutored him in all the proper things to say and do." She stopped and added, almost viciously. "Do you know they're lovers now? It's hardly surprising, though is it? You and she were always very close. Your interests always ran along the same lines."

"Stop it," Briony whispered.

"What's the next stage?" The old woman smiled sadly. "The book is now out in the shops. What else can be done, except destroy Briony Dalton's credibility by exposing her as a liar and a thief? A biography is published exposing Connors' claims, but unfortunately even this plan backfires, because the resultant publicity hypes the book to international best-sellerdom.

"And where does it end up?

"It ends here with the lawyers arguing about it. By the way," she added sarcastically, "I loved the bit about the stolen computer. That was pure genius. It cut the legs out from under Connors' argument."

"I'm glad you liked it," Briony said. She turned back to the machine and switched it off, listening to the descending whine; she didn't think she was going to get any work done today. She could see Constance Park's image reflected in the screen of the computer. "It wasn't until we got back to Ireland that I began to think about stealing the work," she said abruptly. "Although I'll freely admit I had begun to think about it as being mine for a long time before that."

"But do you know what the terrible thing is?" Constance Park continued as if she hadn't heard Briony. "I wish I had the strength of will, the strength of character, the guts, to damn you to hell! It took Howard and myself all our lives to build up this company, and while we didn't have much we had integrity and we had scruples. We've published hundreds of titles — thousands — and yet you've probably destroyed everything we achieved, everything we struggled for, with your one lousy book. I wish I could throw it back at you. I wish I could sue you. But I can't. Because I need the money; the company needs the money. Your book has saved us from ruin; the same book can just as easily destroy us."

Briony broke the long silence that followed. "I can't say I'm sorry, because I'm not," she said, surprisingly calmly. "I did what I had to do. I'll not deny that I'd do it again if I had to." She turned to look at Constance. "And if you're so upset about it, then go to the press, tell them I admitted it, see what happens then!" she added defiantly.

"I lose everything," Constance Park said very quietly. "*Everything*. The publishing company, this house, all the profits from your book, and it will probably take every cent I have just to pay off the legal bills. And at my age what am I going to do?"

Briony smiled wolfishly. "But I'll bet you'll buy the sequel to *A Woman Scorned* if it was offered to you."

Constance Park's face became as hard as stone, her eyes cold, pitiless, abruptly displaying the ruthlessness that had kept the business running through the lean years. "Oh, but we're not going to buy the sequel to *A Woman Scorned*."

Briony looked at her uncomprehendingly.

"You're going to give it to me," Constance Park said. "I'm sure the deal you did with Park & Park eighteen months ago was for a two-book deal."

Both women came to their feet at the same time, Briony white-faced, rigid, Constance suddenly smiling, relaxed. "I'll have the revised contract drawn up immediately." She turned towards the door and stopped with her hand on the handle. "It would be nice to have the sequel within six months."

"You can't do this."

"Why? Give me a reason: because it's wrong, illegal, immoral? Come now: isn't this the sort of thing you'd do if the roles were reversed."

Briony took a deep breath. Finally, she nodded. "Probably."

"What was it you said? Ah yes, well, let me paraphrase I'm doing what I have to do to survive."

"The sequel is worth at least three million dollars," Briony said.

"I'm sure it is, more probably if it went on the open market. I'll offer you the same royalty terms, but no advance."

"This is blackmail."

"Of course it is. But there's nothing you can do about it, my dear. We're both in this together."

"You're a cold-hearted bitch!" Briony snapped.

"That makes two of us, my dear!" Constance Park said tiredly.

Chapter Seventy-Six

Richard Townsend had made his reputation with two spectacular rape trials; in both cases patently guilty men had walked from the courtroom, freed on technicalities.

The tabloids had had a field day with the young, almost effeminately handsome and flamboyant barrister, who favoured Edwardian frock-coats and lurid waistcoats. The lifestyle he courted and led was widely reported. He had been reprimanded on several occasions by the Bar Council for unbecoming conduct and his clientele tended to reflect the type of publicity he received.

He had actually been attempting to reform his lifestyle and had started to refuse particularly unsavoury clients when he'd had an unfortunate accident ... with a pretty young woman named Tizzy and some very pure heroin.

Townsend had known the woman casually for a couple of weeks; they'd gone partying together and although he knew she used coke and smoked a little grass he'd no idea she was into heavier stuff. She ended up dead in the back of his Mercedes, a needle sticking out of her arm and several ounces of white powder scattered over the back seat.

And when you've got a dead body in your car you discover there are not many friends you can turn to. Going to the police with the truth was out of the question — they had little love for him, he had ensured that too many guilty men had walked free — and besides the publicity would ruin him. He might even be struck off.

So what was the alternative? The alternative was to turn to a guy on a manslaughter charge he'd been able to get off on a legal technicality, inadmissible evidence, even though the case against him was cast iron. Townsend figured that if anyone knew what to do with a body, he would. As it happened he did, and he was only too delighted to do a favour for the man who'd saved him from spending at least eight years at Her Majesty's pleasure. He arrived an hour after Townsend had phoned, took the keys of the Mercedes and drove it away. The following morning the car was back in Townsend's driveway and that evening, he read in the newspaper that the girl's naked body had turned up in a squat in Soho. The squat was well-known as a shooting gallery where junkies and pushers met to score and shoot up.

Two days later Townsend got a call from Josef Bach's secretary, making an appointment for Townsend to come and visit. You didn't make an appointment with Bach, he made the appointment for you to see him. Richard Townsend had gone in convinced that he'd just won himself one of the wealthiest clients in the world. Instead, as the young lawyer crossed the floor, hand outstretched, Bach's first words to him were, "I own you now."

And he had the evidence: a dozen ten-by-eight grainy black and white photographs showing Tizzy in Townsend's car ... Tizzy with a needle in her arm, white powder all over the back of Townsend's car ... Townsend looking into the car, pointing at the body ... the car being driven away as Townsend watched ... the naked body being carried from Townsend's car and dumped against a scabrous wall. There were shots of Townsend in a car park handing over a sealed envelope ... the envelope being opened, displaying the money inside...two men shaking hands. There was also a video of the cash being handed over; it showed a tight tracking shot of the white envelope from the moment it changed hands to the moment it was opened. Bach had shown this to Townsend, and then said simply, "Never seal the envelope; it proves there was money in it when you passed it across. Never pay the person directly, always leave it where it can be picked up." His smile had been glacial. "But the golden rule is never get others to do what you can do yourself unless you trust them implicitly, or you own them."

But Josef Bach had not been unreasonable with Townsend. Occasionally he asked for documents to be pre-dated and to prepare legal-looking documents, which were otherwise worthless. He had never asked Townsend to act for him.

Until now.

"It will be a very difficult case," the young man said, staring at the German over the rim of the half-glasses he affected.

"Explain it to me," Bach said pleasantly.

Richard Townsend sat back in the uncomfortable chair and crossed his legs. He wore a Harris tweed three-piece suit that contrasted sharply with his jet-black hair worn slicked back off his face and tied in a short pony-tail at the nape of his neck. His smile was perfect and practised. "One of the difficult problems we have here is client profile. Ours has none, Dalton has it all."

"She is a woman of loose morals," Bach suggested.

"Not germane to this case. Loose morals do not necessarily indicate that one is a thief, a fraud, a charlatan. That's a different matter. Dalton's counsel will undoubtedly bring out a score of witnesses who will swear to the woman's good character and her ability as a writer. What we are trying to establish here is the ownership of the book. They will line up critics, fellow writers, professors of literature, of English, experts in grammar and syntax, all of whom will attest that the book is pure Briony Dalton. Of course, we can have the same, but unfortunately Mr Connors has not written enough for a similar assessment to be made, and he has certainly never written anything like this in order for us or our experts to make a valid comparison." He saw Bach's usually impassive face begin to turn red and he added hurriedly, "I'm only telling you this so you will know what you're up against." He pulled off his wire-framed glasses and polished them nervously with a silk handkerchief. When he looked up again Bach was no longer glaring at him.

"Now, our ace is the fact that we can `prove' Connors sent me copies of his manuscripts in the past. They will undoubtedly question that: we're not dealing with fools here. They will ask how I came to know him, and how he came to be one of my clients; my fees are not cheap, you know."

"I know," Bach growled, never having paid Townsend any fees. "Say you're old friends, that you go back a long way together."

"I cannot," Townsend said softly. "He's been writing for nearly three years; I've only been in chambers for two. He also spent a lot of time abroad before that, so the chances of us knowing each other in the past is slim."

Bach swore softly in German. Why was it that everything associated with this Dalton women was complicated? She was blessed by God, or maybe he was cursed by the devil. He was beginning to suspect it was the latter. Townsend went on:

"We let the people acting for Park & Park and Hall's know that we had copies of *A Woman Scorned* in manuscript. We thought this might panic them into dumping Briony Dalton or arriving at an out-of-court settlement. It did neither, which leads me to suspect that they may have found a way to counter that argument."

"So we have no case?" Bach said simply.

"If they can counter that argument, or at least throw some doubt on it, then no."

"And your advice then?"

"Not to proceed under these circumstances."

"I am committed."

"I can only advise you that you will in all probability lose, with costs awarded against you."

"I am committed," Bach repeated.

"Then dissociate yourself from Connors."

"There is no association between us." Bach smiled thinly. "You should know that. When he falls, he falls alone."

"Do you want to think this over?" Townsend asked.

"With whom? You know there's no one else but me. No, I want you to proceed; do everything and anything you have to do and make it dirty, sling some mud at Briony Dalton. Some of it is sure to stick."

"I don't think it will make much difference."

"Delay as long as you can; damage her as much as possible."

"Are you not just giving them free publicity?"

Bach sank back into the dark leather chair, fingers steepled before his face. "The same publicity should help Catherine's book," he said crisply.

Richard Townsend recognised from the tone of voice that the interview was at an end and stood up, straightening the crease in his trousers. He gathered together the bundle of papers he'd spread out on Bach's desk and slipped them into his pigskin briefcase. "What is my budget?" he asked deferentially.

"Whatever you need." Bach glanced up from beneath bushy eyebrows. "You don't have to be told how grateful I would be if we won this case." He paused and then added, "I'll contact you when I need you." He swung away in the leather chair, and gazed out over the City of London. Reflected in the glass, he saw Townsend make a face and move quickly towards the door. When he'd left the room Bach stood up and approached the windows, his white suit reflecting the late afternoon sunlight. He had an office like this in many of the world's capital cities; it amused him to think that a boy who came from nothing could look down over millions of people. He was wealthy enough to control the lives of many of those millions, decisions he made affected them all in one way or another. There were others like him — the decision makers, the power brokers, whose decisions could affect the world — but they were mostly corporations and governments. There were few individuals like himself. He lifted his hands looking at the blunt, well-manicured fingers. He held the reins of so much power...and yet he couldn't sort out this Briony Dalton problem.

When he had first conceived the idea of buying Park & Park and Hall's and exploiting their backlists he had made tentative approaches to buy the publishers outright, which had been rebuffed. Both companies were family owned and operated, with a tradition behind them. However, both companies were in financial straits. He had coolly analysed the situation and decided that they needed to be put under more pressure, and out of that simple premise the whole deal with Briony Dalton had been born. He'd contacted Terri Fierstein and, for a sizeable fee, she had made all the arrangements, steering the Briony Dalton book towards Hall's and Park & Park even though she could have got a better deal for her client elsewhere. Once the contracts had been signed it was simply a matter of ensuring that the author didn't complete the book. All in all, it had taken nearly two years to come to this stage, but time hadn't been of the essence when he'd first conceived the plan. Now, with the liberalisation of the Soviet Union and the sudden rush of western businesses to invest in and exploit its vast natural and human resources, time had become a major factor, especially now that he'd signed contracts and made promises, committed vast amounts to the Russian project. Josef Bach smiled bitterly. If this failed it could conceivably topple him.

Why had he taken the soft option? He'd never taken the easy path before in his life. He firmly believed that there was nothing for nothing in this world, and that something worth having was worth working for. There were other options, other ways he could have secured the companies; but he'd opted for this way because it had seemed the simplest one. All he had to do was to set the wheels in motion and then forget about it.

Bach hammered on the toughened glass with his clenched fists, making it boom dully.

He was getting old, soft. But not stupid. There were still a couple of choices left; no, he corrected himself, at this stage he had but one alternative, one last chance. It was the idea he'd had in the shower.

He turned back to his desk, the leather chair sighing as he slumped into it. From the bottom drawer of his desk he lifted out his secure phone, with it's completely blank face, the buttons bare. He spent five minutes working through the ramifications of what he was about to do, it's implications, not only to the situation but also to himself. There was some element of risk; he was exposing himself, leaving another loose end that would have to be tidied up eventually. Unfortunately, he had no choice. This was no longer a business decision, this was for his survival.

He dialled the New York number from memory.

Chapter
Seventy-Seven

He was supposed to be some big-name American photographer, but Rianne didn't think she had ever heard his name before.

According to Josef, who had arranged everything as usual, the man, Valdez, had seen some of the work she'd done for *Playboy* in the States and for *Penthouse* in England and had liked it. Bach had added that the man was aware of her porno movies.

Valdez had decided he wanted to shoot Rianne in a raunchy soft-core action set. The pictures would appear in some of the less well known American and South American Spanish-language magazines.

In return he was offering a five hundred thousand dollar fee.

"You know if I do this stuff I'll never work for any of the legitimate magazines again. It's like a page-three girl who does full frontal: she'll never be a page-three again. Once you start going down market in this game you don't go back up again."

"You did," Bach reminded her. He was sitting in the recliner alongside the rooftop swimming pool in his London office. The whole roof was encased in glass, the temperature and humidity carefully controlled to what Rianne called `Sahara Desert temperatures.' Banks of exotic flora surrounded the pool, adding to the moisture and odours in the air, adding to the illusion of a tropical rain forest.

Rianne Moriarty was naked, lying flat on the rounded cobblestones that bordered the pool, one hand trailing in the tepid water. She deliberately rolled over on her stomach and propped herself up on her elbows to look at him, attempting to provoke a reaction.

"Do you think I should do it?"

He shrugged. He was wearing a pair of plain white Bermuda shorts that emphasised his tan. *The Financial Times* and *The New York Times* lay neatly folded and unopened by his chair.

"You've always wanted to be financially independent of me," he said, without opening his eyes, "you've told me that yourself. This job, a single day's work, makes you half a million dollars richer. It will bring your personal fortune close to one and three-quarter million dollars." His eyes opened, bright blue and ingenuous. They moved up and down her body, lingering on the swell of her breasts, her smoothly rounded buttocks. He felt himself stirring and concentrated on her face. "I've told you before, though, that I'll look after you. You don't have to work."

"But I want to," she protested. "I don't want it to seem as if I'm living off you."

"You're not."

"I feel as if I am."

"I've told you before; you can have anything you want. Just ask."

"I know that," she sighed, "but you just don't see it, do you? I need to work, for my own self-esteem if nothing else."

"You don't want to think yourself a whore," Bach said.

"I know what I am."

"You're not a whore," Bach said firmly.

Rianne met his gaze squarely for a moment and then she glanced into the sparkling water. "Tell me about this photographer," she said.

"I know very little about him. I've seen a portfolio of his work; it looked very good to me. He has the usual references, the usual credits. Well thought of, independent, freelance. He's offering the standard contract with full picture approval."

Rianne nodded. She wasn't going to allow any pictures to be published which might be harmful to her career. Crazy, wasn't it? She'd spent years in the porno movie business doing everything imaginable in every imaginable position, and now here she was concerned about a couple of reasonably `respectable' nude shots.

"I'll do it," she said.

"I'll make the arrangements," Bach said quietly, picking up his newspaper and opening it to hide the smile that twisted his lips.

൦ഃ

Valdez turned out to be six foot two, raven-haired, suavely dark and incredibly handsome. His eyes were a deep, rich brown, almost black, and he had a black Zapata-style moustache that she guessed must have taken him years to grow. He was soft-spoken, impeccably groomed and, although she expected him to speak with a Mexican accent, his accent was pure Brooklyn.

She had travelled alone to the hotel in the centre of London, which was unusual; she would normally travel with her own hairdresser and make-up artist, but Valdez had been adamant that he used only his own people who knew his requirements and expectations. He had already designed a very special look for this particular set, and his entire crew had been briefed. All Miss Divine had to do was to turn up; he would take care of the rest.

The hotel suite seemed to be crowded with people and camera equipment was strewn all over the floor. Rianne suddenly recalled Michelle Seigner the French photographer who'd been responsible for the first shots which helped establish Rianne's image. The butch Frenchwoman had always said that you really only needed one camera, and if you couldn't do it with one you couldn't do it at all. Well, maybe that was an oversimplification but there were at least half a dozen cameras either lying on the floor or set up on tripods facing the bed. There was also a video camera on a tripod.

Valdez, who had met her in the lobby, led her through the people, introducing them quietly — the hair-stylist, the make-up artist, his assistant, the prop man, lighting engineer, the script girl.

"It sounds like you're making a movie," Rianne said. "In fact, I think I've made movies with smaller crews."

Valdez smiled politely. He glanced sidelong at her, brushing strands of his fine black hair away from his eyes. "I have seen some of your movies, Miss Divine…or may I call you Rianne? You have a special quality, a fire, which immediately attracted me to you. I even went so far as to attempt to trace you…this would have been three or four years ago, when *Rock and Roll Women* appeared."

Rianne blushed, remembering some of the scenes from the movie. "Yes, that would have been three years ago, I think."

"And then," Valdez continued, "when I saw you had changed your career, I was determined to photograph you. I want you to know that this is a very important shoot for me, Rianne. I have spent a lot of money setting it up, hiring these people, but I intend to sell the photographs to a series of magazines. It will also help promote me as a world-class photographer."

"Josef said you were very well known, but I don't think I know your work."

"I made my reputation in South America, Spain and Italy. But the big money is with the international magazines in North America." His smile was broader now, showing perfect white teeth. "I told a little white lie to Herr Bach."

Rianne blinked. She was surprised he'd even got close to Bach if his credentials weren't in order, equally surprised that he'd lied to the German and got away with it.

"You're not going to walk out on me now, are you?" he asked, handing her a banker's draft drawn on Chase Manhattan for half a million dollars.

Rianne folded the draft and slipped it into her bag. Half a million dollars took care of a lot of questions.

"Where do we start?"

The photo sets were unusual, she had to admit. Each one was scripted almost like a movie. There were photographs taken of her coming into the room and working through a standard strip-tease routine, each item of clothing removed in the prescribed fashion but with her not looking at the camera, which was unusual. Then she lay naked on the bed in a variety of poses, sometimes fondling her breasts, fingers working between her legs. And then she was photographed dressing.

They broke for lunch just after noon.

She had thought with the money he was paying her that Valdez would have lunch sent up to the room, or at least eat in the hotel, but instead he took her out and they spent an hour eating in a local Chinese restaurant, making small talk about their various careers. Valdez did most of the talking, and Rianne suddenly realised that he was actually nervous. She wondered how much he had gambled on the photo shoot.

When they returned to the hotel the best part of three quarters of an hour were wasted while the lighting was checked — why hadn't it been done during lunch? — and a couple of candid shots were taken of her sitting casually, sipping wine, waiting for the crew to get their act together. Every so often Valdez would appear, smile apologetically, get her to smile, and shoot a few more shots.

It was close to two before the afternoon session got under way. This time she was photographed wearing her own clothes and she was given a heavy knife to put in her bag. The prop man showed her how to hold the long, double-edged, needle-pointed knife with her thumb along the flat of the blade. With Valdez dancing around her, camera clicking and whirring, she followed the script girl's bizarre instructions.

"Come in...close the door...turn...walk across the room, pull off your coat, drop it on the ground...open your handbag...take out the knife...drop the handbag. Hold the knife pointing upwards... look towards Mr Valdez. You hate him, show the hate in your eyes, smile savagely... lunge upwards with the knife ... "

She had to repeat the procedure, only this time she had to strip naked before climbing on the bed with the knife clutched in her hand and lunging forward, the knife held in an overhand grip, plunging downwards.

The rest of the shoot went along familiar lines. She undressed and sprawled on the bed, Valdez photographing her as she toyed with the knife, using it with obvious phallic intent and symbolism.

At one point she was splashed with red dye and photographed again, with the dye running down the knife and the length of her arm. Another series of shots were taken of her against a blood-red backdrop on which an alien sky had been painted, and the knife was replaced with a sword. There were more shots of her wearing exotic jewellery. And finally Valdez photographed her as she showered off the red dye and then soaped herself, running her hands lasciviously across her body, watching the photographer closely, attempting to arouse him — and failing. Maybe he was gay but she doubted it; it was as if he just wasn't interested in her. He continued to photograph her as she dressed.

When Rianne returned to the main bedroom most of the gear had been packed away and the crew was leaving one by one, bidding Valdez and Rianne good night. She expected him to invite her for a drink, but he simply took her hand, shook it warmly and then ushered her to the door. As she was leaving, he said, "I've phoned for a taxi. There should be one waiting for you downstairs."

"Thank you ... thank you Mr Valdez." Now that he was through it was as if he wanted to get rid of her. It would have been good manners for her to be escorted down to the cab at least, but then Valdez wasn't a typical photographer. She had been studying him throughout the afternoon; the man was a martinet, obsessed with finding the right picture, the perfect image. "It's been a very interesting day," she added. "I'm looking forward to seeing the shots. I don't think I've ever been on a shoot quite like it."

"You haven't," he assured her.

"Will I see you again?" she asked.

Valdez's lips curled in a humourless smile. "Probably not."

He stood at the door as she walked to the lift and jabbed almost angrily at the button. When it arrived she stepped inside without looking back.

As the lift whined away, the door directly across the hallway opened and Josef Bach stepped out.

挃

By the time Gregory Connors arrived, all evidence of the photographic shoot had vanished. The door was opened by a tall, foreign-looking guy with a drooping moustache dressed like a flunkey, who bowed but said nothing and ushered Greg down into the space which served as a sitting room.

Bach was sitting on one side of the long white hide couch. The German rose as Greg came down the three steps into the room and shook his hand.

"Nice to see you again, Mr Connors."

"And you, sir," Greg said, surprised to see the German.

"You must forgive the subterfuge. But your recent excursions in the press have meant that there is a possibility that someone may be watching you, and there's always someone watching me," he added. "That's why I arranged for you to meet me here and not at the office."

"I understand," Greg said, although he didn't.

The waiter appeared by their side with a bottle of wine in an ice bucket. Without asking he poured two glasses, handing one to Bach, passing the second to Greg.

"Thank you," Bach murmured. He lifted his glass in a toast. "To success."

"Success." Greg sipped the wine, feeling it tingle on his tongue. It was rich and fruity, the tang of the grape very much in evidence.

The waiter reappeared at his elbow to top up his glass.

"Have there been any further developments?" Greg asked.

"Some." Bach shrugged, "But nothing of any importance, nothing we cannot handle. There is the possibility that they will contest your possession of the previous versions of the book."

"I thought that was our secret weapon."

"One of them, my boy." He looked past Greg and smiled. "They will claim you stole the computer and used it to print up copies of the rough drafts."

"But that's nonsense!"

"I know that, my boy. But not to worry. If you've survived in business as long as I have, you always keep something in reserve. For emergency use only."

"I don't understand." Greg said.

Bach moved the wine glass back and forth beneath his nose, breathing deeply, savouring the bouquet. When he spoke his voice was soft, almost gentle, as if he was musing quietly to himself. "I attempted to destroy Briony Dalton's credibility in several ways; they all failed. And then you came along with your tale of woe, and you were a blessing, a gift from the gods. You could save the day, but then circumstances changed, and I'd thought I'd been foolish to pin my hopes on you."

Greg attempted a smile, but couldn't. The man was talking nonsense.

"You see, I thought you could save the situation. And then I thought you couldn't. But then I realised you could!"

The man was drunk and babbling. Greg started to rise to his feet when he felt the ice-cold touch of metal against his neck, then agony flowed through his body!

He slumped limply to the ground as his legs refused to support him and lay there, twitching, fully conscious, but unable to move, unable to speak.

The man he'd taken to be a servant came and stood over him. He was holding a slender oblong box in his hand. The dark-skinned man stooped down and ran the two metal prongs that protruded from the V-shaped end of the box across his face. Greg recognised the device then: it was a stun gun, a semi-legal electrical device that pulsed sixty thousand volts into the body, interfering with the electrical impulses from the brain to the muscles, in effect short circuiting them. The man brought the stungun close to Greg's face and pressed a stud: blue sparks crackled from one metal prong to the other. He suddenly rammed the device up beneath Greg's chin. Greg felt his body twitch as seared nerves recoiled, but he couldn't scream his agony.

The man lifted him up and slung him over his shoulder. He carried him into the bedroom, dumped him down on the bed and began to undress him, his gloved hands moving efficiently, neatly folding and draping the clothes over a chair.

Bach stood at the end of the bed, arms folded.

When Greg was completely naked, the stun-gun was pressed to the back of his neck and triggered. Once again, Greg felt his body spasm as the charge ran though it, but the agony was muted now, the pain little more than a tingling along his nerve ends like pins and needles. But the feeling of helplessness was even more terrifying than the pain.

The door to the bathroom opened and a young woman appeared. She was in her early twenties, dark-haired, slim and naked. Her expression was blank, unseeing, her pupils pinpoints. A tiny bead of crimson rested in the crook of her arm.

She didn't speak and neither man said anything as she climbed on to the bed between Greg's outstretched legs and began to fondle him.

Over her shoulder, Greg could see the moustached man pick up a camera and begin to take photographs.

The young woman aroused him quickly and efficiently and then climbed on top of him, pressing him deep into her body. She posed — there was no other word for it — while dozens of photographs were taken. Then the man put down the camera and the whole process was repeated, only this time it was videotaped with the man directing the girl's movements, like a director instructing an actor. Finally when Greg's orgasm shuddered through him — the moment carefully captured on tape — the young woman climbed off him and returned to the bathroom. She reappeared a few moments later and walked from the room, her expression still glazed.

Greg was beginning to wonder how long the feeling of numbness would last when the photographer pressed the stungun to his stomach and fired another charge into his body. "That'll hold him long enough." The American went into the bathroom and when he reappeared he was naked. He held the stungun in one hand and a long-bladed knife in the other. He was wearing a pair of transparent surgical gloves.

"Remember, don't kill him," Bach said eagerly, his high forehead sheened with sweat. "I want him alive. He must be alive when you've finished."

"He'll live." The man smiled, his tongue moistening his lips. "If you're going to get close, then strip," he added. "Don't get blood on your clothes."

"And he mustn't be able to talk either," Bach said, loosening his tie.

"He won't be," the American promised.

Chapter
Seventy-Eight

"I'm the man who has been making your life a misery."

Briony Dalton lifted the portable phone and walked out on to the balcony of her hotel bedroom. The long white stretch of Miami Beach was still relatively deserted at this early hour, although there were already windsurfers riding the white-capped waves. She took her time settling herself into a wicker chair, and was about to speak when the caller snapped, "Did you hear me? I'm the person who has made your life a misery for the last six months."

"What did you do, rehearse that opening line?" Briony said reasonably. "Listen; the only reason I'm prepared to even talk to you is because you have my phone number and there are damn few people who even know I'm here." Her voice was level, calm, but she desperately wished she had something with which she could tape the conversation. "Now if you've anything to say, then say it."

There was silence, the line almost unnaturally quiet, and Briony was beginning to think they had been cut off when the voice — male, arrogant, with just the faintest trace of a foreign accent — spoke again. "You claim that Gregory Connors stole your portable computer, but you know you were with him when the machine was stolen."

Briony straightened in the chair. Only Greg and herself knew that.

"Aaah, I thought that would get your attention." The voice had relaxed, the shrill edge gone from it. He was in command again. "One of my people stole your machine. But guess what: when we tried to use it the machine ran a programme of its own, blanking the hard disk and then overwriting it so the data couldn't be recovered. You'd incorporated a little security, hadn't you, Miss Dalton? Now how many people knew that?"

"Precious few," Briony admitted quietly. The sun was climbing in the sky and the day promised to be a scorcher, but she felt chilled. "What do you want?"

"I want to talk to you."

"We have nothing to discuss."

"On the contrary, we have everything to discuss. You don't think I'm going to leave it at that, do you? I've spent far too much money ruining you just to leave it at the last post."

"Nothing I've heard so far is very interesting, certainly not interesting enough to make me want to talk further."

"You'll talk with me, Briony Dalton," he said coldly. "You see, I have evidence that proves your daughter, Rianne, murderously assaulted Gregory Connors, tortured and mutilated him. Furthermore I have evidence that links you very closely with the crime."

"You're full of shit," Briony said, moving the phone away from her head.

"Oh, don't put the phone down," the voice said hurriedly. "That is a remarkably pretty swimsuit you're wearing this morning," he added in a completely different tone of voice. "A bit low on the bosom and high on the thigh for a woman of your age, though, wouldn't you think?"

Briony sat up. This maniac was watching her now!

"Yes, I can see you, Miss Dalton. Look straight ahead."

Briony looked out to sea. There was no one on the beach and nothing out to sea but an enormous motor yacht. As she looked, the sunlight winked off glass: someone was watching her from the boat.

"That's right, Miss Dalton. I'm on the boat."

It was the boat which convinced Briony that the man was serious. She knew nothing about boats — apart from her experience on Greg's — but this one was big and she guessed it was worth close to a million. Someone with that sort of money didn't need to play games ... or maybe that's all someone with that sort of money did.

"Would you like to come and talk to me?"

"Do I really have a choice?"

"No, my dear, you don't." She heard a shouted command away from the phone and then a sleek white speedboat came around the bows of the yacht. "I'm sending a boat in for you now. Perhaps you would be good enough to walk down the jetty and meet it?"

Briony hung up without another word.

She dressed hurriedly, pulling on a pair of shorts and a T-shirt over the swimsuit and then took her time strolling down to the jetty. She propped a pair of overlarge Porsche sun glasses on her hair: she read nuances of expression in people's eyes — most people did — and she thought the glasses might give her a tiny edge if the mysterious caller couldn't see her eyes. She had been tempted to phone someone and tell them what was happening, just in case ... just in case what? Just in case she didn't come back? If the madman on the boat had wanted to dispose of her he could have done it very easily. She consoled herself with the thought that people in million-dollar yachts, who sent expensive powerboats to pick you up didn't kidnap you and hold you for ransom.

The pilot of the powerboat looked Mexican and he had to check her against the picture taped to the back of his hand before he allowed her onto the boat. He didn't speak a word to her on the five-minute trip out to the motor yacht, and she amused herself by doing what she usually did in tense or unusual situations: she attempted to memorise the experience and her own emotions; the movement of the powerful boat, the sound it made when it hit the water, the deep vibrant hum of the engine, the wind in her face, the salt on her skin, the way her flesh crinkled. A writer wrote out of experience, so, like most writers, she tended to consciously remember sights and sounds for inclusion in her works.

She thought it might help to distract her from her fear. It didn't. By the time they reached the boat she realised she was genuinely frightened; her mouth was dry, her tongue felt swollen and her heart was pounding painfully in her chest, echoing the pulse in her throat and temples. She was about to come face to face with the man who had attempted to destroy her.

She was also aware that bubbling beneath the surface of her fear was a deep, seething rage.

The powerboat pulled in alongside the motor yacht beside a floating platform. Steps led upwards to the deck. She was met by two more Mexican or Puerto Rican sailors who led her aft, towards the sundeck.

Briony dropped the sunglasses down on to her face as a tall, white-haired, white-suited man came forward to meet her, hand outstretched. He looked so much like a Southern gentleman that she almost expected him to speak with a Louisiana accent. Refusing his hand, she looked into his bright blue eyes and frowned … he was familiar, hauntingly so.

"I am so pleased you decided to join me," he murmured, stopping before her, bowing slightly, traces of a German accent audible. "I am Josef Bach."

It was only with a supreme effort of will that she managed to keep a straight face. She nodded coolly. "I know." She had never met the man before, but he was regular news and gossip fodder. He was reputed to be one of the wealthiest men in the world. But what would he …? Why should he …?

The German indicated two chairs set on either side of a table, shaded beneath a striped parasol. "Shall we sit? We have much to discuss."

Briony sat down and a waiter appeared immediately, placing a beaded ice-bucket by Bach's chair, lifting a slender bottle from the crushed ice and pouring the pale red wine into two fluted glasses in one smooth movement.

Bach saw her looking at the chilled glass suspiciously. "This is from my own vineyards in southern California. The vines are the new larger hybrid which we find gives a fuller flavour. We have scientifically recreated Italian soil conditions and that, coupled with the Californian climate, does the rest." He lifted his glass and sipped the slightly sparkling wine.

She brought her glass to her lips, but didn't swallow.

"I have been an admirer or your work for many years, Miss Dalton," Bach began very carefully.

"Let's cut the shit," Briony said brusquely. "What did you mean on the phone when you said Rianne was involved in the attack on Connors a month ago?"

Bach twirled the glass by its stem. "That was a terrible thing; such a brutal, vicious attack. The man was tortured. Do you know that he was blinded, his ear drums were punctured, his tongue cut out? ... and he was castrated." He looked up at her, a tight smile twisting his lips. "A stungun was used to keep him immobile while he was so savagely violated; the police think he may have been conscious for most of it."

Briony sipped some of the icy liquid, washing away the foul taste in her mouth. She remembered Greg Connors as she'd last seen him, naked and bronzed, handsome, with his easy smile and his sun-bleached blond hair, his laughing hazel eyes. And then her writer's imagination took over and she suddenly saw him lying on a blood-soaked bed, tortured, crippled. ... and emasculated. What sort of person would do such a thing to another human being?

Puzzled, and slightly irritated by the woman's continued silence, Bach pressed on.

"The police suspect Gregory Connors knew his attacker; they even suspect it was a woman." His smile broadened. "A sex attack by a woman, Miss Dalton — why it's a plot worthy of one of your own books, wouldn't you say? But tell me, what would make a woman do such a thing, eh? What would make someone completely destroy another human being in that way — and yet not kill him? It's almost as if Connors' attacker wished to make him suffer for something ... and of course the fact that he was castrated is quite significant." He attempted a laugh. "It is the ultimate punishment for a man, is it not?"

Briony watched Bach closely. She was aware of the muted sounds of the boat, the lapping of the waves against the side of the craft, the low distant murmuring of the foreign crew, the salt smell of the sea tainted by diesel fumes, beads of sweat trickling their way down between her breasts. The sights, the sounds were so ordinary, so mundane, and yet here was this man speaking of ... no, almost gloating over, the destruction of another human being.

She had been horrified when she'd read the reports about the attack on Greg. The details that had been released to the press had been sketchy, but there had been some speculation about Greg's past and the fact that he was once involved with the drugs scene. She had been contacted by various papers and journals but had refused to make any comment, which meant that one of the tabloids had run with the story, Briony Dalton refuses to comment on Connors mutilations. She realised now that it had been one of Bach's newspapers.

"What would you say, Miss Dalton, if I were to tell you that your daughter, Rianne, mutilated Connors?"

Briony straightened in the chair, glad now of the dark glasses to hide her expression.

"What would you say, Miss Dalton, if I were to tell you that your daughter was my mistress?" He noted the sudden tension in her shoulders. "Aaah, you didn't know," he breathed. "So it is true. I didn't really believe it; I didn't believe that a mother simply couldn't or wouldn't or didn't care about her children. I suppose you do know your son is dead?" he asked sarcastically.

"I know that," Briony murmured.

Bach smiled, pleased that he was finally beginning to get through to her. "But you didn't know that your daughter had been living with me while she pursued her career as a nude model? No you didn't," he said softly. "Oh course I had absolutely no idea she was your daughter," he said with exaggerated innocence. There was a briefcase on the deck beside him and he lifted it to the table, snapped open the locks and took out a bundle of glossy British and American men's magazines. "You will generally find her in the centre-page spread," he said, maliciously.

Reluctantly, Briony opened the first of the magazines, flicking past pages of vacuous smiles, tanned, naked flesh, bodies contorted into dozens of impossible positions, legs spread. Rianne — Ryan, as she was called in the article — occupied the centre-page spread. There were eight pages of nude shots, including the double-page spread, of Rianne walking down a golden sanded beach with a spectacular sunset beyond dipping palms ... lying in the shallows with the foaming water washing around her groin, head thrown back in simulated ecstasy ... drinking coconut juice, tendrils of the white liquid tricking down her neck, between her breasts, gathering in her pubic hair ... her mouth in a perfect O as she sucked on a banana ...

She closed the magazine and dropped it on to the table and refused to pick up another. Folding her arms across her breasts, she stared at Josef Bach.

"There are more," he suggested, indicating the pile.

"If you've seen one you've seen them all," she said. She nodded towards the magazines. "Just because my daughter ... " She stopped, realising it was the first time she had used the term, indeed, it was the first time she had even thought of Rianne in that way for many years. "Just because my daughter has appeared nude doesn't make her a murderer."

"Miss Dalton," Bach said, almost angrily, "you take me for a fool!" He lifted a gleaming black box from his briefcase and set it on the table before Briony. The box, which was the size of a large hardback book, was a combination video cassette player and television with a high-definition liquid crystal display screen. "Do you know, Miss Dalton, that your daughter made her living making pornographic movies? No." He sighed, "I see you didn't. You don't seem to know an awful lot about your daughter, do you?" He shook out a VHS video from a cardboard sleeve and tilted it, reading the title. "This one is called *Saturday Night Siren* and features Ryan Divine." He slid it into the small box and leaned over to press the buttons. The picture, when it appeared, wasn't more than a couple of inches square but it was crystal clear. It had obviously been pre-set, and it showed Rianne being penetrated by two men. Briony reached over and turned the machine off, having a sudden vivid memory of herself looking at these types of videos while she wrote the erotic scenes for the original version of *A Woman Scorned*. The thought that she could have been watching her own daughter perform was enough to make her feel physically ill.

"There's more, much more," Bach said. He slid across a typed sheet. "This is a list of her movies; it is by no means complete, of course. There are others in which she is not credited." He reached into his case for another cassette. "Now we come to the business in hand ... "

"I'm not interested in looking at another pornographic tape," Briony said shortly.

"Oh, but I think you'll be interested in this one," the German said very softly. He ejected the first tape and slid in the second. "I think you will find this one very interesting indeed."

Unwillingly, but with an almost morbid fascination, Briony looked at the sharp clear image on the small screen.

A door — with the usual hotel signs stuck on the back of it — opened and Rianne walked into the room. Carefully closing the door behind her, she walked across the room towards the camera. Slipping off her coat, she performed a slow sensuous strip-tease. When she was completely naked, she knelt on the floor and the camera zoomed in as she opened her handbag, pulled out a knife and turned to the bed. The camera moved forward to look over her shoulder at the bed where Greg Connors lay naked, looking relaxed and sleepy, his clothes neatly folded onto a chair beside the bed. The camera came around behind the young woman to show her climbing on to the bed, crouching between Greg's legs, her hands working on him, arousing him. The camera moved in for a close-up as she pressed his erect member deep into her body. Briony Dalton watched with mounting horror as Rianne, her lips twisted in a savage smile, with the knife clutched in a white-knuckled grip, plunged downwards, the blade cutting easily into the man's tanned flesh. The knife came up again, and there was blood running down the length of the blade, twisting along Rianne's wrist. There was then a series of close-ups showing the savage attack. As the knife cut its bloody way down his skin to his groin, Briony speeded up the video, fast-forwarding to the point where Rianne was in the shower washing the blood off her naked body, smiling victoriously at the camera. Briony reached over, turned it off, ejected the video and in one smooth movement picked it up and threw it over the side of the boat. She didn't even hear the splash it made as it entered the water.

Josef Bach sat back in his chair and applauded. "Oh, bravo, bravo! How spirited! And a reaction at last. I was afraid you really didn't care about the girl."

"I don't," Briony said.

"You may lie to me, Miss Dalton, but your actions speak louder than that." He jerked his head in the direction the tape had taken. "I have numerous copies."

"Tell me what you want," Briony said numbly.

"Let me tell you about this tape," Bach continued. "This is the type of video that originally emanated in South America where life is cheap: they usually depicted the ultimate thrill, the death of another human being. They are called snuff films. They are disgusting, perverted, shocking. What would people think if they saw Rianne Moriarty participating in such a video … especially when the victim was the man who had accused her mother of stealing his book?" As he was speaking he began to dole out glossy ten-by-eight colour photographs, spreading them out like cards on the table before her. These weren't stills from the movie, she noted. These were close-up, high-definition shots of her daughter with the knife, and the torture and mutilation of Greg Connors. "Leaving aside the fact that your daughter would go to jail for life, I should imagine that you would spend time behind bars, conspiracy or accessory before or after the fact. Or more than likely you arranged it all. Yes, yes." He was nodding. "I think you phoned Connors and told him to meet you in the hotel room; Rianne arrives, seduces him, and then savagely mutilates him. Surely it would have been kinder to kill him; a man would have killed him, but then hell hath no fury like 'A Woman Scorned'." His smile was triumphant and savage, lending his face a skull-like appearance. "I can prove all this." he added. "Including your phone call to Connors and the fact that your daughter was in the room on that day."

"What are you?" Briony whispered. "What do you want?"

Bach spread both hands, tilting his head to one side. "I am a businessman, and I want to put a business proposition to you. But before doing that I am merely putting forward all the options, letting you see the alternatives." His blunt fingers touched the photographs.

"Rianne wasn't anywhere near that hotel room," Briony said defiantly, though she had already guessed that if Bach had gone to so much trouble to put all this together then he would have taken care of that simple detail.

"Your daughter was in that hotel room," the German said. "A dozen people will swear to it."

"She didn't do that to Connors!" she said desperately.

"No, Miss Dalton, she didn't. But that doesn't really matter, does it? According to these pictures she did and surely you, as a writer, should know that a picture is worth a thousand words. What would happen if these were to get into print? What would happen if this tape were to start turning up on the underground tape market, or was released onto the Internet? Think about that," he said, his temper suddenly flaring. "Try and work it out like the plot of one of your books." He stood up and strode around the table, coming to stand behind Briony, his hands resting on her shoulders. Her neck and shoulder muscles tightened at his touch. "Your conclusions should be ruin, disaster, disgrace, and jail."

"What do you want?" she asked him again, without turning her head.

"You are scheduled to appear on coast-to-coast television tomorrow. If you want to save your daughter, if you want to save yourself, then admit that you stole Gregory Connors book!"

Chapter Seventy-Nine

Constance Park wandered around Briony Dalton's apartment, waiting for her to come out from the bathroom. The old woman felt incredibly nervous and she wasn't going to appear live on coast-to-coast television, so goodness knew what Briony was feeling. And yet the woman seemed perfectly calm, detached almost, and she couldn't help but admire her for that.

The two women had had no contact since their last conversation together. Briony had moved out the following morning and had checked into a private hotel on Miami Beach under an assumed name. However, Constance had met her at the airport earlier that morning when she had flown into New York; not to have done so would have been to excite comment in the press. Both women had been coolly courteous with one another, and although neither mentioned the last conversation they had had together they both realised it hadn't been forgotten.

"You will be speaking to Wayne Kellerman for about an hour," Constance said through the closed bathroom door.

"Tell me about this Kellerman," Briony shouted back, interrupting her, taking a certain amount of pleasure from the fact that the woman was so off-balance.

"He's had this show for about three years now, and he's made his reputation as a no-nonsense interviewer who asks the questions other interviewers won't or are afraid to ask. He makes a point of not interviewing celebrities, but concentrates instead on people in the news … that's how he arrived at the title of his show, *People in the News*. The show is broadcast live every Sunday coast-to-coast and is then syndicated later in the week on the cable channels. It's impossible to estimate audience figures, but it runs into many, many millions. He rarely interviews authors: the last was about a year ago, and he had just won the Nobel Prize for Literature."

The door opened suddenly, and Briony Dalton appeared. "Well, I don't think I'll ever win that, will I?" There was a towel wrapped around her body, tucked down between her breasts, a second towel wrapped around her head. She walked over to the door and swung it open. The two armed guards outside straightened to attention. Briony looked at Constance Park. "If you would care to give me a few moments to compose myself and to dress … ?" she suggested quietly.

The older woman stared at her for a moment and then marched outside with as much dignity as she could manage. Briony closed the door behind her, deliberately turning the key in the lock. She lay back against the door for a moment, breathing deeply, and then padded towards the glass-fronted wardrobes, rubbing at her damp hair — she would have her hair done at the studio — wondering what she was going to wear. Swinging open the doors she looked inside; she had brought a dress, a Dior creation, specially for today's interview, but on reflection she thought it was a little too businesslike, too masculine, not quite the impression she wished to create. Today she was looking for a very particular image.

When she had started writing she had been very conscious of her image; she always dressed to impress, and it was true that her character, her persona, changed according to the clothing she wore. She had always found a subtle combination of masculine clothes and feminine accessories to be extremely effective. Business meetings were always conducted in business suits. Similarly, interviews, depending on the magazine, were always conducted impeccably dressed, perfumed and made up, except, of course, when she wished to unnerve the interviewer, in which case she might choose to appear in a dressing gown which hinted at everything but revealed nothing.

But this interview would be different.

Briony Dalton stood looking in the wardrobe, trying to conjure up the image she wanted to portray.

Bach would be watching this, aseptic in his white suit. She stopped, considering. White; now there was an idea. But no, she couldn't wear white on television. It would shimmer against the screen, reflect back on to her face, leave after images. Black? Basic black was always a useful standby; people associated it with mourning and solidity, steadiness. Respectability.

Would a respectable woman be involved in the terrible thing Bach had suggested? No one would believe she'd even consider such a thing, would they?

But he had the videos. She was sure that modern technology would be able to show they had been spliced together from scores of edits. Or had Bach already thought of that? Of course he had. Maybe the tapes were genuine up to a point. Maybe Rianne had been in the room with Greg, and he'd been killed when she'd left. Maybe she'd been drugged or hypnotised or blackmailed into taking part in the events. Maybe she thought it was just another porno movie. Too many maybes. If Bach released the tapes and photographs there would be an enormous scandal.

But scandal generated newspaper inches and newspaper inches sold books.

No matter what Bach said, she was safe; she'd been in New York with Constance Park when Gregory had been attacked in that London hotel.

She was safe — but what about Rianne?

Briony Dalton looked into the mirror, pulling the towel from her head, shaking her hair, allowing the larger bath towel to fall to the floor. Her body was in remarkably good shape for a woman of forty-five, her flesh was tanned all over, her breasts were firm, stomach virtually flat, and there were a few lines in her face and around her eyes, which she kept because they gave her character.

Rianne was twenty-two. Even if she got life imprisonment, with remand and time off, she'd be out in twenty-five years. She'd be forty-seven then; what would her body look like?

Briony shook her head quickly. This was stupid; Rianne would never go to jail. Bach's scheme would fall down, and he'd be exposed for what he was.

But he was also one of the wealthiest men in the world. And the rich made their own laws.

Briony Dalton smiled into the mirror; she'd been so numbed by Bach's threats that she hadn't even asked him, '*Why*?' She would have liked to have known why he'd done this; maybe she'd get the chance to ask him someday.

But what happened if Bach's scheme didn't fail?

Bach said her prospects would be: ruin, disaster, disgrace, and probably jail. But only for Rianne, not for herself. The thought stopped her cold. She looked at her face in the mirror again, staring deep into her eyes: what was she thinking? She didn't know Rianne Moriarty. The woman was a stranger to her. Did it matter what happened to a stranger?

She was her daughter. The girl meant nothing to her. She was her daughter.

Her children had gone their own way, followed their own paths; they had never looked for help, never wanted help. She had never offered.

Rianne would go to jail, serve a life sentence and emerge an old woman.

Did she care?

Briony Dalton stared in the mirror and a stranger stared back. It came around to that in the end: did she care?

Did she care about her daughter?

Had she ever cared?

She had spent the night thinking about it, working at it like a plot for one of her novels, attacking it from every angle. When she'd finally fallen into a fitful sleep, at some time just before the dawn, she'd even dreamt about it. When she had awoken about two hours later, she discovered she had arrived at the same conclusions:

disgrace, ruin, disaster, jail. On the flight up from Miami, she'd tossed in a troubled doze in which the barely perceptible throbbing of the engines repeated the same cadence: disgrace, ruin, disaster, jail.

Briony dressed slowly, finally deciding on a simple, two-piece charcoal-grey suit and a dove-grey silk blouse with a high Russian collar. She pinned a ruby brooch in the centre of the collar, matching her ruby earrings. She was wondering whether or not to carry a bag when there was a knock on the door and one of the security guards murmured that the car had arrived. She took another few moments to fill an almost flat pocketbook with a few pieces of make-up and, almost as an after-thought, she added her credit cards and chequebook and a copy of the computer disk with the few notes she'd prepared for the new book. She looked around the apartment; there was nothing in it she'd regret leaving behind. Fixing a smile to her lips, she crossed to the door and pulled it open. A tall, uniformed driver saluted smartly. "Good afternoon, Ms Dalton; I'm Gerald, and I'm your driver for the afternoon."

ଓଃ

The large television screen had been wheeled into the boardroom and tuned in to Channel Three. Josef Bach had flown back from Miami to London barely four hours ago, but had come straight to the office and begun work on the final phase of the deal with the Russians. If everything went according to plan he should be able to make preemptive bids for both Park & Park and Hall's when they opened for business tomorrow morning.

If everything went according to plan.

There was still the niggling suspicion that Briony Dalton — who had eluded him for so long — would manage to do so yet again. He buzzed Kaho, calling her into the office, and then handed her a thick brown envelope and a video cassette. "This material is highly confidential and urgent. I would like you to take it to Townsend personally. Give it directly into his hands."

"Yes, sir."

"Order me some dinner before you leave. Chinese — no, make it Russian cuisine," he added with a smile. "I'll be late tonight, here until maybe two or three putting the finishing touches to the Russian contracts. You can stay on, can't you?" he asked, never thinking that she might not.

"Of course, sir."

Bach waited until she had reached the door before he glanced up and said, "It's taken us a long time to reach this point, Kaho, but we've finally got that Dalton bitch." He nodded at the envelope in her hands. "I think it's going to work out very well indeed."

"I am delighted, sir."

Kaho closed the door behind her and immediately opened the envelope. Less than five minutes later her BMW 5-Series screeched from the underground car park. When she was out of sight of Bach's offices, heading across the city in the light Sunday afternoon traffic, she lifted the car phone. There was a moment's hesitation before she made the call, but it was only a moment.

❈

Wayne Kellerman was tall, broad, red-haired and ugly. He looked like a linebacker, which is exactly what he had been until he grew tired of having to have his face fixed up. He was twenty-eight years old, had none of his own teeth, had had his jaw broken three times and his nose broken so often that it now had a distinct kink in it. He exuded an easy Southern charm, and the drawl was pure Texas.

"It's a great pleasure, Ms Dalton." His hand was enormous, and she could feel the calluses as he gently squeezed her fingers.

"Please call me Briony."

"Lovely name, Ms Briony." He smiled. "I think we're going to have a good show today, Briony," he continued, putting his arm around her shoulder and easing her away from Constance Park and the two security men who now accompanied her everywhere. He had met them in the television studio's foyer and they walked down long polished corridors that were buzzing with people.

"Is it always this busy?" Briony murmured, deciding to play up her Irish accent.

"We never sleep, that's our motto," the big American grinned.

"I'm a great fan of your show, Wayne," Briony lied. She rarely watched television and especially detested chat shows. She had never seen the man's show.

"I'm very honoured to hear that, Briony. I think today's will be a goody. Before you're on, I'll be speaking to a preacher who claims that God told him to go forth and impregnate his female congregation to breed a new tribe of Israel — and the guy isn't even Jewish!"

"Wasn't he attacked by some of the men in his congregation?"

"That's the one. They took exception to him forcing his will — God's will — on their womenfolk. They were in the process of ensuring that he would never do it again when they were attacked by their own womenfolk. Seems they were all a bit smitten by the reverend. Wait 'till you see him though: Don Juan he ain't!"

Briony realised that he was only trying to put her at her ease, but she was surprised to find that she actually felt quite relaxed. She knew what she had to do. She had made her decision.

"You'll be on in the second half of the show. That's the better half," he added confidently, "when our main competition, *Friends*, finishes. Once people start flipping channels and see you they'll stop."

"I didn't think I was that good a draw."

"Count on it, ma'am. We'll be looking at audience figures of about one hundred million all told." He had brought her into the studio and walked her around it. *People in the News* went out live in front of a live audience, and the phones were live too. Within a couple of hours to air time, the studio was pandemonium. He stopped at the edge of the stage and turned to face her. Briony found she had to look up at him. "But I got to tell you, Briony, you don't even think of those figures. They can really screw up your head. There's something really scary thinking that every word you say is being heard by people all across the nation."

❧

Rianne Moriarty sat in Kaho's London apartment and watched the video come to an end. The last images were of Greg Connor's mutilated body and then her own smiling face.

Kaho pressed the remote control and the cassette began to rewind. She passed across the envelope without a word. She had picked up Rianne at Tower Bridge thirty minutes previously. The young woman had known something very serious was happening, but all Kaho had said was, "Bach has played his trump card, he's finally found a way to your mother," and then refused to elaborate any further. The Japanese woman didn't know what was on the video, but she had seen the glossy photographs and she had a very good idea what the tape contained.

Kaho's Kensington apartment was discreet and exclusive, decorated in cool and functional metal and glass, the only Oriental items in the sunken sitting room were a pair of Japanese swords mounted on a wooden block above the stone fireplace. Kaho had dropped her coat over the back of a recliner and crouched down before the twenty-eight-inch colour television. The slender matt black video beneath it swallowed the cassette with a metallic whisper.

Neither woman had spoken during the video.

By the time the tape had rewound, Rianne had looked at each of the photographs and returned them to their envelope. And then the shivering began. She wrapped her arms around her body and, throwing back her head, screamed aloud, howling out her rage, her terror. She fell over, curled in a tight foetal ball, shivering uncontrollably, sobs racking her body, tearing through her. Kaho knelt on the floor beside her, tears on her unlined cheeks, sharing the younger woman's terror, her outrage, sharing her feeling of helplessness.

"Your mother will appear on coast-to-coast television tonight," Kaho said. "Unless she admits she stole Connors' book, Bach will release the tape and photographs." She pointed the remote control at the television and the satellite channel appeared on the screen, the colours slightly blurry, the sound muted.

"She won't admit it," Rianne said numbly. She'd been a fool, she realised. She thought she could use Bach and not be used by him in turn. She'd been a fucking idiot to even think it. She was Bach's ace in the hole, his secret weapon. And now he expected her mother to do something to save her. Did the stupid bastard not realise that Briony Dalton did nothing for her children, had never done anything for her children? Briony had — unwittingly — out-manoeuvred Bach at every turn. She was about to do it again.

The shivering began again in earnest as the realisation sunk in that she was going to jail.

⅓

The preacher man had been fun, Briony decided. He was loud and obnoxious, arrogant and ignorant. But Kellerman had been well prepared, had shown that the man's ministerial qualifications had been bought through the post, that ninety-three per cent of all donations went directly into a fund solely administered by the preacher, and that all interest payments on the invested money was drawn directly in cash by the minister.

There had been an extraordinary development when the man had fallen to his knees on the set and, with tears streaming down his face, had begged God's forgiveness. The audience had laughed. The camera had closed in tightly on Kellerman as he quipped, "Maybe the preacher should have looked for forgiveness before he was caught red-handed, eh? We'll be right back after this break." The minister scrambled to his feet as soon as the jingle came over the speakers. He glared at Kellerman, looking for a moment as if he was about to hit him, but then gathered up what remained of his dignity and stalked from the stage to the sound of a single person clapping unenthusiastically and a chorus of boos and hisses.

The floor manager whispered last-minute instructions to Briony as the music swelled and the show came back on the air.

"Until recently the best-selling book of all time has been the Bible, but in the last few months it has been overtaken by the phenomenal *A Woman Scorned*. But it hasn't been without controversy. Let's meet the woman behind this multi-million copy-bestselling sensation: the Irish author, Briony Dalton!"

Briony came on to a sustained round of applause and took her seat directly across from Kellerman. Unlike most interviewers who conducted casual chats on sofas, Kellerman's format was to talk to his guests across a table. It lent everything a slightly more formal footing.

"Thank you for accepting our invitation, Ms Dalton," Kellerman began.

"Thank you for inviting me, Wayne."

"Let's get straight to the business in hand," he said, picking up a copy of the American hardback edition of the book. "Do you know how many copies of this have been sold to date?"

"I haven't a clue," she said truthfully. "Several million? Something like that?" she suggested. "Do you know?" she asked, pencil-thin eyebrows raised in a question.

"Well, we don't have definite figures, but it's been reprinted three times and with the print runs amounting to more than a million copies a run that's at least three million copies of this book in print in this country alone. People who make notes of these things say it's a record that will never be broken." He looked towards the camera and asked, "What makes *A Woman Scorned* different or better than the countless hundreds — what am I saying? — the countless thousands of others on the shelves at the moment?" He turned back to Briony.

"It's so good." She kept smiling, but she felt cold, cold inside. "*A Woman Scorned* is head and shoulders above the hundreds of others in the genre."

"Even if you do say so yourself?"

"Especially because I say so."

"And you wrote it and you should know, eh?

Briony looked him in the eye and said slowly and distinctly. "I did not write *A Woman Scorned*."

Kellerman was turning towards his cue cards when the realisation of what she had just said sunk in. "But your book, I mean ... *A Woman Scorned* ... "

With her hands neatly folded on the table before her, her eyes locked on Kellerman's face, Briony Dalton began the speech she had prepared in the limousine on the way over. She spoke slowly and clearly, all trace of her Irish accent gone now. "Maybe it's time for the truth here. I did not write *A Woman Scorned*. A very talented, very gifted young writer named Gregory Connors wrote the book. I met him on holiday. We were lovers for a while, and I repaid him by stealing the book from him. Oh, some of it is mine, but the heart and soul of it is his."

There was no expression on her face as she turned from Kellerman's wide-eyed startled expression and stared into the camera. "One of the reasons for the success of *A Woman Scorned* is because the reader can recognise and empathise with the emotions in the book. Everything a writer puts down on a page comes from within. There is heart and soul in *A Woman Scorned*, there is tenderness and love and passion. These are the emotions of a young person, vibrant with life. But I think if you look in any of Briony Dalton's recent work you won't find that inner fire ... because the author lost it herself many years ago. To be able to write about love, you have to have experienced it. To write about caring, you have to be able to care. To write about tenderness, one has to be tender. I'm afraid I lost the ability to be tender, to love and care too many years ago when I sacrificed my family to my career.

"And I've discovered — too late now — that some things are not worth the sacrifice."

Briony Dalton unclipped her microphone, stood up and walked away to absolute silence.

જી

The driver passed the car phone into the back seat. "It's for you, ma'am," he said.

Frowning, Briony took the receiver from his gloved hands. Bach calling to gloat; Park or Hall calling to threaten? Reporters calling for interviews?

"Yes?" she snapped.

"Mum … it's Rianne."

Chapter Eighty

It was a simple grave, a black marble headstone, a matching surround, white chippings on the grave itself. No flowers, no jug to put them in.

The woman knelt alongside the grave, opening the bouquet of tiny red roses, peeling off the gaudy paper and placing them on the stones. They looked like drops of blood against the white, she decided. She straightened slowly, her leather-gloved fingers tracing the lines of her son's name carved into the marble.

Matthew Moriarty
Gone but not forgotten

She nodded approvingly.

"I couldn't think of anything else to say."

Briony Dalton turned to face her daughter, Rianne. The two women looked at one another, not speaking, waiting for the other to break the spell. Finally Briony glanced back at the headstone. "I think it says it all."

"So do I," Rianne whispered. Her eyes were huge, magnified behind unshed tears. "I watched you ... I'm sure the whole world watched you. Bach's secretary Kaho told me what he wanted, what he'd done to you. We destroyed the photographs and the tape; Kaho thought they were the originals, but I don't know if he has copies." She stopped, unsure how to continue.

Briony shrugged. "It doesn't matter now. He'll get what he wanted all along, but that can't be helped."

"You've lost everything," Rianne said. "You might even have to go to jail." She stopped, shaking her head, and then asked simply, "Why?"

Briony gazed at her, a hundred answers forming, rejecting them all, then settling on the truth. "Maybe I suddenly remembered I had a daughter." She looked down at the grave. "And a son. I lost my son. I didn't want to lose my daughter."

Rianne put her arms around her mother's shoulders, holding her tightly. "But at what cost? You've given up everything, your career … "

"It was worth it. I thought about you, thought about you going to jail for the rest of your life and I suppose I suddenly realised what my career had cost me. I've got you now."

Arm in arm they walked through the towering headstones and sombre monuments, threading their way along the gravelled paths, the late afternoon sunshine washing them in warm gold and bronze. There was a hint of autumn in the air.

"What are you going to do now?" Rianne asked.

Briony smiled broadly. "Well, you're not going to believe this, but I've got an offer to write a book about my experiences … "

◌

Police are investigating the murder of multi-millionaire Josef Bach, head of the vast Bach Communications empire. He was shot at close range by a small-calibre weapon in his London headquarters earlier today. There was no evidence of a struggle or theft.

In a possibly related shooting, Catherine Garrett, the author and critic, died today having sustained a gunshot wound to the head. Foul play is not suspected and the weapon found alongside Miss Garrett is undergoing ballistic tests. The weapon is understood to be the same calibre as that which killed Josef Bach.

Miss Garrett had been suffering from depression and was under sedation following the recent death of Gregory Connors, the author who contested Briony Dalton's ownership of A Woman Scorned. Mr Connors has been in a coma for the past four months following a savage attack in a central London hotel.

When asked if the two incidents were related, Chief Inspector Margaret Haaren of the London Metropolitan Police refused to comment. However, reliable sources confirmed that Catherine Garrett visited Josef Bach earlier today. Bach's personal secretary, Miss Kaho Tomita, was unavailable for comment. A spokesman confirmed that all visitors to Josef Bach's penthouse suite were screened by a sophisticated metal detector which was monitored by Miss Tomita.